By
ANN YIHYANG KIM

Novels
EYES OF AWAKENING
Eye in the Blue Box
Tree of Eyes

Short Stories
"The Train"
"Half Open"
"The Lilies"
"Two Lines"
"Harvest"
"Memory"
"Whistle"

EYE
IN THE
BLUE BOX

EYE
IN THE
BLUE BOX

Book One of
EYES OF AWAKENING

Ann Yihyang Kim

BLUE WOLF & EYE PUBLISHING • SAN DIEGO

For my husband, who rescued me from the ashes.

CONTENTS

PART I
CREW BLUE

CHAPTER 1

JAMES

Sunlight poured onto the asphalt. The distance wavered in the heat. James Mun hurried across the parking lot, squirming as patches of sweat widened on his back and under his armpits. He threw himself into his car, wrenched the air conditioning to full blast, and rotated all the vents toward himself before driving out of the lot. He willed the roaring, hot air to grow colder faster. He sighed with relief as the air finally began to chill.

After stopping at a red light, he rested his arms on the vibrating steering wheel and lifted his elbows. A smile spread across his face as his sweat circles turned cold against his armpits. His half-open eyes traveled up toward the bright and cloudless summer sky, which seemed to smile back at him. He kept his arms cocked and lifted even as the light turned green and allowed him to drive forward once more. Saliva pooled under his tongue at the thought of making instant ramen for dinner. He would prepare the usual. Three packs of noodles with three raw eggs thrown in. Of course, he'd mix the powdered soup base into the water first before anything else. Only amateurs added the soup base as the last step.

A series of potholes rattled the car. He glanced down at his belly, which bulged slightly against his blue button-up and jiggled along to the car's jolting and shaking. Ramen probably had a lot of calories. Eggs too.

Maybe it would be better to eat something else, something healthy. Losing weight was eighty percent diet and twenty percent exercise, after all. But then again, he was only twenty-five, so his body could probably take the calories. In fact, he probably needed them. He was sweating a lot, and a lot of calories were expended with sweat. And work had been so busy today, as it was every day. Yes, he'd be fine. He could afford to eat ramen tonight. In fact, he deserved a treat for finishing another long day of work.

Despite how fast-paced the office was, he liked this internship the most out of all the ones he'd taken since graduating college. The people were reasonably friendly, his duties were deepening his knowledge of engineering, and he was able to practice the skills he wanted the most improvement in. All the experience was bound to come in handy when he started his master's degree in the coming quarter. The only thing he really couldn't stand about his job was the parking.

A large company had recently moved into the adjacent building and brought hundreds of people who took up all the parking spots, or at least all the good ones closest to the entrances. A lot of his coworkers complained about it too. They'd been there for years, and now this fancy, rich company had swooped in and made parking a nightmare. It was pretty annoying, not to mention rude.

He pulled into his assigned parking space as he arrived at his apartment complex. The steamy images of hot ramen that had filled his mind vanished as he looked at his belly, which jiggled again as the car trembled to a stop. He wondered if it would be a good idea to start working out.

He bypassed the stairs and took the elevator to his apartment on the second floor, playing with his pudge as he went. He threw his keys and wallet onto his desk then hurried from corner to corner, turning on all the fans. After stripping down, he grabbed a pair of jersey shorts off the floor and flung himself onto the stained carpet with a pleasurable groan. He decided that working out was a good idea. Then he opened his laptop.

The sun began to set, spilling its blood-orange light across the white tiles of the narrow kitchen counter. The molten glow turned into the cool gray of dusk before settling into the soft darkness of night. The air became heavy with the type of stillness only summer evenings bring, a stuffy stillness that requires watermelon and cold showers. Pipes gurgled within the walls. The clanging of pots and pans drifted out from neighboring windows. Stray cars whooshed down the street in the distance.

He continued laughing at the Korean variety show playing on his laptop as he rose from the floor and tottered into the kitchen. Noodle bits, powdered soup base, and dried vegetables scattered across the stove as he ripped open three packs of instant ramen. He swung his rear from side to side and blew air between his lips to make farting noises as he waited for the water to boil. After a few slow minutes marked with the annoyance of having an electric stove rather than a gas one, he cracked four eggs into the ramen rather than his usual three (he deserved a treat, after all) and sat down to slurp the noodles from the pot. Specks of oily broth flicked onto his laptop screen as he inhaled the noodles. He only paused in his slurping to laugh along with the audience in the variety show. The dregs of his dinner had long cooled by the time he finally clapped his laptop shut.

He tossed himself onto his mattress, which bounced and squeaked beneath his weight. The sheets felt cool under his skin. He threw out his arms and legs and dragged them across the sheets in sweeping motions, pretending to make snow angels, then rolled around to find the most comfortable position. Yawning, he checked that his alarm was set and recounted several action items for work. He felt confident that he could get through them all in one day. After all, he always did. He smiled as drowsiness blended with consciousness and carried him into a deep sleep....

He was standing in a vast, blurred space. Despite the formlessness of everything and the numbness wrapped around him, he knew, somehow, that rooms and hallways surrounded him and that people were moving about. An inclination to run welled up within him, and he began running through the hallways, passing faceless stranger after faceless stranger as he went. The numbness dulling his senses erased any physical strain that might have tired him and instead, gave him the pleasant sensation of weightlessness.

Gradually, he began to understand that only a part of him, an immaterial and transient part of him, was running through this amorphous space. The bigger part of him, the part that held his memories, his autonomy, and his sense of self, still resided in his sleeping body in a faraway dimension. He didn't know how he understood this. All he knew and all he cared about was his comfort.

A distant sound made him twitch.

A scream. Someone was screaming. She was screaming, "No...."

He shook his head. Did she need help?

He steered his feet into a new direction and followed the far-off echoes of her voice.

A strange sensation began weaving throughout his mind. It was small at first, a kernel of a feeling. Then it grew, sprouting and twisting. The numbness began to dissipate as physical exertion dawned upon him. His feet grew sore as they beat across solid ground. The muscles in his legs burned with the effort of sprinting. His core tightened. His heart pounded. His eyes widened. All at once, the part of his mind that had held his will and his knowledge of self, the part of him that had stayed behind with his sleeping body, expanded until it burst forth, emptying out from the body lying on his bed and pouring into the body that was sprinting at full throttle.

James continued running as he looked around in bewilderment. He was running down an enormous hallway swarming with men, women, and children. The entire hallway, from its expansive walls to its high, vaulted ceiling, was a spotless, snowy white. He did a double take as the crowds suddenly stopped and stared at him. They parted to reveal a black void waiting for him at the hall's end.

He shouted and windmilled his arms, hammering his feet into the ground in a panicked staccato as he tried to stop himself from running into the darkness. But the whole hall tipped like an unbalanced scale as if to prevent his escape, and the black void rose up to meet him, opening up like the maw of a hungry creature before swallowing him whole. He squeezed his eyes shut and screamed out in terror as he plummeted through emptiness like a stone thrown from a cliff.

He was standing. He hadn't felt any kind of impact, yet he was now standing on his feet as if he'd never fallen. For several moments, he simply stood still, shaking and gasping for air. Finally, he dared to open one eye and scanned his surroundings.

Emptiness stretched out in all directions, black, still, and deep.

His terror spiraled into panic, pushing nausea up his throat. What on earth was going on? What was this endless black, and who were all those people in that giant, white hallway? How did he even end up there? Where in the world was he now? He took one shaky step then another before running through the silence. He couldn't tell where he was going or if he was going anywhere at all. He tried to find an interruption, some movement or visual cue to lend him context as to where he was, some sign of life. But he found only darkness.

He stumbled to a stop and wrestled again with the urge to vomit. He tried to calm himself down by saying that this was all a dream. It had to be. There was no other explanation. But if this was a dream, why did everything feel so real? Was it even possible to see this clearly in a dream? To feel the breath in his lungs and the fear in his stomach? To think with this much clarity?

His skin prickled as instinct made him tense. Someone was watching him.

He spun around then jumped. A beam of soft, blue light shone down through the emptiness, spotlighting a small box resting on a stone pedestal in front of him. He swiveled about, his thoughts racing as he tried to piece together how these things had suddenly appeared out of nowhere. He froze as his eyes latched onto the box.

The box. It was deep blue, like ocean turned into stone. Thin, dark lines webbed its polished surface, which reflected the light. It was staring at him. He could feel it. He didn't know how, but he could feel the box staring straight at him. It was staring, calling, asking him to take off its lid. He began to draw closer then stopped.

On the one hand, the box seemed to be the only thing that existed in this darkness other than himself. Inspecting it might give him some clues about where he was and how he could escape. On the other hand, a random box calling out to him in the middle of a vast, empty darkness reeked of danger. Walking away would almost certainly prove to be the safer route. He could simply leave the box and wander off in search for other clues.

But the box. The box was staring, whispering, calling. He knew he couldn't walk away. He reached out with shaking hands, hesitated, then lifted the lid off of the box. He cried out in horror and dropped the lid.

A red eye covered with bulging blood vessels lay on red silk in the middle of the blue box. The eye leaked blood as it throbbed in pulses.

He clamped his hand over his mouth as his stomach spasmed. But despite his revulsion, he found himself unable to turn away from the eye just as he'd been unable to turn away from the box. He didn't know how he even knew that it was an eye. It was bigger than a human eye, and a bite-like crater filled with black liquid lay where the iris and pupil should have been. The thought of someone taking a bite out of the thing almost made him double up again, but even as he struggled to push the image out of his mind, he suddenly found himself gripped with an inexplicable need to finish the job, to consume what remained. Someone had already taken a part of the eye. Now, he had to take the rest.

He tried to stop himself, to walk away, to ignore the sickening task he somehow knew must be completed. But his hand stretched forth against his will. His fingers wrapped around the pulsing, jelly-like thing. And though he turned his face from side to side, moaning and grunting, he couldn't escape as his hand shoved the entire eye into his mouth. He gagged. Then, to his horror, he began to chew. Flesh squeaked against his teeth. Warm, tasteless liquid gushed out and filled his mouth before draining down his throat. A sense of purpose, of responsibility, awakened within him.

He was doing what he had to do. He was doing what he wanted to do. Despite his fears, despite his disgust, despite his desire to escape, this was it. This was it. He had a responsibility. He continued chewing and swallowing with increasing zeal until only one small piece remained. He paused then swallowed with ease.

Thoughts swirled into life within his mind, thoughts that were not his own. Someone was begging him to slay the Beast, the Beast that had survived with the powers of stolen sight.

"What?" he said. "I-I don't understand."

Something suddenly swung his legs up into the air then launched him into the darkness. His arms flapped wildly in front of him as he hurtled backward through the emptiness. He squeezed his eyes shut and screamed for an eternity.

CHAPTER 2

THE FLOWERING

James continued screaming as he flew through nothingness. His feet suddenly jerked up midair, and his head pitched forward. He dangled upside down before his body whipped up and slammed face-down onto a hard, dry surface. A cloud of dust filled his nose and mouth, making him spit and sputter. He rolled onto his back, panting for air. His eyes sprang open.

He was naked.

He cupped his groin as he scrambled onto his feet. Wisps of white smoke were emanating from his naked body like steam rising from a fallen meteor. His hand leapt up to his head as he realized that he was bald. His eyes bulged as they landed on his belly. His belly was flat. His pudge was gone. And not only was it gone, but he had abs. A whole rack of them! He poked his stomach then prodded his pecs as well. They were hard, flat squares instead of the usual soft teepees. He traced the muscular lines on his arms, which looked like they belonged to Greek statues. His stallion-like legs looked like they had been running marathons his whole life. He laughed in disbelief before looking up at his new surroundings.

The endless darkness and the blue box had both disappeared. Instead, cracked, blanched land now stretched toward the horizon beneath a dim sky. Giant plateaus rose up on his far right and curved into the distance.

He slowly pivoted, his mouth half open with awe, as he scanned the massive, white desert. He stumbled back in surprise as he came face-to-face with a gnarled, black tree.

Everything, from its trunk to the tips of its jagged branches, was charred and powdery like charcoal. Single, large eyes that–and there was no other way for him to put it–looked like cartoons hung from the tree's branches. A black iris, lazy black lids that blinked intermittently, and a few long lashes composed each of the identical eyes. He walked to the side of one to examine it more closely. It disappeared. All twelve eyes were flat, completely two-dimensional. They took turns swaying gently on the branches like butterfly cocoons.

He gasped as his gaze jumped toward the view beyond the tree. The biggest full moon he had ever seen hung in the middle of the sky. He nearly dropped his hands from his groin, it was so gargantuan. The moon was streaming down soft, blue light, which surrounded a giant expanse of land like a translucent veil. A myriad of low structures stood on one side of the land. A stone tower stood on the other. His heart melted into the fear that flooded him as his gaze strayed to the land outside of the moonlight. A huge, serpentine creature was diving in and out of the ground like a needle through cloth. He didn't know what the thing was, but even with the distance separating him from it, he was certain that it was headed straight for him.

He scuttled back in a panic. His heel caught on one of the tree's protruding roots. He flung out his hands as he fell then yelped as sharp metal cut open his palm. He moaned and lifted his hand to suck on the wound then stopped. He watched, awestruck, as his skin stretched itself across the cut like webs of glue and pulled everything together without leaving so much as a scar.

The sound of crumbling ground made him snap his focus onto the distance again. Dread shriveled his insides as he saw that the creature had disappeared. White dust clung to his bare skin as he pushed himself back onto his feet. He ran toward the plateaus in search of a place to hide from the creature now burrowing toward him beneath the ground.

He suddenly dropped into ice-cold water.

Bubbles streamed out of his mouth as he screamed. He flailed then kicked up and spouted water as he broke through the surface. His teeth chattered as the cold burned his skin. His surroundings. The landscape. Everything had changed yet again. He was no longer in the white desert but in a murky, green lake, where small waves slapped his face like frigid hands. The sky, no longer dim but blank like frozen fog, encased all that lay beneath it in a globe of light gray. Large sheets of ice floated on the water's surface. A dilapidated dock stood several yards away, leading to nowhere.

He continued treading water as he wrapped his arms around himself and shivered uncontrollably. He was only dreaming. None of this was real. If he waited long enough, he would find himself warm and comfortable in his bed again. But the more he screamed at himself to wake up, the more a small gut feeling thrust aside his denials and demanded that he accept what he already knew was true. Because he knew that all of this was real. He didn't know what crazy world he had been born into or how or why. But he knew the truth deep down. He knew that this world was real.

He winced as the cold continued lancing every inch of him. He would need to argue with himself later. Right now, he needed to escape the pain of these freezing waters! He began doggy paddling furiously toward the dock. His new body afforded him unprecedented power so that he cut through the water despite his clumsy movements.

Something bumped up against him then drifted away. He dismissed it as an ice sheet and forged ahead. Something else bounced off of him, this time pushing him slightly off course. He glanced at the object then swallowed a mouthful of icy water. It was a human body. Stiff and rigid, it floated just below the surface, a frozen smile stretched across its face. He swam frantically away from it as its wide eyes swiveled to fix on him. He reached the dock and clutched at its legs, searching desperately for a way to climb up. He shouted as another body bumped up against him. It turned its head toward him, and though it lay underwater, he could hear its voice as if its mouth were pressed up against his ear.

"*Twelve,*" it whispered. "*The Beast returns. The Beast. The Beast.*"

Panic ensnared him. He gulped down more water as he thrashed about and screamed for help. He knew he was drowning, but instead of encouraging him to swim, the knowledge only amplified his terror. He snatched glimpses of the water's surface before sinking down into bottomless, green depths. As he continued to kick his feet and swing his arms, his hand scraped across the side of an ice sheet and fell into an empty space. For a moment, he thought his hand had fallen through a hole in the ice. Then, with a jolt of realization, he felt that the air was warm. Warm like the summer evening in which he'd fallen asleep.

He twisted around as the shock of the discovery replaced some of his panic with focus. Maybe this was it. Some kind of way back! Gathering every ounce of strength he possessed, he pushed himself through the water. His hand disappeared through the side of the ice sheet as he thrust it further into the patch of warm air. His arm followed then his head. He gasped for air as his head emerged from the water. With one last spurt of energy, he propelled the rest of his body forward and passed completely out of the water.

He landed on his back with a splat and wriggled like an upturned spider before tipping over. Everything spun round and round as he rolled down a long flight of stone stairs. An ominous crunch sounded from his body as he rolled off the last step and landed on grass. He lay still, panting.

He cried out in fear as someone seized his shoulders. A stranger sat him up and shook him. Laughter and whooping boomed in his ears.

"Aw, yes! *Welcome to the Flowering, my friend! Welcome to the Flowering.*"

CHAPTER 3

THE CREW

H ey. Hey, let go of me!" James yelled. He pushed the stranger away.

"And we have an English speaker in the house!" the stranger proclaimed.

James cupped his genitals. The dizziness still rocking his head did nothing to dull his embarrassment of his nakedness. He tried to stand up only to lose his balance and collapse onto the edge of a large, stone step. He continued trembling from the lake's lingering chill.

"Whoa! Take it easy, man," the stranger said, grabbing James's shoulder with a firm hand.

The double images around him began merging together. His panic revived along with the clarity of his sight and mind. He searched his surroundings, thinking of the lake and its prisoners. But both were gone. He now sat at the bottom of a large, stone amphitheater. The night sky above twinkled with stars like jeweled velvet. A full moon sat in the distance like a small pearl. Large steps cascaded down all around him, leading to a semicircle of lush, green grass and an empty stage. Stone fountains stood here and there among the steps and grass, their trickling streams echoing about the theater. The air was warm and fragrant.

A young, Latino man with thick, black hair stood in front of him with his chest thrown out and both hands on his hips. His wide smile dazzled with two straight rows of white teeth, and though his black eyes were kind, a raw energy also rose up from their depths, making them sparkle like fireworks. James recoiled as he saw the guns and knives which hung from the utility belt strapped around the stranger's waist.

"You okay? You focused? You see me? You rolled pretty good, huh? All roly-poly!" the stranger said.

"Who are you?" said James. "And where ... how ... what is all this? What's going on?"

"Yeah. Pretty crazy, huh? No worries. It's always crazy your first time. And your second. And your third," the stranger said, wiggling his eyebrows up and down. "But we'll show you the ropes, and you'll get the hang of it in no time. I'm called Lux, by the way. Pleased to meet you," he said. He extended his hand for a friendly shake.

"Whoa!" James exclaimed as he gawked at the fountain next to Lux instead.

Doll heads made of white porcelain bobbed in the fountain's clear water. Their wide, unblinking eyes were staring at him.

"No worries, man. These things don't seem too bad," Lux reassured him.

He smiled and poked one of the heads to prove it. The head rolled rapidly in the water then stopped and glowered at Lux in response.

"Oh, oops. Uh ... maybe I shouldn't do that," he muttered. He wiped his finger on his frayed jeans as more heads rolled over and glared at him.

Something giant and furry sailed through the air. James shouted as it knocked him over onto the grass. It shoved its wet snout into his face and left snail-like trails around his eyes, nose, and lips as it sniffed him feverishly. He caught sight of several massive fangs. Though he pushed his hands against its chest to try and defend himself, the creature wouldn't budge. In fact, it didn't even seem to notice his attempts. It drew back slightly then let out a sharp sneeze that shot mucus across James's cheek. It whined and whimpered as it began licking him with the enthusiasm of a dog greeting a long-lost friend.

"Bloom, whoa! You're making noises? What? Hey, come on! You need to get off him. Get off," said Lux. He pulled the creature away.

James sat up to find himself staring into the golden eyes of a blue wolf. He'd never seen a wolf up close before but was sure that they weren't supposed to be this huge. And, of course, their fur wasn't supposed to be blue either. The top of the wolf's head would have come up to his neck if he'd been standing, and two people could have seated themselves on the wolf's back. His large fangs and sturdy paws looked like they could maul a bear. A thick tuft of fur encircled his neck so that he looked both ferocious and august, though the curl at the end of his tail also made him look friendlier somehow. But it was the wolf's expression that arrested James's attention. He could see a smile on the wolf's face, a smile that carried both sadness and confusion.

"Lux, what—whoa! Is that a newborn?" someone called from across the amphitheater.

"Sure is!" Lux called back. "This is another member of our crew," he told James. "We call her Honey. Oh, but don't worry. We named her after the food. We're not trying to be all cute or anything like that."

Cute nicknames were the least of James's worries. He curled up and tightened his grip around his groin as a young woman with short, dirty-blond hair jogged over to them. Her sunken, brown eyes glittered above her high cheeks. Her outfit, like Lux's, was composed of army boots, a simple black top, and a utility belt that sported a variety of weapons. The only difference was that she wore black shorts instead of jeans. She came to a stop next to Lux and stared at James with her mouth open as if she couldn't quite believe what she was seeing. Then she threw her head back and filled the amphitheater with hyena-like laughter.

"Oh, boy. What are we going to do with him?" said Honey.

"What do you mean? We're going to keep him, of course. Help him out," said Lux.

"We can't do that!"

"Why not? He's a newborn."

"It's not safe, Lux."

"Move," another voice commanded. "Let me see him."

Honey and Lux stepped aside. A young, Asian woman pushed a sharp dagger back into her utility belt as she walked toward them with quick and purposeful steps. Her black hair was even shorter than Honey's and, like the rest of her body, covered in dirt. She stopped in front of James and looked down at him with coal-black eyes that burned with a fierce intensity. He lowered his gaze.

"And, uh ... this is E, our leader," said Lux. "Look, E. A newborn! Good thing we found him, right?"

E ignored him and continued scrutinizing James. After a few moments, she said, "Bloom, go scout the place. If it's safe, we'll stay here for the rest of tonight. Lux, create some clothes for him. Honey, help Lux. That battle put me down to two creations."

Bloom twitched his tail then ran up the stairs. His blue fur combined with his swiftness to give him the appearance of a speeding nimbus. E stepped past James then paused to examine one of the fountains. She dipped her hands into the water, sipped, rinsed, then spat out grit from her mouth. Doll heads congregated in the water around her hands as she continued scooping and rinsing.

"Wait, E. So, what are we going to do?" said Honey. "We're not really going to keep him, are we?"

"He's a newborn," said E.

"Well, then let someone else take him. How do we know we can trust him?"

"He's a newborn," E growled.

Honey pressed her lips together.

"We'll keep him for now," said E. "Besides, Bloom trusts him."

"Yes, another boy," whispered Lux as he shook a triumphant fist.

Honey sighed but said no more. E continued dipping her hands into the fountain as she began washing away the grime covering her arms, neck, and face.

"It's okay, Honey," said Lux. "E took a chance on us, and it turned out all right, right?"

He smiled and squeezed her shoulder in a one-armed embrace. Honey chewed on her lip as her uncertain expression deepened into fear. As he shook her gently, though, her troubled look slowly gave way to a smile. She cleared her throat, shook her hair away from her face, and straightened her back before turning to James again.

"So," she said, cocking her head to one side and raising her eyebrows, "what should we call you?"

"James," he replied. He tried his best to keep his voice steady despite his complete nakedness and utter bewilderment. "James Mun."

"Wait. Did you just give us your real name?" Honey said. She burst into cackles again.

"Might not be such a good idea to give out your real name around here," Lux advised.

"Just give him a name. Call him 'J' or something," E said.

"What? No!" Lux said, laughing. "That's messed up. Don't just give him a name like that. Give him a nice name, like you did for me."

E rolled her eyes and resumed washing. Lux and Honey looked at each other before bursting into laughter again. The anger that shot up within James's chest burned away his fear and confusion.

"Hey. Hey, what's so funny?" he shouted.

He watched with satisfaction as Lux's and Honey's smiles melted into a look of surprise. This night was by far the worst night he had ever experienced in his entire life! He still had no idea what nightmarish world he'd fallen into or how he had even managed to fall into it, and he couldn't understand what anyone was talking about. The last thing he felt like dealing with was a bunch of strangers laughing at him for no good reason. They had no idea what he'd just been through. And why were they trying to change his name? It was his name! This was ridiculous. He was not in the mood for this.

"My name is James. And I'd appreciate it if someone could explain to me what's going on. What is all this, and who are you? Where am I?" he demanded.

He mustered up the courage to look E in the eye. It was like trying to stare down a dragon. Lux glanced at E then began kicking at a knot of grass. Honey's gaze darted back and forth between E and James. James forced himself to maintain eye contact with E. An interminable silence passed before she smirked.

"Okay. Have it your way then ... James."

The way she had emphasized his name made him feel a twinge of unease. He shunted the feeling aside, though, feeling both angry and justified. E walked away to greet Bloom, who had run back down to the foot of the stairs.

"Shouldn't we still have him choose a name, though? It could be dangerous," Lux called to her.

"He wants to use his real name, so let him. It's common enough," E called back.

Lux sighed and scratched his head. "Well, James is a pretty common name, so I guess it's still safe," he muttered to himself. "Okay, well, then James it is! Nice to have you in the crew, James. We call ourselves 'Crew

Blue.' Or at least Honey and I like to call it that on account of our loveable, furry mascot, Bloom. Oh, right, clothes. Can't keep you all naked and wet like that, though the ladies probably wouldn't mind," he said, wiggling his eyebrows up and down again. "Looks like you went through another plane before getting here. Somewhere wet? Bad luck, man. Sorry we can't afford to create towels right now, but here you go."

Lux knelt down in front of him and extended an open palm. A black tee-shirt appeared in his hand. James stared, then blinked a few times, then stared some more. The shirt had simply materialized out of nowhere. Honey let out a long sigh that clearly conveyed the great inconvenience that this was causing her before extending both of her hands as well. A pair of socks appeared.

"All right, all right," said Lux. "What size are you, James? For shoes."

"Nines," he replied, still dumbfounded.

"Really? You're so tall, though. I thought you'd be bigger."

He handed him a pair of boots before jeans and a utility belt appeared in his hands. James flinched as Honey threw a pair of underwear in his face. She simply smirked at him as he glared back at her. A cocky swagger followed her steps as she walked away to join E and Bloom. James bit back his annoyance at Honey again as he rushed to pull on all the clothes they had given him.

"Hey, E," Lux called as James stood up and finished buckling on his utility belt. "Let's do call and response now. Get it over with."

"You do it," she said as she continued stroking Bloom's mane.

"Aw, come on, E," Lux said. "He'll know you're the anchor this way."

Irritation flashed across her eyes. She hit the step she was sitting on with a sharp slap of her hand then marched over to them. Lux straightened his back as did James. She pierced James with a black glare as she stopped in front of him.

"I want you to know that this is a responsibility," she told him. "It's a pact. It's loyalty. You're with this crew from now on, and we help each other to survive. Bloom trusts you, so we're going to accept you. But I'm giving you fair warning right now. If you do anything to harm anyone in my crew, if you so much as lift a finger against them, I swear I will make you regret it."

James caught himself before chortling. Despite the seriousness of E's tone, the threat had sounded so juvenile. Make him regret it? Really? That sounded like something his little sister used to say whenever they had fought as kids. He crossed his arms. Maybe he had overestimated this girl.

"Do you understand me?" said E.

"Yeah, I understand," he said, giving her a fake smile.

"Good. Now say 'hello' to me in *Our Word*."

The words came out in a language he'd never heard before, rasping, guttural sounds that reminded him of rocks tumbling down the face of a cliff. Yet, he had understood her perfectly.

"No worries, James," Lux said, observing his stunned expression. "*Just speak. It'll come out. Everyone born into the Flowering can speak in Our Word automatically, and good thing too because not everyone around here speaks English.*"

"I–wait, what? I mean, do I just ... I mean–"

"Just speak in another language!" Honey snapped from across the amphitheater.

"*Hello,*" James blurted in Korean, the only other language he was aware of knowing.

A weary sigh escaped from E as if a small part of her were deflating. Honey's laughter bounced around the amphitheater like the jeers of a ghostly audience. James glared at her again, thinking spitefully of how she sounded like a donkey.

"Looks like you're not the only Korean in the crew anymore, E," said Lux. He grinned and nudged her with his elbow.

"At least my Korean doesn't suck that much," she growled. "Say it one more time. *And not in Korean*," she snarled in Korean.

James mustered his focus and tried not to let Honey's sneer or the fact that E's Korean did, in fact, sound much better than his own distract him. He shut his eyes and balled his fists, feeling verbally constipated.

"*Hello*," he finally rasped in Our Word. He grimaced as the language twisted his mouth and tongue in an unfamiliar way.

Lux cheered. Bloom leapt up onto all fours and wagged his tail. Honey rolled her eyes but continued smiling as she looked away.

"*Hello*," E replied in Our Word.

Nothing in particular had happened, no sudden change in his body or his surroundings. Yet, he instinctively felt that something formal had been established. The memory of him nervously accepting admission into college as a high schooler flashed across his mind.

"*You're one of us now*," E continued in Our Word. "*Every night from now on, you'll wake up next to Bloom. He's technically the anchor, but I act as his proxy. Make sure you never say* 'hello' *in Our Word to anyone else because if they answer you, you'll wake up next to them instead*."

He'd understood every word E had said, yet nothing made sense. What was an anchor? And what did she mean, "every night from now on?" She couldn't possibly mean that all this would be a regular occurrence from now on, could she?

"Well, this plane seems safe enough," said E. "You mind explaining things to him, Lux?"

"Sure. Go take a break, E. I got this. I'll make sure he gets the basics down tonight. I can start training him tomorrow too if you want."

"Thanks. That sounds good. But test the plane first before you start. You keep forgetting. I've told you a million times now."

Lux stretched his mouth into a wide, guilty grin as E stalked away once more. Then, with a blurring speed that surprised James, Lux whipped out a gun from his belt, aimed, and shot at one of the fountains. Doll heads swirled as the water splashed from the force of the shot.

"Plane has now been tested. Pellet gun," he added, smiling at James. "Pellet shot straight! We're safe to shoot," he told the others.

James sat down on one of the steps at Lux's invitation. He marveled once more at Bloom's size as he trotted over to them and sat down on the grass. He still felt wary of the wolf, but the calm that dwelled within his golden eyes coaxed him to trust him despite his giant paws and fangs.

"You ready, James?" said Lux.

"Ready? For what?"

"For an explanation, of course," he said with yet another dazzling smile. "Don't you want to know what all the crazy stuff you've been through tonight is?"

And before James could so much as think of another question, Lux began spewing out explanation after mind-boggling explanation, speaking mercilessly without pause before finally announcing that he was tired of talking and calling a break.

"So, yeah. That's the gist of it. Not too hard to understand, right?" Lux said.

James could only respond with a silent look of disbelief.

"I'm going to go over there and clean my boots for a while, so just take it easy here. I'll be back."

Lux hummed to himself as he walked away, leaving James to untangle the mass of information that had just been dumped into his head.

CHAPTER 4

THE WATCH

J ames groaned and pressed his face into his hands as he began separating one thought from another. Bloom cocked his head to one side and gazed at him before shuffling his paws and licking his chops. He spun around in a few circles, laid chin-down at James's feet, and puffed out a sigh through his nostrils.

The first thing Lux had explained was the existence of multiple dimensions. "Reality" was the normal dimension that James lived in. It was the place where he went to work, would start school in a few weeks, and had fallen asleep during a warm summer evening after a pot full of ramen. Currently, though, he was trapped in a different dimension. Called "the Flowering," it was a dimension that only some people were unfortunate enough to be born into.

"Only some people? But then why me? Why did I have to be born into the Flowering? And how did I even get here to begin with?" James had demanded in the one moment he had managed to interrupt Lux's monologue.

"Who knows?" Lux had replied with a shrug. "I mean, no one really does. I don't know. E doesn't know. Honey doesn't know. I guess some humans are just screwed and others aren't."

James had hung his head in defeat as Lux had gone on to explain that some thought it was the mind that traveled between the two dimensions and left the body in Reality to inhabit a more powerful body in the Flowering. Others thought it was the soul. Lux suspected that it was both. Whatever it was, James was stuck in the Flowering until something in Reality jarred his sleeping body awake. When it did–and it was with enormous relief that he remembered setting his alarm before sleeping–he would finally be free to proceed with his normal life. But only for as long as he stayed awake.

It was sleep. Sleep, of all things, opened the gates of the Flowering. Sleep, once the pleasant loss of consciousness that lifted all burdens and worries off of his shoulders, was now a curse that would drag him into a living nightmare each night for as long as he lived. "Living nightmare" was the only way he could label the Flowering, for what exactly the Flowering was no one was able to say. The popular theory was that this dimension was one of several floating somewhere between Reality and dreaming, but that was the closest definition anyone had ever come up with.

He groaned again. The Flowering was assumed to have existed since the dawn of time, yet no one could give him a clear answer as to what it was apart from telling him that it was some soul-sucking, random dimension. No one even knew why this dimension was called "the Flowering." The name had "just always been there" according to Lux. The Flowering, ha! This place was more like a Venus flytrap, a horrible monster of a plant that devoured any poor human who happened to wander into its jaws.

Ridiculous. Just ridiculous. All of this was completely ridiculous and completely unbelievable! Everything had to be a lie, a crazy story that was part of an even crazier dream he had yet to snap out of. He rubbed his bare scalp as he struggled once again to push away the gut feeling that shouted that he was in denial.

Bloom's nose quivered. He jumped to his feet and looked at E, who unsheathed her dagger in a flash of metal. Music suddenly rang throughout the amphitheater. James cried out in surprise as Bloom bit into his shirt and flung him onto the grass. Honey drew her gun from her utility belt. Lux raised both hands to chest level and stood with his legs bent and ready to run. As James opened his mouth to speak, Bloom stomped his paw into the back of his head, shoving his mouth into the ground.

The music was slow and dreamy, a concoction of simple piano chords, drums, and the strumming of an electric guitar. Warm light shone forth from the windows of a small, square adobe house that had materialized out of thin air at the top of the stairs. A silhouette of a woman emerged, visible through one of the open windows. Her powerful voice echoed above the instruments, placing itself at the forefront and fingering each note as she sang about blue moonlight and loneliness.

Bloom sniffed the air furiously then nodded at E. Groups of doll heads turned in intervals to watch her from the fountains as she leapt up the stairs and crept up to the side of the house. Lux drew closer to Honey, who had already aimed her gun at the singing silhouette. E pressed herself against the side of the house then inched closer to the window. She peered inside before leaping through the window and stabbing something on the floor. The silhouette continued singing next to her as she examined the room. She nodded to herself as if satisfied with her findings.

"It was just a small one. One of the Dead," she called to the crew.

The shoulders of Crew Blue relaxed in unison. Bloom lifted his paw off of James's head. Honey returned her gun to its holster, and Lux, who had been standing with only one boot on, sat down again to resume picking out lumps of dirt from his shoe. After giving the house a final scan, E returned her dagger to its sheath and made her way back down to the grass. She gave Bloom a questioning look. He responded with a shake

27

of his head. After a few moments, it was as if nothing had happened. The song that had alarmed them grew into a soothing melody that intermingled with the splashing of the fountains. James coughed as he continued picking out the dirt and grass that had been stuffed into his mouth.

Lux had warned him about the unpredictable nature of the Flowering, but he still knew that it would take a while before he got used to all its instability. There was an infinite amount of different planes within this dimension, and each plane could consist of one or numerous types of landscapes, ranging from freezing lakes to peaceful amphitheaters. Many of the planes were also unstable and prone to changes—or "shifts," as they were called—at any given moment, and the type of shift varied depending on the plane. Random objects or structures, like the adobe house, would appear in some planes. In others, huge pieces of land would fall away as if victim to an earthquake or burst into flames for no reason. Music would start playing. Rain would fall one moment then stop the next.

If a plane proved to be too dangerous or shifted for the worse, the only way to escape would be to find an "exit," all of which were, of course, invisible. It was because James had accidentally passed through an exit leading from one plane to another that he'd been running across a white desert one moment then fallen into an icy lake the next. And it was through an exit that had lain on the side of an ice sheet that he'd miraculously managed to escape the lake on his own. He sat back down on a warm stone step and shuddered as he thought of what might have happened to him if he hadn't discovered that exit.

Bloom laid down at his feet again. James couldn't help but glare at him as he rubbed the part of his head that he had stomped on. His irritation disappeared, though, as he watched the long blades of grass rippling around his snout. His stomach inflated and deflated steadily, rhythmically. His pointed, fuzzy ears twitched intermittently. James hesitated then stretched out his hand. His fingers sank into soft, blue fur before touching warm flesh. After another pause, he gave Bloom a few gentle scratches. His tail began to flop from one side to the other.

The crew was extremely lucky to have Bloom as one of its members. Not only did he have the ability to sniff out exits but he could also smell when a shift was about to occur on a plane. Bloom was a citizen, a creature born of the Flowering, and as such, he understood things about this dimension that humans never would. Citizens existed in countless different forms, from giant, blue wolves to singing silhouettes to strange and monstrous creatures, but Lux had seemed unsure of how many citizens, if any, ever went out of their way to help humans like Bloom did. Citizens and humans weren't known to form a relationship with one another apart from, perhaps, a hostile one, but E and Bloom had managed to become friends somehow.

"All right, all right. Now where were we?" Lux said as he made his way over to James again.

James stood up and watched Bloom trot back to E, who was rubbing off the last patches of dirt caked on her skin. She sat down and ruffled Bloom's mane as he drew near to her. He nuzzled her black hair and licked her cheek.

"You were talking about my weapons and my clothes," said James, "and how I'll find them on me every night the way they were before as long as they're on my body whenever I leave the Flowering." He threw Lux an accusatory look. "And then you stopped and said that you'd tell me the most important thing after you took your break."

"Oh, right. Yeah, so the most important thing. The most important thing is your watch."

Lux held out his right hand for James to see. There were two black, rectangular markings on the back of his hand. One of the rectangles lay horizontally just beneath his knuckles. The other lay just above his wrist, also horizontally. James would have thought that they were tattoos had the rectangle by his knuckles not been steadily disintegrating and adding to the one above his wrist like a strange hourglass.

"So, this is called a 'watch.' Mainly it tells time. I mean, obviously. The name kind of tells you, but anyway. Once this"–Lux pointed to the rectangle by his knuckles–"all reaches this"–he pointed to the rectangle by his wrist–"you'll know that you've gotten eight hours of sleep in Reality. So James, hey, look at me for a moment."

James tore his eyes away from the watch to find a concerned expression on Lux's face.

"I'm about to teach you the most important thing you need to know in the Flowering, okay?" Lux said.

James nodded, eyeing him warily. Lux had explained everything up until now with a smile. The serious look he was now wearing made dread slowly unfurl in the pit of his stomach. What crazy, horrible thing was he going to learn about now?

"Can I ask what time you fell asleep today?" Lux asked.

"Uh...."

James hadn't anticipated such a simple question. Though he wondered what his bedtime had to do with anything, he searched his memories nevertheless. His soft bed, ramen and eggs, Korean variety shows. It all seemed so distant. It took several moments for him to remember that he'd finished five variety shows after he'd arrived at home, which meant that he must have slept at around ...

"Ten-thirty. I think I went to sleep at ten-thirty."

"Good. That's good. No, that's great that you remember because, okay, the thing is ... hm ... how do I put this? You die if you don't get enough sleep."

James blinked. "What?"

"Okay, wait, let me explain that. So, you said that you slept at ten-thirty, right? And you're obviously American, so I'm guessing it was Monday at ten-thirty PM. So by next Monday, ten-thirty PM, you'll need to have slept fifty-six hours. You need to remember that, James. You need to get fifty-six hours of sleep every week. Fifty-six hours by next Monday, ten-thirty PM."

"Okay. Fifty-six hours, and if I don't, I die?" James said, the volume of his voice rising along with his panic. He felt like he was standing at the edge of a cliff with nothing to grab on to as an invisible force pushed him closer to oblivion one inch at a time. "Wait, what do you mean I die? What are you talking about, Lux?"

Lux looked at him with a mixture of pity and sadness. "You die, man. Apparently, it happens through a brain aneurysm. But yeah, you die. It's why we're forced to come back to the Flowering every night and struggle to survive here for at least eight hours. You can't escape it, and it's why your watch is so important. Now, your watch–whoa!"

He caught James as his knees gave way. This couldn't be happening. How had his life transformed into a ticking time bomb overnight? Not only was he forced to return to this nightmarish place night after night, but he had to stay here for at least eight hours and die if he failed to do so. He'd be starting grad school soon. How was he going to get at least eight hours of sleep every single night? How was this going to be possible? Why was all of this happening? He had never chosen any of this. He had never chosen any of this at all!

"Breathe, James! Breathe. I know it's a lot, but you've just got to accept that it's the truth." He lowered him onto the grass and knelt down next to him. "It's crazy, but it is what it is, and we've got to work with it."

James had never felt so many negative emotions in all his life. He tried to determine if he was feeling desperate or sad or angry only to end by asking himself if it was possible to feel all three at once. Confusion began to escalate into irritation. He was about to push Lux away when fur brushed up against him.

Bloom gazed at him before lying down on top of his sprawled legs. Maybe it was the memory of him stomping on his head, or maybe it was his soft, warm stomach lying on top of his legs like a giant, weighted blanket. Whatever it was, James suddenly felt the need for restraint. He gulped then slid a hand into Bloom's coat. His breaths grew measured as his hand rose and fell to the rhythm of Bloom's breathing.

"That's it," Lux encouraged him. "Like I said, I know it's a lot. But we've got each other's backs. It's been almost two years since I was born into the Flowering, but I'm still here. And there are a lot of humans here who are old enough to be my grandparents. It's hard at first, but it gets easier."

James tried not to glare at him. Anything even slightly positive sounded naive and belittling in light of all the horrible revelations he was now forced to live with.

"What were you saying about watches?" he grumbled.

"Oh, yeah. So, all watches show you how much time has gone by in Reality and run at eight-hour intervals. Really helpful considering one hour in Reality can seem like way more or way less when you're in the Flowering. As crappy as the Flowering can be, I guess it gives you help once in a while too. As long as you keep track of your watch and make sure you stay here until the top part goes all the way to the bottom, you'll be good.

"Most humans go back to Reality right after they get their eight hours. I mean, no point in staying here longer than you need to. You can technically keep sleeping after your watch runs out, but your watch won't reset until another eight hours have passed. I don't know why, but this place won't ever let you stockpile on sleep. I mean, if we could do that then I'd just sleep all the ti–"

"What if I wake up before my eight hours are up?" James snapped. He was really starting to get annoyed with just how much talking Lux was capable of conducting on his own. He'd proven himself to be prone to going on all sorts of tangents too.

"You can make up the hours if you wake up early. At least one of your days will be out of whack because you'll need to shift your schedule around to catch up on the hours you lost, but hey, at least you'll live."

"What if something random in Reality wakes me up early, like neighbors or something?"

"Not likely. Once you enter the Flowering, you're out like a light in Reality. You'll see. Even when your alarm starts ringing, it'll probably take a while for you to wake up. Oh, and you go through this weird limbo dimension whenever something in Reality wakes you up, so don't be too surprised when it happens.

"But anyway, you need to worry more about the stuff in the Flowering that can pierce your watch because if anything here pierces your watch all the way through—so if something goes through the back of your hand and all the way through your palm or the other way around—you'll wake up in Reality again, and trust me, this dimension is crazy so it's easier to get this damaged than you think.

"It's kind of a double-edged sword, though, because once your eight hours are up, the easiest way to return to Reality is to just pierce your watch yourself. So piercing your watch in and of itself isn't necessarily a bad thing, but if it gets pierced before you have your eight hours, that's when it starts getting bad. Just always make sure that your watch is okay at all costs until you actually want to pierce it and go back to Reality. Luckily, your watch is always on your non-dominant hand, which keeps it a little safer. I'm a leftie, so mine is on the right, see? Let's take a look at yours now."

James raised his left hand. Bloom lifted his head and bared his fangs.

"What the?" James and Lux exclaimed in unison.

They peered through the wisps of white smoke still rising from James's body to examine the markings on the back of his hand. Like Lux's watch, the markings were black and tattoo-like, but those were the only similarities they shared. In some ways, James's watch looked more like the watches he was used to seeing. For one thing, it wasn't disintegrating. For another, it resembled the face of a clock. Four dots marked the back of his hand, one where twelve o'clock would be, the other at three o'clock, yet another at six o'clock, and the last at nine. From the center of these dots extended a single black line that pointed to twelve o'clock.

"Hey. Hey, you guys! Can you come over here?" Lux called to the others.

"What does he need now?" Honey complained.

E, who had looked at them the moment Bloom had shown his fangs, was already walking over to them. Kneeling down, she gripped James's hand, held it up to her face, then lowered it with a wary expression. Honey stomped over to them as well. Her grumbling subsided as she saw James's watch. She stared at him for a moment.

She whipped out her gun and aimed at his head. James yelled and threw up his hands.

"I knew he was too dumb to be a human," said Honey.

"Whoa, Honey, slow down! What are you doing?" Lux said.

"What does it look like I'm doing? He's not a human. Pin him down so we can check for a mark!"

"What kind of citizen would look like a human, be bald, naked, not know what he's doing, and have all this smoke coming from him? Come on, Honey. The chances are freaking low."

"Then what's with his watch, huh? It's what makes us human. No citizen has a watch, and no human doesn't!"

"I'm human!" James cried.

"Shut up!" yelled Honey.

"E, come on. He's a human. He's a newborn. How can he not be?" Lux said, clearly seeing Honey as a lost cause.

E stared at James's watch again before meeting his desperate gaze.

"I'm human," he repeated. How on earth was he supposed to prove it?

"Bloom," E said. "Is he a citizen, or is he a human?"

Bloom rose onto all fours, shook out his fur, then tucked his nose under James's left hand. He bared his fangs once more. He withdrew his nose, roved his snout around James's face, and licked him. He twitched his tail and parted his mouth into what was unmistakably a smile. E crossed her arms and let out a deep sigh.

"Well, he's a human all right. But something's wrong with that watch of his. Honey, put your gun down. There's something weird going on, but he's a human. We'll just keep an eye on it for now."

Honey glanced at her and pursed her lips before finally lowering her gun. She shot James a look of disgust before marching back to the other side of the amphitheater. Lux heaved a sigh and shook his head. E continued to glare at James.

"You don't have to be angry with me. I don't know either!" James snapped.

"I'm not angry. I'm concerned," she growled. She looked him up and down then said, "What time zone are you in?"

"PT. Why?"

"Lux, can you spot him for now with your watch then?"

"It'd be a pleasure to," he said. "We got lucky, James. I slept later today, but I usually sleep around ten-thirty too. We can look at my watch together from now on, but actually, all of us can help. Everyone is Pacific Time in our crew. Oh! And speaking of time, look whose time is up?"

He held up his hand to reveal a thick, black rectangle near his wrist. The top rectangle had disappeared. Eight hours had passed, which meant that Lux could now return to Reality without fear of losing sleep.

"Well, I guess I'll be seeing you at ten-thirty tomorrow night, then, James. It was nice meeting you. Welcome to Crew Blue!"

Lux unsheathed a knife from his utility belt, plunged it through his watch, and vanished. James couldn't help but gasp. He had wondered what leaving the Flowering would look like and had even formed a small suspicion that Lux would disappear when he pierced his watch, but seeing him there one moment and gone the next was still startling. He turned to face the others.

Then he was floating on his back, ascending through silence. He felt warm and comfortable but heavy too, as if his arms and legs were made of lead. He opened his eyes slowly. What little he could make out had simple shapes and blurry outlines. He closed his eyes, breathed in, and filled his lungs with clean, fresh air. The events of the night, the people he'd met, even his own name. All had disappeared. He simply existed as a living being floating within an immobile body that continued to rise up through a quiet space.

A far-off noise disrupted the silence. He wrinkled his face as the noise grew sharper. He opened one quivering eye then the other.

Morning light streamed through the blinds, creating long, bright rectangles that stretched across the popcorn ceiling. A stray blind swayed back and forth, interrupting the light with metronome-like swings. His alarm clock continued blaring in his ears. His arms creaked as he lifted himself into a seated position and turned off the alarm. He tried to understand why he felt so confused, nauseous even. He felt mildly surprised that he'd been able to wake up at all. Blinking, he tried to shake off the drowsiness clinging to him.

James gasped as if he'd breached the surface of the icy lake again. The eye in the blue box, the tree of eyes, Bloom's warm fur, Crew Blue. A cascade of memories overwhelmed him, clashing with one another like the debris of a falling building. His heart thumped against his chest as he jerked up his left hand. His watch was gone.

He looked at his alarm clock then sprang out of bed with a yell of dismay. He had overslept an entire hour. He was late for work! He shoved himself into the first articles of clothing he spotted on the floor then wrenched the front door open and ran to his car. He half expected his surroundings to change as he sped past other drivers and ignored their angry honking. However, as the landscape remained familiar and stagnant and as the digital clock next to his dashboard blinked on, he became more and more assured.

He was home at last.

CHAPTER 5

THE ROSES IN THE SKULL

J ames stuck one leg out of his car and massaged the inner corners of his eyes. Work had been a disaster today. He'd run into the office, smiling nervously, sweating profusely, and giving quick nods to coworkers as they stared at him or asked him why he was so late. Throwing himself into his office chair, he had braved wave after wave of delayed action items before ending his day with a call into his supervisor's office. He had stood there like an idiot as he was reminded of business hours and the standard dress code. It was only then that he'd realized that he'd been wearing his wrinkled shirt inside-out the entire day. He rubbed and smacked his face with both hands as he relived the mortification. As he dragged his feet into his apartment, his phone began to vibrate.

It was his sister.

A few years ago, his sister had embarked on a "family bonding" mission that included rounding them all up for family dinners at every possible moment. James knew that if he answered the phone right now, a half-hour argument would ensue, during which he'd try to explain to his sister that he simply did not have time for a family dinner on whatever date she was now proposing. The next five or so minutes would consist of a series of "mm-hmms" he'd use to placate her before reiterating that he wouldn't be able to come. Then she'd either accept his answer or initiate the final fifteen minutes of the conversation, the part that underlined the importance of family and her wish that he'd make more of an effort to spend time with them.

James waited until the vibrating stopped then turned off his phone.

He slumped into his chair and rubbed his face again before peering through his fingers at the clock hanging on the wall. He still had several hours to go before ten-thirty. Even with all the chaos at work, a part of his mind had remained fixated on the previous night. He'd thought of Honey when an irritable superior had snatched a document out of his hands. He'd jumped when a coworker had given him a wide, Lux-like grin from across the hallway. Even now, as a dog barked in the distance, he thought of Bloom and his calm, golden eyes, which in turn reminded him of the piercing intensity of E's.

It had all been a dream, hadn't it? He shook his head. Of course it had been a dream. How could anything from last night possibly be anything more than a dream? It really must have been a stressful day today if he was thinking like this. And yet....

The eye in the blue box, the tree of eyes, Crew Blue. The dream had been so singular, so real. But that couldn't mean anything in particular. He had dreamt vivid nightmares before. Besides, if everything had been so real, why couldn't he even remember what E, Honey, and Lux looked like? Sure, he could recall the ghosts of the expressions they had worn, but whenever he tried to recall their faces and what exactly they had looked like, he couldn't remember a thing. It was as if each member of the crew were a drawing that an artist had smudged and left featureless.

Proof. Proof was what it was. Proof that this was all just another dream that would soon fade into amnesia. He'd dreamt a million dreams like this before and had nothing to worry about. He continued to repeat the mantra of "it was only a dream" even as day darkened into night. But no matter how many times he tried to reassure himself, he couldn't help but glance at the clock. He tucked himself into bed well before ten-thirty.

He grimaced as he rolled around on his mattress and massaged his stomach, which was still bloated from last night's ramen and struggling to digest tonight's as well. The ticking of the clock echoed about the room, counting down to ten-thirty. He wrapped his pillow around his ears. It had all been a dream. Ten-thirty meant nothing to him. He would go to work on time in the morning and get through the rest of his action items. There would be no problems tomorrow. He just needed to stop obsessing over this stupid dream and think positively. He was a hard-working, intelligent engineer who would not let one bad day at work freak him out. After heaving a deep sigh, he rubbed his back into the mattress and allowed his exhaustion to carry him into a deep sleep....

"James, don't move."

He jumped. Dread morphed into panic as he saw Crew Blue beside him. He stumbled back and swiveled his head about. He and the crew were standing in front of an enormous hangar housed in a gargantuan warehouse. Bloom's nose quivered as he continued glaring at the closed door of the hangar. Honey and Lux maintained their focus on the giant door as well. Both of them were holding a knife in one hand.

"Stay quiet, James," Lux whispered.

James flinched as E appeared out of thin air next to Bloom. She drew her dagger even before she had finished appearing. She glanced at the door.

"Sorry I'm late," she whispered. "I got tied up because of my mom."

The others nodded.

A moan crawled out of James's mouth. He ignored Honey's vehement shushing and crumpled onto the ground. It couldn't be. It just couldn't be! But the proof was all around him before his very eyes. He was with Crew Blue again. His surroundings were as vivid as they were strange and surreal. Even his body was lean and sculpted again. How could he possibly say that this was only a dream now?

"Get. Up," E growled.

He remained limp even as Lux tugged on his arm, jumping up only as a thunderous boom echoed throughout the warehouse. The door of the hangar craned up to reveal a space filled with people. All of their backs were turned toward the crew.

"Steady," E murmured as the crowd parted.

Under the glow of fluorescent lights stood a monstrous boar. Its numerous black eyes glittered above its curved tusks. Its rough skin was blue and interspersed with wiry, black hairs. Thick saliva dripped from its wide mouth.

The monster reared up onto its hind legs and rent the air with a long squeal. It bit into the torso of a man standing next to it and ripped away his flesh. His intestines fell out in a red, wet mess that slapped onto the floor before he collapsed. The boar swallowed what it had bitten out then squealed once more.

The screams of the crowd and E's command for him to run sounded distant to James. He stood rooted to the ground as the crowd surged toward him. He vaguely registered that many ran past him with unnatural speed. The boar sank its teeth into those who were too slow to flee and tore away mouthfuls of their flesh.

"What is that thing?" James heard himself say as countless people continued to run past.

"It's a citizen, you idiot! One of the living beings that inhabits the Flowering!" Honey yelled from somewhere to his left. "Just run! Run!"

James willed his legs to move, but his thoughts failed to translate into action. Paralyzed by horror, he could only stand and stare at the boar as it continued its gruesome feast. Bloom butted James with his head, bowling him over, then crouched down to catch him before he could fall onto the floor. James remained slumped against him, trembling as his eyes darted about aimlessly. Bloom nipped him in the rear, spurring him to clamber onto his back with a yelp. He remained glued onto Bloom's back as he bolted out of the warehouse.

Bloom's nails clicked rapidly over granite floors as he dashed across an expansive, open plaza and toward a cluster of glass buildings standing in the distance. He weaved through the crowd as it stampeded in the same direction. The boar shrieked with the resounding volume of proximity, instigating screams. James tightened his hold on Bloom's fur. He dared not look behind.

Bloom crossed the last stretch of the plaza and ran into the midst of the glass buildings. Some of the buildings were smooth and circular. Others were composed of sharp angles and jutting corners. Bloom followed a stream of people pouring into a narrow divide that separated two skyscrapers towering up into the sky. Terror choked James as up ahead, men and women began piling against and on top of one another, blocking the way out. Bloom propelled himself forward with a spurt of speed then sprang up and leapt over the squirming pile in a graceful arc before skidding onto dry dirt. He glanced behind at the struggling blockade then ran forward again.

Unlike the smooth, granite floor of the plaza, the ground here was rough and rugged. Dust floated in the air like brown mist, obscuring panicked strangers, who ran about in different directions. Had Bloom leapt through an exit? Was that why the landscape looked different here? No. The glass buildings and the crowd trapped between them would have disappeared if he'd gone through an exit. This was still the same plane, just a different part of it.

Which meant that the boar could still find them here.

James tugged on Bloom's fur in a silent plea to run faster.

"Lux, car!" E yelled from somewhere far behind.

An engine roared into life. Tires screeched before glass shattered. Bloom veered back around toward the skyscrapers. Panic unlocked James's voice.

"No, don't go back! Turn! Run away!"

Two beams of light pierced the dust. Bloom skidded to a halt as a black muscle car burst into view and swerved across the ground to pull up next to them. E swung a door open and lunged out of the car. James flailed and struggled against her in instinctive flight as she dragged him inside. He froze only as she gave him a sharp shake and shouted at him to get a hold of himself. She slammed the door shut after Bloom had hopped in beside him. Honey glared at him from the front passenger seat. No sooner had Lux locked the doors than a nerve-grating squeal sounded from behind them. The crew spun around in their seats.

The dust had parted to form a tunnel of clean air that stretched toward the divide James and Bloom had escaped from. The boar had eaten its way through the human blockade and now stood on a pile of motionless limbs and bodies. Strips of bloody flesh dangled from its teeth. Its many eyes were fixed upon the crew. It tilted its head back and split the air with another shriek before charging down the mound and running toward the crew.

Lux stomped on the accelerator. The car shot forward. Dust swirled all around them as he ran through manicured flower beds, struck people left and right, and missed stone fountains and statues by a hair. James clutched the seats in front of him until his knuckles turned white. He yelped as Bloom shunted him aside. He bared his fangs as he stared out the rear window. E twisted around as well. Her eyes widened.

"It has a mark!" she shouted over the roaring of the engine. "Slow down! Slow down!"

The car dropped speed.

"No!" James cried.

He didn't know or care what a mark was. A monster was chasing them. A monster that looked like it had run straight out of a horror movie! He breathed hard and fast and gripped the side of the car as Honey crawled into the back seat and switched places with Bloom. Up ahead, the plane shifted so that a wide tunnel appeared out of nowhere. A statue suddenly emerged from the dust in front of them, forcing Lux to swerve. Orange light flooded the car as they sped into the tunnel.

"The mark is right there! Under that eye! You see it?" E shouted as she pointed at the boar.

"Where?" Honey yelled.

"Right there! Slow down more, Lux!"

James's scream of terror remained trapped between his clenched teeth. Slow down even more? Was E crazy? What was this "mark" that she was obsessing over? Whatever it was, it was not worth getting torn into shreds over! Did she want the whole crew to end up like all those poor, innocent people back there? He clung to the headrest behind him as he turned slowly around and looked out the rear window. The boar was so close that its nose touched the trunk intermittently, dabbing the car with blood.

"Oh, I see it! It's right in front of me, duh," Honey said. She sighed and pointed at one of the boar's eyes.

James squinted for several moments before finally seeing it too. A small, red circle sat under one of its eyes, etched into its skin like a vibrant tattoo. Was that little, red thing "the mark" that E was making them slow down for?

He recoiled as the boar's many eyes swiveled to fasten on him. It suddenly began to gag and heave deep breaths. With a shower of blood, it vomited up a severed arm. It slowed, falling back slightly, before madness brightened its eyes. It shrieked as it galloped forward again. Panic seized James and wiped his senses clean as it lunged at the car. He grabbed

Honey's gun out of its holster, aimed at the monster, and began firing with wild abandon.

A side window exploded.

Honey shrieked. James saw the bullet holes in her thigh before she pressed her hands over her wounds and fell against E's shoulder. He had shot her in the leg. But how? He had only aimed at the boar behind them.

"You moron!" E raged.

She snatched the gun away from him and punched him in the face. He shouted and cradled his nose.

"What's going on back there?" Lux yelled.

"He opened fire!" E shouted. She yanked James closer to herself. "Guns don't always shoot straight. Shots can go in all sorts of directions if a plane is unstable. That's why you always test the plane with a pellet gun first to be safe. Lux showed you that last night!"

The crew lurched forward in their seats as the boar rammed the car. Lux glared at it through the rearview mirror then clicked his tongue and stepped on the gas. Honey pressed down harder on her leg as blood continued spilling out of her bullet wounds and pooling on the leather seats. E swore and pressed her palms down on Honey's leg as well.

"Hurry up and create some bandages!" E snarled at James.

He stared.

"Now!"

"I-I don't know how."

"What?"

"Oh, shoot! My bad. I didn't teach him how to create last night," said Lux.

"You didn't teach him how to create? Lux!" Honey moaned.

"I'm sorry, I'm sorry, I'm sorry!"

"You've touched clean bandages in Reality, right?" E asked James. "Just remember a time you held them in your hands, and they'll appear."

"E, the bullets," Honey groaned.

E lifted her palms to reveal several bullets squeezing out of Honey's flesh. Honey gritted her teeth to muffle her own cries as E dug her fingers in and started yanking the bullets out one by one. James shook his head slowly as he flattened himself against the door and curled up into a ball. Blood. There was so much blood.

"James, focus!" E yelled.

A giant, steel door appeared in front of them and swung open. Lux slammed on the brakes, but it was too late. The car flew through the open door, which shut behind them before the boar could follow.

James felt the sensation of floating before the car dropped into a free fall. A blinding pain tore into his body as the car slammed into something solid with a deafening crunch of metal. The car continued to fall, rolling over again and again in the air. It finally smashed onto all four wheels as it landed on the floor with a shattering of glass.

James lay still for several moments before spasming and coughing up blood. The stench of hot metal filled his nose and mouth as steam began seeping out of the wreckage. He'd heard several of his bones snap when the car had hit the ground, and pain was now wracking his whole body. He wheezed for air as he opened his eyes.

He was lying on a bed of broken glass at the bottom of a large, tube-like space with smooth, red-orange walls that soared up into shadows high above. A metal, spiral staircase stood several feet away from him and twisted infinitely up. A large archway formed the only opening in the walls of the cylindrical space and led to a wide, empty hotel lobby filled with tropical plants.

James's breath caught in his throat as he saw a piece of glass protruding from his watch. He plucked it out with quivering fingers. The glass would have pierced his watch if it had sunk just a few more centimeters into his hand. If his watch had been pierced, he would have woken up in

Reality. How many hours of sleep would he have lost if he'd woken up now? Enough to fall short of the fifty-six hours he needed each week to stay alive?

E, who lay across the dashboard and through the empty windshield, broke into a fit of wheezing coughs. She vomited blood then looked at Lux, who slowly pushed himself off the steering wheel and groaned. She swore vehemently then flung a bloodied hand forward. Elevating her watch hand, she inched her way across the hood with gritted teeth and blazing eyes, paying no attention to the broken glass digging into her body. Once she had extricated herself fully, she flipped onto her back and lay still on the hood, gulping in air.

She balled up her fists and began to convulse. The bone jutting out of her skin sealed itself back into her leg. The awkward angle in her arm straightened as did her hip. Skin stretched across deep gashes, and after a few moments, she sat up, covered in blood and sweat but completely whole again. She hurried over to Honey, who lay on the floor several feet away from the car. She gasped and choked as E knelt down beside her.

"Try not to scream. I think there's something out there," E said.

She shoved Honey's arm back into its socket. Honey writhed and slapped the floor. E placed a hand on her shoulder to lower her back onto the ground before aligning her legs parallel to one another. A roll of bandages appeared in her hands. She began wrapping the wounds that were bleeding the most. Bloom, who, like Honey and James, had been thrown out of the car, raised himself onto his feet and limped over to the crew, pausing every few steps to lick his wounds. His eye twitched as a protruding rib retreated into his body. James stared at a cut on his arm as it slowly stitched itself together then looked up as E loomed over him.

"The least you can do after all the trouble you've caused is heal yourself," she snarled. She grabbed his feet and remained unmoved by his yelps of pain as she dragged him out of the pile of glass. "You have the least injuries out of all of us. I bet shriveling up into a pathetic, little ball helped with that. Your ribs are broken. So is your ankle. Focus on them and think of them as whole. It'll accelerate your healing. And stop sniveling like you're going to die. Any injuries you sustain in the Flowering will be gone the next night when you return, and none of your injuries will ever impact your body in Reality. So suck it up, and start healing!"

She threw his feet down and turned to leave.

"I'm bleeding," James said, his voice trembling along with his body.

"Then create some bandages. I already told you how to do it in the car. Stopping the bleeding will help with your healing too."

She stormed off to tend to Lux.

James lifted his eyes toward the endless shadows above. Was this really his life now? Was all this pain and struggle really here to stay? He'd gone to work this morning and eaten ramen for dinner. His sister had called to pester him about family like she always did. He'd gone to sleep, ready to wake up to another normal day. But was that life forever gone now? Was he really cursed to end all his nights in chaos and in pain?

As he lay alone, broken in body and in spirit, his thoughts reached for the only people who he knew cared about him. His family. But to his dismay, their faces appeared smudged in his mind just as Crew Blue's faces had appeared in Reality. He delved through the folds of his memory, searching desperately for the faces of his sister, his parents, his grandparents. And as he did, he uncovered a memory that had long gathered dust under forgetfulness.

He remembered the day he and his sister had snuck off toward the forbidden part of the park while eyeing the adults, who were distracted with conversation at the picnic table. Within minutes, his sister had tumbled down a boulder. She had trembled and shrieked so violently as their mother had applied peroxide to her wounds. James had torn through the medicine cabinet, looking for a roll of bandages as guilty tears spilled down his cheeks. He'd given the soft, white bandages to his mother with shaking hands, and though he couldn't recall her face, he knew that she had smiled.

He squeezed his eyes shut and willed the bandages to appear. After a few moments of straining, he opened his eyes. The bandages sat in his hand.

"Hey! You did it, James. You created! Good job," Lux said between pants as he stumbled over to him.

He was battered and covered in blood. James found it amazing that he could still smile.

"Sorry again for not teaching you some of this stuff last night. It's a lot. I forgot. Oh, and by the way, for creating, you can only create twelve things a night, so make sure to keep count. Just thought I'd mention it since E didn't."

Fury at Lux's forgetfulness boiled within James, but he held his tongue. Inspired, perhaps, by Lux's gruesome appearance, he screwed up his face in concentration and pictured himself whole again instead. Slowly, pieces of glass began squeezing out of his flesh. Warmth seeped back into his body. Remembering what E had said about his ribs, he pinpointed his focus onto his sides. He was surprised to feel a rib retreat then click back into place. Try as he might, though, his other ribs, his ankle, and many of his deeper cuts refused to heal faster.

Honey tipped herself onto her feet, careened sideways, then toppled back onto the floor. Lux, likewise, swayed from left to right as he began binding James's wounds. E crept up to the mouth of the giant archway and peered into the hotel lobby. The silence and stealth with which she moved seemed impossible. She looked like she hadn't sustained a single injury to begin with.

"You think there's something out there, E?" Lux whispered.

"Yeah. There's something. Something big."

Bloom bared his fangs at the lobby then sniffed the air. He roved about, sniffing with increasing fervor, before his nails clattered onto the steps of the metal staircase. He climbed, still sniffing all the while, then halted. He leapt over the railing and disappeared into thin air. E slung Honey's arm over her shoulders and helped her to climb as well.

"Come on, James. One, two, three." Lux hoisted him onto his feet.

The pain was excruciating. It stabbed him again and again, waiting futilely for him to die. Hollow clanging echoed throughout the space as he and Lux gripped the railing with slippery hands and limped up the stairs. James looked over his shoulder, hoping that whatever E had sensed in the hotel lobby wouldn't hear them. He muffled a groan as fresh pain shot through his broken ankle. E pushed Honey over the railing and into the exit as they reached her. After throwing Lux over as well, she grabbed James and tossed him over.

A blast of icy air filled his chest, stunning him. Fierce winds cut across his face and through his tee-shirt and jeans. Chunks of snow flew about and broke against his body. E knocked him over into the snow as she entered the new plane last. He remained swaddled in white, panting and grimacing, unwilling to move. His breath rose in small clouds that the icy winds snatched away. E made her way over to Honey and Lux as they helped each other dress into the snow gear they had created. Though James felt that he could have used some help too, he remained silent and steered himself to recall memories of snow clothes. He tried to concentrate on his broken ankle as he dressed alone.

Bloom bounded through the snow then stopped up ahead. He appeared as a pair of golden eyes and a series of blue strokes amidst a flurry of white as he waited for them to follow. E supported Honey again as they walked toward him. Crimson stains trailed behind the crew as they plodded through the snow. Bloom zig-zagged up a white slope, sniffing continually for an exit. James wished that he would slow down. His lungs hurt from sucking in the freezing winds. He kept lurching forward and staggering backward. No matter how hard he tried, his ankle refused to heal, and he was forced to use his hands to move his leg through the snow. His only motivation for pushing forward was his fear of getting left behind.

The slope grew into a steep incline. Small houses with mushroom-like roofs stood ingrained in the snow on either side of the crew's path. Soft, yellow light streamed through the windows and onto the glistening snow. As the crew continued trudging up the slope, the houses grew from the size of snowballs to children's playsets. James would have gladly shoved himself into one of the playset-sized homes, but he was forced to keep marching as Bloom continued bounding through the snow.

The crew finally halted as, up ahead, their path ended at the foot of a massive wall made of towering, black cliffs. Straw huts stood in the snow and on large crags that jutted out from the sides of the cliffs at different heights. Straw curtains hanging from the huts' entrances acted as makeshift doors that flapped about in the howling winds.

Hope sparked within James as he spotted a small group of people dressed in furs. They looked like another crew and were moving slowly about as they searched the snow for something, probably an exit. He hurried over to a woman crouched down in the snow, eager to ask her for more information about this new plane. He was desperate for any clues that would help them escape this unbearable cold. He had almost reached her when Lux tugged him back.

"Just leave her be! She's a citizen too!" Lux shouted over the winds. "She's like all those people back there with the crazy pig thing! She only looks like a human!"

"What?" James yelled.

Lux pointed to the back of his hand then to the woman's. She didn't have a watch. James backed away as she continued digging through the snow with her bare hands.

"Let's rest here for tonight!" E said.

She lifted the curtain of one of the huts, checked inside, then motioned for Lux, James, and Bloom to go in. She disappeared into a separate hut with Honey. James made to follow Lux then strayed a few steps back as he noticed something lying amidst the snow and stone. He stepped closer then recoiled.

Two living eyes stared up at him from within a human skull.

He stared back at the eyes, transfixed by them, and as he did, the eyes began to rot. A rose unfurled from the depths of each socket, blooming into red glory. A luminescent, blue glow encapsulated the skull.

"James!" Lux said, poking his head out from the hut. "What are you doing?"

"There's a...."

The skull was gone.

"What?"

"Never mind," James said.

Lux clapped a hand onto his shoulder and led him inside. They sank onto the floor and leaned against Bloom as if he were a backrest. Though the straw curtain flapped about, the interior of the hut remained free of snow and wind, much to James's relief. Everything, from the rough, stone floor to the air, was warm inside the hut. A tingling sensation overtook the numbness that had stiffened his body as his skin began to thaw. He flinched as his wounds smarted again.

"You okay, James? Here. You can wash off some of the blood," Lux said as he passed him a large canteen. "Trust me. You'll feel better if you're clean."

James winced as he pulled off his gloves then used the warm water from the canteen to wash off the blood and dirt from his hands and face. He sighed deeply. He hadn't expected cleanliness to make much of a difference, but he felt lighter, somehow, and freer without the grime.

"Oh, and sorry that I didn't explain about human-looking citizens before," said Lux. "There are a lot of citizens in the Flowering who look like humans, but you should just give them space and leave them alone if we come across any. You can usually tell pretty quickly that they're citizens by the way they're acting, but the only way to know for sure is to check if they have a watch. You'll get the hang of telling the difference eventually, though. But how is your watch? Is it still all weird?"

"Yup. Still all weird," James grumbled. He glared at his watch. He felt cursed enough for being in the Flowering. At the very least, he deserved a normal watch just like everybody else.

"It's okay," Lux said. "I'm sure it'll get normal one of these nights. It's only your second night, and you're doing good whether or not you have a weird watch. You're already creating and healing. You're doing great, actually."

"I think E and Honey would disagree."

"Aw, it's okay. They'll come around. E didn't like Honey that much at first either. Actually, she attacked her when we first met her."

"What?"

"Yup. Honey wasn't really clicking with the crew she was with at the time, and she was going through some stuff in Reality too, so she kind of tailed us when she saw us. We thought she was trying to stalk us or something, so we waited, and well, E threw her dagger and pinned her arm into the wall."

"Okay…. So, then how did you guys all become friends?"

"Well, like I said, it took a while. Not for me and Bloom. For E, I mean. Me and Bloom begged her to take Honey in right away. Right, Bloom?"

Bloom thumped his tail twice against the ground.

"Honey gave us this really passionate speech, so I told E that she should take a chance on her," Lux said. "Bloom used his puppy eyes on her too, so she ended up agreeing to it, and after a few weeks, Honey earned her trust. So yeah. Don't worry about it too much, James. E'll come around. Honey too."

James sighed. He was unsure of how many more nights, let alone weeks, he could take of E. She was just so rude and rough. She had even dragged him through broken glass even though she knew that he was injured. What if that glass had pierced his watch? He would've lost sleep! The revelation that she had attacked Honey did nothing to brighten his impression of her, though he wasn't exactly a fan of Honey either. He did feel guilty about her leg ... but he didn't see how he could have possibly known about the no-shooting rule on his own. Lux should have given him a thorough explanation if it was that important. Lux was nice and everything, but his lack of articulate language and his inability to give clear explanations continued to annoy James. Bloom was the only crew member he truly liked, but he couldn't help but heave another sigh as he reminded himself that Bloom wasn't even human.

"Aw, come on, James. It's all right. You'll be all right," Lux said. "Honey's never had to accept a new crew member before, and E just wants to protect us. They're awesome friends. I definitely wouldn't have made it this far if it weren't for them, especially E. She saved me the night I was born into the Flowering and taught me everything I know. I owe everything to her."

James hesitated then asked, "What was it like when you first met E? Did Bloom do something to convince her to take you in too?"

"Nope. Not really," Lux said. He laughed at the bewildered expression on James's face. "Hey, man. I know E can be pretty tough, but you've got to believe me when I say she's not that bad. Besides, she took you in last night, didn't she? So why are you so surprised?"

James only shook his head as he handed the canteen back to Lux.

"E's a good person, James. I promise. And if it helps, she's been through a lot of stuff in the past few years. And she's helping take care of her mom right now too. So try to, you know, help her out here and there and be a little understanding. I mean, I know you're trying, but she's going through a lot, and it wouldn't hurt. Just a thought."

James gave him an unconvinced look and continued stretching his fingers. Whatever E was going through, it couldn't be that bad. After all, what could possibly excuse that kind of behavior?

CHAPTER 6

THE MARKED AND THE MOULDED

The crew made their way single file across a series of identical, emerald hills. Wet grass squelched under James's feet as he trudged on at the back of the line. Humidity hung upon him like a fur coat, forcing him to draw in labored breaths. In the endless forest to his left, thick drops of rain splattered onto the leaves of tropical plants and branches of redwoods and aspens. He blinked away the rainwater that rolled down into his eyes before glancing at the fog swirling in the cavernous space to his right.

Lux walked in front of him, separating him from Honey, who, ever since the gun incident the previous month, had refused to speak to him almost entirely. In front of her marched E, who continued scanning their surroundings. Bloom trotted at the forefront, pausing only to sniff the air or ground. Honey glared up at the gray sky and scowled.

"You okay, Honey?" said Lux.

"Yeah, I'm fine. But you know how much I hate the rain," she grumbled.

Earlier in the night, E had commanded the crew to reserve their creations. "We only get twelve a night, so don't waste them," she had commanded. So, the crew had traveled across endless hills without any protection from the weather. James wanted to create something, anything, to combat the sticky moisture and stifling air. He could remedy this weather without a problem. His creating abilities had grown quite a bit over the past few weeks, after all.

He had committed himself to visiting every possible store and museum in Reality and had touched everything that he'd thought would prove useful in the Flowering. His utility belt, which now boasted two quality guns, two topnotch knives, and a sharp dagger, was proof of his growing skills. He'd also been clever enough to realize that expansive, detailed recollections weren't needed to create. Instead, he'd taught himself to recall only the moment he had touched the desired object and in doing so, had learned to create almost instantaneously. Through experimentation, he'd also figured out that he could only create inanimate objects. No live plants. No live animals. Nothing that held even a drop of life.

Yes, he was confident that he could use his intelligence and flourishing skills to whip up something to ease the discomfort of this insufferable weather. If only E would deign to let him try. He shifted his focus onto Reality, but his attempt to distract himself from the Flowering only reanimated a familiar sense of panic. Classes had started the previous week, and the office was as busy as ever. Work of every kind was piling up in every corner of his life. At this rate, it would be only a matter of weeks before he fell irreversibly behind on his studies.

He had photocopied a few pages of his textbook earlier in the day in Reality and created them in the Flowering with the hope of reviewing them during the night. The pages remained folded in his pocket, though, and he doubted he would ever get to look at them. E would be furious if she found out that he had wasted a creation on something as trivial as homework, and there simply was no opportunity to study the pages without her noticing.

He glared at his watch, which remained as useless as ever, then glanced at Lux's. A significant amount of time still remained in the night. He had never felt jealous of any of his fellow students before, but now, all he could think about was how they could stay up as long as they wanted and study as much as they needed to. Meanwhile, here he was, stuck in the Flowering, eight hours a night, every night, unable to review the notes that sat in his own pocket due to E's tyranny.

James collided with Lux as the crew came to a sudden halt. Honey and Lux drew their weapons. James followed suit. E held up a hand as a signal for them to wait as leaves rustled. A man stepped into view amidst a group of golden-leaved aspens and lush philodendrons. He wore a large, gray hood that covered only his shoulders, neck, and head and hid his face in shadows. He stopped and turned toward the crew.

Honey and Lux raised their weapons higher as did James. E and Bloom remained still. Rain continued showering down onto the leaves and grass as the hooded stranger stared first at Bloom then at E. She held up her watch for the stranger to see then inclined her head in a slight bow without breaking her gaze. The stranger stared a moment longer then returned the bow and disappeared into the depths of the forest. Bloom twitched his tail then continued leading the crew forward.

James tapped Lux on the shoulder. "What was that all about?"

"Roamer. You can tell by the hood. They're humans who travel alone in the Flowering."

"You can do that?" James exclaimed.

Honey glared at him. Lux flashed her a smile that asked her to excuse James's outburst before continuing.

"It's not common," he said, "but yeah, there are some humans who do that."

"Why? And how?" James hadn't considered traveling alone in the Flowering to be possible, at least not for an extended period. It sounded scandalous for some reason.

"I don't know too much about it, but E told me a while back that sometimes, when someone doesn't get along with their crew, they kind of strike out on their own. You have to be really tough to do it, though. It's not something just anyone can do. A lot of them don't end up lasting that long because traveling alone makes them too vulnerable to all the citizens and unstable planes. Something out there ends up getting them most of the time."

"Okay, but how do you strike out on your own to begin with? Aren't you stuck with your crew forever? I thought that was the whole point of the 'hello' thing you guys made me do my first night."

"What? You mean call and response?"

"Yeah! I thought I'd wake up next to Bloom every night for the rest of my life from now on. Isn't that how it works?"

Lux chuckled. "Well, yeah. It does. But you can break off call and response too. All you have to do is initiate call and response with someone else and have them say 'hello' back to you in Our Word. That, or you can say 'goodbye' in Our Word to whoever you originally initiated call and response with or to the anchor. The anchor is the very first one in the crew who responded to a call and response, by the way, and you know who that is because you always wake up next to them each time you return to the Flowering. Bloom is our anchor, so that's why we all wake up next to him each night."

"So basically, if I said 'goodbye' in Our Word to Bloom or E, I'd be breaking off call and response with Crew Blue, and I'd wake up alone the next night, right?" James said. "Or I do call and response with another human in a different crew, and that would break off call and response with Crew Blue?"

"Yup. You got it. That Roamer probably said 'goodbye' to a crew he didn't like and is on his way to the City to find a new crew. E told me before that that's what a lot of them end up doing. You remember what the City is, right?"

"Yeah, I remember."

"*And what is it called in Our Word?*"

"*It's called Lapis Lazuli,*" James snapped, speaking in Our Word as well. He'd long ago mastered speaking in the Flowering's language and didn't appreciate Lux testing him as if he hadn't. "I told you, I remember."

Lux lifted his hands in surrender and smiled at the ground. James rolled his eyes then looked up at the sky. A hazy circle of light hung in the passing fog. In the Flowering, a full moon always hung in the sky, sometimes with other moons, sometimes with other suns, sometimes with nothing else at all. On most nights, the full moon appeared as small as a distant star. But on other nights, like tonight, it resembled the moon James was used to seeing in Reality.

Waves of regret pummeled him. Apparently, this full moon was the same gargantuan moon he had gazed at while standing beneath the tree of eyes. The moon's blue light protected a large piece of land called 'the City,' which lay beneath it, and allowed only humans to cross its blue border while guarding against all citizens. As such, the City was a popular resting place for many humans. One only needed to travel in the full moon's direction to reach it. The bigger the moon appeared, the nearer the City was. If only James had only run toward the moonlight the night he'd been born into the Flowering. He could have been sitting comfortably in the safety of the City at this very moment, studying away to his heart's content.

E stopped. "Let's rest here for a while. Bloom isn't picking up on anything, and I want to give that Roamer some space."

The crew groaned as they plopped down onto the soggy grass and settled into a circle.

"What exactly is in the City other than humans?" James said, grasping again for any distraction from the humidity and pouring rain.

"Well, there's the Tower, or *the Abode, if you want to call it by its Our Word name*. It's where all the Shamans live," said Lux. "There's the Market too. That's the Merchants' headquarters and the place where Hedonists live. And Hunters like to visit the Market to buy stuff during their Solstice thing."

James shook his leg as he suppressed the urge to snap at Lux again. He always did this. Lux always assumed that he automatically knew all the terminology used in the Flowering. But just because he knew what Lapis Lazuli was didn't mean he knew everything else there was to know about this crazy dimension! He opened his mouth to ask what Shamans, Merchants, Hedonists, and all the rest were before clamping his mouth shut. It was rare to get a straight answer out of Lux. Asking for clarification would probably end up with him rambling on forever without really answering any of his questions. It would probably save him a lot of aggravation if he simply waited and figured out what everything was on his own later.

Honey wiped the rainwater from her eyes and gave Lux a devious grin. "Bet you'd like to be a Hedonist, huh, Lux?"

He grinned back. "You know it. I'd be very popular in the Market with this handsome face of mine. I'd get all the ladies every night, all night, and I'd provide them with excellent customer service too."

"It's nothing to joke about," E said as Honey snickered.

"Aw, come on, E. You know I wasn't being serious."

"I know, but still. Hedonists are scum," she said. "Hedonists are humans who are addicted to the Flowering," she told James. "They live in the Market and indulge in all the different kinds of sick entertainment they can find there. Merchants aren't much better. They travel throughout the planes in groups called 'bands' and scavenge creations that humans lost or discarded. They prey on crews to take what they want too. Then they take everything back to the Market to add to the variety of merchandise that's sold there." She glared at the grass as if the mere thought of the Market disgusted her.

James shuffled his thoughts around to try and organize everything she had just explained. His thoughts only scattered, though, and transformed into more questions. How could anyone possibly become addicted to the Flowering, and what kinds of "sick entertainment" did they indulge in? Who was in charge of the Market? How was it run? How did all of this work?

"I've always felt that the Flowering is dangerous," E continued, "and I'm not talking about its planes and citizens. Those things are external. They're things that attack you, and all you have to do is fight back. But the powers that the Flowering grants us, our creations, our bodies, all of it. We need to have the good sense to use our powers responsibly. We need to be careful with how we conduct ourselves here."

Grave silence followed her words. Then Lux grinned. He looked around at each crew member with mischief sparkling in his eyes before he began applauding slowly, one clap at a time. Honey burst into cackles before joining.

"Keep it down," E snarled as she checked the forest for signs of danger.

Their clapping escalated into a raucous round of applause. Bloom stared at them with a flat expression. James remained silent, unsure of what to make of all this immaturity.

"You two need to learn to control yourselves. Shut up! I mean it," said E.

Honey and Lux continued to grin even as their applause subsided.

"But it was such a good speech, E," Lux said, his eyes still twinkling. "So serious too."

Honey chuckled. E shook her head, looking unusually exhausted.

"What am I going to do with you two? I try my best but.... What if something happens to me? What if I'm not here in the future?"

"That'll never happen, E," said Lux.

"You don't know that. You don't!"

The earnestness in her expression shrank Honey's and Lux's smiles.

"Well, I guess you'll always have Bloom," E said, more to herself than to anyone else. "As long as you have him, you'll survive, and you'll have a purpose."

"Purpose?" James grumbled. "What purpose?"

E pierced him with a black glare.

"Well, I just feel like we've just been wandering aimlessly through a million planes all these nights. I didn't know we had some kind of purpose," he said, curling up slightly on the grass.

"Is that so?" she growled.

"Sorry, James. I forgot to tell you," Lux said, glancing nervously at E. "The past few weeks have been a dry spell. Actually, I don't think we've had one for this long before. But yeah, our crew does operate on a mission. Other than surviving, I mean. That's always number one, obviously. But–oh, yeah! I never explained about the marked and the moulded."

James pursed his lips. At least Lux remembered that he hadn't explained something this time.

"Marked citizens have a red circle somewhere on their body, and that circle is called 'the mark,'" said Lux. "If a citizen is marked, it means two things. One, it means that their time in the Flowering is up and they have to move on to the next dimension. We don't know what dimension that is, but they need to move on because if they don't, they'll fall victim to the moulded. Which leads me to point number two.

"A moulded citizen is a marked citizen that's combined itself with other marked citizens and turned into this really crazy, evil kind of marked citizen. Like that marked pig citizen that chased us during your second night. That was probably a moulded citizen, judging from how crazy it was acting and how fast it was.

"The moulded just stay in the Flowering and hunt down other citizens to keep moulding with because they get stronger each time they do. And if they mould like a million times, they can start shifting and changing their bodies into different forms at will. It's not totally without consequences, though, because combining themselves with so many different citizens so many times makes them super unstable. Their bodies spazz at random moments, and they can't do anything about it. I guess it's the price they pay for taking so many of the marked, but anyway.

"Only marked citizens can be moulded, so the unmarked ones are safe, but all the marked ones need to watch out because they'll be taken eventually if they don't move on. But that's where we step in. We take down the moulded to stop them from preying on the marked, and we free the marked that have already been taken. Or at least we try. We can't free them all. If a marked citizen chooses to join the moulded out of their own free will–and there are actually a good number that do that–then they get sucked into the moulded citizen and stay as one forever. There's nothing we can do in that situation except to slay that moulded citizen so that it doesn't take any more of the marked.

"But there are also a lot of marked citizens out there with good hearts who don't want to join the moulded even if they do choose to stay behind for whatever reason and end up getting taken. Those ones we can always save. If we slay the moulded citizen that took them, that'll free them and any other marked citizens that were taken against their will. So, yeah. Long story short, our mission is to protect the marked and slay the moulded. Pretty simple, right?"

"Why do you even bother explaining all the details, Lux? It's not like he's going to be useful with any of this," Honey said, jerking her head toward James.

"Aw, come on, Honey. Don't be mean."

James narrowed his eyes and sat up straighter. Despite Honey's remarks and the gun incident with the boar, he was confident about his fighting skills now. For the past few weeks, Lux had been training him extensively in weaponry and agility, and though his shooting skills still needed a little work, he was getting pretty good with knives. He thought he might even force Honey to eat her words next time by saving her from danger with one of his blades.

Bloom sprayed James with rainwater as he shook out his fur. He roved about the grass, sniffing, before raising his head. He walked into the forest, passed behind the thin, white trunk of an aspen, and disappeared.

"All right, Bloom! An exit!" Lux said as he punched the air.

Honey smiled as she slid strands of matted hair away from her face. James sighed with relief. They could leave this miserable plane at last.

"Let's go," E said.

James scurried after Lux through the exit and into the new plane. He stepped down onto the fresh asphalt of a wide, deserted road. His skin prickled, prompting him to scan his surroundings. There was a tension gripping the air. Rows of white clouds stretched overhead toward the distant full moon like nail marks dragged across the sky. On either side of the road stood homes of every kind, from small apartments to mansions complete with protruding balconies and floating fenced yards, all crammed next to and on top of one another without the slightest gap. Some homes displayed only their exteriors while others stood open, revealing their contents like dollhouses. Bloom and E snapped their heads to the right, where the road sloped up into a hill that blocked the horizon in the distance.

Something was coming.

"Guys, in here," Lux whispered.

He crept into a wooden shed jammed into the wall of homes and signaled for them to follow. The crew hurried inside, closed the door, and peered through the cracks between the planks. A figure appeared on the hill, staggering from side to side.

It was a child, a small child wearing a bloodstained dress. Her wails were entrenched in fear and confusion. She stumbled forth on bare feet, wiping her tears away with her fists, until only a few yards separated her from the crew. A small, red tattoo-like circle on her shoulder betrayed that she was a marked citizen.

"No," E said, holding Lux down as he made to open the door.

James gasped and fell back as a swarm of grotesque creatures burst over the hill and spilled onto the street. They were alien-like in appearance. Their slimy skin glistened in the light. Some flailed long limbs that whipped about. Their large, oblong heads looked similar to those of giant squids. Others scuttled forward on pointed, spider-like legs and had bulbous heads like that of sperm whales. All of them shared identical grins that were full of sharp, wet teeth. One of the aliens outstripped the horde. Its taut grin widened as it wriggled swiftly toward the crying girl.

"Bloom, now!" E shouted.

The door of the shed banged open as Bloom dashed outside. Leaping over the girl, he planted himself in the alien's path and bared his teeth. The alien halted, its grin still stretched across its face. E, Honey, and Lux ran out of the shed. Lux grabbed his pellet gun, aimed at the alien's eye, and pulled the trigger. The creature reared back and cried out in a strange voice as purple blood squirted out of its eye. James spotted a red circle on the underside of one of its flailing limbs.

"Safe to shoot!" Lux yelled.

A large assault rifle appeared in Honey's hand. She knelt down and began shooting at the swarm. Several aliens exploded, their limbs and eyes flying through the air with purple mush. Others bore their injuries and advanced relentlessly forward. Still others remained unharmed as bullets bounced off of their shiny skin.

Lux snatched up the little girl into his arms. Bloom charged at the alien that Lux had shot in the eye and tackled the creature. For several moments, all James could see was blue fur struggling amidst a tangle of wriggling legs and gray, slimy skin. The creature shrieked. Purple blood sprayed in an arc as Bloom ripped off the limb that bore the mark and tossed it aside. The leg thudded onto the ground, still flopping.

E sprinted forward and leapt high into the air, flipping then twisting and turning as a black machete appeared in her hand. As she plummeted back to the ground, she drove the blade into the creature's mark with unerring precision, piercing the thick, writhing limb.

The creature vanished.

Another black machete appeared in her hand. She ran into the horde and began hacking away. Purple blood squirted as she thrust her machetes through yellow eyes. Bloom plunged into the swarm as well, ripping apart more limbs as Honey's bullets drilled through the air.

"A little help here!" she yelled at James, who had been standing open-mouthed in front of the shed.

He jumped and looked around in confusion before staring at both of his hands. He needed to create something and fast, but the more he wanted to create, the more he felt immobilized. All of his training from the past weeks had vaporized, leaving his mind blank.

"Hold her!" Lux shouted.

He thrust the crying girl into James's arms and ran to Honey, who created another rifle and tossed it to him. James wrapped the girl in a tight embrace and crouched down as Lux shot at the aliens surrounding E. The girl squirmed in James's grasp.

"*Brother!*" she screamed in Our Word. She stretched out her arms.

James looked up. A small boy stood on the marble balcony of a white mansion high above.

"*No!*" the boy yelled.

An alien dodged E's machetes and ran against Honey's and Lux's bullets with its greedy eyes set upon the girl. James remained frozen as the girl screamed. E hurled a machete before another swarm surrounded her. Her blade somersaulted through the air before planting itself into the back of the alien with a spurt of blood. The creature screamed as it reared up in front of James.

The moment seemed to slow as he stared at the creature then looked down at the girl. She buried her face in his chest and gripped his shirt with her tiny fists. Her hands were only a fraction of his. She could have been a bloodstained cherub.

He drew his knife. Crying out, he thrust the blade into the creature's eye. The creature retreated, shrieking and lashing.

"*Up here!*" the boy shouted to him.

James clutched the girl and ran as the boy unfurled a rope ladder from the balcony of the white mansion.

"*Climb!*" the boy yelled.

"Here, climb. Climb onto my back. Put your arms around my neck. That's it." James tried to suppress the panic in his voice as he coaxed the girl onto his back.

Once sure of her grip on his shirt, he began scaling the ladder, grabbing each rung with frantic hands and focusing on the balcony so many feet above.

"Guys!" he screamed. "Guys, up here! Crew Blue!"

One by one, the members of the crew saw him. Honey and Lux inched backward toward the ladder, still shooting at the aliens, before abandoning their rifles and climbing up as well. E shoved both of her machetes through an alien's mouth then jumped between its legs as the creature shrieked. She dashed toward the ladder. Bloom tore off a final limb then dodged alien after alien before running into one of the homes.

"Bloom!" James cried.

"He'll find an exit on his own! Just focus!" E yelled as she dangled at the bottom of the ladder.

James bit down on his lip and forced himself to climb faster, pushing on despite his burning muscles, hoping beyond hope that the girl's sliding grip wouldn't loosen before he reached the balcony. The aliens swarmed toward the ladder.

"Aim for the eyes!" E said, drawing her handgun.

Honey and Lux whipped out their guns. The popping of bullets and the cries of aliens rang in James's ears as he clambered over the banister and onto the balcony. He paid no attention to the girl as she released her grip on him. Drawing his gun, he shot at the horde below. He felt wildly grateful for Lux's shooting lessons each time an alien exploded or squirmed away from the ladder. He created more ammunition, shooting round after round, losing count of his creations. At last, the rest of the crew reached the balcony too. E swung herself over the banister then cut the ladder. The crew watched as the ropes dropped into the swirling swarm below. James stumbled back and fell onto his knees. The sound of panicked chiding made him look around.

"*What are you doing?*" the boy said as he grasped the girl by her shoulders. "*Why have you returned? What was it all for if you were just going to return?*"

He slid his thumb away from her shoulder. His eyes grew wide with horror as they found the mark. He looked at her, speechless, then said, "*Why are you still here?*"

The girl scrubbed her eyes with her palms as she burst into fresh tears.

"*I said, why are you here?*" the boy said. "*You need to go!*"

The girl sobbed as he shook her.

"*Hey, hey. Easy. Calm down, now,*" Lux said. He separated the two.

"*What was it all for? What was it all for, Sister? Do you want to be moulded like the others?*" the boy cried. He sank onto his knees and buried his face in his hands.

"*But I-I don't want to go,*" she said, stuttering between her sobs. "*I'd … I'd rather mould!*"

The boy snapped his head up, fury and anguish burning on his tear-stained face.

"*I'd rather mould,*" she continued. "*Then I can meet the others again. I can be with our brother and sister who were taken.*"

"*Don't you be ridiculous,*" the boy said. "*You need to go. Now!*"

Lux placed a firm hand on his shoulder as he tried to grab her again.

"*No! I don't want to leave,*" said the girl. "*I'm scared, and I can't just leave you and the others!*"

"*Enough,*" said E.

The children jumped with surprise as a black machete appeared in her hand. The girl shrank beneath E's shadow as she stepped toward them.

"*You know what will happen if you don't leave,*" said E. "*Do you really want to become a monster?*"

The girl looked up at her with a stricken expression.

"*She's right. You need to go before he takes you too,*" said the boy. "*Do you really want to become one of the moulded? Do you want that to be your fate?*"

"*Wait,*" said Honey. "*Who is 'he,' and where is he? How many of your brothers and sisters has he moulded with?*"

"*Our father. He's inside. He's taken two of us already, and when my mark appears, he'll take me too. He'll roam free, taking and taking, growing and growing,*" said the boy. He rounded on the girl. "*And you'll be helping him! You really think we'll be together when we're like that? Don't tell me that that's what you want!*"

"*If you mould now, you'll be doing it out of your own free will,*" E told the girl. "*And if you mould out of your own free will, you can never be freed. When we slay your father, he'll disappear and you along with him. I don't know where citizens go afterward, but I can't imagine it'll be pretty for those who chose to mould.*"

"E, come on. Go easy on her," Lux said as the girl trembled. He knelt down and put a hand on her shoulder. "*I know it's scary, and I'm sorry all this had to happen to you. But you need to leave the Flowering before it's too late. Please. We're begging you.*"

"*We'll look after your brother,*" Honey said. "*And we'll free the others. We promise.*"

James remained silent. He felt that he should say something to comfort the little girl but didn't know where to start or what he could possibly say that would prove useful. After a few feeble attempts to conjure up the right words, he decided to stay quiet. The others were handling it just fine without him, after all.

The girl looked at each crew member as if to implore them to say something else, something to convince her otherwise. She turned to the boy as they did not.

"*But what's going to happen?*" she asked. "*The Flowering is all I've ever known. I'm so scared.*"

Grief pulled at the boy's face. "*I know. I know it's scary, but nothing good will happen if you stay. You need to move on. You need to move on.*" He wrapped her in an embrace.

For a moment, the girl stood still, and the boy shook against her shoulder with stifled cries. She closed her eyes and stepped away from him.

"*I'm sorry,*" she told him. "*Please rescue my family,*" she told the crew. She looked at James. "*Thank you for saving me.*"

She vanished.

More tears dripped down the boy's cheeks. Lux put a hand on his shoulder.

"The girl," James said as he unlocked his voice at last. "Does this mean she's gone now?"

Lux nodded. "She's moved on to the next dimension. She's safe from the moulded now."

James flinched as a deep voice rumbled out from within the depths of the mansion.

"*Boy,*" the voice called.

"*It's him,*" the boy whispered. "*Our father. He'll slay you if he finds you here. Quick, follow me.*"

He hurried the crew into the mansion. They ran through an oval foyer made of marble and surrounded by Roman pillars then into a room covered in dark, green tiles that glistened like snakeskin. Two bathtubs and a sink stood within the small room. Steam swirled up from the murky, green water in each tub.

"*In here!*"

The boy opened the louvered doors of a small closet and closed them after the crew had rushed inside. They watched him through the slats of the doors as he made to leave.

"*Boy,*" the voice rumbled. "*I called you.*"

The boy stumbled back as a man appeared at the doorway. His deep, guttural voice contrasted with his body, which was tall and thin like a dry stalk of overgrown corn. His hair, which lay neatly to one side of his head, matched his trimmed mustache. He wore a tuxedo that perfectly fit his gangly frame. The boy retreated from the man until his back hit one of the bathtubs. He slid down into a trembling crouch. The man stared at him with round, unblinking eyes.

"Why aren't you answering me, boy?"

"I'm sorry. I was only looking for our sister as you had asked."

"Did you find her?"

"No, sir. I was just about to–ah!"

The boy swiveled his head from side to side as he looked at his hands and arms. A luminescent, blue glow had swallowed his entire body. He looked up at the man with a stunned expression. The man returned his stare with bulging eyes. The boy scrambled as the man lunged. He gripped the boy with talon-like fingers as the boy's glow disappeared. A small, red circle appeared on his arm. His mark.

"No!" Honey screamed.

She burst forth from the closet. She grabbed a gun from her belt and began shooting at the man's head. He stumbled back, smiling even as bullets perforated his face.

"Get the boy!" E yelled as she created another machete.

Lux and James sprang out of the closet and grabbed him. Pulling and yanking, they tried to rip him away from the man's clutches. But the boy's and the man's arms had melted into one so that they stretched together like flesh-colored molasses. E hacked futilely at their elongated skin with both of her machetes as James continued tugging frantically on the child.

"The mark is on his chest!" the boy screamed.

The man yanked the boy toward himself, tearing him away from James and Lux even as Honey continued shooting. The boy whipped through the air then collided with the man's chest. The man fell onto his knees as their bodies began to stretch and undulate and mould together.

Honey drew her knife, ready to pounce forward in a blind rage.

"Honey, no!" E shouted.

Honey screamed out in fury as Lux tackled her and pinned her to the floor. The boy's outstretched hand sank into the man's twisting torso. E spread her stance and held up her machetes. James reached for his knife only to realize that he had left it in the alien's eye. With a shaking hand, he unsheathed his dagger instead. The corners of his notes pushed treacherously against his thigh as he adjusted his stance. He couldn't remember how many creations he had used up.

The man's body ceased moulding. He rose to his feet, taller than before. The bullet holes that Honey had put through his head had all disappeared. His eyes bulged as he grinned with a mouth full of yellow teeth. Honey continued struggling against Lux.

"Honey!" E barked. "Calm down. Don't do anything stupid!"

But Honey paid her no heed. For whatever reason, the sight of the man taking the boy had triggered something both wrathful and desperate within her. She shoved Lux aside, jumped onto her feet, and shot the man through the chest. He grinned as he swung a massive fist toward her. Lux pushed her aside. The crew yelled as blood exploded. Lux slammed into the wall then collapsed onto the floor. Blood poured out from his broken skull and onto the glimmering tiles.

Honey drew another gun and screamed as she began shooting with both hands. The man raised his fist again. E leapt toward him before he could attack Honey. Her machetes slashed in unison and cleaved the monster's head off of his neck. His smiling head rolled across the floor. His body continued to move about. Honey threw her guns aside, lunged forth, and began ripping apart the layers of clothes concealing the man's mark. E's machetes slashed again. The man's arms fell from his body before they could trap Honey in a crushing embrace. The decapitated head began to disappear, reforming on the body's neck.

"Gotcha!" Honey screamed as she tore off the last layer.

Over the man's heart lay his mark.

She drew another gun, pushed the barrel against the mark, and pulled the trigger. The man vanished. The boy tumbled out of the air and rolled onto the floor along with two other children. Honey rushed to Lux's side. She stared at his bleeding skull and his bent neck then closed her eyes.

"I'm sorry," she whispered to him. She turned to E. Both regret and defiance wrinkled her face as she said, "I couldn't just watch. You know I couldn't."

To James's surprise, E, rather than yelling at Honey for her disobedience, only sighed and shoved her machetes under her belt.

"I guess it couldn't be helped," she said. "I'm sure Lux will understand too, but try to hold back next time. He shouldn't have to get his head bashed in because of you."

Honey nodded.

"*Where did he go?*" the boy said. "*Is he really...?*"

"*He is,*" E replied. Her voice softened as she said, "*He's gone now. He can't harm you anymore.*"

Joy spread across his face. "*Brother, sister, we're free!*"

One of the children began to cry. The other looked around at the crew as if at a loss for what to make of them.

"*Are there any more of the moulded here?*" E asked.

"*No. It was just our father.*" Tears ran down the boy's face. "*You saved us. I don't know how to thank you all.*"

"*We promised your sister that we'd take care of you,*" Honey said with a firm nod.

The boy did a double take at Lux. "*Will he be all right?*" he asked.

Honey and E nodded.

The children exchanged smiles that mixed sorrow with their joy. They vanished one after another. The boy looked around at the crew a final time.

"*Thank you*," he said.

And then he was gone.

James stared at the spot where the boy had been then groaned and sank onto the floor. Despite the whirlwind of events that had just passed, his thoughts were oddly blank. All he could do was stare at the tiles as his head bobbed up and down to the rhythm of his breathing. He threw his hands into the air and fell onto his back.

"Time," Honey said, holding up her watch. "I got Lux."

She kissed his bloodstained head before piercing his watch with her knife. James didn't bother getting up. Nor did he wait for Honey and E. He simply lifted his dagger and pierced his watch.

He clutched his chest as his eyes sprang open. He remained in bed, trying to catch his breath as the glimmer of the green-tiled room danced about in his mind. Several minutes passed before he was able to get up and start his day.

CHAPTER 7

THE HUNTED

Alarge, finned shadow swam in the clear water below. It glided past the legs of the zigzagging dock on which James stood before disappearing. People laughed and chatted with one another as they strolled up and down the dock. James didn't need to check if any of them had a watch. He already knew that they were citizens. All of them were dressed like they were attending a luau in the middle of summer despite the cold, crisp air making him shiver. Bloom surveyed the dock, ears perked and nose quivering. He looked at E.

"There's one here?" she said.

He nodded.

James clenched his fists and hung his head. The last few nights had been uneventful, so he had hoped that tonight would prove to be quiet as well. But Bloom's nod could only mean one thing. There was a moulded citizen here.

More than a week had passed since the crew had rescued the little girl and her siblings from their moulded father, and they had embarked on several more rescue missions since then. James dreaded their missions because each one ensured such horrendous injuries. Last time, he'd hit the wall so hard that Lux had described his head as looking like a cracked egg filled with red custard. James would never forget that pain. It had blasted away all his senses and washed him in white, thumping agony. Floating as something small and helpless within a shell of a body, he'd been neither conscious nor unconscious as he'd waited for his skull to piece itself back together.

A large, white cloud issued from his mouth as he sighed. It wasn't just the pain and the wounds that made him dread helping citizens, though those were definitely bad enough on their own. Each battle cost him several creations too. He always found weapons missing from his belt afterward, and that forced him to waste more creations in order to refill his belt with his usual weapons.

And then there was the terror. Oh, yes, the terror within each battle. The moment everything became still before chaos burst out all around him. The knowledge that something huge and fanged was galloping after him as he ran. All the shrieks and squeals. Everything. Every single thing terrified him to the bone.

He did take some comfort in the thought that these rescue missions weren't entirely pointless, though. As much as he didn't want to admit it, he knew that helping marked citizens was the right thing to do. How could he say otherwise after saving that little girl and her siblings? There was no way he could deny the good in what they were doing after seeing something like that. A part of him even felt a sense of satisfaction from acting as a kind of protector in the Flowering. But the cost. The cost was always so high. Too high! Yes, helping the marked was great and all, but did the crew really have to go after every single moulded citizen Bloom smelled nearby?

He rubbed his arms as goose bumps rose across his skin. At least E had finally deemed the weather bad enough to let them create some adequate clothing. E, the mean tyrant who always barked out orders and treated him like he was some kind of–

"Down!" E yelled.

James threw himself onto the floor as something enormous and shiny leapt out from the water and alighted the railing several yards away. It looked like a decaying angel fish. Traces of delicate, black stripes were still visible on its rotting scales. Short, sharp spikes protruded from the flesh rimming its mouth. Though he couldn't see its mark, James had no doubt that this was the moulded citizen Bloom had smelled. The crew crouched down and pressed themselves against the railing to avoid the screaming crowds that ran past.

The creature slid off the railing as stragglers fled. Curving its head to one side, it stared at a man standing at the other end of the dock. A man with a mark on his neck. A slimy trail followed the monster as it slid swiftly forth on a stomach that wriggled like snail flesh.

"Block it!" E shouted.

The crew formed a line across the dock. The monster halted. It seemed to contemplate them before speaking in a deep, hollow voice.

"So, you are keeping to the old ways."

Bloom crouched down and bared his teeth. James stole a glance at the marked citizen behind them. He was just standing there with his mouth hanging open like an idiot. He even had a martini glass still stuck in his hand!

"James! Take that citizen and get to safety. Now!" E commanded.

He didn't need telling twice.

"No!"

"Stop!"

"Move! Move!"

James ignored the commotion erupting behind him and continued sprinting. Whatever was happening, he knew the crew could handle it. After all, E could probably chop that thing up into sashimi in a matter of moments. His job was to get that citizen and get out of here. He needed to get out of here. He wanted to get out of here!

He heard the creature inhale a deep, croaking breath from far behind. Then something whistled through the air and slammed into his back, propelling him forward. He stumbled to a stop and dropped down onto his knees as his mind grew blank. The marked citizen stared at him from what seemed like several miles away as pain began spreading throughout his body. He looked down to see the sharp tip of a gigantic, needle-like spike protruding from his chest.

He began to shake and shudder, struggling for breath as he strove to understand what he was seeing. He twisted his head around to see the creature gliding and squishing across the wooden planks. The crew ran after it, shooting their guns, brandishing their blades, and yelling things he couldn't hear. The creature opened its mouth.

He would have screamed had his lungs allowed him to. He saw the creature's pointed teeth and its gaping, black throat before its muscular tongue shot out, wrapped around him, and pulled him into its mouth. The crew cried out as the creature swallowed him whole. He slid swiftly down its throat and into its belly.

The smell of fish and blood overwhelmed him. He choked as a scream struggled to climb out of his throat. Dim light filtered through the creature's skin, revealing the piles of pulsing, raw flesh on which he lay. The spike wedged in his chest grated against his bones and nerves, sapping the strength in his body and what little clarity remained in his mind. Slime clung to him like bloody egg whites as he searched for something—anything—to grab on to. But everything slipped beneath his fingers. Another scream withered inside his punctured chest.

"*Twelve,*" something whispered. "*The Beast returns. The Beast. The Beast.*"

James's mouth fell open. Above him, at the far end of the creature's spine, embedded in its flesh like a bulging tumor, was a grinning face.

He grabbed his knife and pointed the blade at the face as panic surged within him. He struggled to keep his aim steady as his strength continued pouring out of him. He could feel his flesh trying and failing to close around the spike in his chest. The bulging face began to creep toward him. It traveled along the creature's spine, still staring, still grinning as it approached. James floundered about. This was it. This was the end. He was stuck in this rotting, red cemetery and that face was inching closer with every passing moment. It was coming for him, and he was alone. This was the end!

The creature suddenly swerved to a stop. The grinning face halted as well. James heard the muffled sound of E's voice. The crew members' silhouettes raced past, visible through the creature's rancid skin. James's breath caught in his throat as he listened to E barking out orders. Her black eyes seemed to glare at him through the creature's flesh.

He gulped. Still trembling but somehow more clear-minded, he created a spear and threw it toward the wall of sickly skin. A white arm burst out from the piles of flesh and caught his spear. More arms shot out all around him. A cold hand clamped over his mouth. He kicked as hard as he could and fought against the hands that wrapped around his torso, dug into his shoulders, pinned down his arms, gripped his wrist, and–

James's eyelids flew open as he drew a long, ragged breath. He bolted upright in his bed and clutched at his drumming heart. He searched for the face, the hands, the red lumps of flesh. But all he found were textbooks, paperwork, and empty white bowls of instant ramen sitting in the darkness of his room. He pressed his hand deeper into his chest, still panting and fearing for his heart as it continued to race. He raised his left hand, searching for the watch he knew he wouldn't find, the watch that had, at last, been pierced. His mind dropped into a spiraling free fall as he saw his alarm clock.

It was five-thirty AM.

An hour of sleep. He still needed a whole hour of sleep to get his eight hours for the night! He gripped his head and squeezed his memory as he tried to extract everything he'd ever learned from Lux about the rules of the Flowering. He managed to scrape up the recollection that he could make up any hours he lost but that eight hours needed to pass from the time he woke up in order for the sleep to count. Which meant that even if he were to fall asleep right now, the sleep wouldn't count toward the eight hours he needed.

He grabbed his pillow and smashed his face into it. He hated the Flowering. He hated it for everything it had done to him and everything it would continue to do to him. He had never done anything to deserve this!

The ticking of his wall clock reached his ears. He unglued his face from his pillow. He couldn't keep panicking like this. He needed to get a grip on himself. His life depended on it. Time was still passing whether he liked it or not, and he didn't have a second to spare! He forced himself to breathe in deeply before releasing his breath in a steady stream.

He had two options. He could return to the Flowering now and sleep for nine hours straight, or he could get on with his day in Reality for the next eight hours then sleep for one. Would it be better to go back now? But what if the crew was still battling that moulded citizen? No! No. He couldn't go back now. It would be much safer to get on with his day. As soon as one-thirty hit, he would set his alarm to start ringing at two, go to bed, and wake up around two-thirty when he finally heard his alarm. That way, he could get some homework done during the day, make up the hour of sleep he had lost, and go back to sleep at his usual bedtime of ten-thirty. He hated that he'd have to miss class in the afternoon, but what choice did he have?

He hugged his knees then got ready to rush to the nearest drugstore, which he could only hope was open at this hour. He needed to pick up some sleeping pills as soon as possible if he wanted to fall asleep in the middle of the day.

One-thirty seemed to approach both too slowly and too quickly as the day wore on. James rifled through textbooks and paperwork, highlighting, scribbling, and typing, while keeping one nervous eye on the ticking clock. By one o'clock, he'd slurped down two more bowls of instant ramen and shoved some sleeping pills into his mouth. He'd felt so anxious for this time to come and yet, now that it was finally approaching, he only wanted more time. He had managed to finish many of the assignments he'd fallen behind on, but he couldn't help but feel a sinking sense of despair as he looked around at the unfinished projects that still lay scattered across his room. He tossed himself onto his mattress and cursed the Flowering even as drowsiness washed over consciousness.

Bloom twitched his tail and smiled at him. Streams of people brushed past James as they walked briskly by. He and Bloom were standing in a large plaza at the bottom of a square building composed of three stories. The building's cement columns and walls gave it the appearance of a parking structure, though the polished floor of the plaza looked better suited for a luxury department store. Escalators descended into the plaza at random points from all four sides of the building. High above, hordes of people hurried across thin air, creating a moving ceiling. Despite their movements, pale light shone down unobstructed into the plaza as if the ceiling opened up to nothing but a winter sky. Many of the people swung briefcases as they rushed along while others walked dogs or tugged on children's arms to hurry them along. Every few moments, several people would stoop down onto their hands and knees and crawl like insects through a corner on the top floor and onto an escalator. There, they would stand erect again and ride the escalator down into the plaza before resuming their walk.

"Excuse me?"

James jumped as a man held out a map. His eyes darted from the man's smile to his black bowler hat to his hands, neither of which bore a watch.

"Could you please tell me where this might be?" the man asked in a British accent as he straightened out the map.

"I-I'm sorry. I don't know," James said.

"Oh, I see. Well, that's quite all right. Would you happen to know, sir?" He leaned forward and held out the map for Bloom to see.

Bloom shuffled his feet and licked his chops then shook his head.

"I see. Pity. Well, thank you very much. I'll be on my way, then." The man tipped his hat and walked back into the bustling crowds.

For a moment, James could only stand still. He'd had plenty of moments to interact with citizens because of the crew's rescue missions, but apart from the context of battle, citizens seldom engaged the crew in conversation, if at all.

He jumped again as Bloom sneezed. They stared at one another. James had become so used to Bloom's presence that he'd forgotten how miraculous his friendship really was. Lux had explained before that friendships between humans and citizens were rare, and James believed him. He couldn't imagine other humans in the Flowering traveling with a citizen every night like Crew Blue did. How had Bloom formed such a close relationship with the crew and E in particular? Lux had never explained all the specifics.

"Hey, Lux."

He fell silent as he remembered that he was alone. The others didn't know that he had planned on returning at this hour, which meant that he would have to survive whatever dangers the next hour held with only Bloom to help him. And that wasn't his only problem. His heart dropped into his stomach as he realized that, in his hurry to return to the Flowering, he had forgotten to set his alarm. There was nothing in Reality to wake him up, and of course, his stupid watch ensured that he had no way of knowing how much time was passing in Reality. That meant that he was stuck in the Flowering until Lux returned and confirmed the time for him. He rubbed his face. If only his watch wasn't defective. None of this would be a problem if he'd just been born with a normal watch!

"Looks like it's just you and me, Bloom."

Bloom twitched his tail then trotted off into the crowds. James followed him through an archway in one of the walls. They climbed down a flight of stairs and stepped onto a dingy subway platform. People stood in loose lines, craning their heads to check for signs of a train beyond the clear doors guarding a dark tunnel. James followed Bloom to a wooden bench then sat down and eyed the woman sitting on the other end. She smiled at him as her knitting needles clicked away. He hesitated then smiled back.

The doors of the tunnel slid open and ushered in a train with a blast of wind. The crowds stirred before boarding. James hurried after Bloom as he trotted into the train. Inside, people were standing along the length of the train or sitting on metal seats that jutted high off of the ground. Many sat so high up that their heads disappeared through the ceiling. He spun around as the doors clapped shut then fell to the floor as the train jerked forward and rushed down the tunnel. He fumbled about in the darkness that engulfed him then grabbed Bloom's fur. Bloom sat still, a steady pillar of support, as the train continued rocking from side to side.

The sun doused James in warm amber as the train sped out into the open and curved. He rose to his feet, shielding his eyes with one hand, and stepped closer to the windows. Endless green fields flashed by. Honeyed light glinted off long blades of grass that rippled alongside the train. The full moon sat in a soaring expanse of fading blue. And as James gazed at the gold-emerald plains and the wide, deep sky, he forgot for just one moment how much he hated the Flowering.

The wet touch of Bloom's nose pushed him out of his trance. A tickling sensation followed as Bloom licked his fingers. James wiped the saliva off on his jeans and followed him as he sauntered down the train. All was silent except for the clattering of the train's wheels and the clicking of Bloom's nails against the floor. The number of people thinned as they made their way from one car to another until only one or two people stood in each car. Bloom stopped at a pair of doors separating their car from the next.

"What's wrong?" James asked.

Bloom's tail hung low. The sadness in his eyes warned of something unpleasant to come. He scratched at the doors with his paw. James pried them open and stepped into the new car. He gasped and recoiled.

A mutilated body hung from a noose tied to a baggage rack. A black bowler hat sat on the man's cocked head. Bloom walked over to the body and sat down in front it. James drew closer as well. The legion of slashes and punctures covering the man's face made him look like a broken piece of coral. A leg was missing, and a spear had been planted into his chest. The word "PROTECT" had been spray-painted across the man's torso.

James looked away. He couldn't tell if this was the same citizen in the bowler hat who had asked him for directions. He hoped that he wasn't. He stared at the man's brown shoes as they swung gently along with the train.

What was he supposed to do? It seemed only right to cut this citizen free of that awful noose. Or was it better to let things be? He looked to Bloom for ideas only to find himself following his golden gaze to the man's hand. He leaned in closer. The man's fingers. They were disintegrating into thin air.

"James."

He shouted and jumped back.

"Whoa, sorry!" said Lux, laughing. "Didn't mean to scare you."

"What are you doing here?" James said, leaning on his knees for recovery.

"What do you mean, what am I doing here? It's ten-thirty. That's what I'm doing here!"

Ten-thirty. It was already ten-thirty PM in Reality even though it felt like he'd been in the Flowering for an hour at most.

"I tried to come a little early, though, in case you got here first," Lux said. "Did you make up the time you lost?"

"Yeah, I made up the time," James grumbled.

"Nice. Man, sorry we couldn't get to you last night. We gutted that thing and everything to try and get you out, but we were too late. But hey, you probably didn't lose that much time, right? So it's all good. And, oh! I told myself last night that I had to tell you this. You're getting so fast! We were all yelling at you to turn around, but you just kept running so fast down that dock. It was hilarious."

James swallowed the rant that boiled up to his lips as Honey appeared next to Bloom.

"Oh, boy," she said as she saw the swaying body. "Maybe we should go somewhere else. E'll be pissed if she sees this."

"Yeah, you're probably right," said Lux.

"You think they're still around?"

"Don't know. Just got here. James, did you see any Hunters?"

"Uh ... I, uh–"

"Bloom, did you see anyone?" Honey said as she rolled her eyes.

Bloom shook his head.

"Then maybe we should try to find cover. They might still be here," said Honey.

"Sounds good to me."

"Wait," said James.

The others turned around mid-step. He remained next to the body, unsure of how to articulate himself.

"Shouldn't we ... I mean, I think it might be good to ... you know."

"No, we don't know," Honey snapped.

James struggled then said, "It's still a body. I know he's a citizen, but shouldn't we at least cut him down?"

"Oh! No, James. Don't worry about it. It's an unmarked citizen," Lux said, as if that were enough to explain everything.

"Citizens can't mould or die if they're not marked," Honey said, answering the uncertain expression on James's face with an annoyed one.

"Yeah," said Lux. "If they're hurt bad enough like this one, they just disappear from the plane they're in and reappear in a different plane in the Flowering afterward. This guy had bad luck here, but he'll be all right. He's the least of our worries right now."

Honey nodded. "We should be more worried about the Hunters."

"What are Hunters?" said James.

The sigh she expelled reminded him of steam bursting out of a rice cooker.

"Hunters," she said. "Human extremists who go around hunting citizens. A lot of them choose to speak only in Our Word and carry broadswords around with them. Long ones like the ones knights used to carry."

"I think I mentioned them to you before, James," said Lux. "Hunters are some of the humans who visit the City a lot."

"Yeah, but you didn't mention that they go around killing citizens or what they do in general," James seethed.

"Hunters hunt," Honey said. "Moulded. Marked. Unmarked. It doesn't matter to them. They think that all citizens are evil and out to get humans, so they travel throughout the planes in groups called 'families' and torture and kill citizens every night. They say it's supposed to teach citizens to stay away from us humans."

The shift in her tone told James that the disgust on her face no longer had anything to do with him.

"To be fair," said Lux, "they do hunt the moulded like we do, so they technically do help clear some of the dangers in the Flowering. But they make things way too black and white if you ask me. I mean, all citizens aren't evil. Like that little girl and her brother that we saved before. They weren't some kind of threat, even if that girl didn't want to move on. All she really needed was someone to calm her down a little, give her some support, help her to have that space so that she could just think things through and do the right thing. Plus, all that torturing and killing just makes a lot of citizens super paranoid of us."

"Yeah, and it pisses them off too," Honey said.

Uneasiness quickened James's pulse. Were any Hunters still on this train? What would they do to Bloom if they saw him? Would they listen to the crew if they tried to explain that he was harmless?

E appeared next to Bloom. James tensed along with Lux and Honey as she stepped closer to the butchered citizen and glared at the noose from which he hung. She drew Bloom closer to herself with a gentle hand. He stared at her, his eyes more golden than ever in the nectar light.

"Let's find a way off this train," E said.

The crew followed her as she walked to the sliding doors. James took a final look at what remained of the body. The head slowly disappeared, leaving only the noose as he walked away.

CHAPTER 8

RUTHLESS

The giant, rugged gorge stretched on endlessly to the left and to the right. Thick strata of rock formed the gorge's walls, which soared up and tapered into an endless series of massive arches, creating a tunnel-like effect. Everything, from the dirt to the sky to the sun, was red-orange. The only interruptions were the full moon, a small, square bar grafted into the side of the gorge, and a variety of neon shapes floating around the bar. Many of the shapes formed the outlines of drinks, and an unknown language composed of strange symbols created captioned advertisements. Simple shapes, such as triangles, squares, or an occasional eye, also floated around the bar. Honey stood behind the counter. Lux had seated himself on a leather stool across from her, and Bloom was sitting on the ground next to Lux. All three of them were staring at James and E.

"Again!" E shouted.

James's arm shook before faltering. He planted the butt of his spear into the ground and squeezed his eyes shut against the beads of sweat trickling down his forehead. E marched up to him and kicked his spear out from under him. He collapsed onto the dirt then rolled slowly onto his back and remained spread-eagle as he panted for air.

"Up," she growled.

More than two weeks had passed since E had announced that she would be taking an active role in training James. She hadn't explained her reasons for suddenly taking the reins from Lux, but he and James had both agreed that it was a good sign.

"Good job, James. She's investing in you. She knows you're a keeper now. See? I told you she'd turn around," Lux had whispered to him.

As much as he disliked E, James had still felt strangely proud of earning her trust. More importantly, though, E taking over his training had meant that he wouldn't have to put up with Lux's rambling or forgetfulness any longer. He had tried to confront Lux and air his grievances on a few occasions in the past weeks, but he could never bring himself to be honest with him. As annoying as Lux could be, James had begun to regard him as a friend, and he didn't want to risk disturbing their friendship with any unnecessary confrontations.

He had also hoped that E's training would finally enable him to become a proficient fighter in their battles with the moulded. He'd become fairly skilled at binding the crew's wounds and healing his own injuries, and, of course, he'd long ago become adept at creating during battles. He was also the best runner in the crew, for which Lux often teased him. On more than one occasion, he'd managed to grab a marked citizen and run away successfully to safety. Fighting the moulded head-on, however, still wasn't his forte. So, the possibility of becoming skilled in battle had made him look forward to training with E, who was, after all, the best fighter in the crew.

In hindsight, he couldn't help but laugh at himself. He'd expected E's training to be difficult, sure. But he hadn't expected it to be excruciating! Each night now felt like boot camp, and pain followed his every step regardless of whether the crew battled the moulded or not. No matter what kind of plane they found themselves in, E would force him to practice slashing, stabbing, punching, kicking, jumping, and running until his body felt like a white-hot lump of pulsating muscles. His many blisters and bruises reappeared so often that he began to doubt they had ever healed to begin with.

Worse than the physical pain, though, were E's deprecatory comments, flashes of anger, and manhandling. He was always teetering between anxiousness and panic, waiting for her to push him toward one or the other with a harsh insult or a sudden grip on his arm. Part of her training also included stabbing him without warning. "You need to learn how to dodge!" she'd say every time her blade punctured his side. The stabbings had escalated in their level of suddenness and frequency so that terror now seized him whenever her fingers so much as twitched toward her dagger. While he couldn't deny that his fighting skills and even his healing abilities had grown at an unprecedented rate, he also grew more certain with every passing night that if something in the Flowering didn't eventually kill him, E most certainly would.

"Get up!" she shouted.

He gasped and hugged his stomach as she kicked him in the ribs. Anger flashed across her eyes before she hoisted him up by his collar. She shoved him against the rocky wall and forced the spear back into his shaking hands.

"Hey, E! Isn't it time for a break?" called Lux, who now frequently acted as James's guardian angel.

"No. He's not going to slow down our attacks or cower in the corner any longer. He's going to train, and he's going to learn how to fight! Besides, his thrusts are still too weak."

Panic surged within James as E drew her dagger. He fumbled with his spear.

"Aw, come on, E," Lux said. "Let's just have a quick drink. It's my birth night. Honey made a cake and everything."

"What?"

She rounded on Honey and Lux, much to James's relief.

"What do you mean she made a cake? Don't tell me you wasted a creation on a cake!"

"But it's Lux's birth night. And it's Halloween," Honey said.

She tried to smile as she held up a chocolate cake for E to see. The words "The Light of Crew Blue!" decorated the top in white cursive. James could only hope that E wouldn't snatch the cake away and smash it on the ground.

"Have I taught you nothing?" E said. "We still have hours to go tonight. I'm here training this moron, and you guys are over there making cakes and tequila shots?"

"The liquor was already here, E," Lux said. "Come on, we can afford to celebrate. Don't you remember how you found me on this very night two whole years ago? It was one of the best nights of my–"

She turned on her heel and stormed off.

"–life," ended Lux.

Bloom shook out his fur then trotted after her. Lux hung his head and smirked. Honey folded her hands over his, her expression creased with pity. She stared at James as he used his spear like a cane to limp over to them. He paid no attention to her staring. He'd gotten used to her animosity toward him and was too exhausted to care even if he hadn't.

"Hey, James. You're getting so good with your spear, man," Lux said. He made a valiant effort to smile.

"Thanks," James replied in a flat tone.

He slumped onto a leather stool next to Lux, spear still in hand, then stared at the pink reflection on the counter of a neon sign drifting overhead. He remained silent, too exhausted to speak or even to think.

"Still no change with your watch?" Lux asked.

"Nope."

"Man. I thought it would have changed by now. I'm getting kind of worried. I mean, it's working out, you looking at my watch and everything, but still."

James replied with more silence. He didn't have the energy to care about his watch either.

Honey grabbed a shot glass from under the counter. She slammed it down in front of James then poured him a drink. He looked up at her in surprise, but she avoided his gaze. She poured herself a shot as well and drank it in one gulp. The trio turned in unison to watch E as she continued stomping further away into the never-ending gorge.

"Let's cut the cake, shall we?" Honey said after a while.

She reared herself up to her fullest height and shook her hair away from her face before sticking her knife into the counter and rummaging for plates.

"Trick or treat!"

Lux leapt off his stool and unsheathed his dagger. James gripped his spear and assumed a battle stance. Honey's hand slid toward her knife and plucked it out of the counter. Several men had appeared, and more were stepping out of what could only be an exit hanging midair. Two beefy men wobbled forth, struggling with a clear, plastic tub filled with what looked like orange juice between them. All of the men shouldered large backpacks. A few carried metallic boxes as well. Some of the backpacks were so stuffed that they looked like they would burst. One man hauled his metal box forth using both hands, stumbling every few steps as he struggled with the box's weight. But many more men tossed aside flat bags and empty containers. As they observed their new plane, a blond man approached the crew.

"That cake sure looks good," the man said. He held up his hand to show them his watch before saying, "Can I have a piece?"

"Sorry, but this party is by invitation only. No Merchants allowed," Honey said. She wrinkled her nose and threw him a fake smile.

"We're not Merchants," he said as he tossed his empty backpack aside. "We're just posing like this for Halloween."

"We're not interested in doing business with you," Lux said, pointing his dagger at the man's face.

James aimed his spear at the man as well. He tried his best to look intimidating instead of afraid and exhausted. Honey had called these men "Merchants," which meant that they were the scavengers E had talked about before, the humans who traveled throughout the planes in groups called "bands." They picked up lost or abandoned creations to take back to the City so that they could add to the variety of merchandise sold there. They also preyed on crews for goods. James shifted his weight from one foot to the other as the rest of the band set down their luggage and surrounded the trio. The blond man stepped closer to him.

"Nice spear," the man told him. "All right, I'll cut the crap. Look. You guys are clearly outnumbered. You look like nice kids, so tell you what? Just give us those utility belts you have on there, and we'll be on our way. No trouble. No nothing."

Honey puffed out a sound of disbelief.

"I'm serious," the Merchant said, looking annoyed. "We've been going around forever now, but as you can see, we don't have as much stuff as we'd like. All we want to do is get back to the City in time for all the preparations for the Solstice. But there's no use doing that if we don't have enough stuff. So have some pity on us, and hand over your stuff, okay?"

James glanced at Lux, who continued to glare at the man. Honey's spare hand closed around the neck of a liquor bottle. The crew had already tested this plane. Guns were not an option. The blond man looked from the guns in the crew's holsters to the weapons in their hands.

He seemed to understand. Ignoring his pistol, he drew a large knife instead. His band followed his lead.

Silence ensued as the two groups waited for someone to make the first move.

The blond man smacked James's spear to the side and thrust his knife toward his stomach. Chaos erupted all around James as he dodged the man's blade. He evaded attacks to his head, his neck, and his torso before ramming the man's ribs with the butt of his spear and delivering another blow to his spine. The man crumpled. James raised his spear again.

Thick fingers gripped his neck from behind and hoisted him up into the air before he could land another blow. He twisted about, choking and gagging as he kicked wildly and swung his spear about. He pulled at the fingers, but they only tightened. His eyes bulged from his sockets as the fingers began crushing his windpipe. He wriggled desperately, unable to breathe, unable to die.

Something blue soared through the air like a speeding nimbus. A figure bolted down from its back. James dropped down onto the dirt as the Merchant released his grip on his neck. He rolled over, coughing and gasping, then looked up to see Bloom biting into the neck of his attacker. Clouds of red-orange dust blossomed from beneath the man's thrashing legs. His thick fingers fumbled for the dagger on his belt. James jumped up and plunged his spear into the man's stomach before he could stab Bloom. The man's screams and the feeling of human flesh struggling against his spear nauseated him, but he shunted aside his disgust with a determined cry and pushed deeper. Bloom released his bite on the Merchant's neck and dashed into the fray. The man floundered about before gripping James's spear. He pushed himself back onto his feet even as James struggled to keep him on the ground.

Metal flashed.

The man's body jolted as if electrocuted. His head slowly slid away from his neck. James stumbled back in surprise then fell to the ground as the man's body and severed head thudded onto the dirt. His eyes followed the head as it rolled several feet then stopped next to three more decapitated bodies lying motionless nearby.

E rose from her knees.

Wrath possessed her eyes, burning and blazing like wildfire. Blood-stained and holding a black machete in each hand, she looked like ruthlessness incarnate. A predator, who was ready to hunt. A wolf, who was ready to kill. She heaved deep breaths through her flared nose as she scanned the pandemonium raging around them.

Near the bar, Lux was wrestling with a black-haired Merchant twice his size. Broken bottles and upturned stools lay scattered around them. Bloom continued mauling another Merchant, biting deeper into his leg and whipping him about. Honey stepped back toward the rocky wall of the gorge, her knife pointed at two Merchants. One of them used a baseball bat to regain his balance as he shook out broken bits of glass from his hair. The Merchant next to him had taken Honey's utility belt.

E shoved one machete under her belt then pulled out James's spear from the Merchant who had been strangling him. She broke into a run and charged toward the men closing in on Honey. She launched the spear at the Merchant covered in glass. The spear skewered him and pinned him into the wall. He screamed and squirmed as he struggled to free himself. E continued sprinting forth. The other Merchant spun around then froze at the sight of her. He dropped his knife and Honey's belt.

"You!" he said.

She beheaded the skewered man first with the machete still in her hand then drew her other machete from her belt as she dropped down onto one knee. She sliced through the legs of the other Merchant with both of her blades before he could take a single step back. He fell to the ground, screaming. She cut off his arms with blows so swift that James barely saw her blades descending through the air. The man yelled for her to stop. She replied by cutting off his head.

"E," Honey said, cradling her injured arm. "I...."

E ignored her and ran toward Lux instead as he continued wrestling with the black-haired Merchant. Lux cried out as the man stabbed him in the chest then raised his knife over Lux's head for the final blow. E threw her machete like a boomerang. The man yelled as his hand fell onto the floor along with his knife. Lux seized the opportunity and drove his dagger into the man's side. They rolled across the ground, grunting and smearing blood into the dirt. E grabbed the man's knife off the floor and brought the blade down into its owner's back. The man screamed and rolled off of Lux. E slammed her foot into the wound Lux had inflicted on the man's side then lifted her machete. A moment later, the man's body collapsed onto the ground, headless like the others. Lux curled up as he moaned and clutched at his wounds.

E turned toward Bloom, who continued whipping his victim from side to side. A slash of her blade and the man's head rolled across the floor. Bloom turned toward the bar and silently bared his fangs.

"Come out!" E snarled.

The blond man emerged from behind the counter with his hands in the air. She began walking toward him, her eyes still burning with black rage.

"Look, you got us. I get it. I'll go in peace," the Merchant said, placing his hands on the counter.

She continued walking.

"Please. I never beg, but really, I'm a slow healer and my Jackal will kill me if I don't get back in time with more goods for the Solstice and...."

The Merchant trailed off, squinting first at E's face then at the black machete in her hand. Recognition widened his eyes. E's hand shot out and gripped the back of his head before he could make another move. She slammed his face down into Lux's cake then yanked his head back up and pointed the tip of her blade under his chin.

"Don't ever come near my crew again."

The man screamed as she hacked off his hands from his wrists. Gripping him by the collar, she flung him over the counter. He landed next to James in a cloud of dust. She threw aside her machete and pulled out her dagger from her belt. James scrambled back on his hands and feet as she began pumping her blade in and out of the Merchant's stomach. Bloom hurried forward with wide eyes and halted next to James. He pawed the ground and shuffled his feet in agitation as the man screamed and screamed.

James tried to turn away from the sight in front of him, but the man's writhing body enslaved his sight. He couldn't stop watching, couldn't stop the tortured screams and pleas for mercy from filling his ears. E stood up then slammed her foot down onto the man's bones over and over again so that they broke through his skin like large, white splinters. She knelt down then drove her dagger down into his throat so that he choked on her blade. Another machete appeared in her hand. It flashed like black lightning, and the Merchant's blond head parted from his neck.

She stood up, panting, and glared down at the body before walking back to the bar and gripping the counter. James jumped as she snapped around to glare at him with wrathful eyes.

"You moron. Don't just sit there. Get up and help Lux!" she raged.

James tripped over his own feet as he ran over to him. He began binding Lux's wounds with shaking hands as Honey limped toward them.

"You ran out of creations, didn't you?" E snarled at her.

Honey's mouth twisted into different shapes, trying to form the right defense. She bowed her head in defeat.

"Go pick up your belt!"

James glimpsed tears in Honey's eyes as she turned around to obey. For the first time since he'd met her, he pitied her.

"Get any weapons that look useful," E commanded the crew. "Leave the rest."

She lifted a fallen bar stool and sat down without another word. James couldn't tell if it was fury or fatigue weighing down her labored breaths. Blood continued gushing out from the raw necks of all the Merchants she had beheaded, spilling onto the ground and creeping over the dirt in dark pools. Nausea climbed up his throat. His vision suddenly dipped and spun. He shook his head and pushed himself to focus on Lux's injuries.

Many of Lux's wounds were shallow, yet his healing was slower than usual. One glance at his face explained why. Healing looked like the last thing he cared about as he stared into the distance with eyes devoid of their usual sparkle. James had never seen him more depressed. He took a deep breath and stuffed down his nausea.

"So, you were born into the Flowering on Halloween, huh? That's pretty cool," he said, injecting what he hoped was a cheerful note into his voice.

Lux remained as despondent as ever. James couldn't blame him.

"Um ... here."

He checked that E wasn't looking before creating a bracelet made of black, braided leather. He hastily tied it around Lux's wrist then resumed wrapping his wounds.

"I don't know what humans usually do for birth night celebrations. Sorry," he mumbled.

"What is it?" Lux said, lifting his head.

"It's a bracelet my sister made for me a long time ago. We don't get along that much anymore, but I still wear it a lot in Reality. I guess I like it or something."

He finished tying one last knot then pressed his hands down on the wounds that were bleeding the most. Lux touched the bracelet with his fingertips. A smile spread across his face.

"Thanks," he said softly.

Bloom sniffed Lux's wounds then licked his face and laid down next to him. As Lux's smile widened, the blood devouring the white of his bandages slowed.

"Hey!" E yelled.

She marched over to Honey and began berating her for taking something from one of the Merchant's bags. E thought the item was useless and couldn't understand what had made Honey pick it up. Honey remained quiet, looking both anxious and defensive.

James began to register the details of everything he had just witnessed. E had decimated an entire band of Merchants on her own. The crew definitely would have been raided had it not been for her. Their watches might have been pierced too. She had saved them all. But by what means? These men were humans, and she had tortured one. Not in defense of the crew or even self-defense, but out of rage. The anger in her eyes, the hatred. It had been totally out of control. She had been totally out of control! He had never been fond of E, but this. This had been insanity. After all, what sane human could have created such a bloodbath with so little mercy? Who in their right mind would mutilate a human as she had? Would she make him chop off heads and torture humans one of these nights too?

He lifted his hands from Lux's wounds then stared at the blood glistening on his palms and fingers. He'd grown fond of Lux and had always loved Bloom, and even Honey seemed to be warming up to him. But he couldn't slaughter and torture humans like E had. He couldn't follow the lead of someone capable of such savagery for the rest of his life. He couldn't see any way around it. He had to leave Crew Blue. The sooner, the better. He would no longer subject himself to E's cruelty or wait around to witness another slaughter.

He stared up at the distant full moon.

Maybe he would end up at the City after all.

CHAPTER 9

THANKSGIVING

James's family had a set of rituals they followed every Thanksgiving. His father gathered with other Korean fathers to go golfing, his mother took advantage of his father's absence to watch more Korean dramas, his grandmother joined his mother in the living room to watch whatever she was watching, and his grandfather slept on the couch. James sauntered into the house only toward dinnertime after rolling around in bed all day. He loved staring at the strips of autumnal light highlighting the walls and staying warm under his blanket as the November winds shook the windowpanes.

This year, though, all of these rituals had been sabotaged by his sister. She had driven down from L.A. for Thanksgiving break and somehow convinced his parents to spend the entire day cooking a turkey dinner in the name of "bonding." James had tried employing his usual excuses and a handful of other tried-and-true evasion tactics, but his mother had sided with his sister and forced him, under threat of rescinding his rent money, to participate. He'd had no choice but to abandon his Thanksgiving tradition of staying burrowed under his blanket and now sat in his car, shivering in the cold of the morning, just outside his parents' home. He untied his black bracelet and threw it against the glove compartment.

Of all the years his sister could have chosen to herd them together, it had to be this year! The nights leading up to Thanksgiving had been the very definition of the phrase "living nightmare." He'd found himself with a pierced watch and woken up two hours prematurely not only once but twice. He had yet to catch up on the sleep he had missed. His grades were plummeting. Projects lay unfinished. He leapt up from his mattress every morning in a frenzy and ran out the door as memories from the night and to-do lists from the day collided in his head. His sister's stupid Thanksgiving bonding mission was destroying what little time he had left to raise his grades, salvage his job, and most importantly, ensure that he'd live long enough to make it to next year's Thanksgiving. What was so important about cooking together anyway? No one in his family even knew how to cook American food.

Rolling away the crust in his eyes with one hand and gripping his textbooks with the other, he hurried through the morning chill and into his parents' home. As he took off his shoes, his grandfather gave him a swift greeting and disappeared into the spare bedroom for a nap. James wandered into the living room and hugged his grandmother, who patted his hand and continued watching dramas. His mother and sister were arguing in the kitchen. Apparently, his mother believed apples to be the miracle food that would cure the pimples sprinkled across his sister's chin. His sister, of course, had disagreed.

Knowing better than to intervene, James joined his father in mashing the potatoes until his father groaned, stretched out his back, and sank into the couch next to his grandmother. James abandoned the potatoes and switched places with his grandfather in the spare room. As eight hours had yet to pass since his last sojourn into the Flowering, he tossed aside the option of sleeping and plowed through his textbooks instead. He ignored his sister's pleas to return to the kitchen and lost himself in his studies.

Several hours later, he found himself at the dinner table, eating what he had always known they'd end up eating: a normal, Korean meal, which had been prepared almost solely by his mother. The meal consisted of white rice mixed with brown rice, hot doenjang jjigae loaded with potatoes and squash, his mother's hand-made kimchi, a fried fish, and a variety of vegetable-based banchan to supplement the whole meal. The only deviants were chicken, which his mother had bought as a substitute for turkey, packets of ketchup saved from various fast-food restaurants to go along with the chicken, and James's mashed potatoes, which remained abandoned on a corner of the table. Nothing disturbed the silence of their meal except for the clicking of chopsticks. He glared at his sister as she smiled hopefully around at everyone. He could practically feel the awkward conversation just brimming at her mouth.

"*This spinach is really tasty, Heri,*" his mother said in Korean.

"*Really? You like it, Mom?*" his sister said. Her heavy American accent softened and blurred what should have been the hard edges of her Korean. She sat up straighter in her chair as her face lit up at the prospect of breaking the cold silence.

"*Yes,*" his mother said. "*You made it well. You can make it like this when you get married too.*"

His sister deflated. James was glad that she didn't reply. Engaging their mother at this point would only trigger an infinite amount of questions regarding why they both weren't out in a crowd of strangers at this very moment, wooing a significant other with every chance that came their way.

"*This is really good too,* James," his grandmother said. She pointed her chopsticks at the untouched bowl of mashed potatoes.

"*Thank you,*" he said as he shoved rice into his mouth. His grandmother thought anything he did was brilliant. He was the precious first-born son, after all.

"Is school going well?" his father asked Heri.

"Yeah! My *professor* just hired me to help her with a project next quarter," she replied in a mixture of Korean and English.

James didn't know why she even bothered trying to use any Korean when it sucked even more than his.

"Just you?" his mother asked Heri.

"Yeah," Heri said as pride made her sit straighter still.

"Why just you? Why not choose some of the other kids?"

"Because my *professor* thought I was talented, *Mom*!" said Heri. She drummed her feet lightly on the floor in frustration.

"Oh, so only you were chosen," his mother said, her eyes growing wide with genuine understanding. *"Because your professor thinks you're smart."*

"Yes, *Mom*. I have potential. I've been working really hard!"

"That sounds like a good opportunity. You thanked your professor, right? If you haven't already, buy a nice thank-you gift for your professor. If you need money, I'll give you some."

"No! That's weird."

James set down his spoon and tried to convey to Heri through his bulging eyes that she was an idiot.

"Heri," his mother began, *"you need to show respect to your professors. When someone of a higher ranking favors you, you have to show them gratitude. If you do, all of it will come back to you twofold. Buy your professor a gift. I'll give you some money, don't worry. I'm saying all of this for your own good."*

His father carved the chicken as Heri launched into an impassioned defense. His grandfather crept away into the spare room again. His father placed a juicy leg on Heri's plate and eyed James's pudge before placing a bit of dry breast on James's plate. His grandmother chuckled, patted him on the hand, then retired to the couch.

By the time the first episode of his grandmother's drama had ended, Heri had thrown in the towel and mollified their mother with a false promise that she would buy an expensive gift for her professor. His mother bustled away into the kitchen with a satisfied smile then brought back a tray of apples for dessert.

"*Aigoo*," his mother groaned as she sat down. "*It's too troublesome to get the other knife.*" She proceeded to peel the apples with a meat cleaver.

The apple skins swirled onto the plastic serving tray like long trails of pencil shavings under his mother's experienced hand. James didn't know why she had to use a meat cleaver to cut something like fruit. It looked so strange, not to mention dangerous. She used that cleaver to chop through meat–bones and all–for stews. He understood that she didn't want more things to wash after dinner, but still. Couldn't she use a butter knife or a paring knife or any kind of knife, really, that was actually designed for smaller things like fruit?

"*Dad!* After dinner. It's Thanksgiving," Heri admonished as his father straightened out the Korean newspaper with a good shake.

He sighed, folded up the paper, and tossed it onto the floor.

"*Heri, eat apples,*" his mother said, stabbing a large slice with a small dessert fork. She waved it in front of Heri's mouth as she squirmed.

"*Leave the child alone,*" his father said.

Another squabble ensued, culminating this time in a victory for Heri. His mother commented loudly on Heri's anal stubbornness then bustled toward the dirty dishes while grumbling to herself about her disobedient daughter. His father handed Heri the apple slice and nodded gently. She rolled her eyes before cramming the slice into her mouth and crunching away. James waited until most of the slices had disappeared.

"*I'll be on my way, then. I still have some homework to do,*" he said, rising from the table.

"Wait, already?" Heri said.

"*Oh, really? Okay, go study and drive safely,*" his mother said. She hurried out of the kitchen and hugged him with soapy gloves.

He bowed to his father and bid him goodbye. His father nodded and opened up the newspaper. James rushed to the door and stuffed his feet into his shoes. He was stepping off of the porch when his sister opened the door.

"Wait!"

He groaned and turned around.

"Thanks for coming today," she said as she closed the door behind her.

"No problem. Thanks for organizing."

"Actually," said Heri. She caught him by the arm as he turned to leave. "Before you go, I wanted to ask you something." She paused as she put her hands behind her back and glanced down at her feet. "There's actually this trip soon that I'm taking with my friends, and some of them are around your age. And I just thought ... well, you want to come? It'll be fun. Kind of like old times, right?"

The porchlight illuminated the hope shining on her face. James sighed.

"I can't. Sorry."

"Wait, but–"

"But what?"

"I just ... I just thought it would be nice to, you know, spend time."

He rubbed the inner corners of his eyes. He could have caught up on some of his lost sleep today if it weren't for his sister. The least she could do was let him catch up on sleep or even the mountains of work still waiting for him. Why? Why couldn't she just leave him be?

"Heri, why are you doing this?"

"What? What do you mean?"

"I mean, why are you doing all this?" he said, throwing his hand down from his eyes. "I tell you all the time that I'm not up for these stupid bonding sessions that you're always putting together, so why can't you just leave me alone?"

"They're not stupid!"

"Yes, they are!" All the frustration and anxiety that had piled up within him for the past few months churned like poison in his heart and bubbled up into the words he spat out. "They are, Heri."

"Don't say that. Get-togethers aren't stupid. It's not like we're going to have *Grandma* or *Grandpa* or even *Mom* and *Dad* forever. And besides, it's been working. You and I both know that a few years ago we never would've gathered to cook for Thanksgiving, and now–"

"Cook? What do you mean cook? We never cooked. Mom cooked, and she cooked what she always cooks. I wouldn't exactly call that a bonding session. And in case you didn't notice, instead of cooking, everyone went around sleeping or watching TV or doing whatever it is they actually wanted to do today!"

Images of E's wrathful eyes and Lux's crestfallen face on Halloween flashed across James's mind as Heri stared at him. He ignored the memories and pressed on.

"Explain to me, Heri. Explain to me just what you were hoping to accomplish today. Did you want us all to gather and participate with smiles on our faces? For Dad to carve the turkey and hold it at the foot of the table like they do in those Thanksgiving paintings? What? What were you thinking?"

"I was just–"

"There was no pie. There was no turkey. I mean, Mom got us a chicken, and you guys argued about acne for over an hour. You're always trying to make us into some perfect, white-picket-fence family with all the trimmings on the side, but get it through your thick head that that's never going to happen. We're never going to be some supportive tribe that listens to one another and cares about each other's feelings. We have our ways, it's not going to change, if it isn't broke, don't fix it, so give up already, and stop wasting my time! Stop wasting my time. You have no idea how much of my life you're ruining!"

Heri's breaths had grown quick and shallow. James felt a sick sense of satisfaction from watching her tremble.

"Fine," she said. "I'll give you that. I'll give you that one. We won't ever be the family I want or maybe even need. But that doesn't matter. Because we're a family and...." She shook her head as if she were seeing who he really was for the first time. "All I wanted to do was spend time with you and invite you on our trip, and you're saying it's all just a waste of time? A waste of time? You're ... you're a dick. A dick!"

"What? What did you call me? Say that–"

"Dick!" Heri screeched, disarming James momentarily. "I can't believe I never saw it! Oh, James. You may not love our family, but I do. I really, really do! I'm not stupid for trying, and maybe if you took the time, you'd actually see that. For someone who knows so much better than me, you can't even see that relationships are built. They're built! They aren't instant like those stupid noodles you're always shoving down your fat throat! Relationships take time, and they take work, but I'm willing to do it because I love *Mom*, I love *Dad*, I love *Grandma* and *Grandpa*, and I even love you! I just want to get closer to you. Why can't you see that?"

"Oh, my–Heri–you know what–just forget it. Forget it!"

Heri's nostrils flared with each breath. The defiance in her eyes seemed to scorch her tears.

"Fine," she snarled.

James gawked at her as she marched back to the door, stepped back into the house, and slammed the door in his face.

"Happy Thanksgiving!" he bellowed.

He rushed to his car and sped home in a rage. He was boiling as he studied. He was fuming as he tossed himself into bed. All he wanted to do was go back in time and throw his lumpy mashed potatoes at Heri's face. Even as he entered the Flowering and wandered through countless planes, all he could do was seethe with vengeful thoughts.

"Let's rest here for a bit," E said.

The crew broke formation and trickled down the stairs before sitting down with their usual groans. They had traveled through a dark, sepia plane for what felt like hours, descending an endless path of worn steps that snaked through infinite stacks of books. It was as if they were in a singed and faded photograph, journeying futilely to reach a colored world. As James sat down, the words "dick" and "fine" reverberated through his head for the umpteenth time. The defiance that had burned in Heri's eyes remained branded in his mind.

"You okay, James? You've been kind of quiet tonight," said Lux.

"I'm fine."

"You sure? You look kind of pissed."

"That's because I am."

"Oh ... uh," Lux said, "why?"

He stayed silent. For the first time in his life, he wanted to call his sister. Not to make amends but to give her another piece of his mind! He was infuriated that she'd walked away with the last word, though the thought that she must have heard him raging at the front door comforted him somewhat. He silently repeated all the things he could have said, regretting everything he had held back. She was so self-absorbed, always spouting off at him whenever she wanted to, totally incapable of understanding his circumstances.

True, he'd never really given her an explanation. But what was he supposed to say? That he couldn't spend time with her because his soul flew to some weird dimension every night? Knowing her, she'd probably start bugging him to see a therapist on top of everything else. Besides, he was her big brother. Why did he owe her an explanation? No. An explanation or some stupid, touchy-feely heart-to-heart was the last thing he needed right now.

Bloom trotted down the steps then stopped to sniff a stack of books. His nose quivered around the thin, plastic container that lay on top of the stack. He looked up at E, who stood higher up on the steps, elevated above the rest of the crew. He wagged his tail once.

She shook her head. "I want us to rest a little longer before we jump into any rescue missions."

"Wait. Is that an exit?" James asked, eyeing the thin container. "I thought they were all invisible."

"It's rare, but it happens," E said.

"Usually with the ones you can see, you have to do something to get to the next plane," Lux said, looking at the sour expression that had spread across James's face in response to E's curt reply. "You probably have to lift off the lid on that one. We had to do that with another one before too. It's pretty rare, though, like E said. And with exits like these, you usually have to wait a little before someone else can use them again. So Bloom would go, then we'd wait a little, then you, and yeah."

James glowered at the container. It looked like a chopsticks case, and chopsticks reminded him of food, and food reminded him of Thanksgiving, and Thanksgiving reminded him of his stupid sister!

"Create your spear," E commanded him. "We'll go easy tonight. Just practice a few basics then wrap up before we keep moving."

James hung his head and sighed loudly. The crew stared at him.

"I think he's kind of had a rough day," Lux told the others.

"Create your spear," E snarled.

James scowled as he turned toward her. He glared at the ground, arms crossed.

"Hey, man. You sure you're okay?" Lux whispered, glancing at E.

"I said I'm fine. It's just my sister."

"Sister? I didn't know you had a sister," Honey said.

"Well, there are a lot of things you don't know about me."

"Is your sister giving your family trouble?" Lux said, looking concerned.

"Giving my family trouble? You mean she's giving me trouble!"

No longer able to hold back his frustration, he launched into a tirade. His care for restraint and even privacy drained from him as he raved on. Gone from his mind was the fact that he had never spoken more than a few sentences at a time to the whole crew. Vanished from thought was his wariness of E's blade. All that possessed him was the overwhelming need to release his frustration and tell anyone and everyone about the injustice of all that he'd had to endure and could no longer hide.

"And then she slammed the door in my face! After all the time she's wasted from my life. My life!" he said to conclude his rant.

Huffing and puffing, he searched for the outrage and sympathy he'd hoped to find on their faces. Instead, he watched Bloom scratch the underside of his jaw and yawn, Lux cough and kick at a step, and Honey roll her eyes before leaning back on a throne of books. E wasn't even looking at him. She sat perched on a tower of tomes, staring at the city of books.

"Hey. No offense, James. But I think your sister ... I think she's just trying to bring the family together," said Lux. For the first time, he looked annoyed with him.

"What? Are you kidding me? Didn't you listen to everything I just said? You know I lost sleep. She's literally killing me!"

"You only lost four hours this week," Honey said, rolling her eyes. "You can just wake up at six-thirty AM like you always do and take a nap from two-thirty PM to six-thirty PM. You can get all your work and homework done over the weekend. It's not that big of a deal."

"Look," Lux said as James stood open-mouthed, "my family doesn't get along that great all the time either, and it's usually up to me to try and bring everyone together, so I get what your sister is doing."

"So you're siding with my sister?"

"I'm not siding with anyone. I'm just saying it's hard to bring people together. Besides, you're lucky. My sister would probably die before she asked to spend quality time with me like that."

James swiveled his gaze between Lux and Honey before turning to Bloom, his last hope for sympathy. Bloom heaved a sigh through his nostrils, trotted forward, and shoved his snout under James's hand as if to say that he was wrong, but everything would still be all right.

"Unbelievable," he said, tossing his hands up in the air.

"You got to spend time with your loved ones on Thanksgiving. What more do you want?" Honey said.

"It's not about what I want. It's about what I need. I've lost time!"

"But you had time with family instead. Time with family isn't lost time, James," said Lux.

"That's not what I meant!"

"Forget it," E said. "This moron is never going to get it."

She jumped down from the tower of books.

"I've seen kids like him before," she said as she took a step down toward him. "Spoiled, middle-class kids, whose mommies and daddies have done everything for them their whole lives. Their parents slave away so that their children can have everything, and then those good-for-nothing kids turn right back around and forget all about their sacrifices in a flood of self-pity and first-world problems."

She took another step down.

"Pathetic. It disgusts me. There are some of us out here who are struggling to make it, struggling just to survive. And what do kids like you do? Kids who could actually do something to help. Kids who have all the time and money in the world to help your friends and family. What do you do? You go home and complain and complain and complain some more until there's nothing left of you except for your moronic complaints. Never working for anything in your life. Never caring for anyone except yourself. Always taking everything and everyone for granted. Your sister's right. You are a dick!"

She had continued stepping down while speaking and now stood only a few steps above James. She glared down at him, her black eyes full of disdain. Shock and rage created a fog in his mind, jumbling his thoughts and stealing away his words. A barrage of memories converged upon him. The Merchants' screams and headless bodies, E kicking and stabbing him, the piles of paperwork and textbooks on his desk, Honey's glares and sneers, the anger and hurt filling his sister's eyes, Lux failing to explain every important detail imaginable. A tide of despair and indignation rose up within him.

He turned on his heel and stomped down the stairs. He stepped up to the stack of books and placed his hand on the plastic container. Everyone tensed. A small part of him jumped up and tried to assuage his hurt pride and point him to common sense. But he couldn't take it anymore. He shoved aside the regret that was already forming and ignored the alarm in Bloom's eyes and the disbelief in Lux's.

"James, what are you doing?" said Lux.

"I'm leaving," he said, his hand still on the container.

"Don't worry. He's not going anywhere," said Honey. "He wouldn't last a single night on his own."

"Stop that," said James.

"Stop what?"

"Stop that! Why do you always do that? Why do you have to say that? What have I done to deserve this from you? Okay, so I shot you once, but it was my second night. My second night! And Lux hadn't explained a single thing to me about how bullets really work. He forgot to tell me all the details just like he always does!"

Lux jumped with surprise.

"I've never been welcomed by any of you," James said, "but I've been trying my best. And I get it. I'm not good, especially in battles. But I've been trying! And besides, I was the one who saved that marked, little girl. No one's ever given me credit for that. No one ever gives me credit for anything! I've had to figure out everything on my own. No one is helping me. My sister is being difficult. I don't have enough sleep. Work is a mess."

"James," said Lux.

"No!" he cried. He turned his face away, paused, then shook his head. "No. I can't take this anymore. I can't take this nonsense. And I can't take this abuse!" He glared up at E. "I can't take any more of this abuse from a bloodthirsty, homicidal psychopath like you. That Merchant begged you for mercy, but you tortured him. You took all of their heads. Even though they were human beings!"

Bloom stepped forward. His tail swayed gently from side to side as his golden eyes entreated him to stop. But James had made up his mind. He looked E dead in the eye.

"*Goodbye*," he told her.

He opened the container and disappeared from the plane.

CHAPTER 10

RAMIFICATIONS

James splashed through shallow water. He'd done it. He'd actually done it! With that one word of "goodbye," he'd broken off call and response with the crew. He would never wake up in the Flowering next to any of them ever again. White knuckling through E's cruelty and Honey's annoying attitude would now be a thing of the past. He'd probably do better without Lux's inarticulate advice too. He was sure Bloom would learn to live without him. Stumbling to a halt, he rested his hands on his knees and gathered his breath.

Turquoise water as still and clear as glass surrounded his calves. The floor, despite its submersion, looked blanched and parched. Here and there, lobsters with brown, speckled shells scuttled across the floor's jagged tiles. Neon coral and dark tide pools lined the rough walls. A ceiling of black rock stretched overhead and reached into a tunnel of shadows. There, the water splashed with calm waves. James stared into the darkness then behind at the direction from which he'd come. A small part of him couldn't help but wonder if the crew would try to follow him.

He shook his head and sat down on the edge of a tide pool. He looked at his watch. Lux was no longer there to tell him the time. He shook out his hand. It wasn't a big deal. From now on, he'd simply set his alarm earlier so that he'd be sure to wake up at the right time. He didn't need

Lux's watch. He didn't need anyone in the crew. Besides, if it weren't for Crew Blue and all those unnecessary rescue missions that E was always forcing them into, he wouldn't even need to be so concerned with the time. Stupid E. Stupid Crew Blue! He glared at the water as if it, too, were a member of the crew. Honey's words echoed through his head: "He wouldn't last a single night on his own."

What did she know? He was a grown man. He'd survived long enough in the Flowering to make it on his own. He was a strong, independent ... Roamer! He was traveling solo, which meant that he was a Roamer now. Just like that Roamer in the humid forest, the one Lux had said was journeying to the City for a new and better crew.

Yes. That Roamer's path was now his own. This was a new challenge to which he would rise. He would find his way out of this cave then use the full moon to trek through as many planes as he needed to in order to reach the City. There, he would find a new crew and a new beginning. He no longer had Bloom to sniff out the exits he needed to get to the City, but he had found exits on his own before. He had found one his very first night in the Flowering, as a matter of fact. If he could do it then, he could certainly do it now. So what was he waiting for? He slapped his thighs and rose to leave.

Two lobsters froze in the turquoise water. They stared at one another with raised claws as if daring each other to strike first. Waves sloshed in the distance.

Their tails suddenly whipped. White dust flared off the cracked floor. There was a crunch and a violent tug. A cloud of inky-black blood diffused in the water. The two halves of the defeated lobster shuddered then relaxed. Chunks of its flesh sank slowly to the ground.

James stood still as its black blood continued to unfurl and spread in the water. He didn't know why he felt so unsettled. He'd grown used to sights of bloodshed and brutality, and after watching E slaughter an entire band of Merchants, he'd felt that he could stomach anything. Yet, something about this small display of violence unnerved him. It felt like a bad omen.

"*Excuse me?*"

He shouted and crashed into the water. He floundered before sitting up and spitting out saltwater. He locked eyes with a young woman. She stood over him with her hand over her heart and her face full of apology. Her large, dark eyes glistened as she gazed at him. She was pretty.

"*Are you all right? I'm so sorry. I didn't mean to scare you,*" she said in Our Word.

"*Y-Yes, I'm all right,*" he said.

He took the gloved hand she extended to him. Her eyes searched his hands.

"*Don't worry,*" he said, holding up his watch. "*I'm a human. It's just that my watch looks different for some reason.*"

She breathed a sigh of relief. "*Thank you for clarifying. It's always awkward to ask,*" she said, lifting a hand as well.

"*What's with the glove?*" he asked.

"*What, this? For protection, of course. Actually, I'm a little surprised you're not wearing one too.*"

"*Oh, yeah. That makes sense,*" he said, trying his best to sound nonchalant. He wondered why the crew had never thought of such a simple idea before, E in particular. Wasn't it her job as their leader to think of these kinds of things?

"*Here. I have a spare.*" The woman rummaged through a black pouch hanging from the utility belt wrapped around her waist. She handed him a matching fingerless glove.

"Thanks," he said, slipping it on.

"Thanks?" Her English was accented. "*That's the word for 'thank you,' right? Sorry, I must be from a different place than you.*"

"*Oh, sorry. Yes, I meant 'thank you,'*" he said, feeling more ignorant with every passing moment.

"*You can call me Heart. What about you?*"

"James. *You can call me* James."

"*Where is the rest of your crew,* James?"

"*Oh, I'm on my own tonight. We ... we got separated.*" Though he hated to admit it, he couldn't shake E's training. After weeks of suffering under her tutelage, he knew that she never would have approved of him revealing to a stranger just how "separated" he actually was. "*What about you? Where's your crew? Did you get separated too?*"

He hoped that his tone was light and friendly. Though he didn't want to get too excited just yet, he'd met Lux and the others during his first night. Maybe fate had now led him to meet Heart and her crew, the crew he was actually destined to stay with.

"*Yes, I was separated from my crew earlier too,*" Heart said.

"*Oh, wow. Really? You want to stick together for now, then? Help each other out?*"

"*Yes, thank you. That's why I came over to you, actually. I could really use some help. And some company.*"

His eyes lingered on her smile. He drifted along by her side as they began venturing deeper into the tunnel.

"*I'm sorry again for scaring you like that,*" Heart said. "*I didn't know how else to approach you. I watched you for a bit before coming over, and I guess I ended up creeping up behind you.*"

"*That's fine. It's understandable. The Flowering can be pretty dangerous, so it was good that you were cautious,*" said James.

"*Yes, well, hopefully we'll run into one of our crews soon. I've been wandering alone ever since we got separated.*"

"*Does your crew get separated often?*" James asked.

"*Oh, no. Of course not. I'm sorry, I didn't mean to imply that we do. We're very organized. In fact, I'm confident they'll find us soon. We have a system, you see, and my crew would never abandon me. I know they're out there somewhere trying to find me.*"

"*I see,*" James said. "*It sounds like you guys get along pretty well.*"

"*Of course. We always look out for one another. I don't know what I'd do without them. They're my family.*"

"*Wow. That must be nice,*" James said, thinking of Honey's sneer and E's burning eyes.

"*Yes, it is very nice. They're the best crew in the Flowering. Though I don't mean to brag. Or compare. I'm sorry, I didn't mean to imply anything. I know your crew must be just as wonderful.*"

James snorted. "*Well, not exactly. My crew is a little different than yours.*"

"*Different? How?*"

"*Well, they're not as supportive. I don't think they'll even come for me tonight.*"

"*What do you mean? Of course they will. They're your crew.*"

He couldn't help but smile at her naivety. He began recounting the trials he'd faced in the past few months, giving particular emphasis to E's unwarranted cruelty and the bravery he had shown while saving the little girl. The more he spoke, the more he realized the extent to which the crew had failed him. What little regret that had gnawed at him for severing call and response began to disappear. When he'd finished talking, his uneasiness had all but vanished.

"*Wow,*" said Heart after a slight pause. "*I'm so sorry you had to go through all that. That's just awful.*"

He relished the flabbergasted look on her face.

"*It's really unfortunate that you had to meet humans like that,*" she continued. "*Your crew is your family. I didn't even know that humans could act like that toward one another.*"

He nodded solemnly. Heart's compassion felt like the warmth of a heated home after traveling through a long winter night.

"*Thanks,*" he said.

They continued on into the darkness. The water grew shallower with every step. Cracked, white tiles transitioned into dark, rich soil as they stepped onto land. James racked his brains as he tried to come up with a way to continue the discussion about Heart's crew. He would need to meet them in person before making a final decision, but he liked Heart a lot already. Surely, her crew would be just as amiable. She kept referring to them as her family, after all. Her family! He couldn't even imagine calling Crew Blue that. Any crew worthy of such a title had a high chance of being a crew that he'd enjoy being a part of.

Yes, it would be fine. The important thing now was gathering a bit more intel on each member so that he could make a great first impression. That way, when they all finally did meet, he'd gain an invitation into their crew without a problem. He just had to steer the conversation in the right direction to get the info.

Pairs of yellow eyes opened up in the black ceiling above. James unsheathed his knife as they blinked slowly down at him.

"*Don't worry. They're harmless,*" said Heart. She put her hand on his and lowered it. "*I'm glad we found them, actually. They were around the exit into this plane. Let's head further in. My crew might be somewhere there.*"

He didn't like the idea of wandering around in the dark without a weapon in hand. E would have stabbed him just for thinking about it. But he didn't want to ruin his chances with Heart and her crew either. Yes, E wouldn't have approved. But he couldn't live in fear of her any longer.

What had been the point of leaving the crew if he was going to tiptoe around the mere thought of her for the rest of his life? He needed to think for himself. Besides, she wasn't the only one with decision-making skills.

"*Okay, Heart,*" he said. He drew himself up and smiled as if he were meeting a new client in the office. "*I'll trust your assessment on this.*"

He sheathed his knife.

"*Thank you,* James."

He tried to keep his eyes from straying to the ceiling as they continued walking. He flexed his fingers as his body tensed instinctively.

"James, *I don't mean to be rude, but do you think it's a good idea to stay with your crew?*"

He snapped his focus back onto her. Was she about to say what he thought she was about to say?

"*What do you mean?*" he said.

"*Well, I don't want to assume anything. But just from what you told me, I'm sorry, but that* E *sounds so horrible. Our leader would never treat us like that.*"

He swallowed and chose his next words carefully. "*Thanks. I appreciate your concern. But I'd be on my own if I left my crew, and I don't really have another crew to go to.*"

"*You can stay with us! Of course, I'll have to ask the others, but I'm sure they'll approve.*"

"*Are you sure?*" He tried to keep his heart from leaping up into his throat with happiness. "*I wouldn't want to presume anything or be a burden.*"

"*You're not presuming anything. The others will understand when we find them, I'm sure of it. I'll just make sure to give you a good introduction.*"

"*Really, Heart? You'd do that for me?*"

"*Of course. We're always welcoming of newcomers anyway. And you've been kind enough to stay with me tonight. I'm indebted to you.*"

"You're not indebted to me."

"Oh, no. But I am. I am indebted. You've been so kind and brave and— oh, look! The exit. Stay here. Maybe my crew is nearby."

James's heart danced a silent tango of joy. This night was turning out to be one of the best nights he'd had in a while. He admired Heart's slick ponytail as she ran up a mound of black soil up ahead. She really was very pretty.

She approached a lone coat rack standing on the summit of the mound. A gray trench coat hung from one of the rack's branches.

James recoiled.

A pair of bare feet protruded from under the coat, bobbing up and down as if something were sucking on the upper half of its body. No. Not sucking. Moulding! Heart lifted the lapel of the coat before he could stop her.

"Mother," she whispered.

A white arm slid out from between the lapels. James scrambled back and flattened himself against the wall. E's voice roared inside his head, commanding him to make a spear. He obeyed.

The arm waved then wandered down to the ground. Its fingers dug into the soil. A woman's head emerged, dangling silky curtains of long, white hair. Its neck appeared next then its naked torso. It collapsed onto the dirt. Massive coils of hard, segmented flesh followed, dropping like bags of sand and slithering aside. As the tip of the monster's tail glided out from the coat and into the open, it lifted its head and stared at James. Its face resembled a Japanese hannya mask. Thick folds of skin drooped over blood-shot eyes brimming with tears. Fangs protruded from its mouth, which hung open to form a frozen, gaping hole incapable of closing.

The monster drew itself up so that its human half hovered over its unraveling coils. The bleach-white color of its tail and skin was striking even in the dark. The smooth, shell-like surface of its long tail made its coils glisten. The creature turned toward Heart, who had backed away to stand at the foot of the mound as if she were in the presence of royalty.

"*Come*," the monster said.

Heart ran up the mound and dove into the creature's belly. Their flesh began to mould together, and in that moment, James understood that Heart's glove had not hidden her watch but her mark. He ran as the monster slid down the mound toward him. Yellow eyes opened in the ceiling in his wake.

What had he done? Had he really been stupid enough to fall for a trap? Heart's dark eyes. Her understanding. Her compliments. No, not compliments. Her flattery! What had he been thinking? Bloom, Lux, Honey, E. They couldn't help him now even if they wanted to. How could he have thought that he could survive in the Flowering all on his own? He wanted to blame something else. Something else, someone else, anything else for his own stupidity!

But there was nothing.

The horrific danger of his circumstances and the inescapable consequences of his actions would not allow him to crawl under the comfort of pride and deny the cold, hard truth. And the truth was that he had done this to himself. He had done this to himself using own dumb mouth.

What little blood remaining in his face drained as he skidded to a halt. The dark soil beneath his feet transitioned into a path of hard, gray stone before him, stretching down a rocky tunnel and toward a dead end. He turned to see the creature's tail swinging toward him. He clung to his spear as the thick, cold mass slammed into his body. His face split upon the large rocks lining the side of the tunnel. He spat out blood and half a tooth. He could almost hear E yelling at him to get up, could almost feel the sharp touch of her blade in his side.

He scrambled onto his feet and launched his spear. The creature stopped and cocked its head weirdly to the side. The spear whizzed past its cheek, cutting through several strands of silky hair. Its stomach continued rising and falling in small waves. Heart's arms jutted out like misplaced ribs from the moulding flesh. Her head drooped out upside down from the creature's belly. She smiled at him.

"*I told you they would like you,*" she whispered.

He staggered down the tunnel. He tried to shake away the disorientation swirling around his fractured face but succeeded only in colliding with the floor. Glistening coils surrounded him as he patted the ground with shaking hands.

He no longer had a crew. He was low on sleep. He didn't know what the next night would bring. He needed to survive this night, whatever it took. He needed to survive this night! The defiance in his sister's eyes blazed up within his mind as he drew his gun from his belt. He hadn't tested this plane and could only hope that his bullets would shoot straight. He opened fire.

The creature's screams reverberated within the tunnel as his bullets flew into its tail and torso. He cried out in dismay as a bullet zinged into his side. He dropped his gun as he flung himself away from the creature's thrashing coils and rolled across the ground. He grasped rugged grooves in the wall to hoist himself up onto his feet. Another spear appeared in his hand. He hurled it into the creature's chest then stumbled away as the monster shrieked. He scratched himself against the rough stone wall and trampled over rocks and loose gravel. He tried to focus on stitching the bones back together in his face as he neared the dead end. The screams subsided before silence followed.

He looked behind to see the monster crawling swiftly forth on pale, bent arms. His adrenaline fueled his thoughts so that he absorbed a myriad of details in a heartbeat. The creature had grown smaller so that the size of its human half matched his own body. Its tail, too, had shortened. Its face was no longer mask-like, its hair no longer silken. Instead, straggly, yellow strands now tossed to and fro. Humongous, round eyes held pupils the size of pin pricks. A thin-lipped mouth snarled beneath a pointed nose. The flesh of its stomach continued to bulge and stretch, but Heart was nowhere to be seen. Lux had said before that citizens that had moulded countless times gained the ability to shift and change their form. But moulding with so many different citizens also made them unstable and caused them to lose control at random times. There was no way a citizen would choose to shrink to a smaller, weaker size during a fight, which meant that this monster had changed its form against its will. Just how many of the marked had it taken for its own to be so unstable?

He launched another spear. It sliced across the creature's arm before disappearing into the shadows. The monster threw itself at him, roaring as it reached for him with its sharp nails. He fell onto his back and caught its clawing hands. He grunted and shook as it bore down on him. The creature shrieked, its eyes bulging from its witch-like face as, centimeter by centimeter, he pushed its hands away. With a shout and a painful twist of his body, he rolled over and forced it onto its back. Cold and warm flesh tangled together, writhing, scraping, thrashing, thudding as he and the monster wrestled one another.

He gasped as it stabbed his arm with its nails and dug the pointed tips in toward his bone. The creature let out a thunderous roar then reared up and flung him across the tunnel. His head hit the stone wall with a thud that boomed in his ears. The creature crawled swiftly toward him again. He did a double take. A large hole lay at the foot of the wall, barely visible among several boulders.

The creature lunged again. He drew his knife from his belt and drove the blade into its stomach. The cry that burst forth from the creature's mouth seemed to shake the stone walls. Moulding flesh tugged the knife out of his hands. He rammed another spear into the monster's chest as it drew back. Colorless blood sputtered out, thick like sap.

He rose onto his shaking legs, still clutching his spear, and pushed the writhing, screaming creature across the ground. He threw the monster aside with a labored yell then dashed toward his escape. He covered his head with one arm and curled his watch hand against his chest as he threw himself into the hole. Air whistled past his body as he fell into the cold embrace of darkness.

CHAPTER 11

THE LAST SPEAR

James landed on his back with a cough full of blood then flipped onto his stomach. He vomited more blood before scrambling onto his feet. He had to keep quiet. He'd managed to escape from the creature, but he was still on the same plane. It could still find him. He had to keep quiet.

His mind stretched out in all directions as he tried to locate and heal his many wounds. He lurched down a long, dim hall, where beams of light shone down at intervals like spotlights. Cherry wood glinted under his stumbling feet one moment. Shadows swallowed him the next. Identical sets of white, louvered doors lined the left wall. Each pair was missing one of two knobs. A blank wall stretched out on his right, lumpy and reddish brown. Wooden planks creaked in the shadows overhead as if he were lost inside of a haunted ship. Whether the planks were a few or a hundred feet above him, James could not tell.

Up ahead, a cluster of large molecular models floated midair like enchanted science projects. He weaved around them, fearful of making even the slightest noise. His bullet finished squeezing out of his side and fell onto the floor with a treacherous clink. He checked the hall for signs of the creature then looked down at his belt. He had lost a gun and a knife and had used up four creations. Four. A third of the maximum capacity.

He only had eight left. He leaned against the louvered doors. His wounds throbbed and smarted as he tried to stifle his panting in the silent hallway.

Two doors burst open beside him, making him jump aside. A man tumbled out onto the floor. Thousands of small, blue particles were jittering and rolling over his body like bewitched static that had broken free of a television set. The man's wide eyes stared at James from beneath the scuttling layer. James lunged forward to help but stopped short as the man signaled for him to stand back. The light revealed the stranger's watch.

James flipped frantically through his memories as the man writhed silently at his feet. What could he create? What could possibly help? As he scoured the hall for some source of inspiration, the molecular models floating in the air congregated around him like curious spectators. He lifted his hand to swat the models away then paused. Some were bare, but others teemed with the same blue swarm.

Inspiration struck. Grabbing a bare model out of the air, he lobbed it at the man's body. A small sea of particles rushed onto the model, which floated away. He began hurling model after model, unaware of the white mass falling through the ceiling behind him.

The final model floated away, taking away the last particles that had been crawling over the man's body. The stranger remained curled up on the floor with both hands buried in his black hair. James had assumed that he was a full-grown man, but now he saw that he was only a teenager. The boy peeked up at his surroundings. A smile spasmed across James's face as he extended his hand. He was glad beyond all measure to see another human.

The teen's face contorted. He jumped up, grabbed James, and flung him down the hall. Alarm turned into anger as James's bruised and bloodied limbs knocked against the hardwood floor. Despising himself for putting his trust in the wrong person yet again, he rolled to a stop and reached for the knife on his belt. He looked up.

The creature loomed over the teen. Its hair had reverted to white, silken sheets, and its face was mask-like again. But the monster was now bigger than ever before. Its tail had elongated by several yards and thickened. Its human half, too, had grown so that the length from its forehead to chin alone rivaled James's height from head to toe. Its stomach had ceased moulding, and two more white arms had sprouted on either side of its ribcage. All of the wounds James had inflicted had healed. The teen gripped the broadsword that appeared in his hand and assumed a battle stance.

"*Run away and hide! I'll distract it!*" he shouted to James.

Cold, hard skin clamped around James's leg. He snapped his head around, and for a fraction of a moment, saw the creature's white tail gripping him. Then the hall spun as the monster swung him through the air like a club. Bones cracked and metal clattered before James dropped onto the floor.

"No!" he cried out.

The creature lifted the fallen broadsword and cleaved the teen's watch in half. He vanished. The monster's tail wrapped around James's torso. He cursed and pounded on its shell-like skin as it hoisted him high into the air. He tried to squeeze his hands between his waist and the monster's grasp, but it was no use. His belt lay trapped beneath the grip of its tail.

The monster reached toward him with its long, white fingers. He watched, powerless and horrified, as it tore off his belt and dropped it into its mouth along with the teen's sword. The creature jerked its head up and down as it swallowed. His blades. His guns. All the weapons he had relied on as his safety net. Everything was gone. His only line of defense now was his remaining eight creations.

The creature swiveled its head to look at him with eyes that brimmed with tears. James slid his hand behind his back and created the first thing that came to mind, something he knew without a doubt would crack its hard skin.

His mother's cleaver.

His breath caught in his throat as he saw the creature's mark. It lay just above its forehead, hidden among strands of silken white.

"*Why?*" the creature moaned.

He froze. The thing was talking to him. Its mouth remained still, yet it spoke.

"*Why did you leave us, Twelve? You were the last one. You were our last hope. They fell without you. They fell so quickly without you. Every last one.*"

The tears pooled in its eyes dropped and splattered on the floor far below. James prepared to strike.

"*You betrayed us. You lost yourselves to greed. You lost yourselves to pride. What have you become? What did you let us do? Let us become?*"

James hurled his cleaver. The blade stuck to the creature's mark like an ax in wood. The creature's tail tightened around his waist as it screamed. The cleaver remained lodged in its mark. He didn't understand. His cleaver had hit the mark. How could the monster possibly still be here?

"*I didn't mean to kill her!*" it shrieked. "*It's your fault! It's all your faults!*"

Another cleaver appeared in his hand. He swung it down and cracked open the hard shell of the creature's tail. Its coils loosened. He dropped into a free fall. Nails clattered across the floor. A large, furry shadow sailed through the spotlights. Hope blazed into life within James as he saw the blue of Bloom's coat. He twisted around midair, grasped Bloom's mane, and pulled himself onto his back.

Bloom thudded onto the cherry wood floor, swerved, then leapt over the monster's head as it swooped down toward them. The creature began slithering swiftly after Bloom then pulled back. It began to shudder and twitch, cocking its head violently to one side. Straggly, yellow strands of hair replaced its silken strands. Its mask-like face melted and churned before reforming into its snarling, witch-like face. The rest of its body remained the same.

The creature slithered forth once more, pursuing Bloom as he continued dashing toward the opposite end of the hall. Bloom spun around and faced the monster with bared fangs. The creature halted. James thought he glimpsed fear in its wide, unblinking eyes. The sound of running feet reached his ears.

"James! Oh, man. Sorry! You have to shove your weapon all the way through the mark. All the way through it! Man. I can't believe I never explained that to you."

James would have cried had his adrenaline allowed him to. He clutched Bloom's mane and buried his face in his fur before looking up. Lux stood next to him, bloodied and battered. He stared up at the creature with an open mouth before offering James a hand.

"Whoa," Honey breathed as her feet squeaked to a halt next to them. Like Lux, she froze momentarily as she looked up at the terrifying creature.

The monster curled back as Bloom began prowling toward it. It plucked James's cleavers from its forehead and tail and swallowed them. E dashed up to the crew then glared up at the creature without a trace of fear. Both she and Honey looked as ragged as Lux, and all three of them were missing weapons from their belts. The crew must have run into trouble while coming to find him. James lifted his eyes and met E's. Shame made him look away.

"You can't shoot on this plane. I already tried," he said.

He hoped the crew could tell that he wasn't simply trying to exchange information for forgiveness. He knew he didn't deserve their forgiveness.

"It uses its tail to move and grab things. You need to watch out for it."

E's blazing eyes seemed to illuminate his soul as it squirmed in vain for cover.

"Its mark is right above its forehead in its hair. It moulded before you guys came and grew that big after the moulding stopped. It pierced the watch of a human who tried to help me. We need to be careful."

Honey rolled her eyes and shook her head with an expression split between annoyance with James and wariness of the monster. A tomahawk formed in her hand. Lux unsheathed his knife. They both began inching toward the creature, following Bloom's lead. E glared at James a moment longer before shifting her focus back onto the creature.

"Just say 'hello,' James," she growled. Two black machetes appeared in her hands as she readied herself for battle.

He stared at her. She was offering call and response. But he hadn't even apologized to her or to any of them. He had insulted them, abandoned them, and even worse, endangered them. And yet, they had come all this way to rescue him and were clearly offering to take him back.

"E ... I...." He tried to push out the apology that lay jumbled within his mouth. "I'm really–"

"That doesn't sound like 'hello' to me," Honey said as she created a second tomahawk.

James breathed a small sigh of defeat.

"*Hello,*" he told E.

"*Hello,*" she responded with a bite of irritation. "All right, Crew Blue."

"Hey, you finally called us Crew Blue!" Lux said. "Team spirit, man. I love it."

E ignored him. "Go for the arms first then the tail. Chop off as much as you can. We need to weaken it, slow it down, take away as much of its defenses as we can so we can get a good aim at that mark. It's going to be hard to get a spear all the way through its skull with the way that it moves."

Crew Blue nodded as the creature glared down at each of them with its round, unblinking eyes. Its snarl tautened on its witch-like face as it bared its fangs. James created another cleaver and placed one foot carefully in front of the other as he moved in closer with his crew. He couldn't take back what he'd done, but the least he could do was help get everyone out of this mess.

Muscles tensed.

Sweat dripped.

The moment stood still.

Then the monster dove at them. The crew scattered. E leapt forth, flipping and spiraling through the air, her eyes tinted with wrath. Her machetes sliced through the creature's flesh. One of its right arms dropped onto the floor. She sliced and sliced again, and a second fell onto the ground.

Shrieking, the monster reached for her with its left arms. She sent several of its fingers flying then leapt onto Bloom's back. Together, they attacked, Bloom biting and snapping at the lower arm, and E slashing at the upper arm that flailed and dodged her blades. The creature's coils thrashed, writhing in the shadows and swinging through the beams of light. Its torso remained low to the ground as it continued swiping at Bloom and E.

Honey charged forth with a ululating battle cry and sank both of her tomahawks into the monster's torso. Lux's knife whirled forth and plunged into the creature's shoulder. He jumped through the air, his back arched and a gleaming katana held high above his head. He sank his sword into its upper arm.

The creature seized up as it shrieked.

Lux yanked out his sword. E took off its remaining upper arm with her machetes before cutting off the lower as well. Bloom's teeth crunched into the creature's skin as he bit and scratched at its tail.

The creature reared up, raising its human half high up toward the ceiling. James bellowed a wordless cry of determination. He joined the crew as they descended on the monster's tail. Together, they hacked and cut and cleaved. The creature's clear blood splattered onto his face and flew through the light. Soon, only a raw chunk of flesh held the jerking tail together.

The monster swung its tail, forcing the crew to spring aside. The pale chunk of flesh squished about, still bridging the two halves. The creature's round eyes darted about as it looked at its arms strewn across the floor. It stretched open its mouth with two bone-snapping cracks. Its bottom jaw dropped lower. It coiled back as it readied itself to lunge forward and scoop up one of its arms with its mouth.

Bloom snatched up the limb and ran down the hall. Lifting his bottom, he wagged his tail in a jeering taunt with the giant arm still gripped between his teeth. The crew threw themselves aside as the creature hurtled toward Bloom with a shriek of rage. Bloom leapt up, leaving the monster to smash headlong into the floor.

Lux dashed up the creature's back, using the protruding knobs of its spine like steps. Sword aloft, he jumped once more. The creature flipped over, shot forth, and bit into Lux's torso. Crew Blue cried out. The monster shook Lux as a dog would a piece of meat. With a toss of its head, it spat him out. He hit the wall, unraveled in the air, and landed next to his fallen sword. He stirred feebly as blood trickled out of his cracked skull.

"Look out!" E yelled.

Two arms shot out from the creature's ragged, colorless wounds, one from the left, one from the right. The monster slithered rapidly toward Honey. She dove out of the way as it snapped its jaws at her. The creature plucked out her two tomahawks still lodged in its stomach. A third arm burst out of its body.

"Honey!" E cried as she ran forth.

A white coil crashed down, blocking E's path. Bloom leapt to and fro, snapping at the coils surrounding him. The arm in his mouth had disappeared. The wound in the creature's tail continued to seal itself so that the tail no longer hinged on a chunk of flesh but swung as one continuous limb.

James ran to Honey as the creature shot toward her again. She threw herself aside to dodge its hungry mouth. It reached for her as she tumbled across the floor. With all the strength he could muster, James brought his cleaver down onto the creature's wrist before it could grab her. The blade hewed through skin, sinew, and bone. The creature recoiled.

Nails clicked rapidly across the floor. James grabbed Honey and pushed her onto the ground as Bloom whooshed over them with E seated on his back. Bloom spun around to face the creature then leapt forward. A spear materialized in E's hand and whistled through the air. The crew's eyes followed the spear.

A final arm shot out of the creature's side and blocked the fatal blow.

James yanked Honey to the side. Two tomahawks flew into the spot where she had lain. The white tail continued to swing, breaking doors and rattling the ground. Wood flew like shrapnel. Curtains of dust fell to the ground. E hurled her machetes, Honey her knives. The crew broke apart as the monster dove at them again.

James ran down the hall as massive coils pitched and fell around him. He jumped and dodged, cut and cleaved. He flung a knife into the creature's stomach. He split its hard skin with another cleaver. Suddenly, the creature's eyes were before him. Its jaws were open, ready to inflict the same fate upon him as they had upon Lux. It wasn't fear but determination that made him scream, "No!"

He caught the creature's bared fangs with both hands. The impact slammed into his palms, shuddered up his arms, and shook every bone in his body. His feet skidded across the floor before halting. The creature's eyes widened with surprise. The edges of its fangs cut into his hands as he tightened his hold. He would not let go. He had wrestled with this monster before, and he would do it again. But this time ... this time he would not run away!

Honey jumped into view with Lux's sword in hand. She cut into one of the creature's white arms. E leapt through the air, and her machete fell upon another arm. Bloom dashed forward and sank his teeth into the creature's neck.

The creature seized up and screamed as E and Honey cut and sliced away.

Great, white lumps of its flesh fell onto the floor. James glanced at the creature's mark. It was so close. If only he could take a few steps back. He could pierce its mark with a spear!

But it was too late. Honey yelped as an arm twisted her sword out of her grasp. E and Honey leapt out of reach as the creature threw James and Bloom aside. The crew regrouped as the monster reared up again.

"I'm out!" Honey said.

"So am I!" said E. She tossed Honey her machete and unsheathed her last knife from her belt.

James understood. Both of them were out of creations. Out because he'd led them down a wild goose chase and into the jaws of this monster. And now he was completely useless to them as he always was.

No.

No, he couldn't think like that right now. He couldn't just stand around, moping and giving up before he'd even tried. He wasn't strong enough to defeat this creature physically, but that didn't mean he couldn't outsmart it!

And in that moment, he realized what he had to do.

He sucked air into his lungs, and in one long, raging cry, he screamed, "I still have three creations left!"

"No!"

"James. James!"

Honey and E continued shouting at him as he bolted toward the coiling creature. Two knives formed in his hands. The creature lunged. He faltered then froze. The monster smirked before it bit into his torso. He screamed as pain split open his body. He continued crying out helplessly as the monster ground its teeth deeper into him and hoisted him high up into the air. The crew charged forth so many feet below. The monster drew back its arms, ready to strike at them. But James raised his knives and smiled. His plan had worked. The monster had taken him for a coward and fallen into his trap. Now he, James, would be the hunter. He would no longer be the hunted!

He plunged both of his blades into the creature's pupils. The monster opened its mouth as it roared out in pain. He clung to the knives' handles and planted his feet on the bottom row of the creature's teeth to keep himself from falling.

"E!" he yelled. His eyes met hers. He knew she understood.

"Bloom!" She shoved her knife back into her belt and jumped onto Bloom's back.

The creature's head whipped from side to side, sinking closer to the ground in its disorientation. Its tongue smacked against James and painted him with slime. He ripped out a knife from one of its eyes and began stabbing the creature's yellow gums. He drove the blade deeper and deeper, severing nerves and tissue, digging away until he could see the roots of its teeth. The creature yelped and screamed and shook its head. James lifted his knife high above his head. With a long cry of determination, he plunged the blade into its tongue then yanked the knife toward himself in a clean cut that split its tongue in two.

The creature's body seized up as it let out a deafening cry.

Bloom leapt through the air with E still seated on his back. James's twelfth and last creation appeared in his hand.

A spear.

With the precision he had learned from her, he hurled his spear toward E, who caught it with one hand. She sprang off of Bloom's back and launched the spear.

For one heart-stopping moment, the spear sailed through the air.

Then the tip plunged into the creature's mark and reappeared through the back of its head.

The creature vanished.

CHAPTER 12

THE BOULDER

James flailed midair as the bottom row of teeth he'd been balancing on vanished along with the rest of the creature. He glimpsed a frail, white figure hovering beside him in the split moment before he began to fall. He braced himself for the ground and the bones that would break, but instead of hitting the floor, he dropped into inflated plastic. He floundered about as E sank in beside him. Red, yellow, and blue towers slowly craned down and collapsed on them both.

"You all right, guys?" Lux said as he hobbled toward them. Blood had coated him from head to toe so that he may as well have bathed in blood.

"Yeah. Thanks for the ... uh ... castle," James said. "What about your head? Is your head okay?"

"Yeah, I think so. It's still a little tender but–oh, hey! We're twins," Lux said, laughing as James winced and clutched the bite marks on his torso.

"Are you guys okay?" Honey called as she hurried over to them.

Lux raised a thumb. James keeled over as he tried to do the same. Honey ran to him. The castle finished deflating with a splatter of wind, scattering dust and splinters across the floor. E stood up, looking punch-drunk. James breathed out a deep sigh of relief as Honey and Lux began wrapping his wounds with the bandages that had appeared in Lux's hand. He was with his crew now. Everything would be okay.

Bloom walked toward a pale figure crumpled up on the floor. The crew stirred, wary of the dangers that lurked within all unknowns. E held up a hand to command them to stay still. Bloom sniffed the figure, drew back, then cocked his head to one side. He gently nudged the figure with his snout.

A young woman raised her head. Her long, white hair gleamed with an iridescent sheen like a rainbow veil. The mark stood out on her pale skin just above the collar of her white dress. She swiveled her head about, slowly at first, then frantically. Her shoulders stiffened and climbed toward her ears as tears gathered in her eyes. Her gaze latched onto Bloom.

"I never wanted all of this. I stayed behind because I was afraid. I only wanted company. I never wanted to harm anyone. But I killed her. I killed his daughter. I'm so sorry," she said, ending in a whisper.

Bloom's tail twitched. He nuzzled her. E stepped closer.

"Wait, E."

"Don't worry," she told Honey. "I think it's all right."

James exchanged anxious looks with Lux and Honey. Even though he knew that citizens who were freed from the moulded were always safe to approach, getting closer to this citizen was still the last thing he would have advised any of them to do. She was, after all, the last remnant of the creature they had just barely managed to slay.

But as E continued walking toward the citizen, a thought seeped into his mind. It broke apart his fear and told him that this citizen was safe to approach. No, not just safe. They needed to. They needed to approach her. He didn't understand how, but he suddenly knew. He looked at Honey and Lux again. Did they know too? And as his gaze returned to E, he remembered the night he had been born into the Flowering. Thoughts had formed in his head then too, after he had eaten the eye in the blue box. Someone had told him to slay "the Beast."

Tears spilled down the woman's cheeks as she gazed up at E. "*You remind me of him,*" she said. "*But it has been so long.*"

"*Who?*" E said, her voice not unkind.

"*Him. The Twelfth. The Last,*" she said. She looked again at Bloom. "*Is that why you've chosen to be with her?*"

Bloom smiled. His tail swept twice across the floor.

"*And him.*" She stared at James. "*Him. How strange. He is like the Last as well. Not like you,*" she told E, "*but still alike all the same.*"

James exchanged a questioning look with E.

"*I have wandered for so many eras now, so many ages. But I have felt it growing in my bones. It is creeping back into the Flowering. The Beast. The Beast who bleeds and eats with the power of the night.*"

Bloom leapt onto all fours, his fur bristling and his golden eyes wide with alarm. The eye in the blue box flashed across James's mind. The plea to slay the Beast echoed within his head. "The Beast who bleeds and eats with the power of the night." Was it just a coincidence?

"*Beware, my friends,*" the young woman whispered.

She bowed her head and disappeared.

Bloom's eyes continued to dart about in agitation.

"What was she talking about, Bloom?" said E.

He responded with a look that seemed to ask her the same question.

"Hey, what's this?" Lux said, lifting up James's hand.

He was still wearing Heart's glove. Though torn and dirtied, it had somehow survived the battle. He peeled it off and flung it onto the floor.

"It's nothing."

"Guys," Honey said, looking up.

A cloud of molecular models brooded above them, their deadly, blue particles buzzing like angry hornets.

"E!" James yelled.

"Lux, car!" she shouted.

The crew dove into the red muscle car that sprang from Lux's hand as the cloud descended upon them. They slammed the doors shut against the attacking horde. Lux stomped on the accelerator. The louvered doors lining the hall flashed by and blended into a white blur as the car sped down the hallway. The models flew after them. Their blue particles joined to form a giant cloud that stretched toward the trunk and crawled onto the back of the car.

"Check everything!" E yelled.

The crew fumbled about to ensure that the windows were closed and the doors, locked. The particles began spreading over the car like a virus. They occluded the windows before dripping down the windshield. They oozed into the car through the vents and clawed across the dashboard.

"Don't touch it!" James shouted, shoving Lux back as he reached forward.

Lux hissed a curse and turned on the wipers. A thin streak of visibility appeared. A painting hung on a brick wall. Lux hit the brakes. Honey shouted. James's hand shot toward the grab handle. The car smashed through both the painting and the wall and sailed through the air alongside rubble, blue particles, and molecular models. The heads of Crew Blue snapped forward in unison as the car landed. Dirt sprayed as the car swerved to a stop across dark soil. The particles retreated back into the vents and ebbed from the windshield.

"It's leaving!" Honey said.

"Yeah, because look what's up ahead!" James shouted.

The cave they had driven into was shaking and splitting as if on the brink of implosion. Boulders cracked and tumbled. Stalactites dropped and broke in explosions of rubble and dirt across the entire expanse of trembling land before them.

"There!" E yelled, thrusting her finger between James and Lux.

White light illuminated a large hole carved into the far end of the cave.

The engine revved. The car raced forward, bouncing across heaving ground like a boat speeding across stormy waters. James's fingers slipped on blood and sweat as he clung to the grab handle. His body slammed against the door, the glove compartment, the seat. He could hear Bloom's head thumping against the window behind him. The crew yelled as a boulder fell in their path. Lux swerved. The car spun in countless dizzying circles before crashing into the side of the cave. For a moment, everyone lay still. Lux coughed, and Honey moaned.

"Out. Out!" E snarled.

The crew climbed over shattered glass and toppled out of the car. James swayed on the quaking ground. The hole of white light lay several yards away.

"Bloom, lead!" E shouted.

Bloom dashed forth, zig-zagging through the falling rubble. Honey and Lux chased after him. James staggered, his head still spinning from the crash. E suddenly pushed him from behind. He rolled across the dirt as she screamed out in pain.

"E!" he cried.

She lay face-up on the ground, tugging viciously on her right arm, which lay crushed beneath a giant boulder. He opened his hand and thought of his cleaver. But nothing appeared. He'd forgotten. He was out. He fought to keep his dread and fear from morphing into panic as he scrambled toward her. She pushed him away with her free hand.

"Just go!" she yelled.

"Are you crazy?" he shouted. He struggled against her. He needed to get to the last knife he knew was sheathed on the right side of her belt. He needed to cut her free!

"Just go, you moron! Just go!"

She pushed him away again, knocking him backward. He scrambled further back as stones and dust showered down between them.

"Go!" she screamed from behind the rubble.

Hating himself, James ran toward the hole of light. Adrenaline numbed the pain in his body, pushing him forward and carrying him further away from E as he dodged the stalactites and boulders crashing down all around him.

"James!" Lux shouted.

He sprinted forth with all his remaining strength and threw himself through the hole. He tumbled across warm, sandy stone beneath a gray sky.

"E!" he cried. He scrambled past Honey's and Lux's helping hands and back to the mouth of the hole.

"Where is she?"

"E!"

"Right there! Look!"

She was running toward them through the falling debris, her right foot buckling this way and that on a shattered ankle. One hand was pressed over her bleeding shoulder. Her right arm was missing. She had cut it off herself.

A boulder fell from the ceiling down toward her. Honey screamed. E flung herself to the side and rolled across the floor, missing the crushing blow by inches. Her remaining arm shook as she tried to lift herself off of the dark soil. Her arm went limp, and she fell into the dirt. Exhaustion peered out from behind the blood and grime covering her face.

"You can do it, E!" Lux screamed. "Come on, come on! You got this! Come back to us!"

James and Honey joined him. Together, they yelled and cried and begged for her to come back to them. Bloom tossed his head from side to side as a manic grin spread across his face. A familiar flame began to kindle in E's eyes. Gulping in air, she pushed herself back onto her feet. The walls behind her began to crumble and disappear into sinking ground.

"Hurry!" James screamed.

Her broken ankle rolled uselessly about as she ran. Pain flooded her face. She lurched forward, and for a split moment, James thought that weariness had finally defeated her. He watched in awe as instead, she let out a roar of rage and began sprinting toward them. Her ankle straightened. Her eyes blazed like black fire. Her entire being burned with the will to survive as the cave chased her in collapsing waves of debris.

She hurled herself through the hole, and James caught her in his arms. Another boulder fell and blocked the hole for good. He dragged her away from the closed hole and laid her down on the ground. Her eyes remained closed as she continued gasping for air. Lux shoved two rolls of bandages into James's hands.

"You're the best at wrapping wounds, James," Lux said. "I'm out now, so wrap her up carefully."

"Save it for yourselves," E snarled, thrusting out her hand as James made to bind her injuries.

She squeezed her eyes shut again and balled up her fist. Bones twisted out from her shoulder. A skeletal arm began to grow as small portions of muscle weaved together. James couldn't help but pause as he marveled again at her healing prowess. He shouted at Lux and Honey to restrain her. Ignoring her protests, he began tying her wounds even as she squirmed in their hold.

The focus her arm was costing her must have been considerable. The gashes on her body, which were usually such quick fixes for her, had barely begun to heal. Ocean waves surged and boomed in the distance as James continued binding each wound. Though she calmed somewhat as Bloom licked her face, she gave up struggling only as he tied the final knot. The crew broke away from her to give her some air.

Lux stumbled away before falling to the ground with a groan that sounded like something between "umph" and "oh." He unfurled his arms and legs and remained on his back like a panting starfish. Bloom flopped down beside him. His tongue rolled out of his mouth and quivered on the sandy stone with every breath. Honey staggered a few steps forward on her feet, shuffled a few inches on her knees, then crawled to Bloom and Lux. She slumped over next to them, face-down. James's heart continued thumping against his chest. His wounds pulsed as pain jabbed every part of his body. He felt anxious even beneath the calm, gray sky. For a while, no one moved. Then Lux's face slowly split into a grin.

"Now that's ... what I call ... a Thanksgiving!" he said between pants.

Honey rolled onto her back and draped her arm over her eyes. Bloom sucked his tongue back into his mouth with an expression that lacked amusement. E lifted a shaking middle finger. James sprawled out across the warm stone ground and felt light-headed as he began to laugh.

CHAPTER 13

WAVES

G ive me your hand, E," Lux wheedled in a sing-song voice. He grabbed her hand.

"Let go of me," she snarled as she wrested her fist away from him. "Stop being so ridiculous."

"I'm not being ridiculous," he said, swiping at her hand again. "We need to talk. You said so yourself."

"I said we needed to talk, not that we needed to stand in a circle and hold hands like we're in kindergarten."

"But holding hands is conducive to heartfelt conversation. It's a proven, scientific fact!"

"Stop talking out of your ass!"

Bloom shot out a sigh of impatience through his nostrils as E and Lux continued bickering. James scratched him behind the ears to comfort him. The salty scent of the ocean intermingled with the fresh smell of the dark pine trees towering around them. It felt good to be out in the open again with plenty of fresh air.

A sandy trail had led them up a lone, forested hill that bulged out of the ocean's shoreline like a great drop of water turned into a lump of land. The cold, teal ocean surrounding them frothed with seafoam. Instead of crashing into the shore, the ocean's waves rolled perpendicular to the shoreline so that infinite lines of waves stretched into the horizon while surging endlessly to the left of the hill. Seagulls flew overhead in a gray sky that warned of rain. Their caws seemed to complain about the chill in the air and the cold sprays of saltwater. The brisk weather gave the impression of early morning, yet something in the brooding clouds also warned of nightfall.

On their journey up the hill, James had asked Lux how they had managed to find him again. Lux had responded by grinning and pointing at Bloom. He had managed to sniff out James's location using that powerful nose of his.

The crew could have easily given up on him as a bad egg, but instead, they had chased him down even despite other obstacles. Apparently, the black lobsters he had seen were much smaller and tamer than the ones the crew had run into. A shudder unrelated to the cold tingled his spine as he wondered if he would have done the same for them.

The ocean continued surging beyond the trees.

"I barely even have hands right now!" E raged. She smacked Lux's hand away again. "Everyone, just sit down. Sit down!"

Bloom puffed out a sigh and shook out his fur. Wounds stretched and joints trembled as the crew sat down in a circle. James looked at Lux's watch. Only a small bar of time remained. He wanted to discuss everything that had happened tonight before time ran out. He knew that he needed to give the crew a proper apology for everything he'd done, a true apology with a good explanation. But where was he even supposed to start?

"Dearly beloved," said Lux, "we are gathered here today–"

"This isn't a wedding," E snapped.

Honey cackled.

"Well, how else are we supposed to facilitate this very sensitive conversation?" said Lux.

"Just start by telling him what you told us," said E. She glanced at James then looked away with a sigh.

"Wait," James said, interrupting Lux before he could reply. Nervousness, eagerness, and shame all crashed against one another within his pounding heart. "Before you start, I know you guys must have a lot to say to me. But before you say anything, I really just wanted to say...."

He looked around at them, hoping to find the right words. But the more he looked, the more his tongue seemed to shrivel up in his mouth.

"Say what? That you're an idiot for putting us through all this shi–"

"Honey, you said you'd stop," Lux said.

A groan of exasperation rumbled out of her mouth. "I'm sorry, but you know it's true. Tonight was a nightmare and–"

"And you agreed before we went after him that you'd start being nice."

"No, it's all right," said James.

The crew looked at him. He took in a deep breath.

"You're right. I was an idiot. I mean, I am. I am an idiot. Tonight was crazy." He rubbed the inner corners of his eyes. "It was totally unnecessary, and it was all my fault. It was just my ... my...." He trailed off as the words clung to his mouth and refused to let go. He breathed in again and pushed the words out. "It was just my pride. It was all my pride. I'm sorry. I wouldn't have lasted the night if you guys hadn't come for me." He felt the truth of his words even as he said them. He rubbed his face with both hands. "Thank you. For coming back for me."

Bloom nuzzled James then gave him a single, long lick that left a large strip of clean skin on his grimy face. James gave him a small smile before petting his mane. His tail began flopping from one side to the other.

"Well, I for one am thankful for your apology on this Thanksgiving holiday," Lux said. He stuck out his chest only to wince and curl up again. "We're really glad to have you back. And I just wanted to say too, man. If you think I'm not giving you full explanations, or if you don't get something I said, just tell me. It's all right."

The look on his face sank James's heart and filled it with yet another wave of shame.

"I know, I know. I'm sorry. I mean, and I'm not trying to justify anything, but I thought ... I just thought...."

"Spit it out!" Honey snapped, making him jump.

"Honey!" Lux said.

"I'm sorry! But it's just so frustrating when he–"

"I-tried-to-tell-you-I-was-annoyed-a-few-times-but-I-was-being-stupid-and-I-didn't-want-to-talk-about-it-because-we're-friends," James confessed in a single, rushed breath.

"Well, there. He said it after all. Sheesh," said Honey.

"James, man. Look. It's okay. Just tell me. I'm sorry I don't get it all the time, but just argue with me next time. Make me see it, okay? Arguing isn't always a bad thing. Oh, and also," Lux said, jabbing his thumb toward E and Honey, "I made these guys promise to be nicer to you. Honey's going to actually talk to you from now on, and the whole crew will look out for you more. We're a crew, you guys. So everyone will be nicer and acknowledge you when you do something right, and pitch in more when you don't, and say more here and there for your training, and just be more, you know, helpful when it comes to teaching you the ropes. But hey, it might be a moot point. I mean, look at you. I know tonight was a mess, but man. You were on fire!"

Bloom's tail thumped against the ground.

"It's all thanks to you guys," James mumbled, feeling conscientious of the warmth creeping into his face.

He glanced at E as he thought of all the nights she had drilled him. Her yells, her kicks, her stabs. He had resented her for all of it, but now he realized that she had helped prepare him for the worst of the Flowering.

"Yeah, I guess it was kind of impressive," Honey said. "What?" she said as Lux lifted his eyebrows up and down at her. "It's true. Besides, I can acknowledge when someone saves me."

She dodged James's look of surprise.

"I think it's safe to say," said E, "that you don't need training in any of the basics anymore. But as Lux said, we should all try to be more proactive than reactive from now on when it comes to helping you learn. We'll listen to you more too and take your opinions into consideration when making decisions. We'll get better at communicating. Oh, and speaking of. What you said about the Merchants."

"I'm sorry I called you all those things," James said quickly. "It was really rude of me."

E waved aside his apology. "You should know that Merchants are liars. They beg and whine then turn right around and stab you in the back when you show them any mercy. I know from personal experience." She sighed. "I know fighting humans isn't pleasant, and I don't expect any of you to ever do what I did to those Merchants on Halloween, that blond one in particular. But sometimes, there really is no other choice. You've got to understand that this is survival. If it's us or them, I have to choose us. I can't let other humans out here endanger your lives, and I won't just stand around and let them do whatever they want to you."

She winced as a fresh rope of muscles and tendons twisted down her raw arm.

"I ... I understand," James said.

He still couldn't say that he agreed with the level of savagery E had shown on Halloween, but he couldn't argue with what she was saying either. Had she stood around and done nothing, the Merchants would have stripped the crew of their possessions and cut their time short by several hours. Kindness and decency were great and all, but in the face of survival ... of life and death ... they simply became naive hopes. E could be ruthless, sure, but James finally saw that her cruelty didn't stem from a cruel heart as he had assumed but from one that desired to protect.

Silence passed among the crew as the waves continued to crash and boom.

"I wanted to apologize," E said suddenly, "for being so rough on you."

James jumped. Of all the things she could have said, an apology was the last thing he had anticipated. She looked away from him and continued before he could stammer a reply.

"We were all rough on you," she said. "Well, not Lux."

Bloom shuffled his paws.

"And Bloom, of course."

He twitched his tail.

"Also, I wanted to let you know that the stabbing stops tonight. I know you don't like it, so I wanted to make that clear, though again, I don't think you'll be needing too much personalized training in the future."

"N-No! I mean, that's great. I ... I am pretty scared of your stabs. But it helped me so much. When that citizen was attacking me, one of the things that kept me going was the thought of you stabbing me. I know that sounds weird, but it did work. I didn't even realize until tonight how much...." James trailed off, at a loss for words yet again. It was hard to believe that E was speaking cordially to him, never mind apologizing.

"I'm glad the training came in handy, but I still shouldn't have trained you the way that I did. Now that I look back...." She heaved another sigh. "Actually, I wanted to apologize to all of you. I'm your leader, and I'm strong enough to admit when I've gone wrong. I've been unnecessarily harsh with all of you, especially in the past few months. I apologize for that."

"No!"

"E...."

"You're the best leader ever!"

She waved aside the crew's protests. "It's no excuse. I know what it's like to have someone be so hard on you. And it's not fun. It was wrong of me not to realize how I was acting. I set out to protect all of you, but I harmed you instead. I'm sorry."

"No! E, you're the best leader I could have ever asked for. You're the greatest leader...." Lux struggled as if he were about to explode then seized E's hand.

This time, she did not smack him away.

"He's right. We never could have survived this long without you. We owe you so much," Honey said.

"You're the older sister I never had. You both are," said Lux. "And James, you're the older brother I've been hoping for. You know how long I waited for another guy to join the crew?" He grasped James's shoulder.

James's eardrums rumbled. His nose began to sting. The question he'd withheld all night finally came tumbling out of his mouth. "Why did you guys follow me? After everything I said?"

"Well, we couldn't just leave you. You'd be dead meat!" Lux said.

"He's right. As annoying as you are, we couldn't just let you die. I mean, we are a crew, and you were going on and on about how you've missed sleep this week. Not that you missed enough for it to be that big of a deal," said Honey.

James remained downcast.

"I told you your first night, didn't I?" said E. "This is a pact. It's loyalty. You're one of us now."

Bloom lowered himself chin-down onto the ground and closed his eyes. A smile spread across his face as another sigh shot out of his nose.

"But I broke that pact," said James.

"Yeah, well, the pact is active again now, so whatever," Honey said.

"How can you guys forgive me so easily?"

"Oh, my–James, look. We forgive you, and you forgive us. It's fine, okay? That's just how we are," Honey said.

Bloom raised his head, ears perked.

"Quiet. I feel something," said E.

The crew froze.

"Hey. Are the clouds moving, or are we?" Lux said, staring up at the sky.

"Stay here," E commanded. She grunted and swayed as she tried to stand up.

"Oh, no you don't," Honey said. "You don't even have most of your arm yet. I'll go."

"I can handle it," E growled. "Besides, you can't go alone."

"Neither can you."

"I'll go with you, Honey," said James. "I've healed enough."

This wasn't entirely true. He was still losing more blood than he would've liked. But he wanted to prove to the crew that he'd be a better team player from now on.

"See? James can come with me," Honey said. "We all don't have that much time left anyway. It'll be fine, E."

He could tell that Honey wasn't thrilled about wandering into the woods with him and that she was only agreeing with the idea to spare E, but he felt grateful that they were at least on speaking terms now.

"Come on, E. Weren't you just telling us about how you've been too harsh the past few months and that you were going to loosen up?" Lux prodded.

E rolled her eyes. "Fine. Make it quick."

Bloom stood up, shook out his coat, then laid down behind E and Lux so that they could lean their backs against him.

"Well, come on, Benedict Arnold," Honey said, signaling to James as she walked toward the trees.

"You said you'd be nice," Lux called as James hurried after her.

"I'll be nice ... er," Honey added under her breath.

They walked into the woods together and rushed up a steep incline. Their breaths dissipated among the dark green of the trees. Pinecones rolled away as dry needles crunched under their boots. They emerged, at last, at the top of a high cliff. The ocean below them stretched out into the distant horizon. Patches of water sparkled under rays of light penetrating the clouds.

"Well, we're moving all right," Honey said.

The hill no longer stood on the shore but drifted lazily along with the rolling waves. James checked the shoreline. They were neither closer nor farther than before. Nothing seemed to indicate danger. They looked up as thunder rumbled through the sky. Honey cleared her throat, glanced at him, then stared at the ground. After a moment or two, she shook her hair away from her face and gazed at the sky again.

"You know why I hate the rain so much?"

"No. Why?" James said as he continued scrutinizing the clouds for danger.

"My best friend died not too long ago. It rained at his funeral."

He looked at her.

"That, and my mom and dad. It always rained hard whenever they really went at it. I swear, they always acted like they would die if they got along. And it didn't help that my dad was the classic mean drunk who would always beat up his family once he'd downed enough bottles. Always has been, actually, and probably always will be. But it's not a surprise. The rain, I mean. I grew up in a really rainy area, so it's kind of stupid to hate the rain so much. But still. Rain." She wrinkled her nose and shook her head.

James suddenly remembered the boy they had rescued from the moulded father. Honey had attacked that citizen with such ferocity and had gone as far as to ignore E's commands in order to pierce the mark. Had she seen a part of herself in that boy as his father had gripped him? Was that why E had excused her blatant disregard for her orders that night?

"I-I'm sorry," he said, feeling both sympathetic and off-footed. He wasn't sure why she was opening up to him all of a sudden but appreciated her waving a white flag in the form of vulnerability.

"I wasn't always like this, you know," Honey continued. "Maybe if things had been different in Reality, I would've been different toward you. Nicer, probably. More welcoming, for sure. And maybe if I wasn't so afraid of losing Crew Blue like how I lost my friend...."

She sighed and closed her eyes as she shook her head.

"Crew Blue means everything to me. You have to understand that. They gave me purpose, and they gave me meaning. When I was with my other crew, we'd just wander from one plane to another, never knowing where we were trying to get to or what we were even here to do. We all just kind of existed. I think it's like that for most humans out here in the Flowering.

"But Crew Blue. Crew Blue gave me something to fight for, and more than that, they gave me something to live for. They gave me company, and I mean real company, the kind that values each other. They even gave me my name. Honey," she said softly.

Then she scoffed and rolled her eyes. "Not that I really liked the name. 'Honey' sounds like one of those sexist things that misogynistic pigs call women to denote that they're somehow above us! But, well, Lux was really excited about it because he was trying to be all symbolic, and honey has all sorts of uses and medicinal properties, and he thought the name was a nice name so...."

James smiled as she rolled her eyes again. Despite her complaints, he could tell that the amount of thought Lux had put into her name had touched her.

"James," she said, "I never wanted you to be a part of our crew."

"Yeah, I kind of figured that," he said with a grin.

Her mouth twisted, half frowning, half smiling. "Well, you were just some random guy who barely knew how to fight! You even gave us your real name. Your watch is weird, and on top of everything else, you managed to shoot my leg almost as soon as you got here."

"I'm sorry about that. I know I never really apologized for it, but I am."

"It's fine. I'm not asking for an apology. I never was, actually. I just wanted you to leave. I didn't trust you." She stared again at the vast sea. "Anyway, I'm not going to forget any time soon that you left us like that. But at the same time, I can't forget how you saved me from that thing and how you got that spear to E either. Like I said, not bad."

"Well, like I said—"

"I'm going to try trusting you, James," she pressed on. She inhaled deeply and nodded as if to reassure herself. "I'm going to try trusting you. It's why I'm telling you all of this personal stuff, I guess. We need to roll together to survive together. And," she added in a low grumble, "I need to learn to work with others instead of just being scared all the time."

James paused then said, "I'll earn it. I'll earn your trust."

And he meant it.

She smiled at him. "Come on. Let's go. Bet you a new knife E's going to be pissed at us for taking so long."

He chuckled and followed her down the slope. As they weaved between the trees, his thoughts wandered through everything Honey had just told him then back to what she'd said before he had abandoned the crew. "You got to spend time with your loved ones on Thanksgiving.

What more do you want?" was what she had said to him. He'd felt nothing but slighted by her words at the time. But now, he couldn't help but wonder what the day had been like for her. Had she eaten a meal with her family, or were they too dysfunctional even for that? How long had it been since her friend had died? Had she spent the day thinking of him? He thought of his own family. He thought of Heri.

"What took you so long?" E barked upon their arrival.

"Aw, come on, E. It wasn't that long. Besides, guess what time it is?" Lux said.

James stopped in his tracks as Lux waved his watch at him. It was finally time to go home. He touched his waist where his belt should have been.

"Wait," he said. "How are we going to pierce our watches? None of our weapons made it."

"I present to you Exhibit A," Lux said, sweeping a hand toward Bloom.

Bloom sat up and opened his mouth. Lux placed his hand between his fangs.

"Tonight was good. And James. James, I'm just glad things worked out. All right, you guys. See you later."

Bloom bit down, and Lux disappeared. Honey gave James a firm nod and a coy smile before following suit. E reeled him in with a jerk of her head once Honey, too, had vanished. He placed his hand in Bloom's mouth then withdrew it. For some inexplicable reason, he suddenly didn't feel like leaving.

"What's wrong?" said E.

"I.... You go first. I think I'll stay behind for a bit."

"Stay behind? Why? You didn't get enough of the Flowering after tonight?"

"I don't know. Yeah, maybe I am going a little crazy," he said, smirking as he rubbed the back of his head. "I guess I just want to think a bit on my own before going back. Tonight's been a lot. I guess I want to digest things."

She cocked an eyebrow at him.

"I'll be all right," he assured her. "Besides, it doesn't matter if something attacks me now. I've gotten enough sleep for the night, and it seems pretty safe here. And if anyone wants to rob me, hey, they can try. I'm pretty sure they won't find anything."

"Well, okay," she said, looking him up and down. "If you really want to. But don't stay for too long."

She cast him another doubtful look before placing her hand in Bloom's mouth and disappearing. James didn't blame her for looking at him that way. Maybe he really was going insane. He knew, though, that he needed to stay a little while longer, even if he couldn't exactly articulate why. He shivered and rubbed his arms as he sat back down on the ground. Bloom's fur tickled him then enveloped him like a blue coat as he curled himself around him. They stared up at the sky together.

Seagulls floated across a backdrop of rolling, gray clouds. Thunder rumbled like the warning of a celestial beast. Thoughts of family, work, and school drifted across James's mind before disappearing one by one. He nestled deeper into Bloom's fur and breathed in the smell of the trees and the ocean. Cold waves continued crashing against land.

Life felt different after having come so close to losing everything. Things he'd once held as vital now felt trivial. Annoyances and grudges felt foolish. He didn't feel worried, angry, or bitter. He felt calm. He felt grateful.

The waves swelled and burst into white before blending into teal again. When James stood up, his deepest wounds had closed into thin, red scars. He stroked Bloom a final time before placing his hand in his mouth and returning to Reality.

PART II
THE BEAST

CHAPTER 14

THE BLACK ORBS

C rowds of people teemed around the crew as they followed Bloom down another street. On either side of the street, small stores varying in height stood next to one another, creating two long walls of stores. Each store was made of worn, wooden planks and rusting, metal roofs and had been coated with blue paint that had long ago begun to peel. Wooden planks studded the stores' faces, covering large cracks and missing boards. Protruding signs advertised everything from quick bites to eat to peep shows to beach souvenirs. Smoke and reggae drifted out from windows and doorways. White curtains rolled slowly without a breeze.

Bloom seemed to disappear and reappear like a phantom as he passed long strips of the peeling blue paint. He sniffed at fire hydrants, cracks in the pavement, and stains at the foot of the stores as he led the crew to the end of the street. He sneezed with a sharp shake of his head then trotted into a circular plaza surrounded by several stories of small apartments. After crossing the plaza, he led the crew down one of the many streets radiating out of the plaza and into the distance. Wooden stores stood on both sides of this street as well.

James plastered his arms to his sides as he tried to avoid the stream of people walking past in the opposite direction. E had commanded the crew to avoid contact with everyone in the crowds to avoid unwanted attention, but he had no idea how, exactly, they were supposed to do that given the amount of people here. He stifled a cough as they walked through a cloud of skunky smoke that puffed out of an open window. He averted his eyes from the stare of a passing woman and withheld a scowl as a man shoved past him.

"Shouldn't we find cover? This is impossible," he whispered to Lux.

Lux passed the message down the line. E looked back at James and nodded. She prodded Bloom, who acknowledged the concern with a twitch of his tail. More eyes stared and more heads turned as Bloom halted. His nose quivered before he sauntered past a display window full of glass trinkets and into the darkness of an adjacent doorway. With one hand placed over the hilt of his knife, James checked the street for signs of danger before following the rest of the crew inside.

The space within was larger than its small appearance. Sand dripped down in the form of stalactites from the high ceiling above, their granules disappearing midair before they could reach the crew. Plastic tables lined one side of the shop and sported a variety of glass figurines for sale. A dusty cash register sat on top of a long, empty display cabinet on the other side. Behind the cabinet, a man in a welding mask stood in front of a furnace embedded in the wall. Red-orange flames shot intermittently into the air as he sculpted molten glass at the end of a long blowpipe. He paid no heed to the crew.

Honey and Lux wandered toward the glass figurines on the tables. They pointed at the ones that caught their eye and stifled their giggles over the ones that were obscene. James remained at E's side as they surveyed the shop together. Bloom's nails clicked over the cement floor as he walked over to the glass cabinet. The flames extinguished, and the blowpipe rose into the air. The man lifted his mask to stare at Bloom. E shushed Lux and Honey.

After a moment, the man nodded. Bloom smiled as if to thank him then walked down a narrow hall leading to the back of the shop. He slid behind a black, velvet curtain hanging on the wall and stepped out of sight. E signaled to the rest of the crew and followed him. The man's eyes followed James as he hurried after everyone.

"Whoo-hoo-hoo-hoo!" Lux exclaimed.

A gargantuan heap of ice cream lay in a room draped with black velvet. Though colorful puddles oozed from the base of the mound, the ice cream remained soft, fluffy, and whole. Enormous slices of golden pancakes orbited the pastel-colored pile, dripping with syrup.

"Can I?" Lux asked E.

"Remember your promise," Honey said before E could utter a word.

James's mouth squirmed as he suppressed a smile. Two weeks had already passed since their reconciliation among the crashing waves. True to her word, E had stopped stabbing him and putting him through boot camp and instead, had assigned him a specific skill to practice during each rescue mission while giving him supplemental lessons afterward. His battle skills had grown exponentially as a result.

She'd also shown more leniency toward the crew as a whole, and Lux and Honey had wielded her leniency like a golden net to drag in every opportunity to indulge in some of the finer things of the Flowering. They had pushed their luck on some nights, but James had a good feeling about the ice cream.

"Fine," E said after glowering at James. She shook her head in disapproval as Lux and Honey ran to the pile.

Lux began shoveling butter pecan into his mouth. Honey licked strawberry ice cream off of her finger before drawing her knife and scooping large mouthfuls with the blade. James grew queasy as he watched them gorge. Food and water weren't necessary for their bodies in the Flowering. He'd long become accustomed to lasting the night without a bite to eat, and he saw no reason why he needed to start now. Besides, the thought of eating in the Flowering always reminded him of how he had swallowed that gruesome eye in the blue box during his first night. He tore his focus away from the milky residue coating Lux's and Honey's mouths and tried to distract himself from his growing nausea by watching Bloom scratch behind his ear instead. A giant slice of pancake nudged James's head as if to encourage him to take a bite. He pushed it aside with a grimace and watched it drift away.

"You're not going to eat?" E asked him as she helped Bloom with his itch.

"No. I ate something weird my first night. After that, eating just...." He finished with a shake of his head.

"You ate something that night? I don't remember that."

"It was before you guys found me. There was this weird moment."

"Weird moment? You mean your awakening dream?" Honey said.

"What?"

"Your awakening dream," said Lux. "Everyone has one. We all did too."

"You gain full consciousness only after you're born into the Flowering," E explained. "But before that, you can feel yourself gaining consciousness bit by bit in what's called an 'awakening dream.' Supposedly, every awakening dream happens in some sort of bridge leading from Reality into the Flowering. But no one's really sure about the details."

"A bridge? You mean another dimension?" James said.

"I think it's safe to assume that it's another dimension," said E. "But who knows? Who knows what we really traveled through or why we even ended up here in the first place?"

Who knew, indeed. James had long given up trying to guess what, exactly, the Flowering was and why he had been sent here. But something

E had said prodded a sense of uneasiness within him. He'd never really thought about it until now, but he'd always been certain that he had been born into the Flowering only upon reaching the tree of eyes. It was there, after all, that he'd found himself naked and bald. Only there did his skin start to emit steam like that of every other newborn. Which meant that everything before the tree of eyes, including the eye in the blue box, had been a part of his awakening dream. But then that would also mean that he had gained full consciousness within his awakening dream. Was that even possible? It didn't seem like it based on what E had just said.

"I don't remember much about my awakening dream to be honest," Lux said as he ripped off a piece of pancake that had strayed across his path. "It was all just a blur of random things that didn't make much sense. The only thing I really remember is the stuff that happened once I got here. You remember too, don't you, E? The night you and Bloom found me?"

"Yes."

She sat down in front of Bloom and leaned back on his forelegs. He twitched his tail and nuzzled her before smiling at Lux.

"Of course I do."

Something softened in her coal-black eyes. It was subtle, but it was there. It was the same soft something James often saw in the eyes of mothers whenever they smiled at their children.

"Can I tell James about it?" Lux asked.

"I don't see why not."

"James, come and sit here. Have some of this while I tell you," Lux said. He got up, grabbed James, and started dragging him over to the ice cream.

"Oh, no. Lux. That's okay. I don't want to."

"Here."

He shoved a chunk of pancake into James's hands. James looked down at his fingers as syrup dripped between them like thick, brown sweat. He sighed.

"Ah, man. Whoo! Thanks for this, E. Work was rough today. Anyway, my first night. So, yeah. How should I put this? Well, it's like this, James. I'm, well, I'm the head of my family's business because my dad, he was diagnosed with cancer back in '07 and—wow! It's been three years already. Time really flies."

For the first time, James saw the sadness drifting behind Lux's smile. He suddenly felt as if he'd noticed a ghost, some melancholy spirit that he'd always failed to see though it had been there all along.

"I'm sorry," James said.

"Thanks, man." Lux accepted another piece of pancake from Honey as she sat down next to him and placed a gentle hand on his shoulder. "My dad's health wasn't good for a long time, but the cancer. The cancer really did it."

He paused, grinned, then shoved the pancake into his mouth. He commented loudly on how good it tasted before continuing.

"But yeah. Eventually, the cancer got so bad that I decided that I needed to wait on college. I needed to take care of the shop and my family. My dad was really against it, though. He said that he and my mom had worked too hard to get our family to where we were and that they'd done it all to give us a better life. But hey, the hospital bills aren't going to pay for themselves, you know? So my mom ended up sitting me down one night and talking to me. She tried giving me a tough love kind of speech at first, but then she broke down and said that she and my dad were sorry and that they had never wanted me to do this and all this other stuff."

He bowed his head and tried to smile. Honey wrapped an arm around him.

"Sorry. I don't know why it's so hard to talk about this all of a sudden. I've been wanting to tell you forever, and I didn't used to get so emotional while telling it."

"Don't be sorry," James said.

"It's fine, sweetie," Honey murmured.

E remained silent as she stared at the floor.

"Yeah, well, I'm still sorry," Lux said with a laugh. "But yeah. I was born into the Flowering that same night. I was in some kind of broom closet with a sink. It was small and dark, and there were all these things crawling around, some kind of bug or something. I was trapped in there, totally alone and scared out of my mind. And then E found me."

"Yes," she said softly. "You were crying."

"Yeah, and you heard me. One moment, I was crying all by myself in some random broom closet and then the next, the door opens, and there's E and Bloom. You remember what you told me, E?" he said, his eyes misting over with nostalgia.

She hesitated before answering. "I told you that I was sorry that life had taken something precious from you and given you a great burden instead."

"Yup. And then you let me cry it all out and gave me my name. 'Lux,'" he said, puffing out his chest and jabbing himself with both thumbs. "Latin for 'light.'"

A small smile formed on E's face. "I've always been glad that you liked the name. I wanted to give you something that would help you. Something that would give you hope."

"It did give me hope. You gave me hope then, and you give me hope now. I owe my survival and my family's survival to you."

"Lux...."

"Don't shake your head at me like that. It's true. See? What did I tell you, James? I told you she was a good person."

"You didn't think I was a good person?" E said, raising an eyebrow.

"Well–I–I mean," James stuttered.

"Bloom?" Honey called.

James made sure not to distract the crew as they turned their attention away from him and toward Bloom instead. His tail disappeared behind one of the black curtains.

"Good. I needed something to stop me from eating more," Lux muttered. He rose to his feet and stepped behind the curtain after E.

"I'm glad he finally told you," Honey said as she offered a hand to help James up. "I think he's been waiting for a good moment, but you know how things are around here."

He smiled and nodded before stepping behind the curtain too. He immediately lost his footing and slammed onto his rear. He flailed about then gripped his knife and looked all around, ready for danger to fly at him from every direction.

A low stream of water was slowly carrying the crew in a single-file line down a large spiral slide. He dug in his heels and pushed his palms into the sides of the slide. He wasn't surprised when he continued spiraling down as if he were seated on invisible rollers. Smooth, curved walls of reddish-brown composed the long, cylindrical space the crew was sliding through. Large houseplants and stained-glass windows hung midair throughout the space. A pod of smiling dolphins swam slowly by high up overhead. Lux began washing the sticky residue of ice cream and pancake syrup from his hands. Sadness still haunted his eyes despite his usual smile.

Cancer. Of all things. James tried to imagine how he would react if his mother sat him down one night and told him that his father was dying of disease. He shuddered. He couldn't imagine it. It was something he didn't even want to think about. And yet, it was Lux's Reality, his everyday life. It was what he'd wake up to in the morning after surviving yet another night in the Flowering. Not only did he have a father dying of cancer–as if that wasn't bad enough–but he'd also been forced to give up on college, his future, his hopes, his dreams.

James agreed with E. He was sorry that life had taken something precious from Lux and given him a great burden instead. He had always sensed that Lux was younger than himself, but adding up the details now, he realized that he could very well still be in his late teens. He was so young, yet he had the weight of his family on his shoulders and somehow carried that weight with a smile.

Just a few weeks ago, James had been constantly grumbling to himself about how immature and annoying Lux could be, and now here he was, unable to understand even the tip of the iceberg of all his responsibilities. James's parents had worked hard and provided everything he had ever needed. He had gone to college, graduated, and pursued the rest of his life casually at his own pace, following a well-paved road that had already been built for him. Life had never been harsh. It had always been what he had expected. At least, it had been until he'd been born into the Flowering.

The temptation to shove aside the discomfort of thinking raged against him. He wanted to crawl back under the warm comfort of ignorance and resent whatever prevented him from doing so. Thinking about the doom and gloom of life felt so overwhelming. He couldn't begin to comprehend it all because he'd never had to comprehend any of it. But as he tried to bury himself in the excuse of incomprehension, he couldn't help but remember the night of his desertion, the crew's bloodied and battered faces, and his promise to Honey.

He didn't feel happy knowing about Lux's dying father or even about Honey's deceased friend. The most he could gather was a sense of helplessness whenever he thought about any of it. But a strange sense of duty also glowed within him and with it, a sense of satisfaction in knowing that he held his friends' trust. He had promised Honey that he would earn it. The least he could do was listen and try.

"So, did you reach out to your sister?" Honey said.

James snapped out of his thoughts. "Oh, I ... uh ... texted her and told her I was sorry again that I can't go on the ski trip."

The crew groaned. Bloom sighed through his nostrils.

"Come on, James. You said you'd talk to her," said Lux.

"You're lucky to have a sister like her. I would have given up on you decades ago," said Honey.

"We don't live in the same city," James protested.

"It's called a phone call."

"She's not returning my calls. Besides, I'm sure she'll set up another family thing for Christmas, so I'll apologize in person then."

Bloom, E, and Lux twisted around to look at him with dubious expressions.

"Do it sooner than later. These kinds of things don't age well," said E.

"It's true," said Honey. "If I had known that Mark was going to die, I would have told him every day just how much good he's done for me. You just never know."

"You're her older brother, man. Take charge. Be the head of the family," said Lux.

"Okay, okay, you guys. I get it. I'm trying," James said, pumping both hands back and forth to keep all the nagging at bay.

The crew stared at him with expressions varying in their degrees of skepticism before looking away. His sister had been a point of conversation among Crew Blue for the past two weeks. A part of James regretted ever having told the crew about Heri. Now they always pestered him to make amends with her and to spend more time with his family.

"What are you sighing about?" Honey snapped.

"Nothing," James quickly replied.

He tried to ignore the feeling of Honey's eyes lasering into the back of his head. The truth was, he had grown more repentant of his attitude toward his sister. But he simply couldn't find the right words to match his emotions. Whenever he tried to articulate his budding regret, he felt a squirming need to flip over any tables that stood nearby and call the whole thing off due to embarrassment. But he couldn't deny that the crew was right. He needed to start mending his ways with Heri.

He wiggled his bottom around in the water to find a more comfortable position as they continued spiraling slowly down the slide. Monotony began to absorb his thoughts as long moments passed. Action items from work and notes he'd scribbled during lectures floated down through his mind before nestling atop a pile of dormant thoughts. He snapped out of his stupor as Bloom rose onto all fours. E commanded the crew to ready themselves.

The slide deposited them one by one onto a circular, wooden floor. Two tall potted plants stood on either side of an arched door hanging midair a few inches off the floor. Bloom scratched at the door, prompting E to draw her blade and walk forward. The others drew their weapons as well as she turned the knob and let the door swing open.

A flat bridge made of worn wood stretched through a black and hollow expanse, leading to a large staircase made of polished wood. The staircase ascended in square spirals toward a broad, square cut of gray sky. Light, pale and gray like the sky above, shone down on the staircase to create a rectangular column that separated the stairs from the darkness surrounding it. The crew followed Bloom across the bridge and onto the stairs.

Rain began to patter around them then grew into a shower. Streams of rainwater soon swelled into torrents, rushing down the stairs as a river. James gripped the polished railing and continued climbing each tall step as the water tugged at his legs. High above, the moon glowed silver. It looked massive tonight.

"Any change in your watch, James?" Lux asked.

"No. Nothing."

Along with his sister, his watch had also grown into a talking point. More than three months had passed since his birth night. The crew had hoped that the defects in his watch would have disappeared by now, but as far as James could tell, his watch was permanently damaged.

"Man, that is so weird," said Lux. "Hey, E. You think maybe we should take him to the Shamans? Get their opinion?"

"I've actually been wondering that myself. But I'm not sure yet."

"Shamans?" said James.

"They live in the City, remember?" said Lux.

"Yeah, they're humans like us but special," said Honey.

"They have superhuman hearing. And they can read minds!" Lux said.

"See memories is a better way of putting it," said E. "They're best known for their ability to see into another human's memories. They call it 'reading,' and it's considered the root of their infinite supply of supposed wisdom. Humans travel all the way to the City just to visit them for their advice, and they rule the City with their powers. But they have their weaknesses too. They're blind for one thing and limited to six creations for another, and their reading abilities don't work on each other. Still, if there's anyone who's seen or heard anything that's related to your watch, it would be a Shaman."

"But?" James said, hearing the troubled note in her voice.

"But they're corrupt and as greedy as Merchants. Actually, they're even greedier. The place they reside in, the Tower or *the Abode* they call it, it's–"

"Creepy," said Honey.

"Haunted," said Lux.

"It is not haunted," said E. "But the Tower can be difficult to navigate from what I've been told. Very maze-like and a bit of a trap. It's known among Merchants for being a bad place. Plus, payment for a Shaman's advice is really steep, and we'd have to let them read our memories on top of it. The Third Shaman is the most powerful out of all the Shamans and the most powerful human in the City, maybe even the entire Flowering. He'd be our best bet for answers, but I've heard so many shady stories about him. I'm not sure if we should even try. Let me think about it some more."

The crew nodded and continued climbing through the cold rain. Bloom halted then gave E a single nod.

"Brace yourselves!" she shouted.

James snatched his hand away from the railing as the entire staircase as well as the wooden bridge far below began to glow a luminescent blue. The crew's yells of surprise echoed throughout the space as the staircase and bridge vanished. Their clothes fluttered rapidly like flags in a storm as they dropped down through the column of light along with the rain. The light dimmed as they fell away from its reach and further down into the chasm.

James floundered about in the air, grasping at nothing, before forcing himself to relax. The terror of falling began to dissolve within the adrenaline pumping throughout his body as he continued descending through whistling air. The rain petered out into a few drops before stopping.

Honey cheered and whooped as she rolled onto her stomach. She curved her body as if she were skydiving. James's adrenaline spiked as he flipped over and curved his body too. He laughed as Lux began to whoop and cheer. Lux grinned then swam through the air toward him. He put his mouth next to James's ear as if to tell him a secret then whooped at full volume. James pushed him aside as Honey cackled. A small smile played on E's lips as she twisted around gracefully in the air and pulled herself onto Bloom's back. Bloom's tongue flapped about as his jaws opened into a wide, manic grin.

"Come on, James!" Lux yelled. Another shout burst out of his mouth.

James smiled and shook his head. Lux began swimming toward him again.

"All right, all right!" he said. He cheered.

"Weak!" Honey shouted.

James rolled his eyes then filled his chest and bellowed. Lux and Honey clapped and whooped their approval. E shook her head, still smiling. Crew Blue laughed together as they continued falling through the darkness.

Bloom's nose vibrated. He looked at E.

"Single file!" she shouted. "There's an exit coming up!"

James and the others paddled their way through the air to line up behind her and Bloom. The air suddenly became warm. Bloom nodded to confirm that they had passed through the exit. The crew spread out again as they fell toward a vast sheet of brown fog far below them.

"Brace yourselves!" E shouted as the brown mass loomed closer.

They plunged into the fog. James gagged and clapped his hands over his mouth and nose as a horrendous stink overwhelmed him. The stench contained every foul smell possible, from bad eggs to putrid fish to sour feces. He could tell that Honey and Lux were struggling to withhold their vomit too. Only E remained strong as she stared unblinkingly down through the fog with determination glinting in her black eyes.

The smell, the chill, and the whipping winds vanished as they fell out of the fog. Panic seized James as he saw the ground only a few yards below him. But his feet touched gently down onto solid ground as if he hadn't been plummeting through the sky just a moment ago. Lux touched down beside him then collapsed onto his hands and knees and puked.

"Blades out," E said.

James drew his knife before helping Lux onto his feet. Strange structures and objects littered the wasteland that stretched out into the horizon. Complete silence dominated the plane. Bloom stared into the distance with a grave expression that mixed something like scorn with sorrow before setting out into the land. Crew Blue followed with cautious steps.

James felt as if he were walking through an abandoned battlefield. A single lavender eye emblazoned the silk flags scattered throughout the silent wasteland. Upturned baskets spilled out their contents among cracked pillars and fallen statues with missing limbs. Weapons lay in the dirt, all pointed in the same direction.

But what drew James's attention the most were the black orbs perforating the plane.

Small and large, airborne and ground-level, they hung everywhere and had swallowed any part of any object that they had touched. He looked over his shoulder. A massive wall, black like the orbs, stood far off in the distance. He looked closer at the orbs scattered around him. They were black because they were ... empty.

Revulsion squirmed within him. Something about these orbs. Something about them was strangely familiar. Yet, instead of inspiring nostalgia, the familiarity stirred only disgust. Somehow, he knew that he needed to keep the crew away from these things. Bloom seemed to agree, for he paused to stare at one of the orbs before giving James a stern look of warning.

"E," James whispered, "there's something about this place and those black things. We need to get out of here."

"I know. There's something wrong with this place," she said, exchanging looks with Bloom as well. She turned to the others. "Keep together. Let's get out of here as soon as we can. And stay away from those black orbs."

The crew nodded. Bloom quickened his pace. Dust puffed up as he continued sniffing the ground.

"You okay, James?" Lux asked.

"Yeah. At least I think so. This place is–"

"Freaking creepy," Lux finished for him. "Yeah. I don't know why either. I mean, everything is so nice, but still."

"What do you mean?" "Nice" had been the last word on James's mind.

"Well, look at it. It's all so ... nice!"

James's confusion cleared as he shifted his focus. The wasteland's battle scars and the black orbs had preoccupied his attention, but now he saw what he meant. He saw golden thread, purple linens, jewelry and clothes of every kind, gemstone-studded chests sitting on soft furs, juicy meat, pastries with jewel-toned fillings, pitchers full of dark wine, goblets of silver and gold, white scrolls bearing different languages, furniture made of embroidered fabric and carved wood, colorful tents with dark interiors, and golden rods that stood like altars to pagan gods. Many of the goods lay huddled together as if each cluster had belonged to a different owner.

Bloom stopped. A gargantuan folding screen stood stretched across the ground like a wall, barricading their way forward. Colorful scenes had been woven into its many panels. Horns pointed toward the sky from the heads of dark creatures portrayed in the scenes. Veins bulged on their strange bodies. Their sharp claws looked ready to tear their victims apart. All of them were clearly moulded citizens, for each of the ferocious creatures had a red mark.

And standing next to the moulded, holding weapons and ready for war, were humans.

James took a few steps back. Citizens and humans didn't fight together like that, especially not in groups that big. And there was no way the moulded would team up with humans like that. Maybe he was wrong. Maybe the humans portrayed on the screen weren't actually humans but citizens that simply looked like humans. Citizens like Heart, who had wanted to join the moulded.

But the longer he studied the screen, the more he felt sure. These sinister creatures were moulded citizens, and they were fighting alongside humans in battalions. One army held up flags bearing a lavender eye identical to the ones decorating the flags standing throughout the wasteland. They faced another army whose flags boasted a red eye.

"James," said Lux.

He snapped around to see Bloom disappearing through the center of the screen. He rushed toward Lux as he motioned for him to hurry. He was relieved that they were leaving. This plane was chewing through his nerves with every passing moment.

As he made to step through the exit, his eyes fell on a black orb again. The orb had swallowed a weapon on the ground, leaving only the end of an ornate, golden hilt. He suddenly felt as if he'd forgotten something. He checked his utility belt, but all of his weapons were still there. Nothing was missing. He threw one last troubled glance at the orb then stepped into the next plane, thankful to move on and, hopefully, forget.

He stepped down onto gravel. Flaming torches flickered on the walls of rugged tunnels that branched out like hollow tentacles. Bloom roved about, sniffing the ground, then jerked his head up as a yelp echoed from the distance.

"What was that?" E whispered.

The rest of the crew waited for her and Bloom to direct them. But Bloom remained stiff and motionless. Then, without warning, he bolted off, turned the corner, and ran out of sight.

"Bloom! What the–" E sprinted after him.

The others stood still in stunned confusion. Bloom had never run off and abandoned them like this. Honey recovered first.

"Come on!"

She led James and Lux in a chase after E and Bloom. Lux whipped out his pellet gun and shot at one of the flaming torches ahead. It fell from its iron sconce. The crew drew their guns as they ran deeper into the tunnels.

"E, wait!" Honey shouted as they caught sight of her.

"Hurry!" she yelled back as she chased after Bloom's tail.

They hurtled down tunnels and whipped around corners. The torches began to grow sparse, and shadows grew into darkness. The air became colder and wetter, forming a chill, dank mist. James, Honey, and Lux turned another corner and came to a sudden halt in front of a giant chamber filled with torchlight. The dark mouths of other tunnels gaped at them from all around the walls of the chamber.

"Bloom, look at me. What's wrong? Bloom!"

Bloom stood still as E tugged on his mane. On the ground, several yards away, lay a thin, black wolf. Strips of its flesh had been ripped away so that its ribs were bare and exposed. It drew labored breaths through a snout smeared with dirt and blood. To its side loomed a massive ram with a dirty, shaggy coat. Thick horns curled out of either side of its head like a nefarious crown.

The ram lifted its hoof and stomped on the wolf's stomach. The wolf shrieked and convulsed. The ram twisted its hoof before lowering its head. The wolf's screams echoed about the chamber as the ram began feasting upon its flesh.

"Bloom!" E shouted.

He ran from her outstretched hands and charged toward the ram with open jaws. He tackled it to the ground. Bones crunched. Tendons flew. A wild fury burned in his eyes, withering up the kindness that usually emanated from within. E gave her head a quick shake. Anger replaced her shock.

"Bloom," she said, marching toward him. "Bloom, what are you doing? It doesn't have a mark!"

She jumped back as he snapped his jaws at her.

A moment passed in which the crew gaped at him, and he glared back with bared and bloody fangs. Then his pupils shrank. His ears rose as his fur sank. He blinked before looking at E and the rest of the crew with eyes that were no longer wide with rage but alarm. He shuffled his feet and tossed his head from side to side before curling up on the floor. He began to weep. James and Lux looked at one another with expressions that mirrored each other's alarm. They had never seen Bloom lift so much as a paw against E, never mind try to bite her.

E's hand hovered over Bloom's blood-stained fur before gently stroking him. He flinched at her touch then curled up tighter, still weeping. Honey stepped forward and shook out her hair, once more the first to recover. She nodded at James and Lux then began marching toward the remnants of the ram and the wolf. Both lay still on the ground as their bodies disintegrated into an unknown plane. James followed Honey. He, too, wanted to examine the citizens before they disappeared. He wanted to know what about them had upset Bloom so terribly.

Spears, swords, and guns glided out of one of the tunnels like sharks that had sniffed out blood. James, Lux, and Honey backed away from the gleaming weapons, snapping their guns up to eye level and aiming at each of the opposing faces that loomed out from the shadows. The three of them rallied around Bloom and E as the group of strangers encircled them. The torchlight revealed the watches on their hands. A man stepped forward and addressed them with a voice full of authority.

"*Step away from the wolf*," he commanded in Our Word.

CHAPTER 15

THE BROKEN HEART

The man pointed his broadsword at Bloom. The thin creases around his sapphire eyes betrayed age despite his sturdy physique. As James aimed his gun at the man, he couldn't help but feel a small spark of fascination. He had never seen anyone so much older than himself in the Flowering. His intrigue grew as he swung his gun toward the woman next to the man. She looked even older, though her age did nothing to weaken her grip on her rifle. James changed his aim yet again as a young woman pointed her spear at his face.

Her wild, red hair seemed to blaze in the torchlight like an auburn aureole. Her gray eyes glittered above the freckles splattered across her face. Like the other strangers, she wore a loose, sleeveless tunic made of what looked like sackcloth. A black utility belt that cinched in her waist, black jeans, and brown leather boots completed her medieval-looking outfit.

James kept his aim on her as he continued scrutinizing the others. E remained on her knees with one hand in Bloom's fur as one of the strangers pointed a sword at her. Another man inched toward Bloom with his broadsword lifted. A teenager walked out of the shadows, his sword held parallel to his face.

The teen. From the hallway with the snake woman! The one whom James had rescued from the blue particles and who had, in turn, tried to protect him from the creature. James searched for some sign of recognition from him, but the boy only glanced at him before glaring at Bloom again. He shook away the memory of the teen defending him and focused again on the danger these strangers posed.

They carried broadswords like knights of old and were wary of Bloom. That meant that they were Hunters, the human extremists who set out each night in groups called "families" to hunt down citizens. It had been Hunters who had hung that citizen to the baggage rack on the swaying train. They believed that all citizens were a threat to human lives, and such sadistic displays were meant to teach citizens to stay away from humans. But if these Hunters thought that they could string up Bloom too, they were wrong. They would have to hang James first before they dared to do that.

"*Step away from the wolf,*" repeated the man with the sapphire eyes.

The crew responded with silence.

"*Hello?*" said the redhead, her voice full of impatience. "*Did you not hear us? Step away from that citizen!*"

"*Blood Crow, how many times do I have to tell you to stop using that word?*" the man scolded.

"*But Lion Paw–*"

"*No buts. You use that word every time someone annoys you. You know it endangers your call and response. You need to learn to control yourself.*"

The redhead rolled her eyes. The man sighed then looked at E.

"*Are you the leader of this crew?*" he asked her.

"Yes," she said, rising slowly from the ground. Machetes appeared in both of her hands as she stepped in front of Bloom, who, much to James's surprise and annoyance, remained limp and despondent. "Are you the head of this family?"

James silently applauded E for refusing to respond in Our Word. Honey had mentioned before that many Hunters chose to speak exclusively in Our Word. But these Hunters would speak to the crew on the crew's terms, and that included using the language they designated and not the other way around. The man showed no surprise at E's refusal, though, as he continued in a steady voice.

"*Yes. I am the head of my family. You may call me Lion Paw. May I ask what I can call you?*"

"No."

Lux and Honey burst into snickers.

The red head bristled. "*Don't you dare speak to him like that.*"

"*Blood Crow,*" said Lion Paw.

Blood Crow tossed her red hair aside and breathed a sharp sigh of exasperation.

"*We heard the commotion and came in case a citizen was attacking you. We are only trying to help,*" Lion Paw said.

"'Help' is a funny way to describe what you Hunters do," said E.

He stared at her with a contemplative look as if he were wondering how to phrase himself next. He glanced at what remained of the black wolf and the ram.

"*Did you do this?*" he asked.

"We don't harm the innocent like you," E snarled.

"*Innocent? What do you mean 'innocent?'*"

"This wolf is a member of my crew. He's harmless," she said, ignoring his question. "Be on your way. There's nothing to see here."

"*That thing has them good,*" one of the Hunters mumbled.

"*That wolf has you tricked,*" said Blood Crow. "*Just step away from it. Step away from it now before it does anything to hurt you. Trust us.*"

"How about you trust us, and you step away? How does that sound?" Honey said with a wide, fake smile. She pointed her gun at Blood Crow, who glowered back.

"*Please listen to us,*" said Lion Paw. "*I don't know what this citizen has told you, but we know a dangerous citizen when we see one. As I said before, we are only trying to help.*"

"You have a funny way of showing it," James said, his heart pounding with both fear and excitement. He felt the crew look at him but didn't care. If there was ever a time to talk back, it was now. "There's nothing wrong with the wolf, so go on. Get out of here."

"*We will, but only after we've taken a look at that citizen,*" said Lion Paw.

"I'll kill you before I let you touch him," E snarled.

"*But we're your fellow humans!*" said Blood Crow.

E flicked up the tips of her blades. "This wolf is a member of my crew. This is my last warning. Leave us now. I can assure you that he's not marked or dangerous."

The ring of Hunters took another step closer, tightening the loop around Crew Blue. Honey pulled out another gun from her belt and pointed it around the circle.

"Any of you bastards make another move, and I'll blow this one's head off first!" she said, resting her aim on Blood Crow.

Anger twisted the face of the black-haired teen.

"*Steel Heart,*" Lion Paw said to him, a warning in his voice. "*Don't–*"

Steel Heart began marching toward Honey. The Hunters cried out as she opened fire. Crew Blue stepped forward as the Hunters closed in. Steel Heart staggered back then sank onto the ground with one hand pressed against the bullet wounds Honey had inflicted on his chest. Blood Crow remained crouched down on the floor with her arms shielding her head. Her spear lay discarded on the floor. She had dodged Honey's bullets.

"*Enough!*" Lion Paw shouted. "*There was no need to harm the boy!*"

E's machetes glinted. Her feet swirled through the dirt. Her blades found Lion Paw's neck before he'd even had a chance to blink. Gasps and murmurs escaped from the Hunters. Blood Crow looked back and forth between E and Lion Paw as if she couldn't believe what she was seeing.

"Enough indeed," said E.

James and Lux swapped smirks. There were only six Hunters. E could probably take off all their heads without dropping a bead of sweat. But that was no excuse to let her do all the work. James prepared to open fire at E's command.

Raucous laughter boomed out from the depths of one of the tunnels. Hunters and crew members alike snapped their heads toward the sound.

"Whoo, boy! You are kidding me. You have got to be kidding me. The high and mighty Lion Paw. Stuck between two blades like a rat in a trap!"

A young man with light brown hair and pale skin walked out from the shadows of a tunnel. He hugged his stomach as he doubled over with fresh guffaws. More humans emerged from behind him and spread out in the chamber. James cursed silently. Six humans they could've taken easily, but fifteen more now?

The laughing man lifted a hand. The newcomers halted immediately. He walked forward alone as he wiped away tears of mirth. Unlike Blood Crow's family, who wore tunics, this man and his followers wore black tee-shirts, utility belts, jeans, and army boots, much like Crew Blue. His eyes, though, were a strange, copper color bordering on orange. James checked his hand in case he was a citizen, but the man clearly had a watch.

"Blood Crow!" he said. "Blood Crow, is that you? What are you doing at the end of a gun barrel? I thought you were better than that."

"*Good evening, Copperhead,*" Blood Crow replied. Annoyance had flattened her expression. She made to stand then crouched down again with a scowl as Honey leaned her gun in.

Copperhead's smile faded as he spotted Bloom. Then he leered. "Well, hello there, big boy."

Bloom sighed and licked his chops. Lifting his chin higher, he stared into the distance as if Copperhead were unworthy of his attention. James was glad to see that he had finally stopped weeping.

"*We're handling this, so back off. We'll see you at the Feast,*" said Blood Crow.

"Now is that any way to treat someone who can help you out of this mess?" said Copperhead. He placed both hands on his hips with a mock look of offense.

"*We don't need your help,*" said Blood Crow.

"I think he'd disagree," Copperhead said as Steel Heart attempted to stand.

Copperhead's family burst into laughter as Steel Heart toppled back onto the ground. More blood streamed out of the bullet holes in his chest.

"I think you should all leave. How about that?" said E.

Lion Paw stretched his neck higher toward the ceiling as she pressed her blades deeper into his skin.

"Well, look at Miss Fearsome here," said Copperhead. "You must have some pretty amazing skills if you caught this big guy off-guard. He was a Lead at the Solstice, you know. Though, of course, not a two-time winner like, well, me."

He grinned and lifted the necklaces hanging around his neck. Each boasted a single ruby that dangled on a cord of black leather.

"And you must be pretty tough too," he said, pointing at Honey. "Blood Crow won the Tournament two Solstices ago. You should have seen her. I've been trying to recruit her into my family ever since, but this Lion Paw guy. This guy. Boy, he just won't let good talent go."

"*We've already been through this*," said Blood Crow. "*I'm never going to join your family, so stop bothering me.*"

"And why is that, Blood Crow? Why is that? This is so great. We can finally talk without this big guy interrupting. And don't bother giving me any of the typical Traditionalist answers. I want real answers."

She sneered. "*Uh, hello? Why would I want to follow someone who's stupid enough to wear copper-colored contacts every night? They don't make you look any cooler, even though you wish they would.*"

Her family filled the chamber with their laughter. Only Lion Paw remained unamused as his eyes silently reprimanded Blood Crow for saying "hello" so flippantly again.

"As cruel as ever, Blood Crow. As cruel as ever," said Copperhead. The torchlight revealed the slight flush that had crept up into his sharp, bony cheeks despite his enduring grin. "But that's what makes you good for our family. Now stop following this softie here and join us already."

She glared at him. "*I don't believe in torture like you Contemporaries do.*"

"Aw, jeez. Didn't I just ask you not to give me any of that Traditionalist crap? Come on! You can give me better reasons than that."

"*Better? What better reason could I possibly give you? Our way is the pure way, the right way. Just admit it!*"

Though the aim of their weapons lingered on Crew Blue, Lion Paw's family stared only at Blood Crow and Copperhead as the two engaged in a heated debate revolving around the use of torture during a hunt. James had assumed that all Hunters worked harmoniously with one another, united in their common goal of hunting down citizens, but clearly, he'd been wrong. Factions existed. Apparently, one preferred not to use Our Word and believed in torture while the other seemed to use Our Word exclusively and vehemently objected to torture. He didn't see how that made them that different, though. Our Word or not, torture or no torture, both went around harming innocent citizens for no good reason. As Blood Crow and Copperhead's argument escalated in volume, he stole glances at the crew. E gave them a slight nod. Their chance for escape was approaching.

"*It's not the Hunters' way! You know it's not. It's not what the Brave would have wanted!*" yelled Blood Crow.

"Oh, really? And how would you know what that old geezer would have wanted?"

"*His ideals–and I mean his true ideals–have been passed down for generations. You know that. We have to stay true to what the Brave believed in and fight like how he fought. That's how we stay true to the Hunters' way. That's how we stay united!*"

"Yeah, yeah, yeah. Unification. I know how much you like to go on about that. '*That's the whole reason we Traditionalists speak only in Our Word,*'" Copperhead said in a high-pitched rendition of Blood Crow's voice. "'*The true language of the Flowering unites us all, and it's how we stick to our ancient hunting roots. Unification, Copperhead. Unification and tradition!*'"

Blood Crow glared at him as he snorted.

"You have no proof that everything has been passed down exactly the way the Brave wanted. Everything changes with time, and you Traditionalists stick too much to tradition if you ask me. Change is a good thing, and I have the freedom to make whatever choices I want to make for myself and my family. And besides, there's no point in taking down your prey if you can't enjoy the hunt, am I right?" Copperhead shouted as he turned to his family.

They thrust their weapons into the air.

"For life!" some cried.

"Protect!" yelled others.

"*No! No, you're not right. Put your weapons down. There's no reason to celebrate!*" said Blood Crow. "*You need clean kills. You shouldn't risk everything to make sure that citizens feel every inch of pain possible, and you don't always need to exact vengeance, even if they do deserve the punishment.*"

"Oh, they deserve it all right," Copperhead said. His grin wrinkled into an ugly look of resentment. "All citizens are evil. Every last one of them. So I don't understand why—"

"Now!" E yelled.

Her blades sliced together as Lion Paw jerked back his head. Crew Blue's gunfire dimmed the Hunters' shouts of surprise. Blood gushed from Lion Paw's neck as he ran into one of the many tunnels and disappeared into the shadows.

"Oh, no you don't!" Honey shouted.

Her bullets chased after Blood Crow as she scurried swiftly across the floor and dove behind the cover of a large stone crag jutting out from the ground. Hunters fled in all directions, darting into the shadows of the tunnels or behind the safety of stone. James shot at them with one hand while stepping back and retrieving a second gun with the other. He jumped as he collided with Lux and Honey. They pressed their backs against one another and continued shooting. Honey chuckled darkly as more Hunters fled from her fire.

"*We don't want to hurt you! We just want the wolf!*" someone yelled from a tunnel.

Honey answered with more shots.

"He's one of us!" Lux shouted back.

"*Don't trust that thing! We're warning you! This is our last warning!*"

Honey shoved her guns into their holsters and gripped the assault rifle that appeared in her hand. Her bullets drilled through the air and rattled against stone.

"Which way do we go?" James yelled through the din. He knew all the Hunters were still there, surrounding them, hidden and waiting.

"I don't know! Where's E?" Lux shouted.

A bullet ripped into James's leg before he could reply. He knelt with a grunt.

"James!"

"Hands up!" said Copperhead as he hurried forth from the shadows. "I don't want to shoot you again!"

E hurled herself through the air. Her blades flashed. Copperhead cried out in pain as his gun dropped onto the floor. He scampered back, his severed hand dangling from his wrist. E ran forward and leapt up again, her eyes and machetes flashing in the torchlight. She swung down both her blades. Copperhead stumbled as he deflected her blow with the broadsword that appeared in his hand. She jumped up once more, blades lifted high. He raised the hilt and supported his sword with his mutilated wrist as she struck down once then twice. She forced him to kneel with the power of the third then continued pressing into the blow. A trembling grin etched itself together on Copperhead's face as he shook under the weight of her machetes. Blood streamed down his arm as she ground her blades into his sword. He dug the balls of his foot into the ground before pushing up with a shout. E stumbled back. Dirt sprayed as she regained her footing. She rushed at him again.

"Okay, yeah! Let's see what you're made of!" he shouted.

He lurched back, missing the tip of E's blade by a millimeter. She swung again and again, jumping and dodging with an ease and grace that promised Copperhead's defeat. James couldn't tell whether the flush on Copperhead's face stemmed from exertion, admiration, or fear.

"Copperhead!" a voice yelled.

"Stay back!" he shouted.

James, Lux, and Honey kept their guns pointed around the chamber and shot at every sign of movement as E and Copperhead's fight raged on. Hot, shallow breaths pulsed out of James's nostrils as he concentrated on healing his leg. He scoured the chamber for Bloom, feeling relieved at the absence of his blue fur. Hopefully, he had run as far as could from here. Now if only the rest of the crew could escape as well.

Copperhead's sword swung down, shaving past E's body and forcing her to roll across the dirt. He charged after her, hewing the air before she could rise. She crossed her machetes to catch his blade, wincing under the power of his strike. Her arms shook as he continued bearing down and pressing her machetes closer to her face. She smirked.

She slipped her blades out from under his weight and dodged as he fell forward. The tip of his broadsword plunged into the ground. She trapped his sword between her machetes then twisted and forced the sword out from his hands. The broadsword gleamed white in the torchlight as she flung it across the chamber.

Shots rattled out of the tunnels, forcing the two apart. Honey drilled back. Copperhead skidded through the dirt as if on a baseball mound, snatched up his fallen gun, then fled into the cover of the shadows. E shoved her machetes under her belt and fired after him. The gunfire continued for several moments before petering out into an occasional bullet. Then silence abided. James's hair slowly stood on end. The stillness frightened him more than any attack.

"That wolf is still here!" Copperhead shouted from the shadows. "What do you say, Lion Paw? We team up just this once?"

James's breath quickened. A pause, then–

"*Protect!*" Lion Paw yelled in a hoarse, injured voice.

Other Hunters echoed his cry.

"For life!" Copperhead shouted.

"Behind the rocks!" E yelled. "Behind the rocks now!"

Guns fired from all around. For a moment, James could only watch as bursts of red exploded out of him and his friends. He doubled over, grabbed Honey, and forced his legs into a sprint. Lux ran after them. Honey screeched curses over the gunfire as she shot back at the Hunters. James ignored the bullets that plunged into his arm and leg and hurtled toward a tall, jutting crag near the rocky walls.

"Forget it, Honey!" Lux shouted. He yanked away her gun and pushed her forward.

The trio scrambled into the space behind the crag. They flinched as bullets pounded against their cover. James looked down at the holes covering his body, aghast at their number and the blood spilling from them. Gunfire drowned out Honey's voice as she screamed for E. Lux tugged her back from whizzing bullets. Sparks flew off the crag as James clutched his head and went through every weapon he'd ever touched. But it was no use. He couldn't think of anything. No weapons, no means of escape, no way to rescue E. Nothing. Nothing at all!

"Bloom, no!" E shrieked.

Sparks ceased ricocheting off of the crag protecting them, yet gunfire continued to thunder. James flung his upper body out from behind the crag and searched for E and Bloom. They weren't difficult to find. Several yards away in a pool of blood, Bloom lay on top of E. He had pinned her arms and legs down with his body and was shielding her head with his own. She squirmed as she tried to extricate herself in vain. Bullets continued tearing into Bloom, making him jerk this way and that. His eyes were squeezed shut.

"*We've got him!*" Blood Crow shouted as she leapt forward. "*Get him! Protect!*"

The bloodthirsty cries of the Hunters rang out as gunfire ceased. They rushed out of the tunnels and jumped over crags. They converged upon Bloom and E in a thick, wriggling swarm.

"Guys!" Honey shouted.

She tossed rifles to Lux and James and began to shoot. Hunters fired back. A bullet caught Lux by the shoulder, knocking him into the dirt. Blood poured from Honey's wounds, paling her skin into a sickly yellow as she continued shooting. James's hair rippled as another bullet zinged past his head. He withdrew and slammed his back against the wall, willing, forcing, begging his wounds to heal. He lifted his gun again and emerged from behind the crag, spraying bullets. Two Hunters shouted and fell to the floor. Their comrades shot back, forcing James to retreat then fire, retreat then fire. He could see the rest of the Hunters beyond the line of those shooting. Their weapons flew up and down as they plunged their blades into Bloom's body.

"It's not working!" one of them shouted. "It's not disintegrating! Why isn't the wolf disintegrating?"

"*Move! It's mine!*"

The circle parted. Blood Crow drew back her spear then skewered Bloom through the chest. He let out a blood-curdling cry.

Pain, a blinding, white-hot pain, engulfed James's watch, erasing all thoughts and muting all sounds. It splintered his hand, cracked apart his arm, and spread through his entire body with the cold burn of a thousand invisible needles. He vomited.

"James!"

He heard Lux's voice as if he were standing at the opposite end of a tunnel. Everything seemed to jolt up and down as if he were trapped inside a carnival funhouse full of strange lights and saturated colors. Pain continued radiating from his hand and wracking his entire body. He couldn't tell if he was sitting or standing anymore. He balled up his hands and tried to regain some semblance of self-control. He brought his shaking fist up to his eyes.

His watch. His watch was moving. The minute hand was falling steadily from twelve o'clock, turning the skin it passed over tattoo-black as it grated down toward three. He clutched his wrist and held down another wave of vomit. The minute hand glided to a stop, leaving a quarter of his watch black. The pain left him like a fog swept away by the wind, leaving him raw, cold, and shaky.

His watch now read three o'clock.

"James!"

Sound returned at full volume. The frenzied shouts of the Hunters reverberated all around him. James felt pressure on his arm and discovered that Lux was gripping him and yelling words that he didn't understand. Honey littered the air with more bullets and curses before collapsing. Lux hurried to her side with bandages.

A chill skittered up James's spine. He turned to face the rocky wall behind him.

He saw nothing at first. Then the dirt and gravel gave away. Ensconced within a small nook in the rugged wall was an orb. It was the size of his fist and a deep, dark purple. He took one step closer then another, sensing again that terrible familiarity that he didn't understand, the same familiarity he'd felt on the wasteland with the black orbs. There was something. Something wrong.

He saw it. A hairline crack on the face of the purple orb. He stumbled back as it splintered. The cracks grew into the shape of a diamond before a jagged piece fell away like the shard of a hatching egg. Something floated inside. A head. A head of a creature. A head of a calf.

Its matted fur was drenched in blood. Its right eye was closed in deep slumber. Its left eye was missing from its raw socket. A golden orb protruded from its forehead. Three concentric circles were engraved on the golden orb, giving it the appearance of another eye. James jumped as the smallest circle swirled open like an unfurling flower. The middle circle followed then the last. He stared into the darkness within.

A figure wandered about in a hooded robe of blue and white, taking small, tentative steps. Bells chimed from the hem of each sleeve. A red sash lay draped over one shoulder. The figure stopped then turned.

She was a young, Asian woman around his age with skin that was as pale as the full moon. A milky film covered both of her eyes, blurring the strange, midnight blue of her irises. For a fraction of a moment, James knew that she could see him, just as he could see her. They were connected as if staring through opposite sides of a looking glass that had dispelled the constraints of physical space.

Her eyes widened. Darkness enshrouded her. One circle cascaded into another, closing the golden eye ingrained in the forehead of the red, dripping calf.

The calf stirred and twitched. It tossed its head up and down and side to side as if it were struggling to cast off an invisible muzzle. It grew still once more. Its closed eye quivered then cracked open to reveal a dark eye that rolled about before fixing on James.

Darkness poured out from the eye, filling the purple orb and swallowing the creature. James knew, somehow, that it was the same kind of darkness as the orbs on the wasteland, a pitch-black emptiness that would devour all in its path.

For a moment, he dared to hope that that was it, that the creature was gone, that it had disappeared into its own darkness, never to return. But then the black burst forth. It spilled out from the orb, streamed down the face of the wall, and began pooling on the floor. James seized Honey and Lux by their wrists and ignored their protests as he forced them to run out with him from behind the crag.

"Run!" he screamed. "Run!"

CHAPTER 16

LAKE OF FIRE

R un! *Run! Run!*" James screamed at the Hunters. They had to
run away. They all had to. He didn't care how he knew. The
red creature behind them was hungry, and its darkness would
consume them all!

The line of Hunters glanced at one another then turned their guns
away from the crew and advanced with their aim locked on the darkness
still spilling out of the wall.

"What are you doing?" Lux cried.

"Bloom and E!" James yelled.

His hands remained sealed around Lux's and Honey's wrists as he
plunged into the swarm of Hunters. He pushed and shoved his way
toward Bloom's bloodstained body, which lay beyond his reach. Fingers
pulled at his clothes and nails scalped his arms as Hunters shouted at one
another to grab him. He thrust them all aside as he shouted about the
creeping darkness that was coming for them. A scream rang out from
behind him, shrill with terror. He froze. Several heads turned.

"Copperhead!"

"Help! Help me!"

"Hang on. Wait, no!"

James turned his head slowly. Emptiness as black as the mouth of a bottomless well gaped where the crag and rocky wall had been only moments before. Of the line of Hunters that had marched toward the darkness, only four now stood firing their guns at the spreading, black emptiness. The others had disappeared.

James, the crew, and all the Hunters still surrounding Bloom and E watched as a strip of hollow black shot out from the emptiness and swiped at one of the Hunters shooting at the darkness. His foot vanished at its touch. He fell to the ground with a shout of horror. His comrades continued shooting with increased fervor, but their bullets simply vanished into the growing darkness. A small, black wave reared up then lunged forward and covered the fallen Hunter like a blanket.

He disappeared.

"White Scale!" Copperhead shouted.

Another black tongue shot forth and took the foot of another Hunter. She, too, disappeared as she fell forward into the darkness oozing across the ground. One of the remaining Hunters lowered his gun then ran away. The other, a teenage girl, continued to fire.

"Red Rock, fall back! Retreat!" Copperhead yelled.

He sprinted toward the girl as she stood her ground and continued firing round after round. She took one step back as the emptiness continued creeping across the ground, the walls, the ceiling. She dropped her gun with a scream as the darkness lunged forth and swallowed half of her leg. Copperhead gripped her arm and snatched her away from the emptiness before she could fall in. He slung her over his shoulder as he ran for the tunnels.

"Run!" he yelled.

The Hunters scattered. Shouts of "Over here!" and "This way!" sounded from all around as James, Honey, and Lux army-crawled through a flurry of legs.

"Bloom!" James cried.

He threw himself on top of him. Bloom's coat, once soft and brilliantly blue, was now dark and soaked with blood. Bones and guts protruded from large holes in his body. Blood Crow's spear still stuck out from his chest. His eyes quivered open. His tail gave a feeble twitch as he saw James. Despite his gruesome wounds, he continued pressing down on E as she struggled and shouted beneath him.

"*Protect!*" someone screamed.

Knuckles bashed into James's ear. A sharp kick sent him rolling across the ground. A mess of red hair obscured his vision as fingers wrapped around his throat. He gagged and squirmed and kicked as he pushed against Blood Crow's chest and scratched at her neck. She continued choking him and banging his head against the floor. Something tangled around his fingers before he balled his hand into a fist and tried to punch her.

She rolled off of him with a sudden yelp. Honey sent her foot flying into Blood Crow's jaw again then fell upon her with balled fists. James coughed and gagged as he scrambled onto his feet and hurried to Lux, who lay curled up on the floor with his hands pressed against a bleeding wound on his head. A rock lay next him, no doubt the weapon Blood Crow had used to hit him across the skull.

The emptiness continued to consume the chamber.

"Bloom, E, we need to go now!" James screamed. He slung Lux's arm around his neck and lifted him onto his feet.

Bloom blinked at James then slid off of E at last. Something like confusion stirred on his face as his eyes found the growing darkness. Then his eyes closed, and he moved no more.

"Honey!" E yelled. She jumped onto her feet and pulled the spear out from Bloom's chest.

Honey threw a final blow into Blood Crow's nose before rushing over to E. James continued supporting Lux as he hurried over to her as well. E and Honey hoisted Bloom onto their shoulders. The emptiness began gliding toward the crew in a towering expanse of black.

"Bloom, which way to an exit?" E said as the crew shuffled rapidly toward the tunnels.

Bloom twitched as the darkness swept closer. He craned his head up then pointed his snout toward the smallest tunnel on their right. Crew Blue hurtled into the passageway. Flames burst into life on the torches lining the walls within. James glanced over his shoulder and did a double take. Blood Crow was chasing them.

"*Give it back!*" she shouted.

"You're not taking Bloom!" he screamed.

His stomach dropped as he saw the darkness rushing after them in a seamless wash of black. Lux's head flopped this way and that as they continued to run. James gripped him tighter as he stumbled and yanked him forward without breaking speed.

"Come on, Lux! Come on!" he screamed.

Figures stirred in the distance. Torchlight flared to reveal Copperhead and another Hunter crouched on the floor. The teenage girl who had refused to retreat from the darkness sat between them, both hands gripped around her thigh. The bottom half of her leg was still missing. Copperhead's expression wavered between anger and panic as he spoke to her. He sprang onto his feet as the crew shouted at them to move aside.

"Go! Go! Go!" Copperhead yelled.

He threw the girl over his shoulder again and pushed his fellow Hunter in front of him. Crew Blue pelted after them until the two groups merged into a single herd and stampeded down the tunnel together. The darkness sped closer to their heels. Light burst from the tips of the last torches far ahead in the distance. Three cavernous holes stood at the very end of the passageway like a trio of dark mouths. "Choose me," they each seemed to whisper.

"Bloom! Which one is the exit?" E shouted.

Bloom's body jostled up and down on E's and Honey's shoulders. He pointed his snout in an indiscernible direction. His body spasmed before his head dropped back down onto E's chest.

"Bloom!" E cried.

James's legs no longer felt like legs but like two large rubber wheels rolling forth at top speed. He gritted his teeth, fighting to keep up his speed. They had to choose a tunnel. They had to choose one now with or without Bloom's approval!

A low growl rumbled out from the depths of Bloom's throat. "*Le...*" he said.

"*Left!*" E cried.

Crew Blue veered. Amazement swirled within the panic and frenzy tumbling about within James. Bloom. He had talked!

Copperhead glanced behind at the hungry darkness then looked at the three tunnels ahead. His face scrunched up into a grimace that brimmed with self-loathing.

"Do what the wolf said!" he yelled.

"What?" his family member exclaimed with an incredulous look.

"Just do it!" Copperhead shouted before veering to join the crew.

Blood Crow swiped and clawed at James even as she continued running after him.

"Get off of me!" he cried.

"*Give me back my necklace!*" she screamed.

James looked down at his fist as he suddenly registered the touch of leather. Two rubies dangled from the single black cord entangled around his fingers.

"Hey! Come back here!" Copperhead yelled.

"Sorry, Copperhead! But it's still a citizen!" his family member shouted back. He disappeared into the middle passageway as the blackness flew after him.

Copperhead swore and continued running with the crew. The group formed a single-file line then dashed one after the other into the left tunnel and through a dead end. The ground disappeared from beneath James's feet as he ran through the exit. He pitched forward. His shoulder slammed onto a hard surface then skidded across a cold, smooth floor. He quickly raised his watch hand, ready to stop the darkness from taking him. But all he saw was a massive wall of marble.

The darkness. The tunnels. Everything was gone. They had escaped the plane.

Exhaustion and relief made him bow his head. A gentle breeze grazed his cheeks and wove into his hair. The full moon, this time a bright speck, hung far in the distance behind sheer, white curtains wafting upon a long row of marble columns. The sky was purple-blue with dusk. Several yards away, cut into the middle of the marble floor, lay a giant, rectangular pit. A series of immense steps climbed down into its unknowable depth from all four of sides. Shadows darkened the vast space beyond the pit.

James inhaled sharply through his teeth. The pain, which his adrenaline had held at bay, now returned in pulsing stabs. He stared at Blood Crow's necklace still tangled around his fingers then shoved it into his pocket. He wasn't about to hand her necklace back so easily after everything she had done!

He began prying out the bullets squeezing out of his flesh as Copperhead stumbled about and marred the white floor with red-brown footprints. Small shoots of bone and tissue slowly crept out from his wrist, reaching toward the dangling hand that E had nearly severed. He transferred the teenage girl from his shoulder and into his arms before carefully lowering her onto the floor. Skin had sealed the raw end of her thigh, stopping the bleeding. But the rest of her leg still showed no signs of regrowth.

A moan preceded the sound of skin slapping onto the floor. James spun around to see Honey sprawled out and motionless. Her lips were as pale as the floor. Next to her, Bloom remained still with his eyes closed. The blood trickling out of Honey's wounds joined with the blood flowing out of Bloom's so that red pools widened around them. James lurched past Lux, who was now standing steady with his gun glued to Blood Crow's temple. Together with E, James began tying Bloom's and Honey's wounds.

Several moments passed before Bloom's nose began to quiver. His eyes snapped open. He looked at E with an alarmed expression that only danger could incite.

"The plane!" she yelled. "It's shifting!"

Everyone flinched. Copperhead grabbed the girl.

"*Look!*" cried Blood Crow.

A small flame burned at the base of a column, releasing a steady string of white smoke. Another tongue burst into view, then another, and another, until dozens of flames licked at the length of the column. Bloom lifted himself up onto his forelegs.

"No!" E cried, grabbing his mane.

He huffed, rose onto all fours, then pulled away from her grasp. Shaking as if he were taking his first steps, he began sniffing and searching for an exit. The flames lengthened then joined together into a flashing spiral that enveloped the whole column. Fire exploded all around them, first from the other columns then from parts of the floor then the entire wall behind Lux and Blood Crow. White smoke smothered the air and veiled the moon and sky outside. Muffled coughs and the crackling of fire sounded through the thickening smoke. A shiver suddenly ran from the end of Bloom's tail to the tips of his ears. A spurt of blood darkened the bandages wrapped around his chest. He collapsed.

"Lux! Lux, get Honey!" E shouted. "James, help me!"

All around them, patches of black spread across the marble like ink on paper. E and James lifted Bloom onto their shoulders as Lux appeared through the smoke. The crew recoiled with a shout as a tower of fire shot up from the pit in the floor like the arm of a burning giant. The flames collided with the blackened ceiling, which curled away like wood shavings. Smoke streamed through the widening partition and into a dark unknown high above. As the floor began to crumble, the crew retreated toward the blazing wall, where Blood Crow stood with her mouth open. Copperhead slung the girl over his shoulder and joined them.

"Stand your ground!" E commanded. "Wait until the plane stops shifting!"

As the flames disappeared from the bottom up, rugged cliffs formed in place of the flames. With a thunderous crack, the entire floor collapsed in a mass of rubble, leaving the group cringing on a narrow ledge. A burning canyon appeared below them, stretching out into the distance like a lake of fire. They pressed their backs against the rocky wall that had replaced the flames behind them. James gripped Bloom's fur as fire erupted out of the canyon and soared into the black expanse above them. The flames divided into fiery whips that shrank and lashed at the group.

"*Over here! Hey! Over here!*" a voice yelled over the roaring fire.

Blood Crow darted to the left. James watched her as she ran along the ledge and into the distance. Only then did he see a man dressed in the gray, hooded garb of a Roamer standing on a landing high above. A rope ladder unfurled from the Roamer's hands.

"Follow!" E yelled as Blood Crow grasped one of the rungs.

"Hold on to me!" Lux shouted to Honey.

She grasped the back of his tee-shirt with one hand and placed the other on the wall. Still pale and swaying dangerously, she rushed after Lux as he ran to the ladder. James pivoted under Bloom's weight and readjusted his grip on his fur before following. His sweat-drenched clothes stuck to his skin as gusts of scalding heat blew against him. The ground under his feet began to shake as the ledge cracked and crumbled.

"Hurry up!" Copperhead screamed.

"Copperhead, let me down!" the girl yelled.

"No! You'll fall!"

"We'll both fall if you don't!"

James stopped as the ledge quaked violently. He looked behind at Copperhead to see him sliding the girl onto her feet. She clutched the wall and hopped forward on one leg.

"Focus!" E yelled.

James forced his buckling knees to straighten before walking forward again. Rocks scattered from beneath his boots and vanished into the fire. His fingers slipped on Bloom's blood. Lux beckoned furiously to them from on top of the landing as the rumbling intensified. At last, they reached the ladder.

"Here!" Lux shouted. He threw down a net so that it hung open beside James and E.

"Careful!" E yelled. "One, two, three!"

James pulled on Bloom's coat. He rolled off of his shoulder and into the net. Lux and the Roamer began hoisting up the net from high above. James grabbed the ladder and climbed up with fluid swiftness, E just at his feet. The girl scrambled up the rungs behind them as Copperhead struggled to climb with one hand. The ledge gave away in an avalanche of boulders. Flames leapt up and speared the air. The girl screamed. James looked down to see the fire searing and burning away her skin. She squirmed in pain and swatted her body with a frantic hand. She leaned on her absent leg.

"No!" Copperhead screamed.

The girl's sweaty, bloodstained hold slipped from the ladder. She shrieked as she fell. Bloom's muzzle shot out from the net and bit into her outstretched arm. She looked up at him with wide eyes as they began ascending together.

James grabbed the last rung, clambered onto the landing, then clasped hands with E. He pulled her up and dropped down onto his hands and knees to look over the ledge at Copperhead. He was still several feet below, fumbling up the ladder as flames ate away at his skin. Images of Copperhead stabbing Bloom flashed across James's mind. He gripped the hilt of his knife as anger burned within him. He didn't stop E as she raised her dagger high above the ends of the ladder pegged into the floor.

"No!"

James and E spun around.

"Please! Please don't!" the girl cried out as she rolled away from Bloom.

Bloom lifted his head. He looked at the raised dagger in E's hand then at the ends of the ladder stretching from side to side with Copperhead's weight. He laid his chin down between his paws and blinked at E with sad eyes. She glared back at him. Her dagger rose higher into the air then halted. Several moments passed before she lowered her blade.

"Let him climb up on his own," she told James before walking away.

He released his hold on his knife. Confusion filled his mind as his eyes wandered back to the fiery canyon. Had he really just contemplated letting a man burn alive? And for what? Out of fear for Bloom's safety?

Or to avenge him?

"James!"

His stomach lurched up into his throat as the ground gave way beneath him. The flames seemed to part into a hungry mouth as he fell toward the heat. Honey lunged forth, gripped his arm, and pulled him back onto solid ground. Blood Crow rushed out of the shadows and shoved a knife into James's side. He grunted. Honey grabbed a fistful of red hair and wrenched. Blood Crow ripped her knife out of James's side and slashed. Honey pulled back to dodge. Blood Crow pushed Honey.

James reached forth, futilely scratching the air, as Honey's back arched over the edge of the landing. What breath remaining in his lungs left him in a cry of horror as she toppled into the fire with a piercing scream.

CHAPTER 17

HELLO

Honey disappeared into the roaring flames. James's collar tightened around his throat as Blood Crow gripped his tee-shirt and flung him onto the dirt. He rolled across the ground then cried out as she began kicking into the wound that she had inflicted in his side. Something cracked inside his body. His organs squished against her boot.

"*Give it back!*" she shouted. "*Give my necklace back!*"

E thrust two gleaming knives into Blood Crow's neck. She choked and clutched at her throat then collapsed. James curled up and squeezed his concentration into the pain in his side. Down in the pit, Honey screamed and screamed.

"Honey!" Lux cried, running toward the chasm.

"Wait!" James gasped.

He yanked Lux back from the scintillating screen of white-gold flames that exploded out of the chasm. Hot sparks showered down on them.

"*Hey! Come back here!*" the Roamer shouted.

James snapped around, still clutching his side and struggling to breathe. He spotted Copperhead disappearing into the distance with the girl thrown over his shoulder. His eyes fell on Blood Crow and E. A long, dark streak in the dirt marked the path E had dragged her through. Blood

Crow writhed, still choking on the knives lodged in her throat, as E lifted her machete. Her choking intensified as E began hacking off her arms and legs.

"Honey!" Lux screamed as the flames receded.

James tore his eyes away from E and lunged forward to look over the edge of the chasm. He found Honey beyond the blur of raging heat, far below within the flames. Her right hand clung to what remained of the ledge. Her left hand was pressed against her chest in a desperate attempt to protect her watch from the flames. She continued to scream as she stared up at them with bulging eyes. Her skin began sliding off of her bones like hot wax. Lux cried out to her again and again.

"Make me a chain."

E's voice pushed James out of his horrified trance. She stood beside him, gazing down into the inferno with little more than a frown on her blood-splattered face. Her black eyes glinted as she turned away. Honey's screams subsided into an ominous silence.

"Here!" Lux shouted.

E caught the end of the long, metal chain he tossed to her then wrapped the chain around her torso as he ran around her in circles. The Roamer rushed over to them. James grabbed E by her shoulders as she adjusted the chain.

"E, no! I'll do it. It should be me. Honey was trying to save me!" he cried.

Her eyes flashed. She flung his hands aside. "Just help Lux," she snarled. "And don't let go."

Lux fastened the links around her with carabiners. Seizing the loose end of the chain, he dashed to the far side of the landing.

"Yo, James! Roamer guy! Come on!" he shouted.

The Roamer remained motionless with his face turned toward E. His hood concealed his expression.

"Come on!" Lux cried out.

The Roamer ran to join him. James took one step back from E then another before breaking into a run. All he could see was the memory of abandoning her as she lay trapped beneath the boulder that had been meant for him. He despised himself as he shoved his fingers into the links of the chain and prepared for her to jump.

She jogged a few paces away from the chasm then turned her back toward the three men. The fire outlined her figure in a dark silhouette. She turned her head sideways then nodded. James tightened his grip as she sprinted across the landing and dove headlong into the inferno. The chain zipped and swerved through the dirt as it unraveled. The links snapped taut. Their boots skidded across the floor.

"Down!" E shouted.

"Let her down! Let her down!" Lux yelled.

James's veins bulged as he released one link at a time. The chain pulled within his grip, veering from left to right. He shouted as several links rushed out of his hands. What was happening? There was no way E was this heavy. No, it wasn't E. It was the flames! They were swirling and rising and falling, clawing at E as they tried to drag her down deeper into the pit.

"Halt!"

They dug in their heels at E's command. The chain grew still. The flames leapt and crackled.

"E?" Lux said.

She didn't reply. James's breath quickened.

"E!" Lux screamed.

The chain clinked to life. Two sharp tugs reverberated up the chain.

"Pull!" Lux shouted.

James strained and sputtered as they heaved. The chain shuddered midair with each step. Slowly, they drew further away from the chasm. A blackened hand shot into view. The flames suddenly receded.

James ran to E as she struggled to climb onto the landing. Her skin had become a thick, rough layer of volcanic black with cracks that glowed neon purple. Her gritted teeth and remaining eye stood out white and stark on her charred face. As James grasped her, her skin crunched like something that had emerged out of boiling oil. She shouted with pain. He ignored the burn of hot metal as he loosened the carabiners. He scooped her up into his arms and ran into the shadow of a rocky wall. She closed her eyes as he laid her down. Shock stopped him in his tracks as he turned around to retrieve Honey.

She was unrecognizable. Chalky, black stone coated her entire body so that she looked like a vestige of Pompeii. Closed slits sat on a misshapen face in place of her eyes and mouth. Her watch hand still lay curled over her chest.

"James!" Lux shouted, making him jump.

He rushed over to help Lux as he pulled Honey onto the landing. They struggled to lift her up under the weight of her stone shroud. They hauled her body into the shadows and laid her down next to E. James's hands hovered over his two friends. He didn't know what to do. What could he possibly create to help heal such injuries? The Roamer crouched down next to E and threw back his hood.

He was a young man around James's age. His large eyes were brown as was his hair, which seemed to float on his head in short, soft waves. His long nose looked fit for a marble bust of a Roman general.

"She really did it," the Roamer whispered, staring at E with an awe-struck face. "She really dove in for her. She really got her out."

He jumped as Bloom appeared at his side then again as E began to convulse. The glowing, purple cracks on her skin sealed together. Black shards fell away from her body like broken pieces of pottery. Her eyes flew open and locked on James.

"Help me up," she wheezed.

"What?" the Roamer breathed. "But how?"

James hoped that her torso wouldn't snap in two as he raised her into a seated position. A shower of black shards cascaded off of her body, uncovering skin that glowed with thin, neon orange lines, which traced the outlines of the shards she had discarded. She continued to shudder and twitch as she shed the rest of her black shell.

"*What do we call you?*" she growled at the Roamer, still panting and grimacing.

"Phoenix," the Roamer replied, his eyes shining with both intrigue and wariness. "You can call me Phoenix."

James repelled the weight E placed on him as she stood up. She pushed him aside and limped toward Blood Crow. He had forgotten all about her. Her choking had long grown into a background noise engulfed by the sounds of the burning chasm. Blood Crow squirmed, armless and legless, as E came to a stop next to her. The knives in Blood Crow's throat impeded her from hurling the insults James knew were boiling up in her chest. Her anger, though, cast only a thin veil over her fear.

"Phoenix," said E as she glared down at Blood Crow. "Did you want payment in return for your help tonight?"

"No. I only wanted to help. I was planning to leave right after."

E smirked. "'Help,' huh? We've been hearing that word a lot lately."

Blood Crow wriggled like a worm under a beam of burning light as E continued glaring down at her.

"If you don't want anything, I suggest you walk away now. Consider it my way of saying thank you," said E.

"Wait," said Phoenix. "I don't need payment, but I would like to ask all of you some questions. It's been a strange night even by Roaming standards, and I'd like to know what's going on."

Blood Crow continued to jerk and squirm about. James almost pitied her. Nothing could save her from E's wrath now.

E smirked again. "So, you do want something, then. Fine. We can talk. But first." She knelt down and grasped the knives in Blood Crow's neck. "You."

She wrenched out the blades. Blood poured out of the slits as Blood Crow croaked for air.

"You think you can attack my crew and get away with it?" E growled.

Blood Crow writhed. E lifted one of her knives.

"You think you can attack my crew and get away with it?" she shrieked.

Her eyes burned with a wild hatred as she pumped her knife up and down. James looked away. His mind felt numb, his stomach sick. The croaking grew louder, more forceful. He knew Blood Crow would have screamed had she been able to. Lux sat motionless next to Honey with his eyes averted. Phoenix watched without flinching. Bloom struggled onto his feet. With lagging steps that trailed blood, he limped over to E. Lunging forth, he bit into her wrist and pulled her hand away from Blood Crow.

"Let go of me! Let go! Bloom!"

She whipped his head from side to side. He pulled her arm further away then fixed a golden eye on James. A thought floated across his paralyzed mind and blinked into life. He was unafraid of battling moulded citizens. He was willing to fight a horde of Hunters. Yet, here he was, cowering at the prospect of confronting E, his friend, his leader, the person who always had and always would risk everything for them. So why was he just sitting here? He felt his feet moving forward as E began stabbing Blood Crow with her free hand.

"Lux. Lux, help me," he said.

Surprise spread over Lux's face, ironing out the wrinkles that had crumpled it.

"Help me!"

James ran to E, dreading the struggle he knew would ensue. He threw himself on her arm.

"E, stop! That's enough! *Stop it! Stop!*" he shouted, hoping desperately that Korean would reach her better somehow.

Her blade flashed inches away from his nose as she swung around both him and Bloom with lion-like strength.

"*Let go! Let go!*" she screamed.

"Sorry, E!" said Lux. He clinched her from behind.

E's boot sent James flying backward as Lux and Bloom dragged her away. James had already risen to his feet, ready to tackle her again, when a drawling croak made him look down. Blood Crow. She was no longer the proud Hunter who had attacked him so viciously but a limbless mass of punctured flesh forcing out constricted breaths in a pool of her own blood. Her severed arms and legs remained motionless at her sides. James knelt down and looked at his hands. He was almost surprised to see the bandages sitting in his palms.

"James!" E screamed. "Get away from her! *I'll kill her! Kill her!*"

He inhaled, exhaled, then began binding Blood Crow's wounds with swift, sure motions. Hate was a strong word, but he knew that he hated this woman. He hated her, her family, and all those other Hunters. They had riddled his crew with bullets. They had tortured Bloom and set Honey on fire. They would have set him on fire too had Honey and E not rescued him. These Hunters had tried to destroy everything. None of them deserved any help. So why was he helping her? Why had Bloom?

The slits in Blood Crow's throat began to close. Her gagging subsided. James avoided her gaze as she looked up at him with something like wonder.

Honey coughed.

"Honey?" Lux said, pausing in his struggle with E.

The stone layer covering her body had transformed into the same cracked, black skin that had covered E. Bloom threw Lux a wide-eyed look of warning.

"Lux," Honey moaned.

"Honey!"

He released E and ran to her. She sliced off her own hand to free herself from Bloom's bite. Bloom toppled backward then struggled to stand again as she walked toward James. He couldn't tell if the fury in her eyes was a reflection of the fiery pit or the rage consuming her. He bobbed up and down on one knee as panic jumbled his senses. E's kick thudded across his ear. Another kick sent him rolling across the floor. He spat out dirt and scrambled back onto his feet.

"E!" he said, stumbling toward her. "It's too much! *Stop it!*"

A familiar pain lodged itself in his side. He staggered back, fumbling with the hilt of E's knife protruding from under his ribs. He sank onto the ground, feeling more hurt from the fact that she had resorted to stabbing him than from the pain of the wound itself. Bloom began limping toward her once more as she unsheathed a dagger from her belt and pressed the side against Blood Crow's neck.

"Tell me one reason why I shouldn't cut off your head one string of muscle at a time."

"E!" James gasped.

"Tell me one reason why I shouldn't!"

Blood Crow lifted her head and spat blood in E's face. James and Bloom froze.

"*You don't scare me,*" said Blood Crow. "*And you're a fool for trusting that citizen. It has you tricked. You're just too stupid to see it.*"

For a moment, E looked as if she would explode. Then something flickered in her eyes, something that frightened James far more than screams and threats.

"*How?*" said E. "*How could that citizen be tricking us? That's impossible! He's done nothing to harm us all night. How could that possibly be true? You're wrong!*"

Blood Crow sneered before uttering the word James knew that E had counted on, the spiteful word that Lion Paw had warned Blood Crow so many times to avoid.

"*Hello–*"

E rammed her dagger into Blood Crow's mouth before she could speak another word. What little color that had managed to return to Blood Crow's face blanched as E raised another dagger over Blood Crow's watch.

"*Hello,*" E replied.

She stabbed her watch.

Blood Crow vanished.

CHAPTER 18

MORE NEWCOMERS

James gaped at the spot where Blood Crow had been a split moment ago and where E now knelt alone. Bloom slumped down onto the ground.

"E. What?" said James.

She shoved her dagger back into its sheath and sat down in a nook in the rocky wall next to Lux and Honey. She continued heaving deep breaths as James staggered toward them. Bones and tissue sprouted swiftly out of her wrist, forming the hand she had severed.

"E," said Lux, looking just as stunned as James felt. "E, was that ... was that okay? That Hunter girl is going to be stuck with us now. She'll go after Bloom! And what about her family? What if she's the anchor? We'll have to deal with her whole family again!"

"Lion Paw was the head of her family, so he's the anchor. Do you really think I wouldn't think of that? And do you really think I'd be stupid enough to let her into our crew permanently? I'll sever call and response tomorrow night! Bloom will be healed by then. She'll be no match for him!"

"Okay, I mean, I guess ... but I wasn't saying you were stupid–"

"Then what were you saying? What exactly were you saying to me?"

"I just–"

"Stop!" James yelled.

He stopped in front of them and tugged out E's knife from his side. Blood gushed out of the wound.

"James!" said Lux.

Phoenix caught James as he collapsed. He felt as if he were stuck in a movie, a series of images all playing together on a spinning reel to piece together the semblance of something real. E had just tricked Blood Crow. Tricked her into initiating call and response. Tricked her into leaving her family. Tricked her into spending another night with Crew Blue, a night E could use to torture her one more time before dooming her to wander the Flowering on her own.

And it was a done deal. It was a done deal, and there was nothing he or any of the others could do about it. He would just have to accept it, and they would just have to deal with Blood Crow and this entire mess tomorrow night. For now, they were rid of all the Hunters at last, which meant that Bloom was safe. They were all safe. They could finally discuss more important things. They could discuss what had happened in the tunnels.

"What was that thing back there?" he said as Lux and Phoenix tended to his wounds.

"What thing? That black darkness thing?" said Lux.

"Darkness?" said Phoenix.

"I don't remember inviting you into our conversation," E growled.

"You said it would be all right for me to ask you some questions," Phoenix said in an even tone that carried neither fear nor aggression.

Anger blazed in E's eyes. Her hand twitched toward her dagger.

"E, please!" James said. The last thing he needed right now was another bloodbath. "You promised him we could talk. And you've broken enough promises tonight!" He pointed to the wound she had made in his side, terrified by his own audacity.

She glanced at the wound then at Bloom as he continued limping toward them.

"We ran into something weird on another plane," Lux told Phoenix as he cast nervous glances at E. "It was some kind of moving emptiness that swallowed humans and anything else in its path. And speaking of, James. How did you know that we had to run away from it?"

"I don't know. I just knew. And before the darkness came out, this happened."

He held out his hand. His watch still read three o'clock.

"Whoa! It finally changed?" said Lux as the group huddled around him.

"That's a watch?" said Phoenix.

"Yeah, and don't worry. He's really human," Lux said. "He's been with us for months now. It's just his watch that's weird."

"I ... I see. And what about this citizen?" Phoenix said as Bloom laid down beside him with a weary sigh.

"What about him?" said Lux.

"Why is he with you? Why were you helping him?"

"He runs around with us every night. He's part of our crew."

"Every night? How?"

"Call and response."

"What? With a citizen? But that's impossible!"

"Well, man, I don't know what to tell you. It's possible," Lux said, flipping James's hand over from one side to the other.

E snatched James's hand away from Lux to examine it herself. "You said this happened when?" she asked.

James was relieved to see that worry had doused some of her rage.

"Right before I saw the black stuff coming out of the wall. There was this weird purple orb. And a monster."

He described everything to them, from the excruciating movement of his watch to the blood-drenched calf in the purple orb. He told them about the calf's raw socket, the young woman in the golden eye, and the dark eye from which the darkness had flowed. Bloom listened with quickening breaths and an expression steeped in confusion and alarm.

"I made everyone run once the black stuff–the emptiness–started coming out. I don't know how, but I knew we had to. I knew the calf was hungry."

"But how? How did you know?" E demanded.

"I don't know, I don't know!" James said, gripping his head. "That calf. It was different. E, it wasn't like anything we've ever battled before. Its eye, the way it looked, the way it moved, everything. Everything about it was just wrong."

She looked down at his watch again. Despite her silence, he knew that she, too, had felt what he had felt, just as she had on the wasteland. She had sensed the danger within the darkness that had chased them. She, like him, had recognized the presence of death.

"It can't be a coincidence, right?" said Lux. "James's watch changing right before the cow appeared?"

"It was a calf," James said, annoyed. "And no. I don't think it was a coincidence."

"But then, what's going on?" said Lux. "How could your watch be connected to some weird calf citizen?"

"I don't know. I don't get any of it either. I don't get what's going on. I don't know how or why. I don't even understand half the things that are going through my own head right now. Everything is just so ... so ..."

"Spit ... it out."

"Honey!" Lux cried.

Her eyes opened slowly. Several large, black shards had already fallen away from her body. Orange lines glowed on patches of exposed skin.

"Honey, are you all right? Do you need anything?" James said as he scrambled over to her side.

"I need you ... to spit it out!" she said between labored breaths.

A long sigh of relief hissed out of Lux's mouth. He snorted and shook his head. James plopped down onto his rear. Well, at least she was all right.

"Everything is just so crazy," he finished weakly. "But Honey, before that–" His voice caught in his throat. "I'm sorry. I'm so, so sorry. I let you fall into the fire."

"Don't be ridiculous," Honey grunted as Lux raised her into a seated position.

He leaned her against Bloom, who laid down behind her. Black shards continued dropping from her body.

"It was that Hunter," she continued. "I should have shot her in the head when I had the chance. E, did you get her for me?"

E knelt down beside her. "Of course. In fact, you'll be seeing her tomorrow night when I finish the job. I made her initiate call and response."

Honey gawked at her then threw back her head and cackled. "Good," she said as her laughter turned into coughing. "I can spend my day in peace, then."

"You think maybe that Hunter girl might know something about all this?" said Lux.

"Are you a moron?" E said. "Didn't you see how those Hunters tried to fight that darkness instead of running away? They didn't know anything."

"Why do we care about what Hunters know? What are we talking about?" said Honey.

James launched again into his tale of what had occurred.

"Hold on. What did that woman look like? The one in the golden eye," interrupted Phoenix.

"Why?" James said.

"Just describe her for me, please."

"Well, she looked around our age. And she looked Korean, actually. She was wearing a white and blue robe with a hood and a red sash. Really pale skin." Her eyes materialized in his mind. "And she had cataracts. But I could still make out the color of her eyes beneath them. They were dark blue."

"Cataracts? James, did you say cataracts?" E said as shock momentarily cleared all other emotions from her face.

"And a white and blue robe?" said Honey.

"Yeah," James said, startled by the surprise on everyone's faces. "Why?"

"That means she's a Shaman. Right, E?" said Lux.

"Snow," Phoenix murmured.

"Wait. Before we keep talking about all this, who are you?" Honey asked Phoenix. Her skin had repaired enough for her to wrinkle her nose at him.

"You can call me Phoenix."

"And?"

"And I've been in the Flowering for several years now. I've been a Roamer for about two. And, well," he said, looking increasingly uncomfortable as Honey scowled at him, "I was the one who helped your crew. But at any rate, that woman you saw. I know her. I found her as a newborn and returned her to the Tower. She is a Shaman. She's the Twelfth."

"The Twelfth? But why ... how did James see her?" said E. "How did she see him? James, you're sure she saw you too?"

"I'm positive."

"But the Shamans are blind," said Honey.

"I know, but I just know. I know she saw me. I am one hundred percent sure of it."

"Have you ever visited her in the Tower before?" said Phoenix. "Has she ever touched you?"

"No. Never," said James.

"He's never been to the City. He's never been touched by any of them," said E.

"What about the rest of you? Have any of you met with a Shaman before?"

The crew shook their heads.

"Honey visited the Market briefly with her old crew, and I stayed there for a while in the past, but none of us ever met with a Shaman," said E. "Lux is like James. He's never stepped foot inside the City."

"Well, have you seen or done anything in the past that might have given you some kind of connection to the Shamans?" Phoenix asked James.

"No," he said as he futilely racked his brains for a helpful memory.

"You said you found the Twelfth? Was there anything unusual about her? And what's snow? What's snow got to do with any of this?" E demanded of Phoenix.

"There wasn't anything unusual from what I could tell, but then again, we weren't together for very long. I found her on a plane that was close to No Man's Land, and a Runner friend of mine helped us get across pretty quickly. Snow was the name I gave her before I returned her to the Tower."

"And got a fat cut from the Shamans for it," Honey added.

"It wasn't like that. I was just trying to do the right thing."

"Do you think she'd know anything about my watch or the calf or any of the things we saw?" James said, steering the conversation back into place.

Phoenix sighed. "I'm not sure. But if she really did see you, I'd say it's worth paying her a visit. It's weird enough that you'd see her when you've never even met her before. I'd pay her a visit just based on the fact that you managed to see her somehow."

"How much does the current Twelve charge for visits? Do you know?" said E.

Phoenix hesitated then said, "If I go with you, nothing. The reward I asked for finding her was free visitation rights, and that applies to anyone who comes with me. You wouldn't have to search for a Runner either. I could ask my friend, the one I mentioned, and she would get us across No Man's Land for free without a problem."

"Then we should go to the Tower, E," said Lux. "We were thinking about it anyway. We should meet this Snow Shaman and see what she knows. I really think there's something seriously wrong with James's watch, and all this stuff tonight just proves it. It's like we said, right? It's too much of a coincidence? His watch never moves and then the one night it does, a cow head appears and tries to eat us with some crazy darkness, and he sees a Shaman too? Something's wrong. Something's really wrong. We need to ask for help, and you've always said Shamans know way more stuff than anyone else in the Flowering. Now that we have Phoenix, we can go to the City, we can get into the Tower to see Snow, and we won't even have to pay for anything."

James silently agreed with Lux. If the Shamans were as all-knowing as everyone said they were then Snow was bound to know some shred of information that could help solve the torrent of mysteries tonight had loosed. They had to travel to the City. They had to talk to Snow, and with Phoenix, they could have free and easy access to see her.

But something also felt off to James, and E seemed to agree.

"What's in it for you to make the trip all the way to the City with us?" she asked Phoenix.

"I see a lot of strange things as a Roamer, a lot more than what an average crew would see. Citizens aren't as guarded around solitary humans, and in the past months, I've noticed a few of them acting strangely."

The concern on Bloom's face deepened.

"Strangely?" E pressed.

"Yes, though 'restlessly' might be a better word. They've been saying things, the moulded in particular. They keep talking about a growing darkness."

"*It is creeping back into the Flowering,*'" James said, remembering the words of the marked citizen they had freed from the snake woman. "'*The Beast who bleeds and eats with the power of the night.*'"

"You've heard citizens saying things like that too?" said Phoenix.

"Just one. But one was definitely enough."

The eye in the blue box. The whisper that had begged him to slay the Beast. The calf he'd seen tonight. Was that calf the Beast? The Beast who bled and ate with the power of the night? The Beast that needed to be slain?

James shook his head. He still didn't know if everything in his awakening dream had been real. Humans couldn't gain full consciousness within an awakening dream, so for all he knew, his mind simply could have been playing tricks on him before he was born into the Flowering. All he had was a gut feeling and no proof. He couldn't jump to conclusions like this.

"The darkness that chased you," Phoenix said, "and the things I've heard citizens talking about. Something isn't right. I've had a bad feeling about all of this, but after hearing your story and seeing your watch, I need to know what's going on. I can get to the City on my own, but it would take me weeks to get there. I need help if I want to get there faster." He sighed, clearly unhappy about the conclusion he'd reached. "I need a crew if I want to reach the City quickly. I need your help."

E remained silent.

"He's helped us all of tonight, E. Let's take a chance. If he really tries to mess with us, you can cut him up then," Lux said as if Phoenix weren't sitting right in front of him.

"Just because he helped us doesn't mean we can trust him," Honey said, also ignoring Phoenix's existence.

"You said that about James before, and he was fine. You guys are friends now."

She made to retort then stopped short as she looked at James.

He could tell that her mind had snagged on the words she'd told him when they had stood on the cliff overlooking the sea. "I need to learn to work with others instead of just being scared all the time," she had muttered. But was she simply being scared right now? Or was she right to suspect the worst from Phoenix? He was, after all, a human they knew nothing about, and he was a Roamer too. Didn't Roamers usually leave their crews because they couldn't get along with them? How had Phoenix failed to get along with the crews he had met before?

Honey struggled then said, "James doesn't count!"

Lux and Honey continued arguing. James cast Phoenix a furtive glance before speaking to E in Korean for privacy.

"*I don't know what to do either,*" he said. "*This guy seems nice, but something still seems a little weird. Would it really be that hard to get there without his help?*"

"You can leave me at the City after we've seen Snow, if that puts your minds at ease," said Phoenix. His eyes darted back and forth between E and James as if he were trying to guess what they were saying. "Trust me. I wouldn't want to stay with you much longer than that."

"What's that supposed to mean?" James said. This Phoenix guy seemed a little too unhappy for someone who wanted to come along with them.

"I didn't mean anything personal," he answered calmly. "I'm a Roamer by choice. I prefer to work alone whenever possible, so if you're not comfortable around me, you don't have to worry about me sticking around for long."

E stared at the floor then at Bloom. Honey and Lux continued to bicker.

"Shut it," she commanded.

They fell silent.

"Bloom," she said. She paused then drew a deep breath. "Should we go back to the City?"

Something in Bloom's eyes seemed to harden. James couldn't tell what thoughts were flying around behind his grave expression. Bloom hesitated then gave E a single, firm nod. She bowed her head as if he had given her the answer she had dreaded the most.

"It's settled, then," she said. She turned again to Phoenix. "You do realize that if you piss me off in any way, I'll cut off call and response with you before I cut off your head, right?"

"I'm sure you'd do much more than that," he said with a small smile that surprised James.

"And you understand that the only reason I'm taking you on is because of the Runner and the Shaman?"

"Yes."

"We will help you get to the City, and in return, you will obtain a Runner free of charge for us and get us free access to the Twelfth. No other payments, conditions, or hidden terms."

"That's right."

"And you'll take direction from a citizen without any objections or complaints?"

"What?"

"Bloom. His nose will get us there quicker than any route we try to find on our own."

Phoenix glanced at Bloom. "I suppose I've trusted worse, so yes. Agreed."

E glared at him then nodded.

"*Hello*," said Phoenix.

"*Hello*," replied E.

Uneasiness coiled around James and reminded him that nothing was ever as good as it initially seemed. There was nothing about Phoenix that he could point to and call "wrong." Sure, he was a stranger and a Roamer, but James himself had once been a stranger to the crew and had even abandoned them. That didn't mean he was dangerous or out to deceive them. Phoenix had been nothing but helpful tonight. So why did he still distrust him so much? Had innocence always felt this suspicious?

"Great," Honey grumbled. "More newcomers."

CHAPTER 19

HERI

J ames came to a stop at a red light. Electric icicles glowed blue-white along the rims of the rooftops around him. An inflatable Santa stood on one of the lawns, swaying back and forth in the cold night breeze. Projector lights threw shadows across the Santa's face, giving him the appearance of an unhinged murderer. James rested his forehead on the vibrating steering wheel and closed his eyes.

Last night. Last night was all he could think about. The blazing chasm, E stabbing Blood Crow, Phoenix joining the crew, the darkness chasing after their heels, the screams of the Hunters, his blackened watch, the blood-drenched calf, and Snow, the Twelfth Shaman. How had they seen each other last night? What could have possibly forged a connection that could transcend physical space and even blindness? Was it her powers as a Shaman? Was that what had allowed her to see him from within the calf's golden eye?

He shuddered. He could still see the blood trickling down from the calf's raw socket. Its dark eye had fixed upon him as if to mark him as its next target. His gut told him that last night wouldn't be final time he would see the creature. At the strike of six of his watch, the calf would recover more of its strength and appear to him again. And with each strike of his watch, the calf would grow closer to breaking free of the purple orb and returning fully to the Flowering. He shuddered again then stepped on the gas as the light turned green.

Of course, he didn't know how he knew any of this. It was all just a strong gut feeling. And what good was a feeling in the absence of reliable facts? He needed more information. He needed to talk to Snow. Until then, it would be a better use of his time and energy to prepare for other matters, like the chaos that was sure to break loose tonight. E was bound to torture Blood Crow then sever call and response with her. Blood Crow would then be doomed to wander throughout the Flowering alone, maybe even to her death.

He had to find a way to stop E. He could no longer just stand by like a useless idiot and let her continue feeding that wrathful monster that reared its ugly head every time someone attacked the crew. To be fair, though, Blood Crow did deserve some form of justice. And just as E was bound to attack her tonight, Blood Crow was bound to attack Bloom again too.

His heart sank as he remembered how Blood Crow had shoved her spear into Bloom's chest. He had considered sleeping all day just to guard Bloom. Who knew when Blood Crow would return to the Flowering and pick up where she had left off? Sure, E had been confident of Bloom's ability to fend for himself, and James also felt sure that, being a giant wolf and all, Bloom would have a much better chance of fighting off Blood Crow when a swarm of Hunters wasn't attacking him. But still, he couldn't help but worry ... and wonder! Bloom had talked last night. Talked! Well, maybe not talked so much as stuttered. Even one word, though, was beyond anything James had imagined would ever come out of his mouth.

Why had he assumed that Bloom was completely incapable of speech? After all, he clearly understood everything the crew said just fine every night, in English, Our Word, and even Korean, now that James thought about it. Plus, E and Bloom had established call and response long ago, so Bloom had to have talked at least then. Well, wolves never said anything whatsoever in Reality, so that was probably why. But Bloom wasn't part of Reality. He was part of the Flowering. A citizen. And so many citizens could speak. Bloom was a huge, blue wolf who understood multiple languages, yet James had still constricted his capabilities to only what he had considered to be possible. Was there more? Were there other things in the Flowering that had grown into a norm, a backdrop that stared at him each time he passed? What else had he failed to notice for better or for worse?

He groaned as another red light impeded his way forward. The lawn next to him sported a reindeer this time. Its white lights glowed with Christmas spirit. Its automated neck dipped up and down so that it seemed to graze upon the grass. James wanted to jump out of the car, grab the reindeer, and chuck it into the street so that he could run it over with his car! Bloom, Snow, E, Phoenix, Blood Crow, Honey, Lux, the journey ahead, the battle tonight, everything. Everything spun around in his head like a swirling storm. There were so many things to think about, so many important things that needed something done that he didn't even know where to start or if starting on any one thing would even help with the millions of others. He was stuck in the eye of the storm. Whichever direction he chose to walk, he would be swept away into a raging jumble of things and noise. There was no winning.

He dared the lights up ahead to turn red as a green light allowed him to drive forward once more. The storm in his head continued to brew the entire drive, persisting even as his car trembled to a stop in front of his parents' home. He berated himself for failing to exercise. His jiggling fat would have disappeared by now if he'd simply started going to the gym the first time he had promised himself that he would go. The rest of December and all the holiday celebrations stuffed within it were sure to add a few more pounds to his body too. In the Flowering, he looked like a stallion, ran like a deer, and dodged like a viper. In Reality, he woke up every morning feeling like a sack of lard that had somehow sprouted limbs and learned to roll out of bed in the shape of a human. He wasn't quite ready to stop eating instant ramen just yet, but he no longer had any excuse for his lack of exercise. He needed to get gym membership, go for walks, or do something, anything!

He shook his head and chuckled at himself. Of all the things to worry about right now, was he really worrying about something as stupid as his weight? He sat back in his seat and tried to dispel the rumbling, black clouds of thoughts still growing in his mind. It was times like these that he wished all the more that he could remember the faces of Crew Blue. E always said that it was a good thing that they couldn't remember each other's faces in Reality, and after last night, he doubly agreed.

Amnesia, topped with the anonymity of their nicknames, ensured that whatever happened in the Flowering would stay in the Flowering without creeping into Reality. He could only imagine what Blood Crow would do if she ever found out E's face and real name. E would have to sleep sooner or later and then she'd be defenseless in her bed, a prime target for any act of vengeance. Yes, he knew it was better this way, but he still would have liked to have thought of his friends in a way that felt like he was actually remembering them and not like he'd forgotten them long ago.

He took out his phone to check the time then glanced at Heri's text from earlier in the day. Her text had been curt. "Dinner at Mom and Dads. 630." She may as well have added, "You can come if you want, you dick!"

The fury he'd felt upon reading her text had died down so quickly that he had surprised himself. As the crew had warned, the situation with Heri had only grown worse over time. Her anger and his silence now felt like a new norm. This, of course, took care of the problem to a certain extent. If he did nothing, then nothing more would happen. Heri would be frustrated and sullen with him, which would result in less of the dreaded family bonding sessions.

Back in August, he would have sat back and let it all play out without lifting a finger. He would have even seen their Thanksgiving shoutfest as a blessing in disguise. But now, with everything he'd experienced in the Flowering and even the dangers he would have to face tonight, he wasn't so sure that he wanted this to be the new norm. He placed his hand over his black bracelet, thinking of how years had already passed from the day that Heri had given it to him. Had he ever gotten anything for her in return?

He stepped out into the chilly evening and hurried into the house. Upon taking off his shoes, he found Heri and his grandparents congregated around the TV in the living room. A plate of apples sat on the coffee table, each slice expertly peeled and cut so that the core was missing. His mother was in the kitchen, washing dishes as if she'd been there since Thanksgiving.

"*Is that you*, James?" his mother called.

"*Yes. I'm here.*"

"*Oh, good. Are you hungry? There are some apples on the* coffee table," she said.

"I'm...." He trailed off as he saw the look on Heri's face.

Her narrowed eyes were hurling silent death threats at him. She raised an apple slice to her mouth then snapped off half of it with her teeth. She chewed slowly. James gulped then wandered into the kitchen. He feigned interest in the vegetables his mother was rinsing as Heri continued crunching away behind him.

"*Have you been well?*" his mother said.

"*Yes. I've been well.*"

"*What about school?*"

"*School is good.* I think my finals went well."

"*Really? How about work?*"

"*It's going all right.*"

"*What about your professors? Do they teach well?*"

James continued giving generic answers to his mother's questions. He never enjoyed her interrogations, but he couldn't bring himself to leave the kitchen right now and enter Heri's domain in the living room. He could practically hear Crew Blue's disappointed sighs.

"*What about your health? You're healthy these days, right?*"

"*Yes,*" James replied in a monotone voice. Korean mothers shared a universal paranoia about health that seemed to persist throughout the generations like a curse.

His mother lugged a large hobak into a plastic basin she had placed in the sink. She began scrubbing away at the bumpy, green surface of the squash with a pan brush as if she were trying to skin it with the brush alone. Maybe it was the size and weight of the squash or the effort with which she was scrubbing, but James suddenly noticed how small his mother looked. She heaved the squash onto a cutting board then rinsed the basin and set it on the counter. Scratches had long since faded the cartoon family of racoons that had once decorated the bottom of the cheap, pink plastic.

"*How about you, Mom?*" he found himself saying.

"*How about what?*"

"*How is your health?*"

"*Oh, my health is good. Do you remember* Mrs. Ko?"

"*Yeah.*"

"*Well,* Mrs. Ko *and I have been walking in the park every morning together. That park right over here, you know? At first, I thought we were walking too much, but then I noticed that my legs have been getting stronger and that I have more energy throughout the day. Walking a lot must be good for your health. You should walk more too. You exercise these days, right?"*

James dodged the question by asking about the welfare of the Ko family. As his mother entered a lengthy monologue about Mrs. Ko–who, apparently, had a very pretty daughter who attended the same university as him–he felt something release inside his chest. He hadn't doubted that his mother's health was in great shape, not with all the Korean physical wellness shows she watched and the food and health superstitions she clung to. But as he stared at her shrinking shoulders and the white strands of hair that had been absent on Thanksgiving, he was reminded that the Flowering wasn't the only place where time mattered. His mother chopped the squash in half with her cleaver.

"Do you want me to help, Mom?"

"Oh, no. Go ahead and sit down. Go watch TV. Go relax."

James gathered a giant breath into his lungs as if the air would help him float away from the living room into which he was now doomed to walk. He turned his head in increments toward the living room. Heri glared at him. He spun his head back around.

"What are you doing? Go sit. Go relax!"

James accepted his fate. He kept his eyes on his grandparents as he wandered over to the sofa. Only a few dark strands adorned his grandmother's white hair, which had been ink-black when he'd been younger. She had cooked in the kitchen, standing where his mother was now, while scolding his grandfather for teaching him how to play Go-Stop. His grandfather had thrown back defensive shouts and ignored her as she went on about how he was corrupting their precious grandson with a sordid gambling game.

Heri had watched them play from the sidelines, insisting in vain that she was old enough to learn as well. James had taught her in secrecy a few years later during the many nights their parents had been absent. They had both felt lonely on such nights, but he knew it hadn't been easy for his parents either. They had toiled away day and night to make the restaurant into the successful chain that it was now. His father was busy tending to one of the restaurants on this very evening, doing the work James would have done otherwise to pay for his student loans and bills.

Heri squirmed away from him as he sat down next to her. The audience in the TV roared with laughter. James felt likelier to push an egg out of his mouth than to say the right words. It wasn't much help wondering what the crew would do either. E would have stabbed someone, Honey would have said sorry like she wasn't really sorry, and Lux wouldn't have found himself in this situation to begin with. He tried to think of Bloom and his calm demeanor, but he could only recall the wild rage that had burned in his eyes the night before as he had attacked the ram eating the black wolf.

He rubbed the inner corners of his eyes then managed to say, "Thanks for inviting me tonight."

Heri raised her eyebrows. Her arms remained crossed. Though his insides felt like they were shriveling up with both nervousness and embarrassment, he pressed on.

"I know we haven't spoken since Thanksgiving," he began.

Heri leaned forward and reached out her hand to pick up another apple slice.

"But I've been thinking about—what's that?"

His arm shot out. Though his body reacted slower and more awkwardly than in the Flowering, his mind remembered all of his training. He gripped Heri's wrist before she could pull back.

"What's this?" he muttered so that the sounds of the variety show covered his words.

"It's nothing," she said, pulling on her arm.

"It's not nothing," he said. He'd seen too many wounds in the Flowering. He knew what he saw on his sister's arm. "Where are those bruises from?"

She yanked her arm out of his grasp. "It's nothing," she repeated.

He stared at the defiance in her eyes before standing up. "I'm telling Dad when he gets home."

"No! James, sit down," Heri hissed.

"No."

"James!"

"Who did it?"

"James, *what's wrong?*" his grandfather said.

"*It's nothing, Grandpa*," Heri said, yanking on James's wrist in pulses.

Blood pounded in his ears. Heri had never provoked a physical fight with someone in her entire life. She was too nice for things like that. That could only mean one thing. Someone had put their hands on his little sister.

For the hundredth time that day, James saw E pumping her vengeful blade in and out of Blood Crow's body. For the first time that day, he felt glad that she had done it.

"James," Heri pleaded.

She glanced at their grandparents, clearly afraid of drawing more attention to herself, then relaxed as she saw that they were once again entranced by the antics of the Korean variety show.

"It's not what you're thinking, I promise. If you sit down, I'll tell you," she whispered.

His mother clanged pots and slammed cabinet doors in the kitchen. James sat down as her cleaver hit the cutting board in rhythmic chops.

"You'd better tell me the truth," he fumed.

"Don't worry, I will," she hissed. She looked at the TV then grabbed an apple slice as if at a loss for what else to do.

"Well?" he snapped, making her jump.

"Calm down! It's not some kind of crazy ex."

"Then what? It's a boyfriend?"

"No! I don't even have a boyfriend."

"Then what, Heri?"

"Keep your voice down!" She sighed and put down the apple. "It wasn't my boyfriend or my ex. It was my friend's ex. There were four of us in her apartment when he tried to barge in, so we all ganged up on him and kicked him out of the building. There was a struggle, though."

The thumping in James's ears and chest began to slow. A single, long breath calmed him down even more.

"Did you get your arm checked?" he asked.

"No, my arm is fine. Nobody got hurt. It was just some bruises and scrapes."

"And what about the guy?"

Heri slouched against the sofa's cushions as her expression hardened. "I don't know. We're all talking with my friend about what to do with him, but she's scared to death. And I don't blame her. It's a really sticky situation. These kinds of things always are."

The TV exploded with laughter once more. Dizziness replaced the blood that had rushed up into his head. Heri's words sat like a heavy boulder placed upon the growing mountain of his existing concerns. Memories of the Flowering swirled through his mind again before pausing on images of E shooting at Hunters and carving through Merchants with her machetes. Were those Hunters and Merchants scum in Reality too? Did they go around attacking girls like his sister and her friend? Or were they different, somehow, in this dimension? He massaged the inner corners of his eyes again as he wondered why he even cared. He needed to get this night over with. His thoughts were becoming too erratic. Heri glanced at him and rubbed her hands into her thighs before reaching for another apple.

"I'm glad you're helping your friend," James said. "And I'm glad you're okay."

"Yeah, me too."

"Does that guy know where you live? Can he hurt you?"

"I'd like to see him try."

"Heri, I'm serious. You don't know what crazy people are capable of."

"Relax. One, he was drunk, so he probably doesn't even remember that I was there. Two, he doesn't know where I live. And besides, I live with three other people right now, and that guy's graduating next quarter. I won't be seeing him around for much longer."

Heri had always been smart and people-savvy, which meant that she was good at side-stepping trouble, so James felt reassured on that basis alone. But if his sister's fighting skills were anything like his, he knew she'd be in trouble if some psycho were to pick a fight with her.

"If you ever need help, tell me. I'll be there," he said.

Heri pursed her lips and looked away from him. The annoyance on her face was rivaled only by her distrust.

"I'm serious," he insisted.

She slowly turned her eyes toward him again, wincing as if she were afraid of giving him another chance. "You're really worried about me?"

"Of course I am. And if I could, I'd rip that guy to pieces."

A shadow of appreciation softened Heri's smirk of disbelief. James remembered how he had scoffed during his first night in the Flowering when E had threatened to make him "regret it" if he tried to hurt anyone in the crew. Was this the type of fear she had felt? This love? This anger?

"I know I haven't been that ... that supportive in the past," he said. "But this is serious, Heri. I won't just stand by and let someone hurt you."

She pegged herself into the cushions again and remained silent. She looked at his bracelet.

"*Dinner is ready!*" his mother announced.

He knew that the conversation was over as they migrated over to the dinner table, and all too soon, he found himself at the front door, ready to leave. He walked back to his car, deflated at the thought that his talk with Heri had been a total bust. He hadn't apologized for Thanksgiving, and his promise to protect her had probably sounded feeble at best. As he zoomed down the freeway, he wondered if he was simply useless to all of his loved ones.

CHAPTER 20

THE RUBY NECKLACE

At nine PM, James swallowed his sleeping pills. He had decided to return to the Flowering earlier than usual to guard Bloom from Blood Crow. He tossed himself onto his mattress, burrowed into his blanket, then released a deep, slow breath. As drowsiness began eating away at his consciousness, he focused on an image of himself reaching for his knife. His eyes closed in Reality and opened in the Flowering.

He unsheathed his knife.

"Down!" E shouted.

Gunfire rattled through the air as he dropped down onto his stomach. Bloom leapt aside. Blood Crow fell onto the ground beside James. As she scrambled onto her hands and knees, he thrust his blade into her side. She cried out like a hunted animal that knew its last moment had come.

"Handcuffs!" E shouted as she and Honey ran forth.

Honey tossed handcuffs to her before gripping the back of Blood Crow's head and slamming her face into the ground. James wrenched back her arms and held up her wrists. E secured the handcuffs with two swift clicks. He flung himself down onto Blood Crow's back.

"*Lion Paw! Steel Heart!*" Blood Crow cried out as E wrestled with her feet.

"No one to help you now, is there?" Honey taunted as she stood back.

Bloom watched, tense and still, Phoenix at his side. Phoenix had drawn his hood over his head once again, concealing his expression. James's nails scratched the ground in search of a better grip as Blood Crow squirmed beneath him. The floor's surface felt bumpy, rough, neither dirt nor stone. Plastic. A solitary palm tree stood nearby, its branches stiff, the edges of its bark milky. Also plastic. They were trapped on a plastic hump of land in the middle of a calm, flat sea. Pixels of color composed the artificial sky and its motionless clouds. Only the moon and water had an air of the natural.

"James, off!"

He scrambled back at E's command. She kicked Blood Crow onto her back and raised her dagger. Bloom sprang forth. Biting into E's wrist, he pulled her arm away before she could strike. Honey lunged forth and grasped his mane.

"Bloom!" she yelled. "Bloom, stop it! She tried to rip you to shreds last night. This isn't the moment to be nice!"

The chasm's flames reared up in James's memory, stopping him short of grabbing E's arm too. He saw Blood Crow pushing Honey off of the ledge. He heard Honey's screams. He remembered how her skin had melted off of her bones and how his hand had hovered over her still body.

He had stopped E from torturing Blood Crow last night. He had even bound Blood Crow's wounds with his own hands. But with Honey whole in front of him, he suddenly questioned if stopping E right now was the right thing to do. He had made the right decision last night, hadn't he?

E ripped her arm out of Bloom's mouth. Instinct pushed James forward. As he dove toward E, realization then remembrance flashed across her eyes. Her dagger remained drawn back as James tackled her. He braced himself for the pain of her blade in his side and the bone-on-bone collision of her knuckles against his cheek. But she remained still beneath his grasp. Bloom snatched the dagger out of her hand and tossed it into the ocean. He bowled Honey over as she reached for James. He pinned his massive paws into her back.

"Bloom!" Honey screeched. "Get off of me! Get off!"

The hollow lump of land boomed as she banged on the plastic with her hands and feet. James cringed as E glared up at him. Her eyes silently commanded him to move. He swallowed then pressed down on her shoulders.

"I can't let you," he said.

"James, if E doesn't give her what she deserves, I will!" Honey yelled.

"I can't let you!"

"We would have burned alive because of her. She tried to kill us. Your crew. Crew Blue! Don't you care at all about that?" she said as a stifled sob cracked her voice.

"*I didn't try to kill you! None of us did. That's a filthy lie!*" Blood Crow shouted.

"You pushed me into a pit of fire! A pit of burning fire!"

"*I only wanted my necklace back,*" Blood Crow said, her anger suddenly subdued. She sounded desperate, even tearful.

James neither moved nor objected. He cared about his crew. Of course he did. And he knew that the Flowering wasn't some happy place full of sparkles and sunshine, where everyone could hold hands and get along. E hacking Blood Crow into pieces had allowed the crew to rescue Honey. Blood Crow's family would have torn Bloom apart had the crew failed to fight back. Even on Halloween, the crew would have lost all their weapons if they hadn't answered the Merchants' demands with bloodshed. Only fire could fight fire in the Flowering. James knew that.

"James," E said. "I warned you before. I'll punish anyone who touches our crew, and I'll do good on my word."

"You already broke your word last night by stabbing me."

"Don't you guilt-trip me about that!"

"I'm not guilt-tripping you!" he said, quailing as E began lifting herself off the ground. He pressed down harder, hoping the familiar black glint of her machetes wouldn't appear. "I'm just ... you're not–"

Honey whipped out her gun and aimed.

"No!" James cried.

Honey shrieked as Bloom jumped in front of Blood Crow. Her bullet zinged into the water.

"Are you crazy?" she screamed, pounding on the plastic again.

Bloom frowned at her as if to scold her then danced around in front of her as she waved her gun around.

"Move, James!" E commanded.

He knew that the last few grains in the hourglass of her patience were swiftly falling away. The embers of rage were already glowing in her eyes. If they roared into a full blaze, he knew he would stand as much of a chance as Blood Crow had the night before. It was hard to believe that this ruthless E was the same leader who had rushed to his rescue in the hall with the snake woman. The same girl who had looked away from him in shame when the crew had sat down to talk among the crashing waves. The same friend who had defended him from Blood Crow and dived into the flames for Honey.

"James, move!" E yelled.

Bloom sat down in pointed refusal as Honey continued brandishing her gun.

"She's not going to die just because we shoot her," Honey said.

"She will die if you sever call and response," Phoenix said as he stepped forward.

A rush of hope filled James. It didn't matter that he barely knew Phoenix. He was willing to make allies with anyone who could convince the crew to do the right thing.

"What–who–stay out of this, you Roamer! Who do you think you are?" Honey said.

As with the night before, Phoenix showed no signs of irritation or hostility despite the words that were hurled against him.

"I know what you're planning to do after you're done with her," he said. "And from what little I saw last night, I can see that you have good reason to cut off call and response. But Hunters don't stand much of a chance out in the Flowering if they're not with their families."

"Oh, yeah? And how would you know?" said Honey.

"I've Roamed for two years now. I've seen what happens to lone Hunters. They find their life's purpose in going around and attacking any citizen they find suspicious. She," he said, tilting his head toward Blood Crow, "is going to go out there and do the same whether or not she has her family to help her. You know what'll happen to her when she does that."

"I could care less what'll happen to her," Honey said.

"That's not true, Honey," James insisted.

Honey pressed her lips together. Her chest puffed up with outrage. "I regret ever trusting you."

"Honey," James pleaded.

"I saved you from the fire!"

He didn't know what to say. Why couldn't he just push away the part of him that kept nudging his guts and telling him that torturing and condemning Blood Crow were wrong? Why couldn't he just let the crew give Blood Crow the punishment she deserved?

"You heard what Phoenix said," he said, his voice growing weak with the terror of losing Honey's trust forever. "Besides, this just ... this just isn't right. It wasn't right of her to do what she did to us. And yeah, if there's anyone who deserves to burn alive, it's her and the rest of those Hunters. But Honey, do you really want to torture her? Do you really want to stand back and let E torture her? And what if she does wander out there and end up dying? That'll be blood on our hands. Our own hands!"

"Our bodies heal, you idiot!"

"If a band of Merchants comes across her," Phoenix began.

"Really! Who are you? Shut up!" Honey yelled. "I don't care about ifs. I care about what is. And what is true is that she and her whole family tried to kill all of us!"

"*We didn't try to kill you!*" Blood Crow shouted. "*It's against the Hunters' way to harm humans unless it's to protect them, and that's exactly what we were trying to do.*"

"Pushing a human into scorching fire seems a little contrary to what you're saying," Phoenix said. James could hear the eye roll in his voice even with his hood hiding his face.

"*I ... I don't have to keep explaining myself to any one of you. I am a Hunter, and the only humans I ever have to listen to are the head of my family and the Lead at the Solstice. We fought all of you for your own good. You should just accept it.*"

"*The Solstice,*" Phoenix repeated. He paused as if an idea had struck him. "The Solstice is less than two weeks away. Her family is bound to be there! E, if we get to the City in time, we can just leave her there."

"And why would we bother doing that?" Honey said.

"Because you're not a murderer!" James said. "Honey, I could care less about her, but I can't let you do this. I can't let either of you do this. I won't let you torture humans or play around with a human's life. That's not who either of you are. It's not who you were meant to be!"

Honey scrunched up her face, clearly on the brink of bursting into tears. E laid her head back down on the ground and stared at the ocean. As right as James felt about everything he'd just said, he couldn't help but feel like he was defending Blood Crow. Was he acting selfishly somehow? Was he being narrow-minded? Maybe he wasn't prioritizing his loyalty to his friends as he should.

"She'll be useful to us in No Man's Land. It'll be a good idea to keep her for now," Phoenix said.

"Bloom, get out of the way! Go!" Honey shouted, brandishing her gun again and ignoring Phoenix.

Bloom yawned.

E smacked James's hand off her shoulder with alarming ease. She hesitated then placed her hand on his shoulder.

"Let me go," she said softly.

James was both startled and relieved to hear the gentleness in her voice. Maybe he'd done enough damage for tonight. His loyalty lay with E, and he had gone against her wishes for long enough.

"*Wait. Are all of you on your way to Lapis Lazuli?*" said Blood Crow.

"Yes. We are on our way to the City," James replied in an icy tone as he helped E to her feet.

"*What for?*"

"What's it to you what we do?" Honey snapped.

E gazed at the open sea again. Guilt twisted James's insides. All she had tried to do was avenge their crew. He had only managed to defend their enemy. Memories of failure swarmed him, from his failed conversation with Heri to the boulder that had crushed E instead of him to his arrogance the night he had abandoned Crew Blue. Then his mind flashed images of him stabbing the gums of the snake woman and throwing his last spear to E. He remembered the promise he had made to Honey as they had stood above the crashing waves.

Determination flared within him.

He was so tired of being useless!

He shoved his hand into his pocket and pulled out Blood Crow's ruby necklace. Her eyes widened as he dangled the necklace above her head. He didn't know what they were going to do with her, but as long as she was here, he was going to make sure that she would tell them anything they needed to know. E had doubted that Hunters would know anything about the calf and its darkness, but he was still willing to take his chances. Problems were never solved in secrecy, after all, and if any group of humans in the Flowering had ever seen a strange citizen like that calf before, the Hunters would surely be one of them. All they did was hunt citizens.

"Here. Your stupid necklace," he said. "But I'm not giving it back to you until you tell us everything you know, and I'd better be satisfied with your answers, or I will let the others do whatever they want to you. And," he added, coming up with rules on the spot, "and you have to give me your word that you'll stop causing so much trouble. No more pushing, no more choking, stabbing, none of it. Whether it's with Bloom or anyone else here."

"*That's a lot to ask for,*" Blood Crow said. She looked like she wanted to strangle him.

"Well, this is an important necklace, so you'd better behave."

Her eyes followed the two rubies as they swung together like a pendulum. She scowled.

"*What do you want to know?*"

He recounted the events from the previous night, from the calf's appearance to how he had seen Snow in the golden eye. Blood Crow's mouth hung open by the story's end.

"So?" he demanded, trying his best to sound threatening and not completely off-footed. "Do you know anything about any of this?"

Wincing with pain, Blood Crow squirmed into a seated position then tossed her hair aside.

"*I swear upon the name of the Brave that I will tell you all that I know and that all will be the truth.*"

CHAPTER 21

THE BRAVE

The name of the who?" said James.

"*The Brave. The first of the Hunters,*" said Blood Crow.

Honey rolled her eyes so far back into her head that James thought she might catch a glimpse of her own brains. She shoved her gun back into its holster and threw Bloom a look of disgust before storming into the shade of the plastic palm tree. Bloom sighed through his nostrils and trotted after her. Phoenix drew nearer to James. E stared only at the sea.

"Okay," James said, still feeling lost. He shoved the necklace back into his pocket then grabbed his knife still sheathed in Blood Crow's side. He yanked it out and pointed the dripping blade at her face. "Talk."

She gave him a firm nod despite the blood gushing out of her side. "*We Hunters consider it our honor and privilege to protect our fellow humans from the evils of citizens. For countless eras, we have upheld this great duty and passed down our legacy from one generation to another.*"

Honey snorted. Blood Crow glared at her before continuing.

"*We have also made it our duty to preserve the mysteries of the Flowering for posterity. We keep hundreds of stories with us that vary in nature and wisdom, but one story has been with us since the very beginning. It is the story of the Red Calf. Yes,*" she said as James stirred, "*quite the coincidence, isn't*" *it? The story states that the Red Calf was a monster drenched in its own blood. Like so many other citizens, it refused to move on once its mark appeared. Instead of yielding to its fate, it used its gathered powers to devour humans and wreak havoc such as the Flowering had never seen. We Hunters simply knew its hungry power to be an unnameable darkness, but to think that it could have been literal...."*

Honey sat very still for someone who wasn't supposed to be listening. She paid no attention to Bloom as he laid down on top of her outstretched legs and sighed.

"Our ancestors described the evil creature as so powerful and cunning that it was able to steal the sight of the twelve Shamans and retain their powers in a single, golden eye. It was the Brave, the founder of the Hunters, who single-handedly defeated the Red Calf in a fearsome battle. He saved all the humans of the Flowering and ushered in the first of many eras in the glorious history of us Hunters. It was he who laid down the bricks of the Hunters' way, he who taught us our purpose."

A manic passion brightened in her gray eyes so that they glittered.

"If you were to ask me, 'What is your purpose, O Hunter?' I would reply, 'To kill all marked citizens and slay all threats.' If you were to ask me, 'For what purpose, O Hunter?' I would say, 'To defend our own and to protect the Flowering from darkness.' 'For life.' 'Protect.' These are the words that we live by. These are the words that have urged us to protect human lives from the dangers of citizens for generations since the era of the Red Calf. The creature you saw in that purple orb. It's too much of a coincidence. It must have been the Red Calf from our legends. But how. How is the question. How could you have seen the Calf? It has been dead for centuries."

James studied his memory of the creature. It had been drenched in its own blood. The golden orb ingrained in its forehead had resembled an eye. It devoured humans and objects using darkness. It was too big of a coincidence to be only a coincidence. But it was just as Blood Crow had said. The Red Calf had been dead for centuries. It couldn't be the same creature he had seen. But then why couldn't he shake this feeling of certainty, this gut feeling that screamed that the creature in the purple orb and the Red Calf were one and the same? He jumped as Honey burst into cackles.

"That is the biggest pile of steaming crap I have ever heard," she said. "James, you're an idiot. You should've made her say all that before you told her what you saw and seen how well she would've told you the story then."

"*I would never lie about our legends*," Blood Crow said as outrage flushed her cheeks.

"Bloom?" said James as Bloom stood up.

E's hand sprang to her dagger. Bloom's nose scraped against the plastic terrain as he continued roving about the island, sniffing. He slowed then nodded twice at E.

"The plane is disappearing," she said. "Everyone, gather together!"

The group rushed to obey. Blood Crow squirmed on the floor as she tried to join them then yelped as E gripped a fistful of her hair. She kicked and struggled as she dragged her across the ground toward the others.

"*Coconut!*" Blood Crow shouted suddenly.

"What?" James said.

She grunted and jabbed her nose toward the top of the plastic palm tree.

"There," E said, pointing up.

High above in the tree, a luminescent, blue glow had encapsulated a plastic coconut. The light spread down the trunk and across the ground like a phosphorescent disease.

"E?" James said, stretching out his hands to create something, anything, as the glow crawled rapidly across the water and up the sky. "What do we do here?"

"It's the whole plane. There's nothing we can do about it."

"What? What do you mean it's the whole plane?"

"Get ready!"

Everything disappeared. James braced himself for a long fall only to find himself standing on a plush rug. Windows with closed blinds, fabric couches, an armchair, and a large, wooden TV cabinet surrounded the group in a dim room. Dead orchids sat on top of a piano that stood near a locked door. A flight of stairs led from the door to the second floor, where other doors stood ajar with identical, dark gaps. In front of the group, a hallway, short yet somehow long too, led to a room filled with golden light. The room's linoleum floor connected a kitchen, most of which stood out of view on the left, to a cramped dining area on the right. A sliding, glass door, which stood across from the hallway and between the kitchen and dining area, led into the dark of night outside.

The group flinched as bright beams swung through the slits of the blinds covering the windows next to them. Gravel crunched under the weight of approaching wheels before a door opened and slammed shut. Keys jingled as footsteps crunched closer. James pointed his knife at the locked door by the stairs, waiting for the doorknob to turn at any moment. Silence passed in stiff, palpable increments. But the knob remained still. The group lowered their blades then jerked them back up again as pots clashed in the kitchen and rolled across the linoleum floor. A metal lid spun to a halt. Bloom stepped to the front of the group with his teeth bared. Footsteps plodded across the floor of the kitchen.

A corpse appeared.

It paused at the end of the hallway then began walking toward the group. Its rotting flesh had soiled its collared shirt and khaki pants. Strips of skin hung from its head like bleached kelp and dangled with each step. Most of its mouth had decayed, leaving a wide, tattered grin across its face.

Its shoulder smeared brown onto the white wall of the hallway as it swayed then lumbered forth again.

James jumped as Lux appeared at Bloom's side. Lux jumped at the sight of the corpse. He unsheathed his knife and looked at E, who pressed a finger to her lips and signaled for him to come next to her. As he obeyed, Lux twisted his body away from Blood Crow and made a face as if she, too, were rotten and sullied. Blood Crow, however, had eyes only for the citizen.

"*It's Dead*," she said, her voice detonating like a bomb in the silent room.

E yanked up her hair and twisted the tip of her dagger into the skin beneath her eye.

"*No, I mean it! It's Dead!*" she said as she struggled to lean away from E's blade.

"Shut up. Of course it's dead. It's a zombie," Honey hissed.

"*It's a Dead citizen. A marked citizen that can't think for itself. Can't hear. Can't do anything.*" said Blood Crow as if she were addressing someone particularly stupid. She gasped as E's dagger drew a drop of blood.

"We know what the Dead are," E growled.

James nodded along with Honey and Lux as if he, too, were fully knowledgeable of what the Dead were.

"*Then kill it,*" Blood Crow said. She scowled and shook her handcuffed wrists. "*Get these things off of me. I'll kill it for you.*"

Honey rolled her eyes. "How dumb do you think we are?"

"*Dumb enough to miss a mark right in front of your face,*" Blood Crow said. She looked up at E with pleading eyes. "*Above its teeth. In its gums!*"

E slowly lowered her blade as she stared at the citizen. Only then did James see its mark. A piece of flesh dangled over it so that its red hue appeared only in flashes as the citizen advanced with slow and heavy steps. He was surprised that Blood Crow had been able to see it at all.

"I can take care of this if you'd like," Phoenix told E. He stepped forward with one hand held open and ready to create. "It'd be best not to waste more time."

"No, it's mine," Lux said, excitement sparkling in his eyes. "I love zombie movies, zombie shows, anything that has zombies. I've always wanted to kill one."

"Lux, don't be stupid," Honey chided, no longer bothering to whisper.

She groaned in exasperation as he ran forward and thrust his dagger into the corpse's temple. His face fell as it continued walking.

"Sad. They always kill them by stabbing them in the head. Oh, well!"

He shrugged, sheathed his dagger, and with the katana that appeared in his hand, sliced through the corpse's torso. The top half of the body fell onto the floor with a sickening splat. The tip of his sword plunged down into the Dead citizen's gums. The citizen vanished.

"You see that, Honey? I killed a zombie!"

He hurried over to her. Her expression softened as he shook her in a one-armed embrace.

"It wasn't really a zombie," she muttered.

"Aw, close enough."

"*There are bound to be more of them. There always are,*" Blood Crow told E.

James sheathed his knife then squinted down the hallway and through the glass door that led outside. He could make out several human-like figures roaming slowly around beyond a small yard and low fence. Blood Crow yelped as E tugged her up by her hair again and dragged her toward the stairs. She nodded at Honey, who tossed her another pair of handcuffs. She bound Blood Crow to the post of the stairs.

"Crew Blue," E said, stepping toward the piano and ignoring Lux as he grinned. "Huddle. And you stay over there where we can see you," she snapped at Phoenix, who held up his hands and took a step back.

The crew gathered into a tight circle. A sense of foreboding stole upon James. Was E about to make her final decision regarding Blood Crow's fate?

"Honey," said E.

Honey shrank back slightly.

"I know you didn't want the Roamer here. I didn't want him here either, but you know what it's like trying to get a good Runner, and you know what it's like to try and see a Shaman too. If what the Roamer said last night is true, he'll make our lives ten times easier. We need him."

Honey lowered her gaze, looking subdued. "I know," she said.

"Good. Then that's that with the Roamer. As for the Hunter...."

The crew turned to stare at Blood Crow. Her handcuffs clinked against the wooden post as she continued fighting against her restraints.

"What are we going to do with her, E?" Lux said. "I thought you were going to end things with her tonight."

"I was. But James wants to leave her alone, and both he and the Roamer think that severing call and response would be equal to a death sentence. The Roamer thinks we should take her with us to the City and leave her there since it'll be the Solstice soon."

"And you? What do you think we should do?"

"I wanted to ask you all the same thing. What do you guys think we should do?"

Bloom smiled. James exchanged looks with Honey and Lux. Since when had E run the crew like a democracy?

E smirked. "You don't have to look that surprised that I'm asking you."

There was an uneasy silence before Honey spoke.

"Fine. If James is too soft to give her what she deserves, then fine. Sounds like you got her pretty good last night anyway, and I can ... acknowledge ... that torture isn't absolutely necessary, even though I'd call it 'punishment' and not 'torture,' but whatever. Even with all that aside. You guys. It's not okay for us to take her all the way to the City. She speared Bloom and pushed me into the fire. I thought the whole point of us going to the Shamans was to get some answers as soon as possible. She's going to keep making trouble for us, and that'll hold us up forever."

"I'm with Honey," said Lux.

"You didn't even think about it," said James.

"I don't need to think about it. She attacked Honey and Bloom."

"Maybe she can give us some more information if we take her. That story she told us about the Red Calf was more than what we had before," James said.

"That story didn't really explain anything," said E with a shake of her head, "and I'm pretty sure she's just been brainwashed anyway. To be honest, there are so many stories about the Flowering floating around that I've given up listening to most of them. Like the Shamans' sight. The Hunter girl believes that this Red Calf in her legends stole their sight, but the Shamans themselves say that it was the power-hungry Twelfth who stole it and ran away with it."

"The Twelfth? You mean Snow?" said James.

"No. One of her predecessors from centuries ago, or at least that's what the Shamans say. That's why they've always put such a high price on finding the Twelfth every time a new one is born into the Flowering. They're always hoping the new Twelve will be reborn with the power to give them back their sight."

"Either way," said Honey, reeling the conversation back in, "I don't want the Hunter with us. I don't like the Roamer either, but whatever. I'm willing to take our chances with him as long as we dump him in the City. At least he didn't try to kill us last night."

"Bloom, what about you? What do you think we should do?" James said. Maybe Bloom's approval would tip the others in the right direction. E always listened to Bloom.

Bloom's tail flopped from side to side.

"No!" Honey cried. "I—no—E. You guys. You guys never listen to me. I'm so worried!"

"Honey," said E.

Honey balled her fists as if to prepare for E's verdict.

"Honey, if you really feel that unsafe with her, then I won't take her on."

James's breath caught in his throat. Honey's fists slowly relaxed. Lux stared at E, open- mouthed. Bloom beamed.

"I didn't give you a choice with James or the Roamer, but I'll give you the choice now," E said. "I hated her for what she and her family did to all of you, but now I see that I may have been short-sighted. Everyone has a good point—yes, even James—but Honey, this time I'll leave the choice up to you."

Honey bit down on her lip. Hope reignited within James as he saw the turmoil on her face. The responsibility of a heavy decision had never been hers, and now that E had given her the final say, he could tell that Honey, at last, felt the weight of sending Blood Crow to her death. He would've liked to have said "I told you so" were it not for the pity that stirred within him. He knew how much the safety of the crew meant to Honey. The prospect of maintaining call and response with a stranger, let alone an enemy, was surely terrifying for her.

"What if I made her cooperate? Made her behave until we got to the City? Would you feel more comfortable with it?" James asked her.

Though Honey rolled her eyes, she made no objections.

"How?" Lux said.

It was James's turn to ball his fists. If he could just get Blood Crow to cooperate, the crew could take her to the City and keep their hands clean. He marched up to Blood Crow, pulled out the ruby necklace from his pocket, and thrust it in front of her face.

"Swear to me," he said. "Swear to me on the name of the Brave that you will cooperate with every order given to you and that you won't attack Bloom or any other citizen without explicit orders. That you will be fully and completely cooperative until we reach the City."

Blood Crow only glowered at him then continued tugging on her handcuffs.

"You heard what the Roamer said, and you know it's true," James pressed on. "If you don't come with us, you'll wander around just like that Dead citizen until you wind up dead yourself. You have to cooperate if you want to survive to see your precious family again. And if you don't have our help, you'll never reach the Solstice in time."

He had no idea what the Solstice even was, but he didn't care. Whatever it was, it was important to her, and he was willing to prey on everything she held dear. Annoyance flared within him as she continued wrestling with her handcuffs. He grabbed the leather cord of the necklace with one hand and began pulling on the two rubies with the other.

"*Wait*," she said.

He continued stretching the leather.

"*Stop it!*"

"Swear it!"

She gritted her teeth. For a moment, she looked as though she would spit at him. Then she muttered, "*I swear to all that you have commanded on the name of the Brave.*"

"What?"

"*I said I swear on the name of the Brave!*"

"Good." He created a bottle of water then rolled the necklace into a tight ball before shoving the necklace into his mouth.

"*What are you doing?*"

He opened the bottle, took a mouthful of water, and swallowed the necklace whole. Blood sprang into his mouth as the rubies scraped down his throat. He finished the bottle and tossed the empty plastic aside.

"That's for insurance," he said as Blood Crow gawked at him. "And you're not getting it back until we reach the City. Hunters only attack other humans to protect them, right? Well, looks like you'll have to cut me open to get your necklace back or have me take it out myself. Understand?"

Blood Crow snorted in disbelief.

"I said, do you under–"

"*I understand,*" she snapped.

James glared back at her then turned to Honey. "Honey, are we good?" he asked, hoping his actions had proven his loyalty to her.

She exhaled as if she were preparing to leap off a cliff. Then she drew herself up, shook out her hair, and nodded. James caught the keys she tossed to him and held them up for Blood Crow to see.

"One wrong move and I'll let my crew do whatever they want to you. You remember the taste of E's dagger, right?"

He tried his best to curse Blood Crow with his eyes, wishing he could remember exactly how Heri had done it. He grabbed her hands to unlock the cuffs then paused.

She was trembling.

He stamped out his sympathy. Just because he didn't want to torture or murder her didn't mean she deserved to get away scot-free with everything she had done. The least she could do was feel some fear right now. The handcuffs thudded onto the stairs.

"*I wasn't lying, you know. About the Dead,*" said Blood Crow as she rubbed her wrists. She created bandages and began binding the wound he'd made in her side. "*The moulded will come for them soon. We should go slay them all while we still can.*"

"Finally," E said.

Blood Crow flinched as her black machete appeared in her hand. E pointed the blade at Blood Crow's throat and closed one eye as if she were picking out which parts of her neck to carve out first.

"Finally, we have something we can agree on," said E.

CHAPTER 22

THE DEAD

Wait. What exactly are we agreeing on?" Phoenix asked E.

"We're going after the other Dead citizens."

"Why?"

"*They'll mould if we don't,*" said Blood Crow in a tone that suggested that Phoenix was stupid just for asking. She curled away from E as she stepped closer to her.

"You will not speak unless spoken to. And you," E said to Phoenix. "You'll help us slay the Dead, or you'll go to the City alone. And take your hood off while you're traveling with us. I can barely see your face under that thing."

"We're wasting time," Phoenix said in a tone that implored her to listen to reason.

She pierced him with a scorching glare that seemed to burn holes into his hood. He sighed then threw back his hood so that it draped behind the nape of his neck.

"This is important too," she said. "Our crew has always made a point of protecting the Flowering and its citizens, although we protect the innocent the right way," she added, glaring at Blood Crow. "We'll withhold from tracking down the moulded and going on rescue missions while traveling to the City, but we won't ignore the Dead. Not when they're walking around so freely like this."

Bloom pressed his chest down onto the floor as he gave his back a good, long stretch. He leaned forward and stuck one hind leg out after the other as he stretched them too. He shook out his fur then smiled. The group followed him as he trotted down the hallway.

"James," Lux whispered. "You know you need to crap or puke that thing out before the end of the night, right?"

"What? You mean the necklace?" James said, startled. "What do you mean? It's on my body. I'll wake up tomorrow night the way it was."

"On your body. If you swallow something, it just disappears the next night. You really think I would've eaten all that ice cream before if it didn't go away later?"

James gaped. E slid the glass door open and led the group single-file into the darkness outside. They passed through the yard, hopped over the low fence, then gathered under a carport in the driveway. The slimy heads of corpses glinted in the moonlight. Some stood still, staring into space. Others walked with heavy steps down the driveway, passing the garages on either side as they wandered into the street. E clicked on a flashlight before banging the butt of her machete against one of the carport's metal posts. The Dead citizens only swayed or continued walking. She nodded at the others. More beams of light clicked on as the group spread out.

James created a spear as he ran toward a corpse swaying in front of a garage. He inspected its body as he turned it around with his spear, but he couldn't find its mark. There were too many holes, too many layers of decaying flesh and fat. Its clothes complicated matters further. As he wondered with mounting dread whether or not he'd have to strip the corpse to search for its mark, Blood Crow ran up to him.

"What?" he demanded, feeling himself grow small as she scrutinized the corpse.

She sneered at him. Shunting him aside, she thrust her spear under the corpse's sagging collarbone and into the wood of the garage door. The Dead citizen vanished. She tugged out her spear, looked him up and down, then ran off toward the other end of the driveway with her nose held high. He rolled his eyes.

"Make sure they don't touch each other!" E yelled.

"Why?" James shouted as he prodded another corpse with his spear.

"They'll mould!"

He sighed. "Great!"

He raced toward three of the Dead lumbering toward one another and nudged them into different directions before hurrying toward another pair. Bloom bit into a corpse's leg and flung the citizen onto the ground. The citizen disappeared as Honey swung her tomahawk down into the mark on its head. E and Blood Crow had already cleared their areas. Lux and Phoenix were nowhere to be seen. James tailed the remaining corpses as they plodded down the driveway and into the street. He searched for a mark with increasing panic, hoping that the rest of the group were too distracted to notice that he had yet to bring down a single one of the Dead.

The street consisted of two culs-de-sac stretched out and joined together into a long, rounded strip of asphalt. Townhouses loomed side-by-side to the right, forcing the Dead to funnel into the park on the left. The park's lush, green lawn reflected the pale moonlight. Willow trees let down their branches like the hair of mourning women. Small, low hills covered in pine trees formed a spine-like row that reached past a swing set and into the distance. James ran toward a group of corpses slowly congregating amidst the pine trees. As he shepherded them into different directions, he fought down the uneasiness creeping into his stomach. The Dead looked more alive under the shade of the trees.

"Heads up!" Lux shouted.

Beams of light zig-zagged across the grass before fixing on two corpses. James sprinted toward the pair as they leaned into one another. They swayed as if engaging in a strange dance before their flesh began to mould together. He grasped his spear with both hands and aimed. The two corpses merged into one, tall body. The moulded citizen fastened its eyes on him and screamed as it sprang toward him with an open mouth. He thrust his spear through its chest. The citizen shrieked and waved its arms at him. Its flesh slipped along the shaft of the spear as it pushed forward. It bit into James's neck. He looked up at the moonlit sky and screamed.

This was it. This was how it was going to end. A zombie had bitten him, and now he'd be forced to join the army of the undead!

Something flashed. James toppled over onto the grass along with the decapitated body of the citizen.

"Get it off! Get it off!" he cried as he struggled to shake off the head still clamped onto his neck. He shouted with pain as the citizen gnawed deeper.

Phoenix began prying apart the citizen's teeth with a knife as Blood Crow plunged her hands into its body lying on the ground. She flung aside sodden clothes and strips of flesh before standing back and bringing down her spear. The moulded citizen vanished, head and all. James touched the bite marks on his neck with trembling fingers as Blood Crow ran to another corpse. Phoenix inspected the wound with gentle hands.

"James, you okay?" Lux said, hurrying over to him.

"How bad is it?" James asked.

"Oh, man. It's bad. It's really, really ba–oh, look! It's healing."

"The teeth marks are closing," Phoenix said with a kind smile.

James relaxed upon the grass.

"You don't feel any chills, aches, fever? No double vision?" said Lux.

"No," James said, irritated by the excitement in Lux's voice.

"Oh," he said as his face fell with disappointment.

Embarrassment heated James's cheeks as Phoenix helped him back onto his feet. Of course he wouldn't turn into a zombie. This was the Flowering. And these were Dead citizens, not the undead. How ridiculous.

Metal winked at him.

"Whoa. What's that?" he said.

Phoenix was holding the most magnificent sword James had ever seen. Each end of the staff held a large, razor-sharp blade. Despite the length of the sword, which slightly exceeded Phoenix's height, it looked light and easy to wield. One swing would have felled James and Lux both.

"I was going to say. That's one fine sword," said Lux.

"Where did you touch something like this?" James asked. He snapped out of his reverie at the sound of E's voice.

"The plane is unstable!" she yelled from across the park.

The three men assumed battle stances. A large, lumpy staircase had appeared and now stood as a dark blot on the glinting grass. Beneath the willow trees, Bloom yanked a Dead citizen off its feet. Honey brought her tomahawk down into its body. Blood Crow hurled her spear, pinning another citizen into a tree trunk. Phoenix dashed across the lawn to join the fray as E dispatched another moulded citizen.

"Uh-oh. Time. James, time. We need to get that necklace out of you," Lux said, tapping his watch.

"Wait, already? I–no–wait. What do I do?" James said, patting his stomach with frantic hands.

"I don't know. Is there some kind of medicine that can make you throw up?"

"Aren't most medicines supposed to help you not throw up?"

E's machetes sliced through the moonlight. As she stabbed a citizen in the side, a solution dawned upon him. It was a crazy idea, one that filled him with dread, but they were out of time, and they needed something fail-proof.

"E!" he called, waving his flashlight. "I have an idea," he whispered to Lux.

They withdrew into the shadows of the pine trees.

"E, I need to get the necklace out of me," James said, clicking off his flashlight as she ran up to them.

"Just let it disappear. You had a good point about the Solstice. That alone is enough to get her to fall in line," she said.

"No, it still provides a safeguard. If she starts trouble, I can threaten her with it. I don't know why, but she's really attached to it."

"Well, then, get it out. What did you call me here for?"

"I don't want to do it near her," he said, grabbing Lux's flashlight and clicking it off.

E gave James a questioning look then turned off her light as well.

"Just get it out of me for tonight. We'll take turns holding it so that she won't know. It'll throw her off if she ever tries to get it from me."

"Okay," said E, still looking uncertain as to what he was alluding to.

"So, you need to go back on your promise," said James.

He stared at her then at her dagger. He grimaced as he nodded at her blade. Lux gaped at him. E grabbed her blade and slashed before Lux could object.

The pain was sharp and quick. James forced his legs to hold up his weight as E shoved her hand into the cut she had made in his stomach and pulled the necklace out. Lux caught him as his knees buckled.

"Are you guys okay?" Honey shouted from the beneath the willow trees.

Everything disappeared.

He was lying on his back, warm and at peace. His mind was blank like the space around him. He didn't remember anything as he rose through the air. The rotting corpses, the agony in his stomach, the cold shadows of the trees, Blood Crow. Even his own name hung suspended somewhere far away from his mind's reach. He struggled, trapped within his immobile body as a desire grew. A desire to remember. He was more than an empty mind stuck in a void. He was something more, someone more.

But he couldn't remember. He couldn't remember.

Noise echoed through the space, growing into stabbing screeches. His skin prickled under the chill touch of morning as his hand emerged from beneath his blanket and slid across soft cotton. He slapped his hand on top of his alarm clock. Silence followed.

James pressed his palms into his eyes. Scattered images of the Flowering cluttered his mind as they did every morning. E had pulled out the necklace just in time. It was one more thing they could use against Blood Crow, both on the journey to the City and even upon reaching it. He felt the license to breathe a small sigh of relief. Who knew what their future nights held and what trials they would face on their journey? But at least he had managed to tame Blood Crow and keep the crew from staining their hands with needless blood.

He ran his fingers through his flattened hair, shook his head, then walked to the bathroom on feet that felt like sausages. As he relieved himself, he couldn't help but examine the side of his neck where he'd been bitten. Much to his relief, his skin was smooth and bite-free. He scolded himself again as he flushed the toilet and made his way into the kitchen. No wounds in the Flowering ever transferred to Reality. He'd known that forever now. He was stupid to worry. He opened the refrigerator and hoped that the milk was still good as he mixed himself a glass of misugaru. After ripping open a chocolate snack cake and shoving the whole thing into his mouth, he sat down to study.

He had never used his winter break to prepare for the oncoming quarter and cursed the Flowering again for taking away the hours of eating and sleeping which the holidays had always guaranteed him in prior years. However, what preparation he had managed to do so far already showed promising signs, so much so that he knew that he would survive the following quarter, or at least not drown completely as he'd nearly done in the past few months. As he opened his textbook, he couldn't help but feel a tiny ray of gratitude for the spare time, even if it was time he'd always used to relax in the past.

Several hours of studying flew by before he noticed his phone. He flipped up the lid to find a message from Heri.

"Im gonna cook for everyone on Xmas Eve. Wanna help? :)"

He stared at the text for several seconds.

"Sure :0)," he replied.

He clapped his phone shut, smiled, then resumed studying.

PART III
LAPIS LAZULI

CHAPTER 23

CLOSER

James trudged through the deep, empty trench that stretched on toward the full moon. The blue-lavender sky touched a thin line of light bordering the horizon, never fading in the perpetual dusk of this plane. Blades of grass poked over the tall sides of the trench so that their green tips created a ragged fringe on either side. Dust puffed up from the ground as James continued dragging his feet over rocks and dirt, adding to the dryness of the air. They had been walking through this trench forever now, and he was impatient to reach its end.

"I can't believe we're almost there," Phoenix said, staring at the moon.

He had honored E's command to keep his hood off. His wavy, brown hair, now free of weight, floated up and down ever so slightly with every step. James looked at the moon as well. Indeed, it was starting to near the gargantuan size that he'd first seen it as when he'd beheld it from beneath the tree of eyes, though that didn't make him any less impatient to reach the City faster.

"How long did you say it usually takes?" James asked.

"To get to the City? Way more than just four or five nights. I'd say it takes a minimum of a month for most humans. Maybe two weeks if you're really skilled and closer and lucky. But even then." Phoenix cocked his head as if in doubt of the odds.

James looked down at his watch. Three o'clock. Still three o'clock. Over the past four nights, he'd grown a nervous habit of checking his watch, but nothing had changed. His conviction that his watch was, somehow, counting down not only to his next encounter with the creature in the purple orb but also the moment it would break free and return fully to the Flowering had strengthened with the passing nights. Despite E's doubts as well as his own, he'd also grown surer that the creature he'd seen was, indeed, the deadly Red Calf from the Hunters' legends. When he'd shared his thoughts with the crew, they, like him, had been unable to prove or disprove his suspicions, and after several conversations, they, too, had concluded that their hope lay with Snow and the answers she was bound to have as a Shaman.

He rubbed the inner corners of his eyes as he wished for the millionth time that they could reach the City faster. Just when were they going to get out of this trench? He jumped as Bloom shoved his nose into his hand and smiled at him. James scratched behind his ears to thank him for the reassurance then let his hand graze across his spine as he trotted on ahead.

"I never would've thought of using a citizen like this," Phoenix said as Bloom resumed sniffing the dirt. "If I'd known earlier, I might have tried using some citizens myself."

"Well, it's not really 'using.' He's kind of our friend," James grumbled.

"Sorry," Phoenix said, looking sincerely apologetic. "I didn't mean it that way. It's just that it's rare enough for citizens to engage with humans like this, to help us like this. And it's so beneficial. Not just the way Bloom guides us but how we wake up next to him in a safe plane that he finds for us every night. Humans usually don't have a clue about what kind of plane they're going to wake up in. It made Roaming that much more challenging, I can tell you that."

Bloom sneezed.

"Bless you!" Lux called from behind James.

Bloom shook out his coat, smiled, then took a running start before clambering up the side of the trench. He peered down at the group.

"Finally," James murmured, happy to be making more progress on their journey at last.

As Phoenix jumped and struggled to pull himself up as well, Bloom bit into the back of his collar and dragged him onto the grass as if he were an oversized pup. James glanced behind at Blood Crow before taking Phoenix's hand. True to her word, she hadn't raised so much as a finger against Bloom and instead, had remained sullen and silent for the duration of their nights together, though James credited her compliance partially to E and Honey, who had made a point of walking behind her every night.

"How did you guys come across him?" Phoenix asked as he and James pulled Lux up.

"Who? Bloom?" said Lux. "Don't know. E found him. They got along really well, so they did call and response, and the rest is history."

"I see."

"Hurry up!" E barked at Blood Crow from below.

Blood Crow pursed her lips, clearly suppressing a retort. She continued jumping and clawing at the grass as she tried to pull herself out of the trench. James turned his back to her and followed Lux and Phoenix. Bloom's swaying tail and the crisp sound of his paws treading over the grass in quick, even steps led them down endless rows of tents. Blue and ivory stripes decorated the canvases. A breeze wandered through the rows and lifted the corners of the tent flaps to reveal a single cot within each.

"I'm assuming Bloom was the one who got the crew into doing rescue missions?" Phoenix said.

"Probably," said Lux. "I never really asked who started it. I just always thought E and Bloom were on the same page about it from the beginning.

I mean, I don't care. It's the right thing to do, so who cares who started it?"

Phoenix smiled. "True."

Despite James's initial distrust of Phoenix, he was starting to get used to him. In fact, a part of him was even starting to like him. He was calm and polite. He never took offense to anything, and though his questions rubbed James the wrong way once in a while, they tended to be insightful questions. Best of all, he was articulate. At least, more articulate than Lux. Of course, no one, articulate or otherwise, could ever replace Lux! But James had to admit that it was nice having another guy around who spoke in a way he was more accustomed to.

Still, he was far from relinquishing all of his suspicion and was waiting to see if Phoenix would live up to the tough reputation Roamers seemed to have. The Dead had been creepy enough, but they hadn't been anything like the snake woman or even the father in the mansion. If Phoenix fought as politely as he spoke, he wouldn't last long in a real battle. And there was always the possibility that he would turn out to be a coward and abandon the crew in the face of extreme danger. Though Phoenix had grown somewhat close to Lux, he still maintained his distance with the rest of the crew, and James knew that the lack of emotional ties would only make it easier for him to cut ties entirely and run away if needed.

The group stepped into a circular clearing in the grass. A single tepee stood in the middle. The full moon appeared bigger than ever and hung like a giant Christmas ornament over the tepee's peak. Bloom roved around, sniffing and snorting.

"That's close enough," Honey said, placing one hand on her gun.

Blood Crow, who had begun wandering closer to Bloom, halted and crossed her arms with a huff of frustration. Bloom smiled at the group then slipped into the teepee.

"Hey, Phoenix. Ladies first," Lux said with a grin.

"No sexism!" Honey said as Phoenix smiled and followed Bloom.

James stepped into the teepee and walked out onto a sprawling stone courtyard, where Bloom and Phoenix stood waiting for him. At the other end of the courtyard, innumerable steps led to a grand, palatial building with large columns the color of red earth. The building's tiled roof formed a black, trapezoidal mouth against a blue sky. The shadows on the building's face elongated with each step the group took so that the entire structure seemed to lean forward and inspect them as they approached. A large, rectangular plaque hung on the building's forehead, inscribed with the single Chinese character for "sky." Bloom bounded up a few steps then paused and shuffled his paws. He began to run as the group climbed after him.

"Pick up the pace!" E commanded.

The group's feet pounded up the stairs. A stone slab suddenly jutted out from beneath Lux.

"Whoa!" he cried out.

James grasped him, flung him back onto his feet, then spun around with his knife drawn at the sound of a yelp. Blood Crow was teetering on a protruding step. He sheathed his blade and resumed his pace.

"*Hey!*" she yelled.

He sprang aside as a step shot out from beneath him. He regained his balance as he continued running up the stairs.

"*Watch where you're going. If you fall, you fall on me,*" Blood Crow spat.

James rolled his eyes then did a double take as she rushed up to his side.

"Hey! Get away from him!" Honey said. She struggled to aim her gun as she dodged more slabs.

E already had her dagger in hand. No doubt she would have hurled her blade already were it not for the fact that an injured Blood Crow would have slowed down the group.

"*Your reflexes are slow,*" Blood Crow told James.

"You're the one who almost fell."

"*I'm the one who slew the Dead for you.*"

"What does that–" He sighed and shook his head. "Whatever."

"*We're almost at Lapis Lazuli, aren't we? The Roamer is right. This is record time.*"

James kept his expression blank despite the uneasiness that enfolded him. Had Blood Crow been listening in on all their conversations this entire time? Was that the real reason she had stayed so quiet? What had she managed to overhear, and how was she planning to use it against them?

"Hey! I know you heard me!" Honey shouted.

"Why are you so chatty all of a sudden?" he asked Blood Crow. He slipped his hand behind his back and signaled to E and Honey that he was all right. He wanted to find out what exactly Blood Crow had heard and what plots she was concocting.

She glanced at him, hesitated, then said, "*You wrapped my wounds after E cut me up, and you talked your crew into sparing me afterward. I'm taking a chance on you to see if you'll listen to what I have to say. If there's anyone here who might listen, I figured it would be you.*"

"If you're trying to ask about your stupid necklace, I already told you. I'll give it back to you once we get to the City."

"*You mean* Lux *will?*"

She sneered as he glanced at her. They sprang away from a slab together.

"I saw you guys passing it around the other night. Pretty clever. It might have even worked if you had tried it on anyone else. I've always been known for my good eyes."

"Good for you."

"That wolf. It really is different, isn't it?"

"What's it to you what Bloom is?"

"Don't be so defensive. I haven't touched it for the past few nights, just like I swore. And I told you before. We were only trying to help you and your crew."

"By torturing Bloom and gunning down the rest of us? Yeah, sure."

"We didn't pierce your watches, did we?"

"You missed our watches."

"We didn't miss anything!" Blood Crow said, stopping for a split moment. She hurried back to his side as he continued running up the stairs. *"We avoided your watches. We would never pierce a human's watch."*

"Yeah, right. I forgot. You never harm humans. Except when you're shooting them and pushing them into fires."

"I ... that was an accident."

"Try saying that to Honey."

"Why? So she can shoot me?" she said, looking genuinely upset.

James only shook his head in pointed disapproval.

"We honestly thought the wolf was deceiving all of you. You have to believe me. We've never seen a citizen sidle up to a human and mean well. We couldn't take any chances. It's better for you to take a few bullets than to lose your time."

She sighed as James quickened his pace. He shunted aside the memory of Heart luring him into the snake woman's lair. Even if Heart had deceived him, she was only one citizen. Hunters had no right to suspect every single citizen out there of evildoing. After all, Bloom was living proof that some citizens could be trusted.

"You've never lost anyone to the Flowering, have you? Someone in your crew? Someone you really cared for? Once you lose someone here, you learn not to take any chances."

James snorted. "You're torturing and murdering innocent citizens. There are no excuses for that."

"They're not innocent. They never are. Maybe the wolf's acting nice right now, but it won't last. Not forever. And another thing. My family doesn't torture. We kill the marked and the moulded and teach lessons to the unmarked ones that are acting up or look suspicious. If they really do look harmless, we leave them alone, and I'm telling you, that wolf isn't harmless. You guys need to listen to me and part ways with it. It's like the Roamer said. It's just not normal!"

"I don't care!" he said, stopping in his tracks and rounding on her.

She blinked rapidly as blush filled in the spaces between each of her freckles.

"I don't care. You and your family are cruel. Stop talking about Bloom. You don't deserve to. Just save your breath because you'll never convince us to leave him behind."

She stood still as he started climbing again. Listening to her had been a stupid idea. She wasn't scheming anything. She was just brainwashed, just like E had said. Maybe he should have let Honey shoot her. Although if he had, he wouldn't have found out that she had noticed them passing around the necklace. At least he had that to help rinse the bad taste out of his mouth. Stupid Blood Crow. He stomped up the last step and paused to catch his breath. The building seemed to stare down at him like a king upon his throne. He hurried after the others as they headed inside.

The air held the stale scent of dust and age. Rectangular, wooden posts interrupted the shadows, which extended into the far borders of the wide, empty building. The group ventured further in, passing post after post. James searched for the right moment to tell E and the rest of the crew what he'd learned about the necklace, but the surrounding silence amplified everything from the sound of his boots stepping across the wooden floor to the air flowing in and out of his nose.

Bloom sat down. His snout arched through the air before he nodded at E. He walked through one of the posts.

"This is it. No Man's Land," she said.

James's pulse quickened. They had traveled for several nights now, and they were finally about to step into the plane where the City resided. He hoped Phoenix's Runner really was as reliable as he had claimed. E had explained on a previous night that the land surrounding the City was infamous for its treacherous nature. Known as No Man's Land, the land shifted so quickly and frequently that even Bloom's nose would have had trouble keeping up with all the changes. Without a Runner who knew the way across, any crew could easily be destroyed, though finding a trustworthy Runner was a difficult task in and of itself. Many Runners demanded payment upfront before abandoning the crew that had hired them. Others barely knew the way across but pressed forward regardless, only to walk straight into disaster. A good Runner, though, ensured that a crew crossed No Man's Land in one piece and reached the City within the night.

He checked his watch again before following Lux through the post. He stepped into a bamboo forest. A breeze ran its fingers across the leaves, making them rustle. A stray leaf twirled at the end of an invisible thread. The yellow hue of decline colored the entire forest, yet each tree stood straight and tall with the strength of life.

"All right, Phoenix," said E. "Where's–ah!"

James drew his knife and scoured the forest for danger. But the only unusual sight he found was the stricken look on E's face.

"E?" he said.

She blinked.

"Phoenix, where's this Runner of yours? Let's not spend all night," she said as her usual stern expression fell over her face.

"We're in luck," Phoenix said. "She has a lot of posts in this forest. Follow me."

Honey ordered Blood Crow to move forward. As Blood Crow passed by, James glared at her and silently dared her to speak to him again. She merely stared at the ground, looking subdued. Bloom trotted alongside him as he made his way to E at the back of the line. He decided to use Korean just in case.

"*We need to be more careful with what we say around her. She's been listening to us all talk. She said that she saw us passing around the necklace.*"

"*Really?*" said E.

He waited for her to say more, but she only continued to walk with a far-off gaze that cared little about him or Blood Crow.

"Uh ... you okay?" he asked.

She remained silent. Most humans would have said that they were fine just to be polite, but of course, E was curt even without words. James wondered whether it would be better to walk away or to take the risk of inquiring further in what was already promising to be an awkward conversation. After a few moments of internal vacillating, he gathered his courage and decided to take the risk. E was their leader and their best fighter. If there was anyone in the group who needed to be on full alert right now, it was her. Besides, the worst that would happen was that she'd get angry and stab him, and he was used to that anyway.

"E, what's wrong? You don't seem like yourself right now."

"It's nothing. I'm just worried about the Runner."

"Okay. Is that really all?"

"Yes!" she snarled, making him jump.

He lifted his hands in surrender. He'd forgotten that E attacked with her words as well as her blades. Half wishing that she would have used a blade instead, he reached out to pet Bloom in an attempt to comfort himself. E closed her eyes under the weight of remorse.

"I'm sorry," she said.

He relaxed. "It's fine."

"It's not just the Runner or Phoenix or the Hunter. It's everything. It's the City. It's...." She fell silent again, looking more upset than ever.

"Uh-huh," he pressed.

"Have ..." she began. She ended with a sigh. Her face scrunched up, creating an expression similar to the one she wore whenever she was struggling to cut through an exceptionally large citizen. She breathed out a sharp sigh before continuing.

"Have Lux or Honey ever told you about my family?" She stared at the ground as if she were too embarrassed to look him in the eye.

"No," James said, surprised.

E had never talked about her personal life before, though he wasn't sure why she'd feel so embarrassed to talk to him about it either. But then again, she wasn't exactly the type to jump into such conversations.

"What's up with your family?" he asked.

She continued staring at the ground.

"E," he prodded as she sank into silence again. Why did she even bring it up if she wasn't going to talk about it?

She sighed again. "My mom ran into some health issues a while ago. I've had to take care of her ever since. Nothing like Lux's dad," she added, as if to assure him that her situation was nothing in comparison to Lux's. "It's not so much an illness as it was too much labor. Her body just kind of gave out at one point, and of course, I was conveniently born into the Flowering not long after her health went down the drain. I was born in the Mountains, actually. Here in this forest."

"Here? In this forest?" he exclaimed. He stooped his head slightly, glancing around for any danger his voice might have attracted. He still wasn't sure what exactly to expect here in No Man's Land. He relaxed, though, as Bloom gave him a smile that assured him all was well.

The tightness in E's expression began to loosen. It was if James's nervousness had triggered a reminder that she, as his leader, had to maintain her composure in his stead.

"Yes, in this forest," she said. "Sort of a wild coincidence. The last time I was here, my first crew was on their way to the City too. Pretty crazy, huh? Well, no. No, it's not. Most humans who come through No Man's Land only come through to get in and out of the City. I don't ... I don't know what I'm talking about anymore. I'm sorry," she said. A frown tightened her face again. She placed a hand on her forehead. "I-I know that I should talk about the things that are bothering me, and I know it's supposed to be helpful, but I just ... I don't want to either. It's all really hard to put into words. I don't know where to start."

Bloom doubled around James and nuzzled E's arm. James tried to decipher what she'd just said but came up empty-handed. Not only was she speaking in vague circles but the sight of her so clearly distressed was both concerning and slightly alarming.

"Is your mom all right? Is that what's bothering you so much right now?" he asked.

"Yes. And no. I'm always upset because of my mom. She's always in pain, and she can be so ... so difficult. I know it's not her fault, but I couldn't go to grad school because of everything. I had to work."

"What about your dad?" He regretted the question immediately.

"He's dead. Car accident. On Christmas Eve. Not too long before I was born into the Flowering, actually. I guess coming back to this forest, it just reminds me of that time. And, well, it reminds me of certain people and certain memories I'd rather forget."

"I-I'm sorry," he said, unsure of how else to reply. Maybe getting E to talk about her troubles was simply agitating her even more. Had he made her speak for nothing?

"Yeah. I'm sorry too. But," she said, lifting her chin high, "the past is not the present. You're right. I'm not myself right now. I should focus. I need to focus. It's not safe."

He pursed his lips, unconvinced that she was really okay. She did a double take at the look on his face.

"I'm fine now. Really. I'm focused, James. Besides," she said, giving him a small smile, "who else is going to take care of all of you if I don't?"

He hesitated then smiled back. "I don't know, E," he said, hoping that picking up on her joke would cheer her up further. "Maybe you should take a break. You protecting us and saving us all the time, it's starting to get old. Maybe even a little annoying. I don't know."

His grin widened as she nudged him gently in the ribs. Blood Crow twisted around to stare at them. She withdrew her gaze as E put a threatening hand on the hilt of her dagger. The flames of determination within E's eyes flared into a full blaze.

Maybe she really was okay now.

"*Did she say anything else?*" E asked.

Her firm tone further convinced him that she was all right.

"*No*. She just went on and on about how Bloom is a danger to us all," he said, shaking his hands in mock terror. "Basically, she was trying to convince me that we should ditch Bloom."

"What a moron. I wouldn't even be here if it wasn't for Bloom. He's the one who was there for me when I was all alone and needed help. I wonder what she'd say to that?"

"She'd probably say you're wrong somehow. You know what they say about the truth."

"What? That most people are too stupid to see it?"

"I was thinking more along the lines of it being a pill hard to swallow, but sure, I guess that works too."

She smiled again. Bloom's eyelids drooped as she massaged his head with her fingertips. Her smile waned.

"Bloom has something hurting inside of him too, you know. Something broken. Something that won't heal. I never knew what it was, but that black wolf the ram was eating in the tunnels ... it made me wonder if he had family issues too."

"Here!" Phoenix called.

They followed his voice into a rectangular clearing. Yellow leaves trickled down from the sky and carpeted the floor. A large human skull hung from the end of a spear that had been planted into the ground in the middle of the clearing. Someone had spray-painted an "A" on the skull's forehead, and the paint had dripped down into its sockets like bloody sweat. A red bandana had been threaded through its nostrils as if to mimic a nosebleed. Phoenix reached under the skull and withdrew a walkie talkie.

"Alex? Are you there?" said Phoenix.

"Alex *is the Runner you know?*" Blood Crow exclaimed. "Alex Lin?"

"Shut it," Honey warned, pointing her knife.

Static sounded for a few moments before a woman's voice answered in Our Word. "*This is Alex. How may I help you?*"

"Alex! It's Phoenix."

More static then, "Phoenix?"

"Yeah!"

"Roamer Phoenix?"

"Yes, this is Roamer Phoenix."

James jumped as a young woman burst out from behind the spear. Her shaved head, which sported wavy lines and zig-zags, combined with her long shorts and black tank top to give her a resolutely tomboyish appearance.

"Phoenix!" She broke into a wide, sunny smile as she clasped hands with him and embraced him. "*And Blood Crow–whoa! A knife!*" she said, staring at the blade Honey had pressed against Blood Crow's back. "*And new crew members? Where are Lion Paw and Steel Heart? Where's your family?*"

"*I got separated from them and put on house arrest for hunting that thing,*" Blood Crow said, flicking her head in Bloom's direction.

"*Whoa,*" Alex said, craning her neck forward to study Bloom with wide-eyed fascination. "*A Hunter and a citizen? Together? And not killing each other? You're going to tell me that you're in love with Copperhead next.*"

Blood Crow scoffed then smiled as Alex offered her a hug.

"So, I'm guessing you need a Runner," Alex said, smiling at Phoenix.

"We were told you'd do it for free," E said before he could reply.

"Oh, of course, of course! For Phoenix, everything is free. You don't find grade-A guys like this any old night, after all. Always willing to help others. Really a friend worth having. Just an all-around great guy. But, oh! I do have to warn the ladies here. He's already got a girlfriend," she said with a wink.

Lux oohed.

"Alex," Phoenix muttered, glancing at E.

"What? I still think Snow likes you. You really should think about it, you know. You guys would make a good couple."

Phoenix cleared his throat. "It's James's and Lux's first time in *the Iris*. Maybe you should give them the rundown."

"Oh, all right, all right. I'll lay off. But I'm just trying to look out for you. Anyway, it's whose first time?"

"Me, James. Nice to meet you."

"And me, Lux. I'm the other virgin," he said, lifting his eyebrows up and down.

Alex laughed. "I can tell we're going to have a fun Run already," she said. She shook hands with Honey and E as they introduced themselves as well.

"And this is Bloom," said E. "He's a member of our crew too. He'll be coming with us to the outskirts of the City. I'd appreciate it if you could refrain from mentioning him to other humans, though. His presence tends to draw unnecessary attention."

"Really? He's a member of your crew?" said Alex. Her smile stiffened on her face as concern widened her eyes.

"It's all right," Phoenix reassured her. "He won't cause any problems. I've been with them for a few nights now. There's nothing to worry about when it comes to Bloom."

Alex's smile defrosted. "I see. Well, then, awesome! I'm glad to have him with us."

Bloom twitched his tail. E gave Phoenix a nod of thanks, which he returned with a smile.

"Well, if there are no other concerns to address, let's get down to business! I'm known as Alexander the Great, but you can call me Alex Lin or just Alex for short. I've been a Runner for around five years now, so I'm already halfway through my tenure. I'm hoping to become an official Runner someday, though, so if you happen to run into any Head Runners in the future, I'd appreciate you putting in a good word for me. Their heads are shaved like mine, but they just have one line on the side here," she added, looking at James and Lux and pointing to the side of her head. "And their last names are always '*Shadow*.' Runners are the only group of humans in *the Flowering* that use last names, though I'm sure you already knew that."

"You're waiting to be tested? So you're a Merchant Runner?" E said, glaring at her.

"I am indeed. And I'm guessing you're not particularly fond of Merchants? Yes, I understand. No one really is, after all. I, myself, had the bad luck of being tricked into debt by a few Merchants pretty early on. That's how I ended up here to begin with. But Running turned out to suit me better anyway, so it all worked out. But anyway," Alex said, clapping her hands and rubbing them together.

"A quick rundown of No Man's Land before we proceed, especially for our newcomers here! You may know already that No Man's Land, also known as *the Iris* in Our Word, is the land surrounding the City, otherwise known as *Lapis Lazuli*. Of course, *Lapis Lazuli* is well known for the Market, the Shamans, the Tower, which is also known as *the Abode*, and of course, the shield of moonlight, which allows only humans and human creations to enter.

"That's right! Anything of *the Flowering* will be prevented from crossing into *Lapis Lazuli* by the moonlight, both citizens and objects made by *the Flowering* alike. But enough about *Lapis Lazuli*. What about *the Iris*? We know so much about *Lapis Lazuli* and what's in it, but what about the land surrounding it? What makes this land so unique? Would anybody like to take a guess? Anybody?"

"*The Iris is composed of nine distinct territories, each one known for its own geographical makeup,*" said Blood Crow.

"You want a gold star for that?" Honey grumbled.

"Wonderful answer and correct, but that would actually earn a silver star because that's not the only thing that's unique! *The Iris* is a stagnant plane, the only one that we know of in *the Flowering*. It'll never glow. It'll never disappear. A lot of shifting and changing does occur in each territory, though, with the one exception of *the Desert*. All shifts occur in clear patterns that change from month to month, and of course, we Runners work hard to track all of those patterns.

"Luckily, the boundaries of each territory never change, and certain key markers also remain stagnant, including certain rivers and specific hills and such. There's other stuff like being able to use exits to go back to the same location you were in before, all exits staying stagnant for a month before changing again, a few exits being big enough to allow large groups to go through in one go without going single-file, citizens being able to use most of the same exits as us humans, and of course, the fact that there tends to be a lot less citizens around here. The Solstice is right around the corner too, which means our Hunter friends have already started performing their annual extermination for us. Always helpful, those Hunters," she said with a wink in Blood Crow's direction.

Blood Crow raised her nose proudly in the air. E drew Bloom closer to herself.

"And now," said Alex, rubbing her hands together again and pressing them against her nose.

Her silence made James lean in closer.

"A quick rundown of my ground rules! Rule number one, always follow me. Never stray off the path or go on before me. Are we absolutely clear on rule number one? Okay. Rule number two, no guns. Guns are a no-no. Bullets and *the Iris*. Not a good mix. Neither are planes or helicopters or anything like that. The air around here isn't normal air, as is the case in most of *the Flowering* as you all well know. Rule number three, no talking from here on out unless spoken to or until I give the okay to talk again. This part of *the Mountains* is really safe, but once we get further away from here, things will get less stable. And rule number four, run like the wind if a citizen does come after us. Not a high chance but still a possibility. I'll run toward the nearest exit, and you all will follow me. Worst case scenario, we fight back together, in which case, feel free to break formation. Yes! Question."

"Which territories will we be going through?" E asked.

"Great question! We'll be going through *the Mountains* for a while longer before going over *the Great Sea* and into *the Desert*. And from there, of course, we'll cross *the Desert* and go into *Lapis Lazuli*. Any other questions? No? No? All right, then. Let's put the third rule into effect right now, which is?"

"*No talking*," said Blood Crow.

"Awesome! You guys got it. And Honey, I must ask that you not point your knife at Blood Crow and that you please return it to your belt. We're a team here, everyone, a team," Alex said as she signaled for the group to form a single-file line behind her. "All right. We'll be having a safe and hopefully fun Run tonight. Are we all ready? Great! And to James and Lux in particular, *welcome to the Iris*."

CHAPTER 24

THE IRIS

The air was cool and sweet. Ivy hugged the pine trees like green lace. The group passed mossy boulders, crossed a waterfall that fell like a bridal veil, and walked through patches of sunlight filled with the sound of chirping. As they made their way past peridot fern, a pillar of earth suddenly erupted out of the ground beside them. A tall tree on top of the pillar snapped in half, creaked forward, and stopped midair just a few feet above the group. James lowered his arms from his head as the pillar sank back down into the ground. The broken tree simultaneously sealed itself back onto the base of its trunk. Alex continued leading them forward as if nothing had happened.

Taking Phoenix along for the journey really had been the right call. If it hadn't been for him, who knew what kind of Runner the crew would have been stuck with or if they would have been able to find a Runner at all?

A waterfall thundered down into a rushing stream as the group hurried across a fallen log and toward a lush jungle. Alex ushered them one-by-one into the shade then seized E's arm and pulled her off the log just before the log shot into the air. It transformed into the size of a toothpick as it disappeared into the gray sky. Alex gave the group a bright smile and two thumbs up. She retrieved a pen and pad from a pouch on her utility belt and scribbled a note for them to read.

"Great job! Next exit leads to *the Barren Isle* then just one more exit until *the Desert*," the note read in a mixture of English and Our Word. James had never seen Our Word written out before but wasn't surprised to find that he could read the language as fluently as he spoke it.

Alex flashed a smile and lifted her thumbs again before crumpling up the note and swallowing it. They passed beneath rope-like vines and stepped over large roots that dug into the ground like fingers reaching into the warm comfort of the jungle floor. She pushed aside a cluster of gigantic leaves and stopped in front of a murky pond. Dragonflies flitted about, visiting each of the many lily pads floating on the water. She walked around the rim of the pond with both arms held out like a trapeze artist, motioned for them to follow, then jumped feet first into the middle of a ring of lily pads. James teetered along the rim before holding his breath and jumping in as well. His feet landed with a thud on wooden planks.

"No, no, no! Oh, why?" Alex tossed her hand up and groaned loudly.

"What is it?" Phoenix asked as he appeared.

"This!" she said, throwing out her hand.

James wondered what exactly he was supposed to find so offensive as he stared at the empty dock they were standing on.

"*Is this the Third's doing?*" said Blood Crow.

"Probably," Alex grumbled.

"The Third Shaman?" James said.

"Yes, the Third Shaman," said Alex. "The all-powerful Third! He's been building all around *the Iris* for the past few months. I mean, okay. Look. The man's done a lot for the Market for better or for worse, and I recognize that he's a businessman. But this? Building a dock on *the Iris*? Is he insane? Oh, if I get my hands on the Runner who sold out to him.

That Shaman is blind in more than one way! Who does he think he is? Does he really think that he can tame the territories? This land has been here since the beginning of *the Flowering*. Have some respect!"

"It is very disrespectful," Phoenix said.

James could tell that he was trying to placate Alex, but instead of calming her, Phoenix's agreement only seemed to fuel her anger.

"It is! It is disrespectful! But oh, no! I forgot. Shamans can't respect anything. Not *the Iris*, not the territories, not even *Lapis Lazuli*!" She stomped her foot then spun around to face James and Lux. "Those Shamans don't even use the territories' *Our Word* names when they talk to us. They don't use *Our Word* names for any parts of *the Flowering*, period! They just use whatever language they want, even though all the planes have been here way longer than any of us. Using the ancient language of *the Flowering* is one of the easiest ways to show respect to the land, but do they do it? No! Just no respect whatsoever. Blatant disrespect. And now they're building all this crap all over *the Iris*. Look at this. Look!" she said, stabbing her finger at the dock over and over again.

"Maybe you can come with us to the Tower. Talk to the Third, give him some feedback on all this construction," Phoenix suggested.

"No, no. I'll be in line for half the month before I get a meeting with him. And it's not like he'll care about some lowly Merchant Runner and her opinion, especially when he's not the one who has to dodge splinters and pick through rubble when all this gets upended next month!"

She drew in a deep breath then pushed her hands down as if to depress a rising column of stress. A manic smile stretched across her face.

"I apologize for the unprofessionalism, everyone. Please, follow me. We'll reach *Lapis Lazuli* soon. And, as you may have guessed, no need to use silence on *the Isle*. Once we get to *the Cliffs*, that's when the real fun will begin. Once we're there, you can just jump after me, spread out your arms, and flap like a bird. Flying is very intuitive. You'll get the hang of it without even trying."

"We're going to fly?" Lux exclaimed.

"Yes, indeed-y," Alex said. Her smile grew genuine as Lux grew wide-eyed with excitement.

E had said before that the Third was the most powerful Shaman in the City. That meant that he was likely the most powerful human in all the Flowering. Despite this intimidating reputation, though, James thought that the Third sorely needed some lessons in elementary engineering. The dock still smelled of fresh sawdust, yet it creaked and swayed as if on the brink of collapse. He doubted that any of the streetlamps lining the sides of the dock worked. Why would the Third even bother building something so big and useless on such unstable land? The whole project seemed futile and half-hearted to begin with.

Alex leapt and sidestepped across the rickety dock as she led the group forward in a single-file line. As they approached the last stretch of the dock, she stopped and squinted. Turning to the group, she held up a finger to her mouth.

A large creature hung upside down from the last streetlamp up ahead.

"No worries. I've seen this citizen before. It isn't aggressive. As long as we keep our distance, we should be fine," Alex whispered.

The creaking of the dock grew louder as they picked their way toward the citizen. It hung from its tail, which was long and tapered like a bull whip. The bony lumps of its spine protruded from its brown, lizard-like skin as knuckles would on a clenched fist. Though its face was curled into its stomach, James could still hear its deep, measured snores rumbling out from its throat.

The group followed Alex to the end of the dock and stepped onto flat, open land. Wilting grass grew in patches all across the land, which sprawled out toward a black and barren forest in the distance. The group began walking forward then stopped as Bloom halted with one paw cocked. His nose quivered before he spun around to face the citizen with bared teeth. E's machetes appeared. Crew Blue drew their weapons. Blood Crow stepped forward with her spear.

"Guys!" Alex exclaimed.

"*Lower yourself, monster! We know you're marked, and we know you're hungry!*" Blood Crow shouted at the hanging creature. She glanced at Bloom as he joined her at her side.

Four large eyes appeared, each black and round like those of a tarantula, then a grin full of sharp, triangular teeth as the monster rolled its face away from its stomach and unraveled its body fully. The dock groaned under its weight as it settled its claws onto the planks, unwound its tail from the streetlamp, and pressed its chest down into a luxurious stretch. It turned around on all fours to face the group, smiling all the while, then tilted back its head and sucked in a deep breath through its flat, bat-like nose. A black hole on either side of its lumpy head formed its ears, and a thick, pale roll of uninterrupted flesh lined its entire mouth, forming its lips. Its grin widened as it exhaled.

"*Ah, if it isn't a young Hunter. Away from your family, I see. A shame, really, that you failed to listen to the Runner. I really wouldn't have attacked. And–oh, my. What is this? Can it be? Can it truly be? A Castaway! And one of the Last's wolves at that. You're the rogue one who left the pack if I'm not mistaken. Yes, the mute.*"

Bloom's fur bristled as the monster threw back its head and filled the sky with its laughter. Honey drew a second blade.

"*Oh, but my friend. How the sight of you brings back memories. How many eras has it been since the nights of the Last, of true, seeing Shamans? Those were glorious nights, were they not? I'm sure you crave to see the Last again as much as I yearn to see the Third.*"

Bloom pulled his lips back further to reveal more of his teeth. Blood Crow's eyes darted back and forth as she continued scanning the monster's massive body.

"*Its mark is somewhere in a crevice. A wrinkle on its face, its armpits, under its tail. It's not on any visible surface,*" she told the group.

"*We can't battle here. Just leave it!*" said Alex.

"*But it's already made up its mind!*" said Blood Crow.

The monster's eyes widened as they fell on E. "*Why, but my dear. We've crossed paths before. In the hotel lobby. Surely you remember? Though perhaps we may have been acquainted before that. Your scent is familiar, somehow, as is your friend's,*" he said, nodding at James.

E lifted her machetes higher. "*I'm afraid we've never met,*" she growled.

"*I see,*" said the monster. It picked beneath its chin with a sharp claw. "*Ah, Castaway. Are not the generations further polluted with every passing age? Straight into battle without so much as an introduction. How absurd. I do miss the eras gone by.*"

"Lux, car!" E shouted.

An open off-road SUV sprang from Lux's hand. The monster leapt into the air and landed on the car, crushing the frame and blocking their way forward. The group scrambled back onto the swaying dock as the monster tossed aside the flattened car with a swat of its tail. It prowled toward them with a widening grin and glittering eyes.

"We need to get off this dock. We need to get to the edge of *the Isle*," said Alex.

"Bloom and I will distract it! Everyone else, follow Lux!" E commanded.

"What? No! It's too dangerous!"

E leapt onto Bloom's back as he ran forth. The monster sprang toward them. Bloom jumped up and sailed through the air. Fangs and machetes sank into the monster's neck. The monster roared and floundered. The dock began to splinter and sway as James and the others ran forward and threw themselves pell-mell into the new SUV that flew out of Lux's hand. Lux stomped on the accelerator. The car shot toward E and Bloom. Phoenix and Alex squished themselves into the front seat while the rest of the group forced themselves into the back. E slashed at the monster's clawing hand then somersaulted into the air. Bloom released his bite and kicked off of its neck. The group threw their weapons and forced the monster to retreat as the car swerved to a stop.

E maintained her hold on her machetes even as she slammed down arm-first onto the roll cage. She hopped down, pegged her legs in behind James to remain standing, then healed her broken bone with a sharp whip of her arm. The windshield smashed as Bloom landed on the hood. He shook out his coat then jammed himself into the back seat as well. The car sped across the dock toward land. Lux jerked the steering wheel from left to right to dodge the monster's stamping feet and lashing tail. Two rows of sharp teeth snapped inches away from the group as the car zoomed onto dirt. The monster sprang off of the collapsing dock then galloped after them. The group grated against one another as they turned around in their seats to face the monster.

"*Hold me!*" Blood Crow yelled as a spear appeared in her hand.

James and Honey gripped her legs and waist as she stood up. E leaned to the side to make room for her spear. Blood Crow drew back her spear, aimed, and threw. The monster dodged with ease.

"Do you see its mark?" E shouted over the whistling winds as Blood Crow created another spear.

"*No! Not yet!*"

"Wait! Give it here!" E yelled. She shoved her machetes under her belt.

Blood Crow handed her spear to E then crouched down to give her a clear aim. E gripped the roll cage with one hand and placed one knee on

James's shoulder. He hooked his hand over the calf of her bent leg and wrapped his arm around her other leg to secure her balance. She took careful aim then sent the spear flying into the monster's forearm. The monster stumbled before crashing into the ground and rolling across the dirt.

"*Yes!*" Blood Crow cried.

Lux and Honey cheered.

"Just keep driving straight! We're almost there!" Alex yelled.

Clouds of dust billowed behind the car as they whooshed onto a dirt road leading deep into the forest. All of the trees were black and bare like the remnants of a forest fire. Far ahead, the road ended at a cliff overlooking the sea. Bloom's nose vibrated as he sniffed the air feverishly.

"Drive the car off the edge of the cliff! Right there!" Alex shouted. "And remember to flap your arms!"

The monster jumped out of thin air. Honey screamed as the car veered. Bloom leapt out of the car and bit into one of the monster's eyes. The monster roared as it whipped its head from side to side. E hurled her machete into its neck. Spears, tomahawks, and scimitars studded the monster's body as Bloom tugged and wrenched at the monster's flesh. It let out a deafening cry as he ripped out its eye. It writhed and rubbed its face into the ground as Bloom spat out the black mess and leapt back into the car. Lux thrust his foot against the pedal. The wheels tossed up dirt. The car catapulted toward the cliff.

"What do we do?" Lux yelled as yards shrank into feet and feet shrank into inches.

"Let go of the car, and flap like a bird!" Alex bellowed.

The car shot off the cliff then dropped away from the group. For a moment, James floated, and all around him, the group hung suspended like feathers tossed into the air.

The monster lunged.

"James!" Lux cried.

Blood Crow grabbed James and flung him away from the monster's jaws. Its saliva flicked onto his face before he plummeted toward the sea. He flapped his arms then beat them fiercely as the ocean drew nearer and nearer. He struggled to catch sight of the crew but found only gray skies. He tried to grab onto something but discovered only air. He plunged face-first into the water. With bated breath and eyes shut tight, he waited to sink.

But he wasn't sinking. He was gliding. Gliding across the ocean's surface like a bird skimming the water! With his face still submerged, he gazed down at the ocean's floor. A pride of lions ran across the sand as if traveling across the Serengeti. A giant, serpentine creature slowly uncoiled and sank deeper into an underwater canyon. James lifted his head from the water. With a sweep of his arms, flew up toward the sky. Salty air streamed past his face.

The ocean stretched out far below him to meet with the murky sky in the fold of the horizon. Flocks of seagulls drifted like clouds around towering, rocky cliffs, their cries mingling with the sound of the waves below. James reveled in the vastness of everything, the openness of everything. He was no longer chained to the confines of the terrain below but was weightless, emancipated, flying free through wide, open air.

The sound of crumbling rocks made him twist his head around. The monster sat on its haunches at the edge of the cliff. Crimson blood continued dripping down its face as it glared at him with its remaining eyes. It turned and ran back into the forest. An image of the Red Calf flashed across his mind. He dipped in the air then flapped frantically to regain his balance.

"That's it!" Alex said, sweeping down to his side. "Just keep flapping! You can take a break by holding out your arms like this. There you go! That's great! Just keep gliding like that."

The tips of Blood Crow's hair fluttered like candlelight in the wind. Bloom, who lay draped across E's back, smiled down at James. Lux whooped from somewhere behind him. The group soared past the island and over miles of blue water until parched, white land appeared.

James suddenly realized that he knew this place. This was where he'd been born into the Flowering. He was back where he had started.

They flew by the Desert's massive plateaus then down toward its dry, cracked ground.

"When I tell you to, just close your arms tightly to your sides and aim for that!" Alex said, pointing.

James's heart skipped a beat. Far below, black and jagged, stood the tree of eyes.

"Fold your arms ... now!"

James pressed in his arms and zinged toward the ground like a bullet. He mimicked Alex as she lifted her chin and opened up her arms. Air blasted against his body, and he slowed as if he had opened a parachute. Together with the others, he drifted toward the tree of eyes with his arms held wide. He touched down toes-first onto the Desert.

"Excellent, excellent, excellent!" said Alex. "Flying! It never gets old. And, of course, my sincerest apologies about that citizen back there. Hopefully, next time, we'll all learn to follow directions a little more," she said, lifting her eyebrows and looking at no one in particular. "But for now, welcome to *the Desert*! This territory is known as the one that citizens avoid the most, so let's take a small breather here before making the last sprint. You all right, James?"

"Yeah, I'm good," he said, tearing his gaze away from the tree. "It's just that this is where I was born."

"Really?" Alex said, looking pleasantly surprised. "You know, in Runner tradition we say that those born into *the Iris* are destined for great things. Maybe we'll be seeing great things from you, James."

The smile with which he responded disappeared as he saw E. She stood alone beneath the tree of eyes, staring down at its protruding roots. Was she still thinking about her dead father, her ill mother? Would it be weird for him to go and comfort her?

The ground rumbled. Bloom whooshed past James. The monster that had chased them to the Cliffs suddenly burst out from beneath the arid tiles of the Desert in an explosion of white dust. Black flesh bubbled out of its socket as the eye which Bloom had torn out in the forest continued to heal. Its remaining eyes glinted with its hunger for revenge. Bloom leapt toward the monster with bared fangs.

"Watch out!" Lux shouted.

The monster slammed its tail into Bloom. James and the others ran after E as she sprinted forth. Blades flashed. The monster roared. E skidded to a halt, her eyes wide with surprise.

Phoenix slashed through the tendons of the monster's hind leg. As it stumbled, he ran toward its left hand and spun and sliced with his double-bladed sword until its clawed hand buckled on its wrist. He threw aside his sword, pulled out two knives, and leapt up before the monster could make another move. He climbed swiftly up its arm using his knives and created a new sword as he flipped onto its back. He plunged one end of his sword down between its shoulders and ran along its spine, ripping open its skin. He dodged its flagellating tail as he jumped up, blades still spinning. He landed on the ground, ready to strike again. Blood scattered across the white ground as the monster fled from him. Its limp hand began sealing back onto its wrist as, twitching and spasming, it stomped in a circle far away from the group.

James and the others stared with open mouths.

"C-Car!" E yelled, making them jump out of their amazement. "Lux, car!"

They piled into the car that sprang from his hand then zoomed past the tree of eyes.

"That was pretty hot!" Lux shouted to Phoenix.

He simply smiled in response.

The monster began galloping after them. Hope burned brightly within James as he saw the City up ahead. The monster wouldn't be able to pass through the moonlight protecting the City. Once the group crossed its blue border, they would be safe.

"What about the wolf?" Alex yelled to E.

James's eyes snapped onto Bloom. Bloom was of the Flowering too. He wouldn't be able to pass through the moonlight.

"I'll stay behind with him! Just go on without us!" E shouted.

"You can't stay!" Honey yelled.

"I won't leave him!"

"*You have no choice!*" Blood Crow shouted.

Bloom began to pant and heave. He shuddered like he was about to vomit as he stared at E. "*O ... kay. I pa ... p-pa....*"

E's face lit up. "*He can pass through the moonlight!*"

"That's impossible!" Phoenix shouted.

"Go full throttle!" E yelled.

"Yes, ma'am!" Lux shouted back.

James clung to the edge of the seat as the tires of the car whisked over the ground.

"Step on it! Step on it! Go! Go! Go!" Alex yelled.

The moon hung above them like a huge, silvery planet. They were so close to the City now that James could see the empty windows of the Tower and the countless tents he knew must belong to the Market. The monster snorted hot puffs of air as it drew closer to the car. It dodged James's and Blood Crow's spears and Honey's tomahawk and continued chasing them even as E's machete flew into its shoulder. A guttural growl rumbled out of its mouth. Bloom bared his teeth.

"Go!" Alex screamed.

The monster roared as it leapt toward them. E hurled her dagger into its face then threw her arms around Bloom as the car shot through the moonlight. Lux wrenched the steering wheel to the side. The car swerved to a halt.

The group sat still in their seats as the dust settled, their labored breaths mingling with the whirring of the engine. James unglued his hands from the seat then let out a sigh of relief as he saw Bloom safe and whole in E's arms. The group turned in unison toward the monster. It was prowling back and forth on the other side of the blue veil of moonlight, glaring at them with a face full of malice. Its missing eye bulged black and red as it continued to regrow.

"*This is not farewell,*" it rumbled.

It galloped away from the moonlight, leapt up toward the dim sky, and disappeared from sight.

CHAPTER 25

THE ABODE

What a good boy. Yes, that's a good boy. Where can I get me one of you? Where?" Alex cooed as she ruffled Bloom's mane with both hands.

"Alex, here. I know how much you like these."

"Oh, Phoenix. No," she said, backing away from the massive bag of sour candy he held out for her. "You know I always Run you for free."

"She had better Run us for free. That thing nearly ate us," Honey hissed into James's ear as Phoenix continued pressing Alex to take the bag.

James chuckled and leaned back further onto his hands. It felt good to be out of the car and sitting on solid ground. He could have sat there in the dirt forever, but he knew that they needed to get going. They needed to see Snow. They needed to find out more about the Red Calf. Time was slowly running out. He could feel it.

"Oh, and just so you know, James, the rules are kind of different here," Lux said.

"What? What rules?"

"Oh, jeez. No wonder you got so fed up with Lux before. You really do need to do better, Lux," Honey scolded.

"Sorry," he said with a grin.

"Things work a little differently when you're inside the moonlight," Honey explained. "Bullets always shoot straight as long as you're in here. You should watch it if you're too close to the moonlight, though, because stray shots that make it out of the moonlight come right back at you. Also, all humans within the City wake up the next night exactly where they were before and not on another plane. Call and response doesn't matter here either, which means that even if Bloom stepped outside of the City, Crew Blue would still wake up where we were before and not next to him like we usually do. It's one of the things that makes the City so special, but it also means that we have to stick together to stay together."

"What if we went outside of the City, and Bloom stayed inside?" James said. He wanted to make sure that he knew every rule there was to know if there was a chance of getting separated.

"Then that would be an exception. Since Bloom is the anchor, we'd all wake up next to him inside the City if we stepped out. In any other scenario, though, we'd just wake up where we were in the City regardless of where Bloom was."

"I see," James said as Phoenix finally shoved the bag of candy into Alex's arms.

"Oh, come on. You can't take a tip from an old friend?" he said.

"Oh, all right. But only because you already created it. And because we're near one of my storage units. But really, it wasn't necessary. It was a treat to see you in action again with that sword of yours. That was payment enough. And you know I owe you forever for how you rescued me."

"Stop saying it like that. It was what any decent human would have done."

"Well, there aren't that many decent humans, Phoenix. Especially around here! But yeah, you come back to me when you need another Run back. And you guys do me a favor, and take care of him for me. He lost his crew helping me out a few years back–don't try to stop me from saying it, Phoenix! He had to switch crews a lot after that but always ended up getting stuck with a bunch of bad eggs, which is why he became a Roamer. But, well, you guys seem like a decent bunch so maybe keep him around. He's kind of handy with a sword, you know?

"And you too, Phoenix. These guys seem all right, so don't be afraid to open up a little, grow more attached. No more of this giving up on everyone and being a lone ranger thing. I know you've been through a lot, but you can't just keep traveling on your own forever. It's not healthy or safe, and it makes me sad to see you wander off into *the Flowering* on your lonesome every time we see each other."

"Thanks, Alex," Phoenix said as she shook him gently by the shoulder.

"Well, all right, my friends! The Tower is over there, as you can see. I'd recommend just driving the car there and parking it. The Bodyguards will tell you what to do. It was a great pleasure Running all of you tonight. Not exactly the calm Run I'm used to giving, but hey, we made it! And it was free. I sincerely hope we meet again. *Say 'hi' to Lion Paw and Steel Heart for me when you see them again, Blood Crow.*"

The group waved goodbye to her as she saluted them and walked out of the moonlight.

"Let's get going," said E.

James jumped into the backseat with Bloom and Honey. Phoenix took shotgun as Lux took his place behind the wheel. E paused as she made to climb in then turned to face Blood Crow, who alone had remained still.

"Give her back the necklace," E told Lux. "A deal's a deal."

He pulled out the ruby necklace from his pocket and tossed it back to Blood Crow. She caught it with one hand.

"*Goodbye,*" E told her.

And that was it. The ending of Crew Blue's call and response with Blood Crow. This would likely be the last they would ever see of her. James stroked Bloom's mane and kept his eyes locked on his blue fur as E jumped into the backseat. The engine started.

He couldn't quite describe what he was feeling. Sadness? But what reason did he have to feel sad? Images of Blood Crow hurling her spear at the monster and pulling him away from its jaws as they fell from the Cliffs drifted across his mind. He tried to shake the memories away, but even as he did, he wondered if things would have been different if Blood Crow hadn't been a Hunter.

"*Take me with you,*" she said.

James looked at her.

"Go," E commanded. She gave Lux's seat two swift pats.

He accelerated then braked abruptly as Blood Crow threw herself in front of the car.

"Please!" she said.

Blood Crow's use of English surprised James almost as much as the first time he had heard Bloom speak. E bowed her head with suppressed rage then unsheathed her dagger and jumped out of the car.

"Please, I need to know what's going on," said Blood Crow, backing away. "Our legends state that the Red Calf nearly destroyed everything in the Flowering the last time it was here. If it really is returning, everyone will be in danger, including us Hunters."

"I don't care about you Hunters," E growled.

"I know you don't care about us!" Blood Crow cried out. "I know you hate Hunters, but you care about human life, don't you? If this really is what I think it is, then the darkness in those tunnels killed those Hunters. Killed, E! They died back there, and there'll be more deaths if I don't find out what's going on. I don't care if you hate us. We're still humans, and you need to care about that. Unless," she said, her face scrunching up with both fear and resolve. "Unless all of you are too scared to care about anyone else besides your own crew. Is that it? You're all just cowards?"

E's dagger flew into Blood Crow's shoulder. She yelped and fell to the ground. James and Bloom leapt out of the car.

"E. E, let's go. It's not worth it," James said, grabbing her shoulder before she could start beating Blood Crow.

"I promise I'll behave," Blood Crow said, yanking out E's dagger and curling her hand into a fist. Tears gathered in her eyes. "I won't touch the wolf. I won't touch any of you. I'll fight as much as you need me to, against citizens, humans, anything. But E, please. I need to warn the others if there's something bigger at play here."

E drew another dagger. Bloom bit into her shorts and tugged.

"We're wasting time. Let's go," said James.

"No! I won't let you leave!" cried Blood Crow.

Lux groaned. Honey stood up and aimed her gun. Phoenix stared in silence.

"I'll follow you. I'll follow you for as long as I have to! I can't just let you leave like this," Blood Crow said, standing up with E's dagger in hand.

"You can't follow us if I blast out your brains. Now move aside!" Honey shouted.

James's hand slid down toward E's wrist as he tried to devise a strategy to get her back in the car. Sure, he didn't want to torture Blood Crow or send her to her death, but to go as far as to include her in their visit with Snow and maybe even beyond. He wasn't so sure about that.

But even as he secured his fingers around E's wrist, he remembered the Hunter girl whose leg the darkness had taken and how her leg had shown no signs of regrowing. He remembered the Hunters' screams before they had disappeared and how he had felt the presence of death in the tunnels.

Was Blood Crow right? Would it be better to bring her along so that she could warn other humans of whatever dangers the Red Calf posed? James looked at his blackened watch then jumped as he realized that E was glaring at him.

"*I should've gotten rid of her before instead of listening to you. If she does something now, it'll be your fault!*" she snarled at him in Korean. "Get in!" she yelled at Blood Crow before he could stammer a reply. "We're wasting too much time."

Relief washed over Blood Crow's face as she hurried with them into the car. She squeezed herself onto the floor of the backseat and handed E her dagger.

"I know call and response isn't active in the City," said Blood Crow, "but just in case we have to go outside the moonlight for whatever reason–"

"Just do it," E growled.

"*Hello,*" Blood Crow said softly.

"*Hello,*" answered E. "Now let's move!"

Lux stepped on the pedal once more. An uncomfortable silence sat with the group as they jostled over the bumpy terrain. Honey stared at the empty land surrounding them with a sour expression that clearly marked her displeasure at Blood Crow's continued presence. In the rearview mirror, Lux's eyes flickered between Honey and the Tower. Phoenix glanced at E, who looked even more disgruntled than Honey. Blood Crow remained curled up in a tight ball on the floor. Bloom simply smiled as he stared at the vastness around them. James quickly abandoned any hopes of remedying the awkwardness in the car and instead, twisted around to take a last look at the Market behind them.

Whenever he had listened to Lux talk about the Market before, he had always painted a gilded picture of a peaceful, five-star lodging in his mind, a place where he could rest and study to his heart's content. The city of ramshackle tents he now saw completely shattered those fantasies. What few humans he spotted kept their heads low and scurried like vermin into the Market's many dark entrances. Bloom shoved his wet nose into his face and licked him as if to comfort him.

"We should hide Bloom before a Bodyguard sees him," Phoenix said. "I'm sure the Shamans will want to inspect him, especially the Third. He'll want to know how he passed through the moonlight."

Images of robed strangers dissecting Bloom on a metal table flew through James's mind. He clutched Bloom's mane. Bloom gave him another gentle lick before resting a serene gaze on E. She stared back at him with a sad expression before nodding. Shouts of surprise rang out as Bloom leapt out of the car and disappeared into the dust trailing after them.

"Don't," E said as Lux made to turn the car around. "He'll find us later."

A sudden gust of wind kicked up a thick haze of dust, obscuring all the land around them. James forced his attention back onto the Tower up ahead. The massive structure leaned back slightly as it stretched up toward the moon. Rows of large archways lined each story of its circular, stone body. James glimpsed through the swirling dust a power plant station puffing out white steam as it fed electricity to the stone behemoth. Bells chimed softly in the distance.

"Phoenix," said E.

"Yeah?"

"I'm going to need your help navigating things once we're inside. None of us have been in there before. Plus, you're the only one who knows Snow."

He glanced at her then said, "Understood. Leave it to me."

Another blast of wind parted the dust, revealing a man with dark brown hair jogging toward them. The thick fabric of his black vest bulged out to form a large "X" across his chest. Numerous weapons and objects varying in size and function hung from his utility belt. The dust began to settle around them as Lux pulled the car up next to him. E rose slowly from her seat.

"*Good evening. Purpose for visitation?*" the man asked. A bracelet of bells jingled on his wrist as he clicked his pen and held up a clipboard.

"*We're here to see the Twelfth,*" Phoenix said, leaning forward.

"*The Twelfth?*" the man said, raising an eyebrow. He did a double take at E.

"Marcus," she said.

"E! What the–"

The man burst into laughter as she leapt out of the car. She clasped hands with him before flinging her arms around his neck. They laughed together as he squeezed her in a hug and spun her around.

"E, how are you? What are you doing here?" the man exclaimed as they stepped apart.

"Just a quick visit with one of the Shamans, but never mind me. Look at you. A Bodyguard! I mean, you know I always believed in you but to actually see you like this. In full gear and everything!"

James stared as they continued talking. He wasn't sure what threw him off more, the fact that E was chatting and laughing like a normal girl or that she was so well-acquainted with someone outside of Crew Blue. He looked at Lux and Honey. Both of them shook their heads, wide-eyed and clearly clueless.

"Where are your machetes? You still use them, right?" the man said.

"Of course. I'm way better with them now too," E bragged.

"Better? Oh, man. I really won't stand a chance now."

"How are the others? Are they still around?"

"Some of them made it, but a lot of them found crews and left the City after the Combats finished. I guess the Flowering isn't so scary anymore after all that training. But anyway, look at me just standing around and not doing my job. What can I do you and your crew for?"

"I'm called Phoenix," he repeated as he leaned forward again. "I was given immunity from reading and payment for returning the Twelfth a little over a year ago. My name should be on the list."

"Oh, yeah! I remember you. You came here with Alex Lin, right? Let's see here. Ah, yes. There you are. All right, then. You guys are all checked in. I'll let the guys up front know that you're here," he said, patting a walkie talkie on his belt. "If you guys can park your car around the side of the Tower over there then go to the front, one of the other Bodyguards will see about getting you to the Twelfth. It shouldn't be that hard. No one really visits her."

"All right. We should get going, then. But it was so nice seeing you again, Marcus," E said, embracing him once more.

"Same here. Man, I so wish I weren't on duty right now! I'd take you out for a drink for old time's sake."

"Why? So I can clean up after you? I'm tired of mopping up all your puke, Marcus!"

They laughed again and began reminiscing about nights full of brawling, eating, drinking, and vomiting. James exchanged looks with Honey and Lux again.

"Ah, E," said Marcus as he grinned and rubbed tears of laughter away from his eyes. "Those nights really were the best. I really miss the old crowd. Oh, but uh...." His smile faded. "Speaking of the old crowd, just so you know. Kit is still in the Market. He's been looking for you."

E stepped back.

"Sorry! Sorry if I ... I just thought you should know."

"No, no. It's good that you told me. I'll keep that in mind. Thanks, Marcus. I-It was really great seeing you again."

He nodded and waved them off as Lux drove to the side of the Tower.

"What," said Honey, snapping her head toward E, "was that all about?"

"Who's Kit?" said Lux, frowning.

"*You used to party with Bodyguards?*" said Blood Crow. Her expression seemed to question the balance of all she knew.

"I thought you said you'd never been in the Tower before. At this rate, you'll be the one who needs to take the lead inside," said Phoenix.

"Everyone, hush," E said. She smiled as she shook her head. "Marcus is an old friend of mine. We used to train together when he was a Bit. Bit stands for 'Bodyguard in Training,'" she added, looking at James. "I used to fight a lot of Bits, actually. They're tough, and they have good sportsmanship."

"Well, that explains where your fighting skills came from," Phoenix mumbled.

"And Kit?" said Honey with a sly grin. "Who's he?"

"He's nobody, Honey."

James remained quiet despite his strong suspicion that Kit had been much more than a "nobody." Honey and Lux continued peppering E with questions as the car's wheels rolled onto smooth, black pavement. Squadrons of men and women appeared far off to the group's right, standing straight-backed and silent as a man in a black vest shouted orders. As another black-vested Bodyguard waved a traffic wand and guided Lux to an empty parking space, the squadrons cried out in a unified, "*Yes, sir!*"

A raucous din of tinkling bells broke out as the men and women paired off and began sparring with one another. James winced as a woman kicked in a man's teeth then hurled another kick into her opponent's neck. James climbed out of the car and quickened his pace as she swung her foot down into the man's testicles.

"So, you used to practice every night with guys like that?" Lux asked E with a dumbfounded expression.

"Yes, Lux," she said with a small smile. "Is that so surprising?"

"I-I guess not. I mean, you can kick anyone's ass. We all know that. But still!"

They found a long line of humans standing in front of two humongous, wooden doors that marked the Tower's entrance. Every age and ethnicity looked accounted for in the diversity that composed the line. Words had been carved into a stone arch above the doors in Our Word.

"*The strong will aid the weary*," James read aloud as Phoenix approached a Bodyguard.

"*You'll have to wait until tomorrow night!*" the Bodyguard shouted at a gray-haired woman in line. "*The Third is a busy man. You're not the only one who wants his advice!*"

The bells on his wrist jingled as he raised his baseball bat and made to hit the woman. He paused as Phoenix tapped him on the shoulder.

"*What do you want? Get back in line!*"

"*We spoke with* Marcus *up front. We're here to see the Twelfth.*"

"*The Twelfth? Oh, right. The guy with immunity. Fine. Follow me.*"

The woman in line cowered as the Bodyguard feigned a strike to her head. He walked to the doors, banged his fist on the wood, then spat on the ground. The rusted, brass hinges emitted a long groan as the doors cracked open. Bells shivered from all directions as the group stepped into a vast lobby made of stone. Several other Bodyguards heaved their weight against the doors, making them boom to a close.

The place smelled old, like rotting velvet. A large, round stone platform stood under a blue beam of moonlight spilling down from the Tower's open ceiling high above. Pillars and gaping, dark archways encircled the wide space. What people were present stood huddled in groups, muttering and hissing their conversations.

"*Wait here*," the Bodyguard said before sauntering off.

The group watched him hail another Bodyguard standing beneath one of the archways. He snickered and whispered with his friend as they disappeared into the shadows together.

Honey rolled her eyes. "Anyone want to make any bets on how long he's going to take before coming back?"

"I'll create any car you want if he comes back before I count to nine hundred," said Lux.

"He's not really going to take that long, is he?" James asked Phoenix as Honey and Lux shook hands.

"I don't think so. It might take a little longer if Snow's Guide is doing his regular round of business in the Market right now, but even then, as long as she approves our visit, we'll see her within the night."

James stared up at the open ceiling. After a few moments of restless fidgeting, he sat down on the moonlit platform. He stared at his watch as Honey and Lux sat down on either side of him.

"No other changes. Right, James?" said Lux, peering at his watch as well.

"No. Not yet."

"*Do you still feel like it's counting down to the next time you see the Red Calf?*" Blood Crow asked.

"And to when it breaks free from the purple orb and returns fully to the Flowering?" added Phoenix.

"My gut instinct says 'yes.' But like we all said before, there's no way to prove anything I'm feeling," James replied. He sighed again and rubbed his forehead. "I just hope Snow knows something about all of this."

"She will, James," said Lux. "You guys saw each other in that golden eye. There's a connection there. And she's a Shaman. She'll know something about all of this."

"Did you say something about a golden eye?"

James's hand sprang to his knife as the group whirled around. A pale-skinned man beamed at them. Suspicion wriggled within James despite the stranger's smile. Maybe it was the manner in which he had combed his hair neatly to one side or the way his suit matched his body in perfect, tailor-made fashion, but the man reminded James of the moulded father in the white mansion.

"*Snake Eyes*," Blood Crow said, spitting out the name as if it held a foul taste. She stepped up to front of the group. "*What business do you have with us?*"

"Oh, my apologies. I overheard your conversation and thought that we could have a light chat."

"We're not interested in doing business," Phoenix and E said in unison.

"Oh, come now. Don't jump to conclusions! This isn't about business. There's no better place than *the Abode* to make some new friends, and there's not exactly a lot to do while waiting around here besides talk with one another. Plus, I think Three would be very interested in what you all were talking about. I'm the Third's Head Merchant, by the way. And as your friend just pointed out, you can call me Snake Eyes."

"*Be gone from us! We have no interest in conversing with a traitor who left the Hunters' Way to pursue goods and power,*" said Blood Crow.

Snake Eyes chuckled. The bells on his wrist clanged in dull, flat tones as he folded his hands over his stomach. "Oh, Hunters. Always yelling about something. And you all wonder why I left the fold."

"Snake Eyes," a deep voice called from the shadows.

"Certus!" he said, throwing his arms wide. "We have some visitors here. They were talking about a certain Red Calf and a golden eye?" His brow creased just enough to create a perfect balance of curiosity and concern.

Bells rang low and mournful from the belt of the man who walked toward them. Massive muscles covered his body like heavy slabs of armor. His long, black hair lay on the nape of his neck in a low ponytail. His dark brown eyes darted from Snake Eyes to the group. Snake Eyes's smile hitched up slightly to one side, transforming into a sneer, before sliding back into a cheerful smile.

"Well, Certus? Do you think the Third would be interested in meeting with them?" Snake Eyes asked.

"We are here for the Twelfth, not for the Third," E growled.

Snake Eyes paid her no attention but continued smiling at Certus, who glared back at him for several moments before addressing the group.

"I apologize for the inconvenience, but I must ask that you all come with me. I am called Certus, and I am the Third's Guide. I assure you that the Third will reward you handsomely for your time. Please, follow me. I will take you to the Twelfth afterward."

"We are here only for the Twelfth!" E snarled.

Certus waved a massive hand. More bells jingled to life as Bodyguards poured out from the shadows and surrounded the group.

"Don't!" Phoenix said as E's machetes appeared in her hands.

Honey aimed her gun, Blood Crow her spear. Lux held up his katana. James held out his knife with one hand and raised his spear above his head with the other as he crouched into a battle stance.

"E, it's against the laws of the Tower," Phoenix said in a low voice. "If we break the laws now, they'll never let us see Snow."

Blood Crow and James drew closer to one another. He scanned their circle of enemies. If these Bodyguards were anything like the ones training outside, the fight would be a brutal one, though with E and Phoenix, the group could definitely take them on. How many more Bodyguards lay hidden and ready to join the fight was the real question.

"Again, I apologize for interrupting your time with the Twelfth. The sooner we meet with the Third, the sooner I can escort you to her," said Certus.

E glared at him then at Phoenix, who held her scorching gaze. Uneasiness stirred on the Bodyguards' faces as she pierced them each with a black glare. Several of them shifted away from her. Certus frowned at his men as E lowered her machetes.

"Stand down," she commanded the group.

They obeyed. James remained wary of any sudden movements as he sheathed his knife and set the butt of his spear down on the floor.

"Thank you for your patience. I'm afraid I must ask you to hand over any weapons that are larger than a dagger as a safety precaution before we proceed," said Certus.

"'Safety precaution,'" E said with a snort. "Adding to the Third's stash of large weaponry tonight, is that it? How many other crews have you stolen from so far tonight?"

Certus didn't answer but nodded at a tall Bodyguard whose large muscles nearly rivaled his own. Though the man stepped toward E in response, he avoided eye contact with her and made no attempts to take her machetes. She snorted again then held out her blades. He hesitated then took them with two hands as if he were accepting a sacred gift. He gave her a deep bow before scurrying back. Curiosity stirred in Certus's eyes as he looked at the Bodyguard and E.

"Please put these on your wrists and follow me," Certus said as he handed over several bracelets with bells. "Snake Eyes," he said before turning.

Annoyance twitched on Snake Eyes's face. He snapped his fingers. A group of men who'd been lazing about on the opposite side of the lobby jumped to their feet. Some snatched up the boxes and bags strewn around them. Others hoisted up a wooden litter that boasted giant cuts of cooked meat. As the Bodyguards hurried the group past stone pillars, Blood Crow passed James one of the bracelets. The cold metal of the bells kissed his wrist as they moved deeper into the shadows.

A cloud of jingling followed the group as they marched swiftly through long, stone hallways, along balconies, and up countless stairs smoothed by the hundreds of feet that had preceded them. James leaned away from the Bodyguards and tried to mask his growing urge to grab his knife again.

Why was the Third so interested in the Red Calf and its golden eye? Snake Eyes's eagerness to learn more about the group's conversation and the way in which Certus had forced them to come with him implied that any information about the Calf was of great importance to the Third. James wondered only briefly if he should tell the Third about anything he'd seen before deciding to keep his mouth shut. Any man who leapt to using coercion to get what he wanted was not a man he could trust.

The Bodyguards led them down a cold corridor, where bright lamps hung down at intervals from the ceiling. Thick cords snaked along the ceiling and walls. The clamor of the bells dimmed into sporadic jingling as they halted in front of a door made of handsome, dark wood and wrought iron. Certus waved his hand. All but two of the Bodyguards marched off. He stared at Snake Eyes, who flicked his hand as if swatting away a fly. The band of Merchants set down their goods then disappeared down the corridor with the remaining two Bodyguards. A burst of muffled laughter sounded from behind the door. Certus rapped his knuckles on the wood before pushing. Warm air and the rich, chocolatey aroma of fresh coffee welcomed the group in.

CHAPTER 26

THE THIRD

odyguards stood sentinel along the smooth, curved walls of the Third's opulent office. Black bookcases with diamond-paned glass doors showcased gilded books, gold and silver trinkets, and large cigar boxes. A black table with lion claw feet displayed desserts, pastries, coffee, and tea. Silverware and china sparkled on both ends of the table.

In the middle of the room, a group of men and women were seated on velvet furniture. They whispered to each other in rapid Spanish as they clutched cups of steaming coffee and reached in turns for an assortment of biscuits on a low glass table. Traces of laughter lingered on their faces as they gave their rapt attention to a man sitting behind a solid, wooden desk.

The Third Shaman.

James might have thought the Third's garb to be peculiar had he not already seen Snow wearing the same red sash and blue and white, hooded robe within the Calf's golden eye. Abundant, pitch-black hair lay beneath his hood. Only a few wrinkles traced his smooth skin. The cloudy film of blindness barely muted the colors of his eyes. Unlike Snow's eyes, which had been dark blue, shocking turquoise colored what should have been the whites of the Third's eyes and blended into the golden brown of his irises. James continued studying his face as he tried to determine if he looked more Korean or Chinese.

A man sitting on one of the velvet couches turned to speak to the Third. *"Thank you, Three,"* he said in Our Word. *"We've been having this argument in our crew for a while now. It's a relief to finally come to a conclusion."*

"It was my pleasure. And I'm glad we were able to examine a few of your battle memories as well," the Third replied with a sincere smile.

"Absolutely. A poor grip on the hilt. Who would have thought?"

"Who would have thought? Certus, Snake Eyes, *did you know our visitors traveled for nearly four months to see us? I think that's a new record, don't you?"*

"Yes, my liege," said Certus.

"Definitely a record!" said Snake Eyes, throwing his arms wide and beaming. *"If you'd like, I'd be happy to have some of my boys show them around our claim. All of the best spots."*

"Oh, no," the man said. *"That won't be necessary. We couldn't impose on the Third like that after all of his advice. Receiving his wisdom is more than enough for me and my crew."*

"Oh, come on. Don't be like that," said Snake Eyes. *"Our claim has the best casinos, dining experiences, drinks. And I'm sure you've heard about our weapons. The best in the Flowering."*

"W-Well, yes, of course. Everyone knows how splendid Turquoise is, and the weapons too. But the best spots in Turquoise. Well, the payment can be—"

The man gasped then clamped his mouth shut. One of his crew members elbowed him. Several of them looked at the Third with terrified expressions. The Third, however, responded with a pleasant smile devoid of offense.

"My Head Merchant and his men will be sure to show your crew a wonderful time. Please wait for him in the lobby. This week will be on me. A gift for all the effort you and your crew have made to see me."

"Oh, th-thank you! Thank you very much. This really is a gift," the man said as his crew members' terror turned into glee. *"Are you really sure there's no other payment we can offer you before we leave? You've seen the places I've been to. I can create some great dishes for you if you'd like."*

"Oh, no. That's perfectly fine, but thank you very much for the offer. And thank you again for stopping by. I hope we can meet again very soon."

The visitors shook the Third's extended hand before bowing to Certus and following a Bodyguard out of the room.

"Certus, my apologies for the delay," said the Third as the door closed. *"I can hear that you've brought me some visitors."*

"Actually, these are my guests," said Snake Eyes, shoving his way through the group.

"Is that so?" said the Third with a hint of sarcasm.

Certus smirked. Annoyance cracked Snake Eyes's smile.

"Three," Phoenix said, stepping forward. "I'm called Phoenix. You granted me immunity over a year ago when I brought the Twelfth to *the Abode*. This is my crew, which I know my immunity applies to as well. We came here to speak with the Twelfth, but your Head Merchant and Guide demanded that we be brought here instead. We don't quite understand why."

"We befriended one another in the lobby over a conversation about the Red Calf and its golden eye," Snake Eyes interjected. "They wanted to speak to Twelve about the matter."

The Third's expression remained blank in the brief silence that followed.

"I see," he said. "Well, I certainly remember you, Phoenix. You made quite an impression the last time you were here. A very positive one, of course. Please, sit down. Would any of you like some coffee or tea? We have the best of both here."

"No, thank you," Phoenix replied as Certus gestured for the crew to sit.

"Are you sure? Magnus, can you get me some more coffee, with cream this time? Well, we'll set out some refreshments just in case you change your minds during our meeting. Aren't our bodies in the Flowering wonderful? We never have to worry about what food allergies anyone might have!"

Snake Eyes chortled as did a few of the Bodyguards. Honey turned to stare at James with an expression that asked, "Really?" He patted her on the shoulder and steered her toward the velvet couches. He was used to sycophantic behavior. An abundance of it always followed the executives in his company. However, the level of ingratiating attitude in the room and Snake Eyes's slimy behavior in particular not only made James want to take a shower but also provided irrevocable proof that the Third could not be trusted. After all, a man who loved flattery was no man at all.

The warmth that lingered on the fabric of the couch made James grimace despite the memory foam that molded around his body to form the perfect support. The bells on the group's wrists jangled softly as they, too, sat down. A Bodyguard brought the Third a new cup of coffee before throwing the previous cup into the trash, saucer and all. Certus replaced the biscuit assortment that had been sitting on the coffee table with a large tray of pastries, cookies, coffee, cream, and sugar for the group to enjoy.

James gazed at the swirls of steam rising from the cups. In Reality, most humans avoided coffee out of fear that the caffeine would ruin their sleep cycle, and of course, most would never waste a creation on something so trivial in the Flowering. To see cups of hot coffee right in front of him–coffee that he could actually drink–felt as surreal as many of the citizens and landscapes he had seen out in the planes. Lux closed his eyes as he breathed in the aroma.

"Well, then. On to business," said the Third. "Snake Eyes, do you mind postponing our meeting by a few moments so that I can speak with your guests privately?"

"Absolutely. Take your time. Oh, and your tribute is outside. The Bodyguards in particular will love what we've brought tonight."

"Wonderful. And do you mind if we conduct your reading before you leave? We can dive straight into business afterward that way."

"Now?" said Snake Eyes, glancing at the group.

"Yes. I'm sure your guests won't mind. They are your guests, after all," the Third said with a pleasant smile.

"W-Well, yes. Yes, of course. That sounds fine."

Snake Eyes swallowed then stepped up to the Third's desk. The bells on the hem of the Third's sleeves chimed as he rose from his seat. Striding past Certus and rounding the corner of his desk with quick and sure steps that seemed to defy blindness, he came to a stop in front of Snake Eyes, who knelt before him.

"May I?" he said, holding out both of his hands on either side of Snake Eyes's head.

"Of course."

The Third placed his hands against Snake Eyes's temples. Snake Eye's gaze grew distant so that a slack, unfocused expression replaced the slyness that had lurked on his face. The Third glared into thin air as if he were focusing on an invisible book hanging open in front of him.

"This is my first time seeing this," Honey whispered to James.

"Seeing what?"

"A Shaman reading memories. They can read any and all of your memories from the Flowering and Reality, even the ones you can't remember, and they're in total control while they do it. See? He's practically a vegetable."

The Third removed his hands. Snake Eyes blinked then looked up at the Third, his eyes clear and focused again.

"I'm glad to see that your daughter is doing so well in high school, and I see you've mended your argument with your wife. I hope my advice came in handy?" said the Third.

James squirmed in his seat and clamped his hand over his wrist to silence the bells on his bracelet. No matter how detestable Snake Eyes was, it was still wrong for the Third to address his personal details from Reality so publicly. Was this the Third's way of asserting his dominance over Snake Eyes? A subtle threat to let him and everyone else know that he was in control?

"Your advice always comes in handy, my liege. You know how much I value your wisdom," said Snake Eyes.

"Good. I'm very glad to hear that. We'll discuss your vacation plans tonight as well. You deserve some rest and relaxation."

"Thank you for remembering. I look forward to our discussion."

"Aurelius, Cyrus, please escort Snake Eyes to the lobby and remain there until Certus sends for you. Magnus, Felix, please take our tribute to the Black Room."

Snake Eyes followed the Bodyguards out of the room and closed the door. The group now sat alone with Certus and the Third.

"I apologize on behalf of my Head Merchant," said the Third. "I saw how he inserted himself into your conversation down in the lobby. I'll be sure to remind him to treat our visitors with more respect. It's no excuse, but I'm sure you know how Merchants are. Always trying to get ahead, especially with their superiors, even if said superior can read their memories. A bit moronic really, but well," he said, leaning back in his chair and sighing. "Let's have some proper introductions. I'm Three, and you've met Certus, my Guide. By what names may we call all of you?"

Starting with E, the group took turns introducing themselves.

"Wonderful. And what brings you to our side of the Flowering, and how may I help you with it?"

"We came to see the Twelfth," said Phoenix. "I told my crew about how I had rescued her. We thought we could come pay her a visit."

"Pay her a visit so that you could discuss something about a golden eye?"

"It was just something we saw," Phoenix with a shrug. "We thought it might be interesting news from the outside since she can't ever leave the City and see the planes for herself."

"I see. Now, pardon me for asking, but in the lobby, Lux mentioned something about James and the Twelfth seeing one another in a golden eye, which, I'm assuming, belonged to the Red Calf you were all talking about. Could you please elaborate on that?"

James could sense the group's unease despite their silence. The Third might as well have been standing with them in the lobby earlier. His physical blindness only made his omniscience more unnerving.

"I'm afraid our conversation had nothing to do with business matters or even the Shamans at large. It was only a matter of friendly conversation, so I'm uncertain where your concern is coming from," said Phoenix, who remained as calm as ever.

"I understand," said the Third. "And what about James's watch?"

"What about it?" Phoenix asked politely.

"Is that something I can help you with?"

"It's not something I like talking to strangers about," James said quickly.

"Strangers including the Twelfth?"

"I'm sure the Twelfth will be all right," E interjected. "I think it's reasonable to feel uncomfortable showing something strange about yourself to someone who keeps asking rather than someone you intended to tell. Although we do appreciate your willingness to help us."

Though E's tone had remained even, James felt a prick of annoyance in her words.

The Third grinned. "My apologies if I was too intrusive. I appreciate your acknowledgement, however, of how I'm only trying to help. It's my duty to keep on top of all the on-goings in the Flowering, both for the good of the other Shamans and, of course, for those visiting *the Abode* for our advice."

"Yes, we've heard about the many things you've done here in the Tower as well as in the Market. You're a shrewd man. It would be moronic to think otherwise," said E.

James couldn't tell if she was giving the Third a compliment or a back-handed insult. He was glad to see Phoenix lean ever so slightly against her arm in a silent warning to stop. To his surprise, though, the Third's grin only widened. He seemed rather amused, even impressed, with E's daringness.

"Yes, well, I'm not going to be modest about how hard I've worked to build what I have. Or, should I say, how hard we've worked to build what we have. Certus and my Bodyguards make quite the team here, making sure that everything is spinning the way it should. Of course, I've received my fair share of criticism for what I've done, with the Market in particular. But no one can deny that there's more space than ever before for humans who wish to find rest, or even to stay permanently, if that's their situation."

"The City definitely offers protection and rest for many humans in need," said Phoenix, bringing the topic to an end.

The Third leaned back in his chair again. Though his blind eyes stared into emptiness, they seemed, somehow, to contemplate Phoenix as if there were something about him that he couldn't quite place his finger on. Blood Crow snatched up a cookie from the coffee table, shoved it into her mouth, and chewed loudly before slurping down some coffee and setting the cup forcefully back down onto its saucer. Honey and Lux began eating and slurping as well. Their eagerness to leave couldn't have been clearer. The Third chuckled.

"Well, I apologize for taking up so much of your night. You must be tired from your journey. Certus, can you please show our visitors to the White Room? They can wait there for the Twelfth."

"That won't be necessary," Phoenix began.

"Nonsense," the Third said, cutting him off. "You can hold your meeting there. I doubt the Twelfth's quarters are nearly as comfortable. Certus, take the others and escort our visitors to the White Room then bring Snake Eyes to me."

"Yes, my liege."

A buzz sounded as the Third reached under his desk. A knock immediately rapped against the door before Bodyguards marched into the room. Phoenix and E rose from the couch, their faces devoid of the panic that had begun to surge within James. Was the Third so intent on learning what they'd seen that he was willing to hold them hostage now?

"It was truly a pleasure meeting all of you. If you need my help with anything, please don't hesitate to ask," said the Third.

"We'll keep that favor in mind," E retorted.

The Third grinned once more.

Certus and the Bodyguards surrounded the group then led them out of the room and down the corridor. As they hurried along a balcony, a burst of laughter rang out from the lobby far below. James peered over the parapet to see Snake Eyes and his men engaged in what appeared to be a highly amusing conversation. Blood Crow looked down at them with a livid expression bursting with the desire to spit on them all. James half wished that she would.

The group hadn't traveled far from the Third's office when they arrived in front of a pair of wide, iron doors. The Bodyguards formed a semi-circle around the group as Certus unlocked a large padlock, removed the chain wrapped around the doors' handles, and opened the doors to a conference room. A few ceiling lights illuminated identical, white office chairs and a long, oval table in the otherwise dimly-lit room. A projector hung from the ceiling above the table. A massive dry erase board hung on the right wall. The countertop running along the back wall flaunted a display of wines and liquors, boxes of cigars and cigarettes, as well as finger sandwiches and other hors d'oeuvres.

"Please help yourselves to any of the refreshments. I will bring the Twelfth or her Guide to you once they become available," said Certus.

E marched past him without a word, leading the group into the room. Once he had closed the door, she held a finger to her mouth and leaned her ear against the door.

"He's locked us in," she said. "He's leaving a few of them behind to guard us."

The group groaned. Lux wrapped his arms around his head as if it were about to explode. James slumped into a chair and massaged the inner corners of his eyes.

"Great. That's just great," said Honey. "First that monster out in No Man's Land and now the Third. Does the whole universe just not want us to meet with Snow?" She threw herself into a chair and allowed velocity to wheel her across the room.

"Blood Crow, you've been inside the Tower before with your family, right? During the Solstice?" said Phoenix. "Has anything like this ever happened to you before?"

"*No,*" she said, plopping down into a chair with an exhausted sigh. "*We were never hauled off like this. Or imprisoned.*"

"The Third's seen something too. There's no other explanation," said E, leaning both of her hands on the table. "I got the feeling that he's in the dark about a lot of this, though, just like we are. There was something about his voice. Did you guys get that feeling too?"

"I don't know. I couldn't tell," James said. "Whatever his deal is, though, he has questions and wants our full cooperation."

"Well, he's not getting it. I'm not selling out to some rich, creepy guy," said Lux as he pulled himself up next to Phoenix. "He had us dragged all the way up here and locked up. No way I'm cooperating."

"You said it, Lux," Honey grumbled as she rolled up next to him.

"*At least the Third's behavior confirms that there's something bigger at play. Maybe his interest in the Red Calf is confirmation that it really is returning to the Flowering,*" said Blood Crow.

The group murmured in agreement.

"Do you know where Snow might be? We need to find her," James said to Phoenix.

"I don't know exactly where, but if I had to guess, she's probably on one of the lower floors. I think we're on one of the higher levels for the Shamans' offices right now, and if the most important Shaman gets a higher floor for his office, then Snow would probably get one of the lowest for hers. Her living quarters are probably near the base of the Tower too."

"*I think I've heard rumors along those lines,*" said Blood Crow.

"Me too," said E.

"She's really that low on the totem pole? I thought the Shamans prized the Twelfth," James said.

"They prize finding the Twelfth," said E. "Once they confirm that the new Twelfth can't give them back their sight, they send the Twelfth straight to the bottom as punishment. It's been like that for every Twelve that's ever walked into the Tower."

James swallowed the rant of frustration that threatened to erupt out of his mouth. Even if the group managed to knock down the door and overcome the Bodyguards outside, the Third had a whole army of other Bodyguards that would be sure to intercept them. Plus, the group didn't even know where Snow was located. Which of the many hallways would they need to travel down? Which of the countless flights of stairs?

Metal scraped against stone somewhere within the walls. James crossed his arms and attempted to ignore the teeth-clenching noise. He flung his arms away from himself as metal scraped again.

"What is that?" he complained as he searched the ceiling.

"*Don't yell. They might hear us outside,*" Blood Crow said suddenly. She pointed at one of the walls.

There, in a large, rectangular hole where the grate of the air vent had once been, was a pair of eyes staring out at them from within the dark.

"You," said a voice in the wall. "You're the one who saw the Twelfth, aren't you?"

CHAPTER 27

SNOW

hairs rolled and toppled as the group sprang to their feet and pointed their weapons. The voice in the wall scowled. The eyes retreated. A pair of feet swung out and landed on the floor. A tall, Black teenager with a shaved head and wiry muscles stepped into the light.

"You. In the middle. You're the one who saw the Twelfth, right? In the golden eye?" the teen said as he pointed at James.

"Who wants to know?" said E, her dagger at the ready.

"I'm called Zilch. I'm the Twelfth's Guide. Follow me. I need to get you all out of here before the Third tightens security on you guys."

James's eyes swept across the teen's belt. Unlike Certus, he wore no bells.

"Show us your identification," Phoenix demanded.

"Never mind identification. We don't have time!" hissed Zilch.

"Do as he says," E snarled, holding up another blade.

The teen pursed his lips then rolled his eyes. He marched over to the table and flung his foot onto the surface. He unlaced his boot, tugged down the collar, then pulled back the hem of his black jeans. James flinched. The number twelve, written in Our Word, bulged out above the teen's ankle like a small, mutated bone. The shape slowly traveled a centimeter in one direction before traveling another centimeter toward the other, stretching and pushing against different parts of the teen's skin as it tried to find its way out of a body that wanted to reject it.

The mutilation had obviously been purposeful, but James doubted it had been self-inflicted. Someone else must have cut open his skin and shoved the number inside before allowing his natural healing abilities to seal in the shape. He hadn't known that it was possible to manipulate healing in such a way. It was revolting.

"Satisfied?" Zilch said as he tied his laces again.

"Yes," Phoenix said, sheathing his dagger. "Thank you for showing us."

E nodded at the others. They lowered their weapons as well.

"Good. Now that we have that out of the way," Zilch grumbled. "All of you, take off your bracelets. Just leave them here, and follow me. Whatever you do, do not make any noise. We won't be soundproof."

"Where are you taking us?" said James.

"To the Twelfth, of course. Who else? Now be quiet and follow me."

Zilch ran back to the wall and leapt up as easily as if he had wings. Gripping the sides of the air vent, he slid inside then dropped down one arm to help up each member of the group. Once they had all climbed in, he refitted the grate and signaled for them to follow. James struggled to keep his elbows and knees from thudding against the metal panels as he hurried after Zilch, who, in contrast, army crawled down the vent with the swiftness and silence of a lizard. James glimpsed stairs, corridors, and groups of marching Bodyguards as the group passed grate after grate.

They had crawled through what felt like miles of the Tower's metal intestines before Zilch stopped. Curling up, he gripped one of the metal panels, wrenched it away from its identical siblings, and led the group into a tunnel stuffed with humidity. They scurried across worn, wet stone toward an absinthe-green glow at the tunnel's end. The laughter of women rose up from below in a ghostly echo that shivered through James. Zilch twisted his head around.

"Just follow me," he whispered.

He crawled out of the tunnel and, to James's surprise, began crossing the thin air on his hands and knees as if he were making his way across an invisible bridge. Two women reclined in a bubbling pool far below. Bright lights illuminated the green, steaming water. James prepared himself with a short exhale then crawled out of the tunnel too. Mosaic tiles of midnight blue, sparkling gold, and pearlescent white covered everything, from the floor below to the dome above, so that the two women seemed to float in a misty, green nebula ensconced among shimmering constellations. James might have appreciated the beauty of the chamber had the terror of falling or being noticed by the women not constricted his senses. One of the women tilted her head back and sank deeper into the murky water as the group continued creeping across the air above her.

"*Well, I suppose Three will get what he deserves in the end,*" she said.

"*But not from us,*" said her friend.

"*Oh, of course, not from us. We can't do anything. But he's growing his claim too much too fast if you ask me. It will catch up to him. You just wait and see. The mighty always fall, and they always fall hard.*"

"*Well, Four will be happy if that ever happens. I know he's been frustrated with some of the sanctions that Three put on him lately.*"

"*Oh, well, I can't fault Three for doing that. Some of the things Four does in his claim…. I haven't met any of his girls, but the stories I hear make my skin crawl. You can't help but feel for those poor girls. They're women just like us, after all.*"

Water splashed as she sat up in the pool. The sizzling water had turned her skin a raw, pinkish red that reminded James of a freshly steamed crab. He desperately hoped that she wouldn't stand up.

"*That pervert,*" her friend said with a shake of her head.

"*Oh, and speaking of perverts. Did you hear about the fiasco Ten had the other night in his little strip club?*"

Water splashed again, this time as her friend sat up. "*What happened? Was it another fire?*" she asked eagerly.

"*It was.*"

Her friend pumped her fist in the air. "*Looks like you'll be getting more traffic into your claim!*"

"*Yes, and you can be sure whose claim I'll be referring them to afterward.*"

As the women laughed, James crawled onto a warm, stone ledge then slipped into a large gap in the wall. He stood up on shaking legs and waited with Zilch in a column of wavering, green light as the others joined them. Zilch hurried into the surrounding darkness toward a lone strip of cobbled road lying like a petrified mat on the floor. The even black of the dark swallowed him in greedy mouthfuls as he rushed down a flight of stairs and disappeared from sight.

James's hand skimmed the wall that rose up at his side as he, too, rushed down the slippery steps. The warm moisture clogging the air began to lift. The steady dripping of water grew distant. A damp chill stole over his skin and soaked into his bones. The stairs curved along the walls in massive, winding spirals, bending at random intervals and climbing down into long, flat bridges before leaning against the wall again. One hundred ... two hundred ... three hundred.... He lost count of the stairs as he continued climbing down step after step and passing door after door. His hand had long grown raw from grazing the walls when Zilch came, at last, to a stop.

"We're here," he said, panting.

"*How did you find all these paths? I've never even heard of these parts of the Abode before,*" Blood Crow said between heavy breaths.

"I was only nine when I was brought here. Not much else to do in a place like this at that age except explore," Zilch said.

He coaxed a switchblade into a small crevice in the wall then began lifting, turning, and jiggling the handle. James leaned his back against the wall and tried to tame his breathing. This was the longest night he had ever endured, and his body was, at last, beginning to succumb to weariness. Though Blood Crow held her nose high in the air, her drooping shoulders and limp arms betrayed her exhaustion. Lux wrapped one arm around Honey, who rested her head on his shoulder and shivered. E's fierce determination still burned in her eyes like an undying flame, but James knew that even she had her limits. Phoenix's eyes continued to flit toward her, full of the same concern that James felt.

"Got it," Zilch mumbled.

A click preceded a low rumbling. The outline of a door cracked into view.

"Keep your voices down once we get in," said Zilch. "I don't think the Third knows anything yet, but if any Bodyguards hear too many voices in Snow's room, it's game over."

He heaved his weight against the stone. Excitement quickened the breath James had managed to calm as the door opened noiselessly. This was it. They were going to meet Snow, the mysterious Twelfth Shaman for whom they had traveled so long and braved so much to see. Zilch stood back and motioned for him to go in first. James took a deep breath, stepped across the threshold, then stood still.

She stood with her back toward him, just as she had in the golden eye. Moonlight spilled through an open, arched window, making the contour of her robe glow a bright blue-white. The bells on the hem of her sleeves chimed as she spun around. Her long hair swung away from her pale, translucent skin. The milky film of blindness dulled the color of her irises, which were the same blue as that of the moonlight protecting the City.

"Z?" she said.

James remained silent. All he had wanted for the past few nights was to meet Snow, but now that she stood before him, he didn't know what to do or say. Her figure seemed to crumple like a flower shriveling under quickened time as she stepped away from the moonlight. The ethereal being at the window vanished, giving way to a young woman who was petite in stature and anxious in spirit.

"*Who are you, and where is* Zilch?" she demanded.

"Move!" Zilch hissed, snapping James out of his trance. He pushed past him. "I'm here, Snow. I got him. Him and his crew."

The tenseness that had seized her loosened. She placed a pale hand over her chest and breathed out a sigh of relief. The rest of the group took up half the room as Zilch waved them in. In contrast to the Third's office, only a few pieces of well-worn furniture and an outdated television set occupied Snow's room.

"I was getting so worried," she said. "I was starting to think the Third had gotten you somehow, Z."

"Nope. Not yet." He grunted as he threw his shoulder against the stone door again.

"Are you hurt? *A-Are any of you hurt? Did anyone harm you?*" she asked.

Phoenix spoke before James could summon his voice.

"Snow, it's me. It's Phoenix. And no, no one was hurt. Everyone's all right."

She tensed again as her breath caught in her chest. "Phoenix?" she whispered.

"Hi, Snow," he said. "It's really good to see you again."

Shock unwound into joy on her face. She stretched out her hands, searching for him. She grasped his arms as he walked over to her. He smiled and squeezed her arms in response.

"Phoenix," she said. "You're really here. I can't believe it."

"I'm back, just like I promised. And with others too. This is E. She's the leader of this crew."

E simply glared at her. Honey, Lux, and Blood Crow greeted Snow in whispers as Phoenix introduced them.

"And last but not least," Phoenix said, turning to James.

Zilch yelled. The group spun around as he thrust his finger toward the window.

It was Bloom.

"Bloom!" E exclaimed.

He hopped down from the window then leapt across the room and knocked Snow onto the floor. Zilch cried out, drew his knife, and ran forward. E swung her knee into his stomach, dropping him to the ground. Bloom shoved his snout into Snow's face, licking and whining as she yelped and thrashed about.

"Z! W-What is this thing?" said Snow as Phoenix and E grabbed fistfuls of his fur and dragged him away.

"It's a citizen. A citizen!" Zilch gasped as he clutched his stomach. "But there's no way. No way can citizens pass through the moonlight."

"He's part of our crew," E snapped. "Yes, he's a citizen, and yes, he can cross the Blue Border. We hid him because we didn't want the other Shamans finding him."

She pinned Zilch with a sharp look that threatened more than a blow to the stomach should he make a bigger deal out of this than he already had. Zilch's lower jaw shuddered before he gulped and closed his mouth. He looked too stunned to raise any objections. E turned to Bloom with worried eyes.

"Are you crazy? This is the Tower. You shouldn't be here," she whispered as she stroked his cheeks.

Bloom merely smiled and twitched his tail. As Snow staggered onto her feet and wiped away Bloom's slobber from her face, James discovered his voice at last. He uprooted himself from the floor and walked over to her.

"Snow, I'm the one you saw in the golden eye. You can call me James. We've traveled a long way to meet you. We were hoping you could give us some answers about everything that's been going on."

"James!" she said. "It's you! You've come. I-It's such a pleasure."

She gasped suddenly then snapped her head toward the window. Bloom turned his head as well.

"What's wrong?" James said as fear reared up within him.

"I hear bells," Snow whispered. "The window."

James had forgotten. Shamans had a superhuman sense of hearing in addition to their reading abilities. His heart sank into a white panic as he and the others rushed over to the window to look outside. Down below, Bodyguards skittered around the base of the Tower like ants in search of food. James could just make out the insidious jingling of the bells on their wrists.

"They know you've escaped," Zilch said. "Snow, are you ready?"

"O-Of course."

The bells on her sleeves chimed as she cast aside her robe. She was wearing black clothes, a utility belt rife with weapons, and a sturdy pair of boots. E and Phoenix looked at one another. Zilch pushed past James again as Snow tied back her long hair.

"Snow, what are you doing?" Phoenix said as Zilch knelt down in front of her.

"I'm sorry, but we can't stay here anymore. We can talk about everything once we've escaped," she said as she clambered onto Zilch's back. "We all need to get out of the Tower immediately. We have a place in my claim where we can hide for now."

"You're leaving the Abode? But you're a Shaman!" Blood Crow said as Zilch flung aside a chair, pulled back a desk, and began patting down the wall.

"We'll explain everything later. Please, just follow us for now," said Snow.

"But it's too dangerous for you," Phoenix protested.

"Before it was Z, it was you who carried me, Phoenix. Don't you remember? If we did it then, we can do it now," she said as Zilch continued running his hands along the stone wall.

She gasped again. Bloom bared his teeth.

"Everyone, quiet," E commanded.

Several moments passed before James heard the distant echo of Bodyguards marching down the corridors. Zilch slapped his hand against the wall.

"Got it," he said as the stone slid open to reveal a descending passageway.

"We can talk later. We need to escape first," E said as the marching grew louder.

The group rushed into the passageway. Zilch grabbed a walkie talkie hanging on the wall and held it up to his mouth.

"Curly, we're coming. We're going to the rail right now. Be ready for us. And get a bigger cart," he said, glancing at Bloom.

"On it," was the immediate answer.

Zilch clipped the walkie talkie to his belt and hitched up Snow on his back. James stayed close to her as Zilch slapped his hand twice against the stone and sealed the wall shut.

CHAPTER 28

THE MARKET

Wooden steps creaked beneath James's boots as he hurried down into a cavernous tunnel. Darkness enveloped the group as Zilch slowly closed a pair of steel plates overhead.

"Okay, we're out of the Tower now," Zilch said. He clicked on a flashlight then rushed down the stairs with Snow still curled up on his back.

James exhaled. He had hardly dared to breathe for most of the nerve-wracking journey out of the Tower, fearful that one of the many Bodyguards passing above, below, or around them would discover them.

"Good. Then explain to us what's going on and where you're taking us," E demanded as Zilch hurried past her and positioned himself at the front of the group.

"We're going to the Third's part of the Market, his claim, Turquoise. The tunnel we're in right now is one he built a long time ago. It was meant to be a rail system between the Tower and the Market, but he gave up on it after someone tried to bomb it while he was down here."

"Wait, wait, wait. You're taking us to the Third's claim? So we're heading straight into enemy territory again?" Honey said, outraged.

Lux groaned. E looked ready to draw her dagger.

"Look, I know it sucks, but we can't go above ground. Bodyguards will catch us, and this is the only other way we can escape. Our friend will pick us up in Turquoise and take us to a safehouse in the Last."

"What's the Last?" said James.

"It's the name of Snow's part of the Market, her claim," said Zilch, stomping his foot. "We can talk more about the details and what's happening once we're at the safehouse. Our friend will find a way out of the Market and into No Man's Land while we wait there, so just follow me. We've had all of this planned out ever since Snow saw James in that eye."

A motorcycle sprang from Zilch's hand. James bit down on his lip and shook his head. He agreed with Honey that rushing into the Third's claim wasn't exactly an ideal plan, but he also didn't see what choice they had. The Third would surely capture them again if they stayed here. The group seemed to share his thoughts, for no one objected as E commanded Lux to create three more motorcycles.

Honey seated herself behind Lux as James hurried toward E with the intention of siting behind her. He didn't know how to ride a bicycle never mind a motorcycle. He stopped in his tracks as E signaled for Phoenix to sit behind her.

James groaned then made his way over to the last motorcycle on his own. He cursed Phoenix as he swung his leg over the seat and fumbled with the handles. Blood Crow hopped onto the seat behind him and wrapped her arms around his waist.

Shivers suddenly ran from his waist, billowing up to his head and down to his toes. Her arms were warm against his stomach, her body soft against his back. Suddenly, he wasn't a weary and desperate fugitive within the dark confines of an endless tunnel but a boy with something fast dissolving in his chest like ice under hot water.

He jumped as motors revved. He fumbled again with the handles. Bloom trotted up to him and smiled. James narrowed his eyes at him. Was he giving him his usual smile, or was he grinning at the blush that had spread across his cheeks?

"You don't know what you're doing, do you?" Blood Crow yelled above the din.

James sighed. "No," he confessed. "Do you know how to drive this thing?"

The others began to depart.

"Move over."

She took his place. As he wrapped his arms around her waist, the dissolving thing in his chest melted completely so that his heart dropped into his stomach. The motor revved into life. With Bloom at their side, they sped after the others into the darkness.

Blood Crow's hair fluttered against James's face in a soft barrage of wild, red strands. He swept aside the stream of hair then wrapped his arm around her again. He jerked his head back as he felt himself leaning into her. What was happening to him? And how long had his palms been this sweaty? He fought off the urge to wipe his hands on his jeans. What did he care if his hands were a bit sweaty? The whole group was dirty and battle-worn, especially Blood Crow. A crazy Hunter girl like her was sure to have seen far dirtier humans during her nights in the Flowering. And he wouldn't have cared even if she hadn't! He jerked his head away from her once again.

For the rest of the ride, he made sure to maintain a minimum of an inch between her body and his. Once the group slowed to a halt, he leapt off the seat before the motor had even silenced. Zilch unclipped the walkie talkie from his belt. A spurt of static followed.

"We're here, Curly," he said.

James's hand flew to the hilt of his dagger as metal dragged across the ceiling. He blinked and squinted as a manhole opened up above them like a waning eclipse. A figure peered down at them.

"Hurry! News hasn't spread in the Market yet," the figure whispered.

Snow climbed onto Zilch's back. James followed them up the stairs and surfaced on a long, deserted alleyway. A man stood next to the mouth of the manhole, gesturing for the rest of the group to hurry as they climbed out as well. His golden, curly hair dangled around his thin face as his green eyes swept from one end of the alleyway to the other. Bloom emerged from the darkness. Zilch clapped his hand over the man's mouth to muffle his scream.

"Curly. Curly! Calm down. Let's get out of here first," Zilch hissed as the man flailed within his hold. "We can explain later."

Zilch gave him a sharp shake. The man froze then nodded. He continued to stare, pale-faced, as Bloom jumped into a giant cart near them. Zilch gently lowered Snow into the cart before climbing in as well. The man threw a large tarp over them, hooked the sides down, then pushed the cover of the manhole back into place.

"I-I'm sorry," he told the group, his eyes darting back and forth between them and the cart. "I just wasn't expecting a citizen, of all things!" He shook his head. Sweaters, each of which were worn-out and over-sized, appeared in his hands. "Please, put these on. Pull down the hoods, and cover your faces as much as you can. We're in the Third's claim, so we need to be extra careful to make sure that no one notices you. You can call me Curly. It's a pleasure to meet all of you."

With a strength that seemed to defy his gangly frame, Curly picked up the giant cart's protruding handles and began pulling forward. Phoenix hesitated before pulling off the gray Roamer hood still draped behind the nape of his neck. He shoved the hood into the cart before dressing into the black sweater he'd taken from Curly. He rushed to the back of the cart to help push it along.

Neat rows of red bricks provided a smooth path that felt soft and strange underfoot after the gravel in the tunnel and the Tower's roughly hewn stone. Tawny walls of stucco reached up on either side of the group. Large pieces of tarp and linen stretched into a multi-layered canopy overhead. Metal mesh screen doors guarded closed wooden doors along the right wall. Each screen door bore a unique design, from metal vines that twisted up iron bars to large cornucopias filled with meat and fruit. As the group passed an open door, the sounds of sizzling meat, live jazz, and light-hearted laughter floated through the screen. Saliva welled up beneath James's tongue as the smell of fried chicken, butter, herbs, and garlic filled his nose.

Lux breathed in deeply. "Man, that smells good," he murmured.

James swallowed then yanked down the rim of his hood to conceal more of his face. He thought of the gruesome eye in the blue box and tore up the desire for fried chicken that had mushroomed in his stomach. He couldn't afford to drop his guard for a mere piece of chicken. Not when the Third was on their tail.

A door banged open up ahead. A thick, hairy arm appeared, its meaty hand gripped around the collar of a bearded man.

"Just keep walking. Don't look," Curly muttered.

The owner of the large arm slowly closed the door so that it shut quietly behind him. He began wringing the bearded man by the collar.

"How many times do I have to tell you not to do that with the plates?" he shouted. "Someone complained about it again last night! You want them to start complaining to Snake Eyes next?"

"S-Sorry, Bear. I got distracted. It was just a lot of work tonight."

"'It was just a lot of work tonight,'" Bear repeated in a mock voice. "Creating ten desserts isn't exactly a lot of work. I swear, when I find someone who can create a better crème brulée than you, you'll be out of my shop, out of this claim, out of the City, and out of No Man's Land, you pathetic Hedonist!"

He flung the bearded man from the porch. The man landed face-first on the street. Bear continued to rage as he climbed down the stairs and kicked the man repeatedly in the stomach. James kept his eyes averted as the group stepped out of the alleyway and onto a wide street made of cobblestone.

Soft piano music played from speakers hanging from ornate streetlamps. Chatter, music, and the clinking of glasses sounded from the myriad of restaurants that lined both sides of the street. Passersby stopped at intervals to examine menus or to ask stationed waiters questions. Everyone wore clean clothes. Even the Bodyguards, who slid in and out between the crowds as they watched for signs of trouble, looked impeccably clean. Only the occasional band of Merchants, immediately recognizable by their large carts, tubs, and bags, looked as grimy as the group. James had feared that eyes would linger on their bloodied, dirt-stained jeans as well as their giant cart, but the group simply looked like another band of Merchants.

Like the screen doors in the alleyway, each restaurant boasted a unique style. White paint, sand, and colorful glass created a beachfront atmosphere for a spacious, outdoor patio, where smiling waiters refilled glasses for men and women gorging on crab and lobster. Further down, dark tiles, plastic plants, and golden letters constructed a slick and modern exterior of an expansive bar. Large, open windows revealed guests sipping on craft beer, biting into crispy, fried shrimp, stretching apart quesadillas oozing with cheese, and shoving hamburgers stuffed with multiple patties into their mouths. Raucous laughter, clapping, and the blare of rock music promised good company and even better memories. Across the restaurant, a throng of giggling women burst out of a white door, clutching cones stacked with scoops of ice cream. An invisible cloud saturated with the sweet smell of sugar encompassed the group as the door swung shut.

Lux licked his lips.

"What's that on their hands?" James asked E as he stared at one of the laughing women.

The number three, written in Our Word, had been stamped over the woman's watch in red and was circumscribed by a large circle, also red. Her friends bore stamps of black, dark blue, and light blue. James could hardly spot a human whose watch bore nothing at all.

"It tells how much you've paid to stay in the Market," said E. "You can stay longer and access more stores depending on the color. Black, like that guy over there, means he paid minimal payment. The Third made it black on purpose to match the watch. It makes it more difficult to read your watch and easier to lose track of time."

Blood Crow gasped and ducked her head.

"What? What is it?" Honey hissed.

"*Hunters,*" Blood Crow whispered. "*They know me!*"

Up ahead, a man and a woman stepped down from a red carpet that covered a cascade of marble steps. They were both heavily armed and dressed in the same medieval-looking tunic that Blood Crow was wearing beneath her sweater. As they turned toward the waiter who had followed them, Crew Blue surrounded Blood Crow to block her from their view.

"*Thank you very much for choosing our shop again this year. It's always a pleasure doing business with your family,*" the waiter said.

"*Of course,*" replied the woman. "*Several families at last year's Feast commented on the quality of your wine. We wanted to make sure that we ordered the same for this year as well.*"

James didn't relinquish his guard over Blood Crow until the group had walked far away from the Hunters' line of sight. As they turned a corner, a bombardment of lights assaulted his eyes. Bricks of pure gold paved the street, reflecting lights that sparkled, lights that streamed, neon lights in pinks, blues, and purples, and lights that blinked and winked. Couples sat on benches, kissing each other or sucking on cigars. Images of cocktails, cigarettes, cards, and chips rolled along the screens above their heads. Thick glass windows revealed people standing at slot machines, their faces alight in the glow of one-armed bandits. Cheers erupted around a man who pumped his fist in victory at the roll of a dice. From poker to blackjack, baccarat to craps, pachinko to mahjong, no game seemed to go unaccounted for on this golden street.

"Lucky Lane," E told James and Lux. "The best gambling shops in the Market. A lot of humans come here every year just for this street."

"I don't blame them," Lux whispered, his eyes glistening in the lights.

"I don't know," said James, coughing as they passed through a cloud of cigar fumes. "Everything is kind of extreme. And tacky. I mean, the street is literally paved with gold."

E and Blood Crow smirked. Honey let out a low cackle. Curly shushed her as a pair of Bodyguards burst out from a shop. The woman between them writhed and screamed within their grips. She stopped only as one of the Bodyguards punched her in the stomach.

"Probably a Hedonist who's late on paying tribute," E said.

James steered himself to stare straight ahead as the Bodyguards threw the woman onto the ground and began beating her with batons.

"You said before that Hedonists are humans who are addicted to the Flowering, right?" he asked E.

"Right. But I guess it would be more accurate to say that they've become addicted to the Market and not to the Flowering as a whole. Hedonists are humans who want to stay within the comfort of the moonlight so that they don't have to risk their safety out in the planes every night. That, and they love indulging in all the things the Market has

351

to offer, even at the expense of being at the bottom of the totem pole and getting kicked around by Merchants and Bodyguards all the time. They're allowed to live here in exchange for labor or a certain number of their creations every night, which they call 'tribute.' Usually both. Most of the food, merchandise, and supplies in the Market come from their tribute, and if they're late too often on paying up, Jackals will give the okay to have them kicked out of the Market permanently."

"What are Jackals?"

"Jackals are Merchants who are at the top of the food chain. There are at least two or more Jackals who oversee each of the Shamans' claims in the Market. They supervise all of the Merchants who belong in their claim too. The only ones higher up than Jackals are Head Merchants, like Snake Eyes, and there's only one Head Merchant per claim. The only ones who are higher up than Head Merchants are the Shamans."

"So, from the bottom up, it's Hedonists, Merchants, Jackals, Head Merchants, Shamans. That's the org chart of the City?" said James.

E chuckled. "I never thought of it as an org chart, but yes, that's the general structure. There are a lot of subcategories too, though."

"What about Bodyguards? Where do they belong?"

"It's hard to say. They're kind of in a different branch all together, and there are different ranks of Bodyguards too. Generally speaking, though, they're treated as more important than Merchants."

"And Guides?"

"They're more powerful than even the Head Merchants since they work closest with the Shamans. They're second only to the Shamans, actually." She glanced at the cart then leaned in closer to James. "I don't think Zilch has much power, though, because he's the Twelfth's Guide. The fact that he's so young probably doesn't help either."

"I see," James said. He had assumed long ago that the Market would have some kind of system of organization in place. After all, it was a market. But he had underestimated how sophisticated the system really was. How old was this place? It had to have existed for a while now to have grown this large and complex.

The group turned into a dark and empty alleyway away from all the lights. James felt himself relax. As much as he'd grown to associate darkness with danger, the shadows of the alley were far preferable to the outrageous glamor of Lucky Lane. The absence of Bodyguards helped too.

A strange mélange of clashing smells grew into a foul odor as the group continued down the alleyway. They stepped out onto an asphalt street lined on either side by red-brick apartments. The entire street overflowed with trash bags. Cakes, meats, and noodles dribbled out in globs from the side of a ripped bag. Another bag vomited up fried fish, plates, and loaves of bread still whole and untouched. Rolled up carpets, curtain rods, and a glass chandelier protruded from one of the many dumpsters.

"All trash," E said, "and unwanted leftovers from the restaurants."

"What happens to all of it?"

"Merchants take most of it out of the City and let the shifts in the planes take care of it. The rest is distributed to Hedonists."

She fell silent as the group drew nearer to a band of Merchants transporting their goods into one of the apartments. A man with a clipboard stood on the porch, glaring down at the band. He held out his clipboard to stop a Merchant as he made to cross the threshold.

"This isn't enough," the man said.

"It was rough out there. We tried," the Merchant replied, panting as he shifted the bulky bag on his shoulder.

"I don't care if you tried. You think Snake Eyes is going to care? You think the Third will? This is barely enough to satisfy ten of his Bodyguards, never mind his shops."

"We'll try harder next time."

"You had better." The man raised his voice as he turned toward the rest of the Merchants at the bottom of the steps. "I'm not going to let Snake Eyes take another shop away from me just because you all can't meet your quota. I'm giving you all one week off!"

"One?" a Merchant exclaimed.

"Yes, one. You're lucky I'm even giving you one. If you want more, you bring in more!"

The man stormed into the apartment. The Merchants groaned. Several of them threw down their goods. One of them cursed and spit on the ground. The group passed the band, leaving them far behind before coming to a stop at the end of the street, where a large garage door impeded their way forward. The number twelve had been written on the door in white chalk.

"This is Snow's claim, the Last," Curly whispered before lifting the door.

A song floated out to greet them as a distant echo, describing summer days and an aching heart that beat for the singer's darling love. It continued playing in the background like elevator music in the otherwise silent claim as the group followed Curly down a worn, dirt road.

Makeshift walls of lattice fencing and chicken wire conjoined one empty stall after another. String lights zigzagged overhead and, along with Christmas lights, draped the interiors of the stalls to create a pervasive glow of soft, golden light. Squares of artificial grass formed a green carpet in each stall, though many of the squares had come loose and now lay discarded on the dirt road. Each stall also displayed various items, from wrinkled shirts and jeans hanging from spindly, metal racks to plastic earrings and bulky necklaces that hung from the loops in the chicken wire. No one sat in the metal, fold-up chairs manning the stalls. The group was entirely alone.

"We're here," Curly said as he came to a stop. "The safehouse."

He unhooked the tarp cover from the cart. Zilch stood up and watched Bloom leap out before helping Snow onto his back.

"My lady," Curly said, kneeling.

"Curly, you don't have to call me that. I've told you so many times now," said Snow, frowning slightly.

He simply smiled then stepped into a stall where empty picture frames covered walls of lattice fencing. He dragged back one of the walls to reveal a gigantic piece of sheet metal, which he pulled aside as well. Rickety steps led down to a small room in a sunken cavity.

"We'll hide in here for now while Curly finds us a way out of the Market," said Zilch.

James and the others climbed down into the room. Stained couches, an armchair missing its seat cushion, and an old coffee table fit for the corner of a thrift store created an air of decay and neglect. Brown stains ran across the ceiling and down the cement walls. Dirt, shreds of paper, and human hair planted in a large, faded rug amplified the room's woeful appearance.

"I'll be back soon," Curly said as he pulled on the sheet metal.

"Be careful," Snow said.

The sheet slid back into place, securing the group within the safehouse.

CHAPTER 29

CONNECTION

Lux and Honey sank down into one of the sofas. James seated himself opposite of Snow and Zilch. E waited for Phoenix and Blood Crow to take the cushioned seats on the couches before taking the shabby, cushion-less armchair as her own. Bloom laid down at her feet and sighed through his nostrils. E glared at the cement walls and the sheet metal sealing their way out.

"Your friend is incredibly loyal for a Hedonist," she growled at Zilch.

"Curly is different," he retorted.

"Different enough to not go and sell us out to the Third right now while we're all trapped in here?"

"Curly wouldn't do that," he said, rising from his seat.

"Z," Snow said.

He glanced at her then sat back down. He crossed his arms and looked away from E.

"I don't trust all of my Hedonists, so I can see why you'd be worried. But Curly and I have a very good relationship," Snow said.

"You guys had better have a good relationship," Zilch blurted. "You took him into your claim when no one else would. He owes you his life. Him and his whole family."

"Curly has some extenuating circumstances in Reality, and he was losing too much sleep," Snow explained to the group. "You'd be surprised at how many Hedonists have circumstances like that."

"Yeah, and most of them are in your claim," Zilch muttered.

"Well, taking them in is the right thing to do. They wouldn't have a chance otherwise. All the other Shamans require an insane level of quality for their tribute."

"How long do you think it'll take for Curly to come back, Snow?" said Phoenix.

"He'll be back soon. He's gone to talk with a Jackal in another claim. They discussed terms before, but Curly needs to check if he's still willing to help us and finalize payment details if so."

"He'll help us out," said Zilch. "That Jackal is definitely the type of guy who can be bought. The price will be high, though."

"So, we have the word of a Hedonist and the partnership of a Jackal. Wonderful," E growled.

"Z," Snow said, stopping him as he began rising from the sofa again. "I know it's not ideal," she told the group. "If I weren't the Twelfth, I might have been able to do more, pull more rank. I'm sorry for all the trouble."

E responded with a piercing look loaded with suspicion.

"It's fine," James said, gesturing for E to back down. "We're out of the Tower now, so maybe we can talk about some of the things that have happened. How did we see each other in that golden eye? Why is the Third so interested in it? What's going on?"

Snow took a deep breath as if she were digging deep to search for the confidence she needed in order to speak. She began rubbing her knuckles as if they were prayer beads. Then she deflated and leaned back into the cushions.

"I don't know where to even begin," she said.

"Just tell us what you know!" E snapped, making her jump. "We've gone long enough tonight waiting for you to give us some answers."

James signaled for her to back down again.

"Th-Three's always been obsessed with the Red Calf, the one the Hunters talk about in their legends. He's convinced that the Calf is real and that it really does have a golden eye, just like their legends say," said Snow.

"He's been doing crazy amounts of research on the Calf for years now behind everyone's backs. I know. I've been spying on him through the passageways," added Zilch.

"His research shows that one of my predecessors, a Twelfth Shaman from ages back, somehow gained the sight of all the Shamans," Snow said. "But then either by choice or by force he gave our sight to the Calf. Then the Calf kept the Shamans' sight in its golden eye and disappeared from the Flowering. Three isn't sure why it disappeared, but he's never agreed with the part in the legends that says the Brave killed it. He thinks that it's trapped alive somewhere, gathering its strength, and that it'll eventually return to the Flowering."

"And that led him to send Merchants and Bodyguards out on secret missions over the years to try and find the Calf," said Zilch. "Or at least to find out as much as he can about it. He thinks its golden eye can give all the Shamans their sight back, so he's desperate to find out whatever information there is out there. That's why he wanted to talk to you all so badly tonight and why he tried to keep you imprisoned. We had to run away with you guys too because he thinks only Snow can take back the golden eye from the Calf. He would try to imprison her too for good measure and find ways to control her now that he's finally found humans who have seen the Calf and its eye."

"Why would he think that only Snow can retrieve the eye?" said Phoenix, looking concerned.

"Because it was originally one of the Twelfths who took the sight of the Shamans all those ages ago," said Snow. "Three hadn't been sure which new Twelve would be able to retrieve the eye, but then he found out that I'd had a different awakening dream, and that convinced him that I was that Twelfth, the Twelfth who could restore the Shamans' sight."

James's heartbeat quickened. "What do you mean you had a different awakening dream?" he said.

"Well, I-I don't know if you know this, but all Shamans find themselves fully conscious during their awakening dream, and all of our awakenings are similar. We become conscious in a big, dark space where there's a ring of keys next to a barred cell with moving faces. Off to the side, there's a pair of giant, wooden doors and a sound or smell that attracts the Shaman. When the Shaman opens the doors to investigate, they're blinded. Right after that, they're born into the Flowering."

James's heart thudded harder against his chest. So, it was possible to become fully conscious in an awakening dream. He hadn't been imagining things. But he wasn't a Shaman, so how...?

"I didn't know that," said Honey.

Snow nodded. "It's the same for all Shamans, but I was different. Three was too, actually, but he never told any of the other Shamans about it. I only know because Z listens in on his meetings with Certus. Tell them what he saw, Z."

"Three went to open the doors in his awakening dream like all the Shamans do, but then he saw his son's face in the cell and tried to help him instead. Then the doors opened and revealed a golden eye. He was blinded right after he saw it." He scowled and crossed his arms tighter. "His awakening dream. It's the whole reason he started hunting for the golden eye to begin with. Any time his research came up empty, he'd point to his awakening dream and say that it was some kind of sign that he was still destined to find the eye, even with all the setbacks he's had. It's what's kept him going for all these years."

"Okay, so that's the Third. But what about you, Snow?" said James. "What happened in your awakening dream? How was yours different?"

"Well, it started the same. I entered the dark space like any other Shaman, but then I totally ignored the doors and grabbed the keys instead. I opened the cell to free the faces. They were calling out for help, and I couldn't just...." She sighed. "But when I unlocked the cell, I found this blue box, and it had an eye. Not a golden eye like the Calf's. This one was really"–she swallowed–"red."

A rapid succession of images rolled through James's mind, swirling around his memory of the eye in the blue box.

"And I-I know it sounds weird," Snow continued, "but I–"

"You ate some of it," James said quietly.

Everyone's focus latched onto him.

"How did you know?" exclaimed Snow.

He rose to his feet, unable to stay seated as adrenaline flooded his body. "Because I found the box after you."

"Huh?" Lux and Honey said in unison.

"What are you talking about?" said E.

Phoenix leaned back in his seat. Zilch leaned forward in his. Blood Crow's face slowly creased. Bloom's entire body had grown rigid.

"I never mentioned it before because I wasn't sure if it was even real, but I became fully conscious in my awakening dream too. I found the same box in my awakening, and I ate what was left of the eye."

"You ate the rest of it?" Honey exclaimed.

"Why'd you do that?" said Lux with a wide-eyed look of disgust.

"I couldn't stop myself," James said, pacing back and forth. He quickly summarized his awakening dream.

"It was like a pull, wasn't it?" Snow said softly as he finished.

"Yeah." He stopped pacing and stared at her.

"It was a pull. A calling," she said. She balled her fists. "I knew I couldn't eat all of it, though. I knew the rest was for somebody else. It didn't feel right taking the eye all for myself. And now I see that the other was you, James. It was you all along."

"Wait. Is there something weird about you too?" Zilch asked him.

Several eyebrows cocked at him. Zilch shifted in his seat.

"I mean, is there something you can't do that most humans can? Like Snow. She can't read properly like the other Shamans, and I always thought it was because of that eye."

"You're still having trouble reading?" Phoenix asked.

"You failed to mention that tiny detail," E growled, her eyes flashing.

"It's not his fault," Snow pleaded. "We both thought it was normal for newborn Shamans to have trouble reading."

"And to be fair, most Shamans do need a lot of practice to get the hang of it, and some are way better at it than others," said Zilch. "But it's different with you, Snow. It's just not right. It's too different."

"I know, I know," Snow said, rubbing her knuckles furiously.

"Well," said James, "as far as weird things go, my watch isn't normal. It doesn't tell time like it should."

"Let me see," Zilch said. He murmured a description to Snow as he inspected his watch.

"Snow," said E. "Have you ever seen or heard of anything like James's watch before?"

She shook her head. "No. And as far as I know, none of the other Shamans have either. I have no idea why his watch would look the way it does."

James's heart sank. The rest of the crew stared at the ground in disappointment too.

"I-I'm sorry I don't have a better answer," Snow said.

"That's all right," James said, collecting himself. "It's not your fault. Zilch must be right, though. There must have been something in that eye we ate. It impacted your ability to read, and it changed my watch."

"Yeah, and it connected you guys to each other," said Lux.

The group stared at him.

"What? The eye messed with parts of James, but I bet you anything it's how him and Snow were able to see each other that night with the Calf too. There's a connection between you two, and that connection is in the eye you ate. It gave you powers or something."

James stared again at the blackened portion of his watch. "I don't know if 'powers' is the right word, but yeah, that eye definitely changed my watch and made some kind of connection. It might also be why my watch is counting down to the Calf's return. Or at least I think it is."

"Counting down to the Calf's return?" Snow said. "What do you mean?"

James described how his watch had changed right before the purple orb imprisoning the Calf had begun to crack. He told them of how the Calf's darkness had consumed the Hunters in the tunnels and how he could somehow sense the Beast's impending return.

"I see," said Snow, her voice trembling slightly as he finished his story. "Well, it definitely seems plausible that the Calf would be returning based off of everything you saw. And like I said before, Three's always believed that it would return, so it makes sense."

"The pieces do seem to fit," Zilch murmured. "And whatever eye you guys ate in your awakening dreams, it has you connected not just to each other but to the Calf too. That's why James's watch is counting down to its return and why he senses all these things. And that's how Snow was able to see it and James the way that she did. I just don't understand how, though. What exactly was that eye you guys ate, and how did it make all these connections?"

James and the others fell into deep contemplation. They had found some answers to their questions, but those answers had only opened the gates to more questions. At least one thing seemed sure, though. The Red Calf of the Hunters' legends was, indeed, returning to the Flowering, and he and Snow were somehow connected to its return.

"*We should hunt down the Red Calf while we still can,*" Blood Crow said, breaking the silence. "*Our legends say that it nearly destroyed everything with its darkness when it last walked the Flowering, and you all saw what it did in the tunnels. We can't let that thing come back to full strength. We should go find it and kill it now while it's still weak, while we still have the chance.*"

She looked at E, her eyes all earnestness. E stared back at her then nodded. One by one, the others nodded too. James knew from their weary expressions that no one wanted to embark on this hunt, but he also knew from their solemnity that they understood what would happen if they didn't. It was only a matter of time before the Calf would break out of the purple orb and come for them all, citizens and humans alike. Then it would swallow them just as it had swallowed the Hunters in the tunnels. The group couldn't wait around until that happened. They had to do something. They had to take action. They had to slay the Beast, just as how that mysterious whisper in his awakening dream had begged him to do.

But how were they supposed to defeat the Calf? Running back to the tunnels now would only result in the Beast unleashing its darkness upon them, just as it had before. And even if they did somehow manage to evade its darkness, how were they supposed to kill it? From what James had been able to see, it didn't have a mark, and he didn't want to gamble everything on the expectation of finding one.

He looked up as Bloom shuffled his feet and tossed his head from side to side in agitation. He couldn't quite make out what he saw in Bloom's expression. Confusion? Denial? But what was there to be in denial about? E stroked his mane with a worried look as he continued shuffling his feet. He looked at her with wide eyes as he opened and closed his mouth. E's worry turned into sadness as he snorted and shook out his fur in frustration. James knew that she, too, was wondering what words were trapped within that silence which Bloom could never break.

Snow suddenly let out a shaky laugh. "Z, can you imagine what Three would do to have all this information? To know that the Calf is in those tunnels?"

"He would literally kill to know," said Zilch. "And if he does find out all this, he'll use James's watch to keep tabs on the Calf's return and use all of you to go out and track down the plane it was on again. Once you guys find the Calf, he'll make me carry Snow and have her fetch the golden eye for him. Then he'll probably have his Bodyguards capture the Calf and keep it in the name of 'research,'" he said as he rolled his eyes and used air quotes. "We're all doomed if he catches us. We're his ticket to getting his hands on the most dangerous citizen to have ever existed. It's the last tool he needs to make himself invincible."

"But he's more concerned with the golden eye than with the Calf itself," Snow said. "He wants his sight more than anything. It's what every Shaman wants more than anything."

"*I don't suppose he'd take into consideration the fact that the Red Calf eats humans alive with its empty darkness?*" Blood Crow scowled.

"And that he could essentially be sending us to our deaths?" E added with a grim look.

"He kind of would care. But not really," said Zilch. "He'd just make us all go out there again and again until he either gets what he wants or we die trying. He's just too obsessed with getting the golden eye. Everything and everyone else come second. Always has and always will. Like I said, he thinks he's destined to find the eye."

"I don't think we can blame him for being so desperate, though," Snow said. She slowly stopped rubbing her knuckles as she murmured, "To have sight. To be free of the Tower. Think of what our lives would be like, Z. How our nights would change."

Something like hunger stirred feebly within her milky eyes. Zilch sighed and patted her arm. E snorted.

"Shamans," she growled. "The Market is bad enough. I can only imagine what they would do to the rest of the Flowering if they could see."

"Thank you. We appreciate that comment," Zilch snapped.

Sorrow and weariness overshadowed the hunger lurking in Snow's eyes as she sighed. "No. E's right. Three in particular would set out to rule the entire Flowering if he could see. The other Shamans wouldn't be much better. I guess it is better this way." She paused then said, "I knew you'd come to the Tower to find me, James. After I saw you in the eye. And I guessed that you would have more information about the Calf and that Three would try to imprison us. So Z and I kept quiet and waited. We'd hoped that we would meet you first when you arrived."

"But we failed," Zilch said. He heaved a long sigh. "I failed. I saw you guys too late in the lobby. Snake Eyes got to you first."

The group fell back into a tense silence. E leaned her elbows on her knees as her eyes darted back and forth across the ground.

"Fine. That's that, then," she said. "We'll all just have to run for it. Get out of the City before the Third finds us. We'll get out of the City then figure out a plan to kill the Calf once we're safe."

"So, by 'we,' do you mean we can come with you?" Zilch said, peering at her as if afraid of her answer.

"The Third is after everyone in this room. We might as well stick together for now. You keep carrying Snow like you've been doing. I don't know how we're going to keep carrying her out there in the planes, but we're just going to have to figure it out."

Bloom shuffled his paws, clearly still distraught, as the group murmured in agreement. Honey pressed her lips together but nodded nonetheless. James gave her a small smile and a few nods to reassure her that adding Snow and Zilch to their group was the right decision.

"Well, then ... *hello*," said Zilch.

"*Hello*," E responded. "You too, Snow."

"*Hello*," Snow said, rubbing her knuckles again.

"*Hello*," E answered.

The sheet metal shifted. The group jumped out of their seats.

"We need to hurry," said Curly as he dragged the sheet aside. "The Third's Bodyguards are on their way to the Market. They'll be making an announcement soon too."

The group rushed out of the room. Bloom laid down next to Snow once Zilch had lowered her back into the cart. She hesitated then buried her hands in his fur and nestled herself against his side. She smiled as he licked her forehead.

"So he'll do it?" Zilch asked as he climbed into the cart.

"He will," said Curly.

"And what does he want for payment?"

"I tried to get a firm agreement upfront, but he kept saying that he'd see about payment 'once her highness gets here.'"

Zilch rolled his eyes and threw the tarp over himself.

"We'll leave the Last, go through the rest of Turquoise, then into Lavender. That's where the Jackal is," Curly told the group. "From there, he'll get you through the Doors in Caved. You can escape past the Blue Border and into No Man's Land from there."

Blood Crow stepped up to James's side as Curly began securing the tarp over the cart.

"*Lavender is the Tenth Shaman's claim*," she told him.

His heartbeat accelerated at an alarming rate.

"And Caved is the Seventh Shaman's claim," she continued. *"Oh, and the Doors are basically a series of big storage houses all lined up together. They're on the outer border of the Market and lead back out into the Iris. And, well, the Blue Border is obviously the moonlight."*

"Oh, uh ... thanks for, uh, explaining."

He stared at the ground then at Lux, who had waved away Phoenix and positioned himself behind the cart instead. He cleared his throat and swayed back and forth on the balls of his feet.

"So, what's with the weird names for the claims?" he asked. Why was he continuing this conversation? His mouth was moving all on its own!

"They're named after the Shamans' eyes," said Blood Crow. *"I think they call the Twelfth's claim 'the Last' to be mean, though."*

"Oh."

The group began hurrying down the dirt road. James nearly punched himself in the eye as he yanked his hood back down over his forehead.

"What's wrong?" Phoenix asked, looking behind them.

James turned around to find E standing still.

"Nothing," she said. "I just wasn't expecting to go to Lavender."

She swept past them without another word.

The group hurried past countless stalls then helped Curly and Lux heave the cart up a flight of steps, through a pair of red doors, and onto a cobblestone road, where families of Hunters stood examining vast arrays of weaponry displayed behind polished windows.

"We're back in Turquoise now," Curly murmured.

The group surrounded Blood Crow again, hiding her from the Hunters as they walked on. They traveled past innumerable stores before coming to a stop at a set of giant, purple curtains hanging in the middle of the street. They were drawn closed as if to hide the stage of a theater. E drew her hood lower over her face. James made sure to do the same.

"This is the entrance to Lavender," said Curly. "Stay close. There isn't much light in this claim. Visitors tend to get lost."

Tassels brushed against James's skin like soft fingers as the group stepped past the velvet curtains. The dim light of Victorian gas lamps gleamed against the street's polished, black tiles. Humans drifted by like shadows as they walked down the street. Red lamps, which hung from the many stores standing along the street, cast a bloodstained glow over half-naked women posing behind windows. Some of the women wore see-through lace. Others wore spikes and leather. A few wore nothing at all.

James did a double take. The Hedonist from the alleyway, the bearded man whom Bear had flung onto the street, stood whispering with another man guarding a store. They exchanged nods before the Hedonist stepped inside and groped one of the women. James slid his hand onto the hilt of his knife and stepped closer to Blood Crow. Brotherly instinct spurred him to glance at Honey and E as well. Both of them stared straight ahead with fearless expressions.

After walking down several blocks, they turned the corner and onto a street that was, to his relief, devoid of red lights. They stopped in front of a large, multi-storied home covered in the same black tiles as the street. Curly lifted the garage door and ushered everyone inside before checking and double-checking that the door had closed completely behind them. Everything within the room, from the tapestries draping the ceiling and walls to the cushions and hookahs strewn across the floor, held a rich, crimson hue like the flesh of a ripe cherry.

"I'll go get him," Curly said, wading through a pile of velvet cushions. He stepped past a sheer curtain then disappeared down a hall.

Only a few moments passed before a voice sounded.

"So where is her royal highness? In here?"

A tall, young Asian man pushed back the sheer curtain. For a moment, he stood with his head turned slightly toward Curly. He was handsome, model material even. His black sweatpants hung loose and low on his shirtless body, which displayed an eight-pack that was impressive even by the Flowering's standards. In fact, his whole body was defined by handsomely shaped muscles, which together with his height, created a presence that roared of strength and power. His strong jaw and night-black hair combined into a smoldering look which ensured that heads would turn wherever he went. He turned to face the group.

"So let's see what...."

The annoyance wrinkling his face slowly smoothed into stunned recognition as his eyes fell on E.

"*Oppa*," she breathed.

"E," he answered. "*You....*"

He took a few steps forward as if in a trance. Then he strode across the room. Placing one hand behind E's waist and another behind her neck, he pulled her in and kissed her.

CHAPTER 30

THE JACKAL

What was James watching? Was it really E? Kissing? And she had called him "Oppa!" Of course, "Oppa" was a Korean honorific all girls had to use to address any boys who were older than them by a year or more. But it could also be used as a name for someone special.

For a lover.

E squirmed in the Jackal's embrace then tore her lips away from him. The tarp ripped open as Bloom leapt out of the cart with his fangs bared and his eyes dilated with fury. The Jackal leapt back and dodged him with ease.

"You're still with that thing?" he shouted at E.

A bright and murderous hatred burned in his black eyes as he glared at Bloom. Bloom's fur bristled as his lips continued curling back to reveal more teeth. Slowly, they began circling one another. Phoenix drew his dagger. The rest of the group waved their hands over their weapons in flabbergasted confusion before finally following suit. E took a step back. Her face was pale, and her eyes were wide. She was shaking.

"Hey! No brawling!" Zilch shouted as he bolted upright in the cart. "You are in the presence of her lady, the Twelfth Shaman. I suggest you show her some respect, Jackal!"

He ignored Zilch and continued crossing one foot over the other, his focus fixed solely on Bloom. He flexed and curled his fingers into claws that seemed intent on gripping Bloom's coat and ripping him apart. The rage in his eyes burned brighter with every step. E exhaled a trembling breath. She walked over to Bloom and placed a hand on his back.

"It's okay. Not now," she said.

Bloom halted but continued bristling with a silent warning. James looked around at the others for some clue as to how to react. Was he supposed to defend Bloom and attack the Jackal who had promised to help them? Was he supposed to leave E and the Jackal alone? What was he supposed to do?

Honey's and Lux's dumbfounded expressions offered no help. The sight of E kissing seemed to have tangled their abilities to think as well. Blood Crow's gaze flickered back and forth between the Jackal and Bloom. Phoenix walked swiftly over to E's side and pointed his dagger at the Jackal's face. The Jackal's eyes darted from him to E then back to Bloom. The wrath in his eyes blazed brighter.

"Jackal," said Snow. She rose to her feet with Zilch's help. "If you'd like payment, I suggest we hurry. Curly informed you about payment, I presume?"

Her tone maintained a perfect balance of firmness and nonchalance that surprised James. For a moment, she had sounded almost as authoritative as the Third.

The Jackal slowly straightened his posture. Bloom simultaneously sank down onto his haunches. Only as Bloom sheathed his fangs did the Jackal look away from him. As he raised an eyebrow at Snow, his wrathful expression diminished into an irritated look that, far from ruining his handsome features, accentuated them with a tinge of haughty rebelliousness.

"Yeah, he told me about payment. But I didn't make any promises," he said.

Snow's face settled into a grave expression. Her blank eyes suddenly appeared eerily focused as if she could see the invisible which others could not.

"Well, then. Instead of fighting and wasting time, perhaps we should begin with negotiations," she said.

The Jackal placed his hands on his hips and exhaled long and loud. He shook his head as if to clear it then smirked.

"All right. What are you willing to pay?" he said.

"We are willing to pay with ten of my Hedonists, who will use all of their creations for you every night for the next thirty nights. A handsome reward. I'm sure you'll agree that it's more than enough."

The Jackal slowly traced the inside of his cheek with his tongue then smirked again. "It would have been if it were just you and the others like your boy Curly here had promised. I'm not so sure now with the wolf."

"I can personally pay you more if you want," said Curly. "Like we discussed before–"

"I wasn't done," said the Jackal. He pinned Curly with a lethal look.

Curly fell silent.

"Name your terms, then," Snow commanded.

He glared at Curly a moment longer before crossing his arms and narrowing his eyes at her. "You guys are being hunted, aren't you?" he said.

"W-What?" said Snow.

Zilch pursed his lips. Curly glanced at Snow then at Zilch then at the ground. James stood as still as possible, hoping that his surprise would remain hidden behind his poker face.

"Curly here did a pretty good job of selling me some sob story about how you wanted to get out of the Tower with some friends of yours. Said you were sick of all the stuff everyone in there was putting you through. I didn't buy it, but the payment sounded good, so I played along. But now that you're here, tell me. What did you all do? Who's after you?"

Snow opened and closed her mouth like a fish out of water.

"It's Three, isn't it? That bastard wants something from all of you."

Snow cleared her throat. "I see. So, this is how it's going to be. Well, if you're not willing to help us, we'll be on our way. Come on, Z. Come on, Curly, everyone. This Jackal obviously isn't interested."

James seized her bluff as did the others. They sheathed their weapons and turned toward the door as Snow and Zilch sat back down in the cart. E and Bloom remained still. A crooked grin slowly lifted a corner of the Jackal's mouth.

"Hey, hey, hey. You guys didn't even hear me out. I'll do the job. Don't worry about it."

The group turned to stare at him with dubious expressions. He chuckled and shook his head.

"I'm fine with helping humans if the occasion calls for it, especially if it has something to do with going against Three. You know everyone outside of his claim hates him, and that includes me. He's a tyrant. You guys should've just told me the truth. I'll do the job. And I'll do it for free."

Curly jumped. Snow frowned. Zilch stared in disbelief.

"For free," Zilch repeated. "You will do something like this for free."

Blood Crow snorted and rolled her eyes.

"Hey, don't laugh. Not all Jackals are bad, you know?" he said with a smile that carried both bemusement and sincerity. "Some of us are here in the Market because we needed to find a place in *the Flowering* to survive. You shouldn't judge. And besides, E is an old friend," he said, turning toward her. His grin dissolved into a hard stare. "And I don't abandon friends."

Her eyes snapped onto him. Flush as red as the cushions replaced the pallor on her face as she glared at him. His eyes softened. He seemed to wilt a little.

"*I don't know what's going on, but it's a relief to see you alive,*" he told her in Korean.

The hostility on her face split like cracking glass. She dropped her gaze onto the floor. Bloom rose onto all fours and bared his teeth again. A deep sigh rose out from the Jackal's chest. He closed his eyes and nodded as he stepped back. He walked back to the sheer curtain. When he turned around again, the weariness on his face had vanished, and he pierced the group with a steely expression that made clear that each and every one of them was to give him their fullest attention.

"You can call me Kit. I'll get you guys past the Doors in Caved. The plan is to pretend like you're some of my subordinates and that you're helping me haul some of my personal goods into *the Iris*. I like to go out as a Merchant Runner whenever I'm on break, and I have several storage units out there as well. Most of the Merchants guarding the Doors know this about me, and I'm on good terms with most of them too, so no one should raise any questions as long as all of you stay quiet and play along. Understand?"

James nodded as did the others.

"Good. One problem, though. Merchants never look that dirty when they're leaving *Lapis Lazuli*. Change out of those, and we'll get going. I have some clothes up here on the second floor. Free of charge like everything else."

"We don't have time," E said. She had reassembled her face into her usual look of fierce determination. "We can just create some clothes."

"*Listen to me, and don't be so stubborn,*" he said.

His use of Korean made him seem closer to E, somehow, like they were well used to speaking casually with one another in a language that many around them couldn't understand. His fluency in the language added to the impression. After all, it was rare to meet a Korean American who spoke Korean as fluently as English and jumped from one language back to the other with equal ease. Kit and E belonged to a rare breed.

"*And are you really going to talk to me like that?*" he continued. "This is the first time we've seen each other in over two years! Just ... don't waste your creations. I have tons of clothes here. You guys need to look like well-rested Merchants who are helping out your supervising Jackal. And besides, you guys could use a makeover."

"We need to get going," E insisted. "We don't know when we might get caught!"

"Hey, you," Kit said, pointing at Lux, who jumped. "You want some free, clean clothes before you go out into the planes again? I have some pretty good stuff."

"Well, I-I mean," Lux stuttered. "I guess it wouldn't be bad to have some new clothes." He shrank back from E's scorching gaze.

"See? It wouldn't be bad to have some new clothes. And I really mean it. You guys might draw a lot of attention if–"

"Fine. Let's just get the clothes and hurry up," Zilch said, hopping down from the cart and reaching up to help Snow. "We're wasting more time by not doing it."

Kit grinned then waved a hand for the group to follow as he slipped past the curtain.

"I should leave, then, my lady," said Curly.

"Thank you for everything, my friend," said Snow.

"I'll keep watch over everything, your grace. Just leave it to me. And you know where to find me if you need me," he told Zilch as they clasped hands.

After giving a quick nod of farewell to the group, Curly cracked open a side door and slipped outside. The group hurried past the curtain after

Kit. A dark hallway and stairs led to a spacious, well-lit room. Contrast startled James as he entered. Not a single drop of red colored this room. Instead, large bamboo panels lined the white walls, washing the room in a palette of neutral colors that soothed the senses and reflected a simple yet modern taste. Sparse furnishings, which included a round bed, a bookcase filled with books, and a few artificial plants, further invited James to relax and clear his mind. Kit tugged on one of the bamboo panels. Long racks laden with clothes rolled out of the wall.

"Take whatever you want," said Kit. "If you don't see your size, just look further in. Girls can choose something from that room over there. There might be some stuff in the room down that second hallway too, but let me know if you can't find anything. Happy to help."

Honey stood back and watched E with a worried expression as she and Bloom walked into the room which Kit had indicated. Blood Crow's eyes flitted between Honey and the floor before she muttered something to Honey. Honey only frowned at the ground then at the room into which E had disappeared. She turned to Blood Crow, looked her up and down, and sighed before nodding. The two women followed E together.

Zilch and Snow sat down on the bed as James joined Lux and Phoenix in shuffling through the racks of clothes. James plucked out the first tee-shirt he saw, eager to change and continue their journey.

"So, what should I call all of you?" Kit said as he joined them.

As James, Lux, and Phoenix introduced themselves and identified the rest of the group, Kit tossed his sweatpants onto the floor and chose a pair of black jeans and a black tee-shirt from the rack. Both fit him perfectly.

"Nice to meet all of you," he said with a firm nod.

He pulled on another bamboo panel. Dozens of gleaming blades appeared alongside numerous guns varying in caliber.

"You guys can take some if you want. I don't mind," Kit said, doing a double take at Lux, whose eyes had grown round.

"Really?" Lux ventured.

"Yeah! Go on. Take some."

Kit's easy grin compelled James and Lux to smile back.

"No, thank you," Phoenix said as he dug deeper into the closet. "Come on. We should hurry up and pick something," he told James and Lux.

Kit raised his eyebrows at Phoenix then smirked and shook his head.

"Anyone's first time in the Market?" he asked as he took a large dagger from the wall.

"Yeah. Me and James," said Lux.

"Yeah? And what do you guys think about it so far?"

James's hand faltered as he reached for a pair of pants. All of the Market's gaudy attempts to impress him had only left a negative impression that lingered like a bad aftertaste.

"It's awesome," Lux said.

James frowned at him.

"I knew it," said Kit, grinning. "I'm glad you guys are enjoying it. What's your favorite part so far?"

James's frown deepened as Lux launched into an enthusiastic monologue that glorified everything from the affable waiters to the golden bricks of Lucky Lane.

"That's nothing," Kit said, waving a hand. "I mean, okay. I'll admit that Three has a lot of quality service in his shops, but our claim is where all the really good food is. Sure, maybe some smiling waiter isn't going to be there to kiss your ass, but who cares when you're busy eating the best food in the Market?"

"So, there's food in this claim too?" Lux said. "I mean, I just thought that, well, you know."

"That we were just a red-light district," said Kit, putting his hands on his hips.

Lux's grin betrayed that he was guilty as charged.

"Well, there is a lot of sex stuff you can do here, and it's the best here if you're into that kind of thing. But there's other stuff too. When you guys come back, I'll show you around."

"Really?" said Lux as his face lit up.

"Yeah, sure. Why not? I supervise half of Lavender. The non-red-light district half, mind you, contrary to popular belief. But yeah, I can show you everything."

"Man, that'd be nice. To just relax a bit. Do some fun stuff for once," Lux murmured.

James resumed his search for fitting pants. On the one hand, he felt disappointed in Lux for succumbing to the Market's allure. On the other hand, he couldn't help but feel sorry for him and even a bit ashamed of himself. Maybe the only reason he was immune to the Market's charms was because he didn't have a father with cancer and a family business to take care of.

"That's what the Market is here for. It's hard enough surviving in Reality without having to make it in *the Flowering* too," Kit said as if he had peeked into James's head and glimpsed his thoughts. "You guys are welcome to come by any night once whatever it is you have with the Third is all over. I'll show you everything for free. Any friend of E is a friend of mine."

"Really?" said Phoenix. "She didn't seem too happy to see you, though."

"Yeah, well, I kind of took her off guard with that kiss, I guess. But how could I stop myself? I promised myself I'd do it if I ever saw her again. Those eyes. There's fire in them. And tragedy." He sighed, looking troubled. He drew himself up and said, "Yup, she's still as beautiful as the night I found her."

"Found her?" James said as he tossed aside yet another pair of jeans that had proven too small.

"Yeah. I found her as a newborn. Convinced the crew to take her on while we were crossing *the Iris*. I'm the one who gave her the name 'E.'"

Kit shook his head, grinning again, as James and Lux exchanged looks of surprise.

"I guess she never mentioned me?"

"No," said Lux as something like hurt wrinkled his expression. "Not even once."

"That's all right. I know she likes to keep things private. It's a good thing. But yeah, I found her and trained her. And trained her some more once we came to the Market. I wasn't a Jackal at the time–ditched my boss and joined a crew because he conned me on a promotion–but I still had enough connections to help her get stronger. Really amp her up, you know? They were good times. The best."

"Kit," E snapped from across the room.

"Yes, ma'am," he said, jogging over to her.

"There's only lingerie in here. What were you expecting us to do? Wear it?" she snarled.

"*Hey, hey.* I told you to call me over if you couldn't find anything. Here, let me–"

She flung a lacy thong into his face. He sighed as he hung his head and placed both hands on his waist. Bloom crept into the room with his head low and his eyes locked on Kit.

"There's some less girly stuff in the other room. Here, I'll show you," he said, leading her away.

Bloom followed them, his narrowed eyes still fastened on Kit. James picked up a pair of socks and continued dressing. He wasn't sure what to make of Kit. Sure, the way he'd kissed E had been surprising, to say the least, and the on-going tension with Bloom didn't help. But his generosity and willingness to help seemed genuine, and he was chill in a way that made James want to get to know him more.

Maybe Kit was right about the need to reserve judgment before getting to know a person. Blood Crow, for example, wasn't nearly as bad as James had originally thought her to be. Brainwashed, sure, but not bad at her core. Maybe Kit was just a normal guy trying to survive, like Curly. And hostility with E and Bloom was only to be expected if Kit had had a bad breakup with her, though it definitely seemed like he'd been the one to get dumped and not E.

And E! How could she have failed to tell the crew that she'd been in a relationship with a Merchant before? And not just any kind of Merchant, but a Jackal. The top of the food chain! Was that why she hated Merchants so much? Because they reminded her of Kit? James spun around as E marched back into the room. She was still wearing the same, dirty clothes.

"*I told you to stop being so stubborn!*" Kit shouted.

He reached for her wrist. Bloom lunged. Kit scrambled back. Hatred blazed in his eyes again. E's voice shook as she spoke.

"*I'm not going to do whatever you tell me to do now.*"

"'*You? You're really not going to call me 'Oppa' anymore?*"

"*You don't deserve to be called 'Oppa' anymore!*" she shrieked.

James and Lux glanced at each other again. They'd never heard E yell like that before. Kit clenched his fists. His cheeks had turned red, and he, like E, was shaking.

"That's right. I forgot. Ever since that night, you started calling me Kit!"

"That is your name," she said, turning away from him.

"Why did you leave me?" he shouted in a voice filled with fury and pain.

E flinched. Bloom looked at her with worried eyes.

"Without so much as another word! Do you know how much I looked for you afterward? I thought you were dead! The number of men I sent out. For over two years, I ... you...." He struggled then raked his fingers through his hair. He took a deep breath and exhaled. "You could have at least told me something instead of just leaving like that!"

"Stop pretending like you cared," said E.

Kit jumped. He looked like she had slapped him. Bloom began prowling toward him again. Anger gnarled Kit's face.

"Easy, doggie. Last time I checked, you all still needed to get past the Doors–"

Bloom leapt.

"No!" E cried.

Bloom twisted midair. Kit rolled across the floor with his dagger in hand. E rushed over to Bloom's side. Kit expelled an empty sound of disbelief.

"So I'm worth less than a dog to you now, is that it?" he shouted.

Bloom shook out his coat, turned his rear toward Kit, and swished his tail. E glared at the floor.

"Why is it so noisy out here? What's going on?" said Honey as she returned to the room with Blood Crow. Both women were dressed in a new set of sleek, black athletic gear.

Kit hung is head again as he sighed. He breathed in deeply then said, "Nothing!" He pressed his lips together into a flat, forced smile. "Let's get going. Sorry for the wasted time."

Worry stirred in Honey's eyes again as she stared at E. Blood Crow muttered something into her ear. Honey nodded in response. The group followed Kit back into the red room downstairs. As Snow, Zilch, and Bloom climbed back into the cart, Kit tore off one of the tapestries from the ceiling. He fastened it over the cart to replace the ripped tarp cover. He kicked open a large trunk and doled out new black sweaters to the group.

He held out the last one to E. She turned her face away from him. He sighed yet again.

"*Wear it. It's a lot better than the one you're wearing right now,*" he said.

"Let's go," she replied, her face still averted.

He glanced at her waist. "What happened to the dagger I gave you?"

"I got rid of it."

He stared at her with the sweater still held limply in his hand. James couldn't help but pity him. After all, he'd been scorned by girls he'd liked in the past too, though definitely not this brutally. The sympathy on Lux's face indicated that he felt the same way. Phoenix walked up to E and tapped her on the shoulder.

"Do you want to get in the cart too?" he asked. "You've had a long night."

"That dagger belonged to one of the original Shamans. I gave it to you because it was priceless," Kit said, ignoring Phoenix.

"Good thing I got rid of it, then," she snapped. Her piercing glare softened as she turned to Phoenix. "I'm okay. I should stay on the outside in case anything happens. Thank you, though."

Kit watched as she placed a gentle hand on Phoenix's arm. She walked away.

"You want to pull the cart this time since Curly isn't here?" he asked Phoenix.

"Sure."

Kit grasped his shoulder and gave him a slight shake before letting go.

"Hey, Lux," he said.

Lux paused as he made to push the cart from behind.

"Why don't you switch with Honey for a while? You look tired. You mind, Honey?"

"Oh, that's okay. Honey's tired too," said Lux.

"No, you do look kind of burnt out," she said. She shooed him away from the back of the cart. "It's fine. We'll switch again later."

Kit gave her two thumbs up then strode to the front of the group. "Stay in line, keep your heads down, and let me do the talking once we reach the Doors. If any of the Merchants there or anywhere else try to talk to you, just ignore them. I'll take care of it."

He opened the garage door and led them out into the street. E stayed close to the cart, away from Kit and close to Bloom, who lay hidden beneath the red tapestry. The group turned onto another block where red lights glowed. James cringed as they passed walls that muffled loud moans and open windows that broadcasted lewd yelping. With a jolt of unease, he saw Lux's gaze stray toward some of the women behind the windows. Kit seemed to notice as well. He began pointing to certain shops and describing their histories to Lux. The twinkle in Lux's eyes brightened as Kit spoke.

The group turned the corner and, at last, made their way down a well-lit street teeming with people and devoid of red lights. Unlike the Third's claim, the restaurants here looked more or less uniform, varying only intermittently in size or color. However, the smells that floated out from each shop carried a savory depth that the restaurants in Turquoise had definitely lacked. Streams of girls eyed Kit as the group continued making their way through the crowds. Many of them burst into giggles. Kit didn't seem to notice.

"This part of the claim isn't mine, but it will be soon. You just wait and see," he told Lux. "I'm going to become Head Merchant and show Orion how it's done. Orion is my boss, the Head Merchant of Lavender. But yeah, when I take over these restaurants, everything's going to be renovated and not in a way where it looks like some old guy is trying too hard like in Turquoise. I'll even surpass the First Head Merchant with all the new things I'll build and do."

"Ha! That's quite an aspiration to have," Blood Crow said with a sneer.

Kit grinned at her. "Ah ... so you were a Hunter before? Or maybe you still are? You've got the necklace. Well, I don't blame you for not liking the story. It doesn't really say a lot of good things about the Brave, now does it?"

"It is a false story," she hissed.

"If you say so," Kit said with a shrug.

"The story states that the First Head Merchant was originally a Hedonist," Blood Crow explained to James, catching his confused look. *"He supposedly convinced the Brave and his Hunters to help him scavenge goods by striking some sort of deal with them, and that helped him to climb the ranks and become the First Head Merchant. A lot of Merchants say that the whole Market is here thanks to him and the deal he made with the Brave, but it's obviously a lie. Scavenging is an evil idea that the Merchants came up with on their own. It has nothing to do with the Brave. The Brave was a valiant and noble man who founded the Hunters' way. Merchants are just trying to drag Hunters into the story so that they look less shameful."*

"Hey, hey. We're not trying to drag anyone into anything," said Kit. "You Hunters need to stop putting yourselves on a pedestal. You guys do plenty of bad things. In fact, one might even argue that Hunters are known to do cruel things and maybe, just maybe, dumb things."

He grinned at Lux, who grinned back.

"At least we didn't try overthrowing the Shamans and get ourselves killed like your hero, the First Head Merchant," Blood Crow retorted.

"Ah, but that's why I said I'd surpass the First Head Merchant," said Kit, wagging a finger at her. "I'm not dumb enough to try and take down the Shamans. You guys know what they do to humans they don't like, right?" he asked James and Lux. "Ever since the fiasco with the First Head Merchant all those centuries ago, the Shamans have read the minds of all their subordinates on a regular basis. Merchants, Bodyguards, Guides, everyone. If any one of them steps out of line, all a Shaman has to do is give the command and someone's name will be called out over the speakers here along with all their personal information. It usually only takes one or two nights for something bad to happen to them in Reality, and almost all of them wind up dead in their sleep."

"*It's a barbaric practice,*" said Blood Crow.

"True," said Kit. "But also effective."

They walked down an alleyway and into a wide street covered with black tiles. Trash lined both sides of the dimly-lit street. Bands of Merchants scurried about as they transported goods into black apartments. Several of them did double takes before dropping their bags and greeting Kit with low bows and terrified expressions. He, in turn, gave a flippant nod to a few and paid no attention to the rest.

"How much further do we have to go?" James asked as a Merchant stared at E.

"Not much. Hey, Lux. Looks like Honey's kind of tired back there. Same with Phoenix. You and Blood Crow want to switch off with them?"

"Sure," Lux said.

Blood Crow rolled her eyes but marched to the back of the cart nevertheless. James wondered if he should offer to take her place. She looked exhausted. Kit glanced at Blood Crow.

"*Hey. Do you like her?*" he asked James in Korean.

Sirens went off in his head. "W-What? What?"

Kit grinned. "*I said, do you like her? And don't try to get out of answering me by pretending like you don't understand Korean. I can already tell you speak it.*"

James hoped that the dim lighting would conceal the blush glowing on his cheeks and neck. He hoped in vain.

"Hey, look at you, getting all red! It's okay. Why are you embarrassed? She's cute. You guys look good together."

James grunted, neither agreeing nor disagreeing.

"I'll be cheering for you guys from the sidelines," said Kit, shaking his fists in preemptive celebration. *"If there's any way for me to help, just let me know. I'll help you."*

"You don't have to do anything," James mumbled.

"Why? You're around the same age as E, right? So I'm probably a year or two older than you, which makes me your Hyung. And since I'm your Hyung, I'll look out for you. I always look out for my juniors."

James rubbed the back of his neck, feeling both pleased and mortified. Kit continued grinning as he opened a large door, which bore the number seven in wrought brass. The group stepped out onto a bustling street paved with marble tiles. Behind the shops' ceiling to floor glass walls, mannequins flaunted brand-name clothes and quality sports gear for every climate.

"Hey, Phoenix. I haven't really gotten a chance to talk to you yet. Come over here. We can get to know each other a little better," Kit said, twitching his fingers at Phoenix.

Phoenix glanced at E before joining Kit and James.

"So, what's your story? How long have you been traveling around with these guys?" Kit asked.

"It hasn't been too long. I'm actually a Roamer."

"A Roamer? Wow.... So you're kind of a badass!"

Phoenix shrugged and gave him a hollow smile.

"Don't be so modest. And loosen up, man," Kit said, grabbing Phoenix's shoulder and shaking him. "You're always walking around like you have a stick up your ass."

Lux laughed. "Hey, that's kind of true, Phoenix."

"Kit," E snapped.

"What? It's true. Oh, come on," said Kit as she continued glaring at him. "He knows I'm only joking. Besides, he has good reason to be walking all uptight. I mean, I'm just saying. I don't think I'm the only one here who wants to make out with you."

James stopped in his tracks. Lux's scandalized expression verged upon laughter. Honey looked down at the ground with lifted eyebrows as if to say, "Well, can't deny that." Blood Crow continued pushing the cart.

"Kit!" E said. She marched forward and planted herself in his path. "Stop it. That's enough."

"It's all right, E," said Phoenix, who, despite the redness that had spread over his ears, looked nonplussed. "He's just teasing. Don't bother."

"Yeah, E. I'm just teasing," said Kit, grinning down at her. "I can't even joke around now?"

"You're not joking."

"All right, all right. I'll calm down. *You* calm down *a bit too*, okay? Calm down," he said in a mixture of Korean and English.

He put his hand on her waist and began pushing her gently to the side. She jumped away from him as if she'd been electrocuted. He tossed his hands up and tilted his head back as he groaned in frustration.

"Must you be so difficult?" he demanded.

"Don't touch me," E growled.

He rolled his eyes then lifted his hands in surrender. "I'm not touching right now. See? Damn! No wonder Phoenix likes you. Both of you are so damn tight-assed!"

The group cast furtive glances at Phoenix as they turned away from the crowded street and into an empty alleyway.

"*Good evening, Lapis Lazuli!*" a voice boomed.

Everyone jumped except for Kit and E.

"Well, what do you know? It's Snake Eyes himself," said Kit. He smirked as he threw a finger up toward the speakers hanging from the brick walls surrounding them.

"*We apologize for this brief interruption,*" Snake Eyes's voice boomed. "*We wanted to notify you that unauthorized trespassers have entered the Market. There are six trespassers in total.*"

James gulped as Snake Eyes began describing each member of the group. Kit's eyes glinted as he turned around to look at them all.

"*The Third himself will grandly reward anyone with information on these trespassers. If you do have information, please speak to a Bodyguard, and they will be happy to assist you. Again, the Third will give a generous reward to those with any information. Thank you very much for your cooperation.*"

Silence followed. The cart swayed from side to side as one of its occupants stirred.

"Those bastards," said Kit. "'*Unauthorized trespassers,*' my ass. They're too embarrassed to admit that you guys slipped past them. And they didn't even mention Twelve. Well, I guess it makes sense. Politics, you know?"

He resumed walking.

"You're going to turn us in, aren't you?" said E, standing still.

He continued walking. "Maybe. Maybe not," he said with a shrug.

E remained motionless. Kit shook his head and chuckled as he turned around again.

"I'm not going to turn you in. Don't worry. Besides, we're all getting along, and you guys have me outnumbered. I couldn't turn in any of you even if I wanted to, and Mr. Roamer here would probably kick my ass if I tried."

"You would win," E said quietly.

"Ho! So you do remember something about me," said Kit, looking pleased. "I mean, it's pretty deep down there in that cold, black heart of yours, but I guess it's still there."

She didn't reply. Kit sighed then walked up to her. She glared at the ground as he placed his hands on her shoulders.

"I'm not going to turn you guys in. If Three captures your crew, he captures you. No matter how much you think I didn't care, I did." He hesitated then said, "I still do."

She looked up at him. He slid his hands down her arms and smiled as he gave her hands a gentle squeeze.

"Besides," he said, walking away again, "I know how much you like that damn dog. Three will turn that thing into a science experiment if you guys get caught. So come on. We'll probably have some trouble now at the Doors with that announcement, but whatever. We'll deal with it when we get there."

They approached the end of the alleyway. Spotlights illuminated countless large, metal roll-up doors embedded along an endless cement wall up ahead.

"Like I said before, you all stay quiet," Kit commanded. "If it does come down to a fight, no guns. Any stray bullets that make it into *the Iris* will come right back. Plus, the gunfire always attracts other Merchants who want to shoot things for fun. Just make a run for it and pierce your watches once you get past the moonlight if it comes down to it. You guys doing all right on time?"

"Yeah, I think most of us just ran out," said Lux, checking his watch.

"Good."

Kit strode up to one of the doors then pounded his fist on the metal. After a few moments, the door rolled up with a loud clatter. Dozens upon dozens of Merchants sat drinking, smoking, and playing cards in a giant warehouse filled with crates. Behind them, a long stretch of empty land led to the veil of blue moonlight. Grassy hills and tantalizing freedom lay just beyond. Kit cursed as a man with a buzzed haircut rose from his seat.

"Well, look who needs to get through tonight," said the man. "Kit. The mighty leader of Merchants. Looks like I chose the perfect night to be on rotation, after all."

"Get out of my way, Quail," said Kit.

"Why? What's the rush? You had plenty of time before to report me to the Butcher. Why not sit down for a while, play cards with us, take a break from all that backstabbing you do?"

"Get out of my way," Kit repeated, looking bored, "or I'll tell everyone here what you did with Shelley the last time you visited my claim."

Quail stiffened. Blood rushed up into his cheeks and across his scalp as his fellow Merchants stared at him.

"What do you need to get through for?" he asked through gritted teeth.

"What do you think?" Kit said, flicking his head toward the cart. "Are questions part of a new protocol now? Get out of my way. It's the last time I'll ask nicely."

"I didn't know you could do anything nicely," Quail muttered as he sat back down.

"Hey, I'm a nice guy, even if you won't admit it," said Kit, grinning. "And I've still got my balls too, unlike some Merchants here. I, you know, actually go out into the planes instead of holing up at the Doors on 'guard duty' every night."

His grin widened as several Merchants rose from their seats.

"You need this many men for one cart?" said Quail.

"Just thought we'd have some fun out there," Kit said with a shrug.

"Ha! I forgot. You're always fooling around with some girl. Which one is the new one? The Chinese one?" Quail said, looking at E. "No, no. You usually go for white girls, so it must be one of those two. Or maybe both. That's more likely. Plus, the Chinese one is all dirty. But hey, maybe that's a turn-on for you. I've heard the stories."

Kit smirked. Then he drew his dagger with lightning speed. His grin transformed into a glare that made his eyes burn bright.

"Oh, ho, ho!" said Quail, looking around at the others as they jeered. "Looks like I touched something there. Well, whatever, Kit. But I guess I can see where you're coming from. She's not that bad under all that dirt."

"How much you want for her?" said one of the Merchants.

James and Phoenix stepped closer to E.

"Yeah, Kit. You're a man who can always be bought. I thought that was your motto," said another Merchant.

Kit's muscles tightened as if he were a lion readying to leap upon his prey. Several men continued to jeer. A few stared at E as if she looked familiar.

"Maybe she's worth a lot," someone said.

"Hey." A man rose from his seat and squinted at the group. "These guys. Aren't they–"

Kit's dagger flew through the air and plunged into the man's forehead.

"E!" he yelled.

For a fraction of a moment, she hesitated. Then she drew her daggers and ran after him.

"Protect the cart! Get past the moonlight!" she yelled at the group.

A spear appeared in Blood Crow's hand and the double-bladed sword in Phoenix's as they flanked the cart. Lux's veins bulged as he pulled the cart forward. Honey and James rushed to push the cart from behind. Up ahead, Kit and E battled back-to-back one moment then sprang apart the next as they carved down waves of Merchants in perfect, terrifying harmony. E's machetes glinted like onyx in fire as blood sprayed in all directions. The huge, curved swords that had appeared in Kit's hands flashed like strikes of lightning as he roared. The same wild and ruthless rage possessed their black eyes as they continued clearing a path for the group.

"E!" Kit shouted.

He dropped his blades. She jumped up onto his laced fingers. He flung her into the air before kneeling down, grabbing his swords, and cutting a man in two. E twisted midair before bringing her machetes down on the skulls of the men who had rushed toward Lux. Blood Crow threw her spear into a Merchant who lunged at Honey. Phoenix's sword whirled about, adding to the bodies on the floor. Lux released his hold on the cart as he parried a Merchant's knife with his katana then dodged another blow. A group of Merchants flung themselves at Phoenix, forcing him to stumble back as he repelled them with his sword. His back slammed into the cart. James gripped the red tapestry as the cart tilted. The tapestry ripped, and the cart toppled over. Bloom, Snow, and Zilch tumbled out onto the floor.

Merchants gaped at Bloom as he shook out his coat. He bit into a man who tried to grab Snow. James shoved Honey aside and grunted as a knife flew into his stomach. He created a spear then threw it into his assailant's chest. Honey fended off two more men with her tomahawks.

"*Oppa!*" E shouted.

Kit's blade swung through a Merchant's neck. Drops of blood and sweat flew from his hair as he turned and sprinted toward Bloom. His sword flew like a massive silver bullet and shot through the chest of a Merchant who had raised his blade above Bloom's head. Kit leapt onto the fallen cart as tables and crates toppled and crashed all around them.

"Take the Twelfth!" he yelled at Bloom before bringing his blade down again and again with raw, piston-like power upon the heads of the Merchants still bearing down on Phoenix.

Bloom shoved himself under Snow then shot toward the moonlight as she clung to his fur.

"Follow Bloom! Follow him!" James screamed at Lux and Honey.

Lux hurled one dagger into the eye of a Merchant stumbling toward James then another into the head of a man charging toward Honey before jumping over bodies and dashing toward the moonlight.

"Just go!" James shouted, pushing Honey after Lux as she continued throwing tomahawks at oncoming attackers.

James wrenched out the knife in his stomach, gritted his teeth, and began sealing the wound as she threw a final tomahawk and sprinted toward the moonlight. Zilch screamed behind him. James whirled around to see Blood Crow spearing a Merchant standing over Zilch. Kit's sword flashed, and the Merchant's head rolled across the ground.

"Look out!" James cried.

A Merchant jumped up onto the cart and swung an ax. Kit roared with rage as his hand dropped onto the floor. James stabbed the Merchant in the foot. The Merchant seized up as he screamed. Kit ripped open the man's stomach with the sword in his remaining hand. A new hand swirled out from his bleeding wrist. James stumbled back, momentarily stunned by the instantaneous healing. Kit reached into the man's opened stomach with his healed hand and ripped out his guts. Then he sliced off the man's head, kicked him off the cart, and jumped back into the fray.

"Come on!" James shouted to Blood Crow and Phoenix.

Together, they began dodging, kicking, pushing, and stabbing their way through the warehouse and toward the rest of the group standing on top of the hill beyond the moonlight. Phoenix ran forward to intercept the pack of Merchants who charged at them. Blood Crow cried out as daggers flew into her torso. James caught her as she fell. Phoenix whirled his sword about and felled Merchant after Merchant until they lay in a pile of limbs at his feet. James ran to him with Blood Crow in his arms.

"Take her and go!" he shouted.

"But—"

"Go!" James bellowed.

Phoenix slung Blood Crow over his shoulder and ran. James hurled his blades into the Merchants blocking Phoenix's path. He created more knives as he depleted those in his belt. He picked up the weapons scattered around him as he ran out of creations. He flung one last blade and screamed out curses as a horde of Merchants tackled him. Fists pummeled his face as metal tore into his sides. He heard a man shriek and glimpsed a body being tossed up into the air. The Merchants attacking him scattered as Kit descended upon them. He slammed his fist into noses, took off heads, and ripped out the organs of screaming Merchants. Quail bellowed a long battle cry as he charged toward Kit with a group of men.

Kit shouted for E, who sliced off another head before running to him. As he knelt down, she gripped one machete between her teeth, jumped up, and sprang off of his back using her freed hand. She flipped in the air, brought her machete down on Quail's skull, then released the machete in her mouth and began slaughtering the others with both of her blades. Kit's swords flew past her and plunged into her would-be assailants with the force of cannonballs. E ducked as Kit ran up behind her. He cut off her opponent's head with another roar of rage. E sliced the man's torso in half with a cry equally ferocious. She and Kit spun around to face James.

"Go!" they screamed.

James stumbled then, with a last spurt of energy, sprinted toward the moonlight as the remaining Merchants rushed toward Kit and E. James fled across the expanse of dirt beyond the warehouse and didn't stop until he had run past the moonlight and into No Man's Land. The group ran down to meet him as he rushed up the grassy hill. He only made it halfway up before he crumpled on top of the grass. Blood Crow propped him up as Lux and Honey began binding his wounds. Phoenix skidded to a halt next to him and created more bandages as Snow climbed down from his back.

Bloom shuffled his paws, watching as E and Kit ran over to Zilch, who lay curled up on the warehouse floor. The two of them began circling Zilch as Merchants surrounded them. The men pointed their weapons but maintained their distance. Kit jerked up a threatening fist, making several of them recoil. E smirked. Humiliation flashed across the Merchants' faces before they attacked.

E shouted at Zilch. He threw his hands over his head. James watched, his nerves fraying to a thin line bordering on total panic, as E and Kit engaged in a macabre dance that left bodies felled and twitching in their wake. Both of them were down to their last creations if they hadn't run out already.

"Should we go back?" asked Blood Crow, her voice squeaking with the panic James was barely managing to suppress.

"No. It'll only cause more trouble," said Phoenix as his wide eyes followed E.

"Wait, no!" James shouted.

Kit pulled away from his opponents, spun, and took the blow that had been meant for E. The man stumbled back then ran away from Kit as he advanced with the man's ax still embedded in the side of his neck. He hurled his sword into the man's back, yanked the ax out of himself, and began hacking into the man's body. E stuck her machetes through the chest of a screaming Merchant then crossed her machetes and took off his head. Together, she and Kit converged upon the last two Merchants. Silver and black flashed in unison. The Merchants collapsed, headless.

The group remained still for a moment, frozen and breathless.

Then sighs of relief broke out among them. Lux and Honey hugged each other as Blood Crow held up a fist and let out a triumphant battle cry. The last bit of adrenaline that had kept James sitting up left him. He fell back onto Blood Crow's chest, feeling equal parts nauseous and relieved. They had won. The night was finally over. They had made it out of the City. He chuckled as he spotted Zilch, who lay unharmed and quivering on the warehouse floor. Phoenix began describing the details of their victory to Snow. Bloom stood still, his watchful gaze still on E.

Kit turned to her, his face flushed and his eyes still burning. She stared back at him, panting and dripping with the blood of the fallen. He stepped closer to her. They stood still for a moment, simply looking at one another. Then Kit tossed his blades onto the floor and slowly raised his hand. His fingers traced E's cheek before finding the bottom of her chin. He spoke to her, and she listened without a word. He hesitated for a brief moment before gathering her face into his hands and kissing her gently. She seemed to stiffen. Then her machetes clattered onto the floor. Her hands slid onto his chest as she leaned in. Her arms wrapped around his neck.

Blood Crow stopped cheering and cleared her throat. Lux, in contrast, broke out in raucous laughter. Honey stared at the kissing couple with an uneasy look as Bloom shuffled his paws in agitation.

"W-What is it?" said Snow.

James couldn't help but glance at Phoenix, who had fallen silent.

"Uh," said James. "E and Kit are, uh–"

"Making out!" Lux said, bubbling over with fresh laughter. "Yeah! Go Kit! Go E! Woo-hoo!"

Kit and E broke apart slowly. He kissed her on the forehead then wrapped her in his arms again. He leaned his cheek against her head and murmured to her. Zilch staggered onto his feet and began walking toward the moonlight.

A Merchant moved. Zilch's hands sprang up to cover his head. Kit pushed E onto the ground and flattened himself on top of her as a knife spun through the air and found Zilch's watch. Zilch vanished. Kit's blade flew, and the man slumped back down onto the ground. The group stared in silence.

"Oh, no," Blood Crow said.

James felt the horror on her face transferring to his own as he realized what this meant. Any human within the moonlight would wake up the next night exactly where they had last been. Call and response didn't make a difference. It couldn't take Zilch out of the City. He was trapped.

"What's happening?" said Snow. "Is it ... where's ... Z. Zilch. Z!"

More Merchants began to stir. A man with a bashed skull raised a gun and began firing. Some of the Merchants who had managed to stand fell once more as bullets shot toward the moonlight and zinged back into the warehouse.

"Go!" Kit shouted, pushing E toward the moonlight. "I'll get the kid when he comes back! Go!"

She hesitated.

"Go!" he roared.

She snatched up a machete and sprinted toward the Blue Border.

"Watches! Now!" Kit yelled at the group. He grunted as a bullet tore through his leg.

"No! Z!" Snow shrieked. "Z! Where are you?"

"I'm sorry," said Phoenix. He gripped Snow's wrist and pierced her watch.

"Watches!" E shouted.

Lux and Honey vanished. Blood Crow glanced at James before disappearing too. Bloom turned and dashed up the hill at full speed.

"James! Phoenix!" E screamed.

Phoenix vanished as she hurtled past the moonlight. She pressed the tip of her machete into her palm. Kit gave a firm nod of satisfaction then turned to face the rising Merchants. James grabbed one of the knives Lux had pulled out of his side, stabbed his watch, and woke up gasping in the warmth of his sweat-soaked bed.

TO BE CONCLUDED IN

TREE OF EYES
BOOK TWO OF EYES OF AWAKENING

TREE OF EYES

BOOK TWO OF
EYES OF AWAKENING

COMING JANUARY 2026
AVAILABLE FOR PREORDER

FOLLOW ON INSTAGRAM FOR UPDATES
@ANNYIHYANGKIM

ENJOYED *EYE IN THE BLUE BOX*?
WANT TO SUPPORT THIS AUTHOR?

• *Leave a review online*
(Online reviews are **crucial** for a
book's success!)
Amazon, Goodreads, Barnes & Noble

• *Follow the author on Instagram*
@annyihyangkim

• *Subscribe to the author's blog*
ann-yihyang-kim.com

THANK YOU FOR SUPPORTING
INDIE AUTHORS!

ABOUT THE AUTHOR

Ann Yihyang Kim graduated with an English major and Korean minor from the University of California, Berkeley. After finding herself successful yet unhappy with her professional life, she remembered how much joy writing had once brought her. She subsequently wrote her debut novel, *Eye in the Blue Box*. Her short stories have appeared in multiple literary magazines. She lives in San Diego, CA with her loving husband and their rambunctious dogs, Max and Volk.

ann-yihyang-kim.com
Instagram: @annyihyangkim

www.ingramcontent.com/pod-product-compliance
Lightning Source LLC
Chambersburg PA
CBHW020541120726
47903CB00001B/80